New Halem Tales

13 Stories from 5 NW Authors

Kate E Thompson
L. C. Mcgee
Catherine Kigerl
Gwendolyn Van Hout Knechtel
Charles Thompson

New Halem Tales, 13 Stories from 5 NW Authors is a work of fiction. Names, characters, places, and incidents are the products of the authors' imaginations or are used fictitiously. Any resemblance to actual events, locales, or persons, living or dead, is entirely coincidental.

Beach Edition

ISBN 978-0-9906998-3-5

Ebook ISBN 978-0-9906998-5-9

Map Illustration by Kelsey Thompson

Cover Photo adapted from "Rockaway Beach, Oregon" by David Wilson Some rights reserved http://www.flickr.com/x/t/0093009/photos/david-wilson1949/8365211743/

Seagull text icons adapted from flaticon.com Some rights reserved www.flaticon.com/free-icon/beach-view-of-sea-sun-and-seagulls-couple_34940

Seattle, Washington
www.TwoNewfs.com

13 Stories from 5 NW Authors

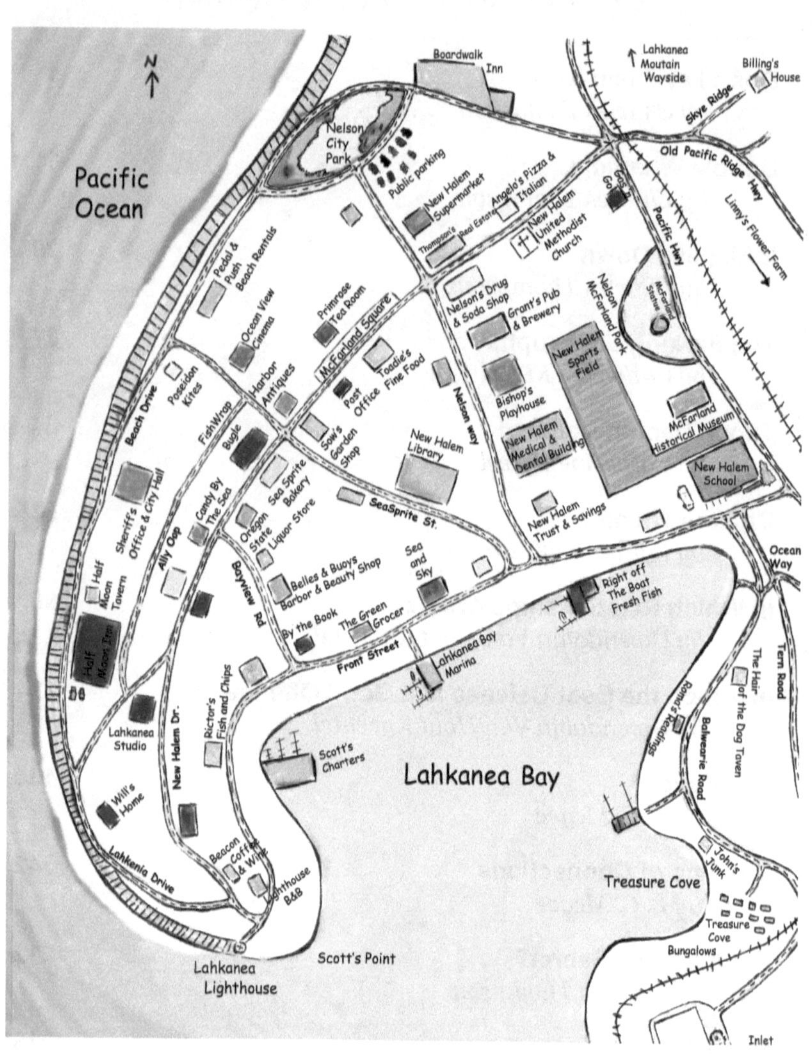
N
Pacific Ocean
Boardwalk Inn
Lahkanea Moutain Wayside
Billing's House
Skye Ridge
Nelson City Park
Public parking
Old Pacific Ridge Hwy
New Halem Supermarket
Angelo's Pizza & Italian
Thompson's Real Estate
New Halem United Methodist Church
Pacific Hwy
Linny's Flower Farm
Pedal & Push Beach Rentals
Primrose Tea Room
McFarland Square
Nelson's Drug & Soda Shop
Grant's Pub & Brewery
Nelson McFarland Park
McFarland Statue
Ocean View Cinema
New Halem Sports Field
Toadie's Fine Food
Poseidon Kites
Harbor Antiques
Post Office
Nelson way
Bishop's Playhouse
McFarland Historical Museum
Beach Drive
FishWrap
Bugle
Sow's Garden Shop
New Halem Medical & Dental Building
New Halem Library
New Halem School
Sheriff's Office & City Hall
Candy By The Sea
Sea Sprite Bakery
SeaSprite St.
Ally Oop
Oregon State Liquor Store
New Halem Trust & Savings
Half Moon Tavern
Bayview Rd
Belles & Buoys Barbor & Beauty Shop
Sea and Sky
Right off The Boat Fresh Fish
Ocean Way
Half Moon Inn
By the Book
The Green Grocer
Front Street
Lahkanea Bay Marina
Tern Road
The Hair of the Dog Tavern
Rictor's Fish and Chips
Lahkanea Studio
New Halem Dr.
Roma's Readings
Bulwearie Road
Scott's Charters
Lahkanea Bay
Will's Home
Beacon Coffee & Wine
John's Junk
Lahkenia Drive
Lighthouse B&B
Treasure Cove
Treasure Cove Bungalows
Scott's Point
Lahkanea Lighthouse
Inlet

Don't Let Them Know!

by Charles Thompson

Oregon Coast Event Celebrates Pirate Lore

The Oregonian

New Halem, Ore.--- Arrgh, here be pirates! This weekend pirates, treasure hunters and northwest history buffs will celebrate New Halem's maritime history and mysterious pirate lore during the annual Beachcombers' Festival in this quaint Oregon coastal village.

The festival will feature a street fair with food, plenty of grog, live music and a treasure hunting contest. In addition, a local community theatre group, The Lahkanea Players, will populate the crowd with colorful pirates and swashbuckling action. Local restaurants will sport English and Spanish themed pirate menus. The McFarland Historical Museum, named for New Halem's sea captain founder, Nelson McFarland, will highlight rare items from their collection.

Samuel Weston, curator museum, says the annual event, held Memorial Day weekend, will raise the region's profile as an important historical site and encourages further research into the local artifacts.

"Native legends of the misty Lahkanea Mountain speak of great 'winged canoes' fighting off shore and buried boxes of treasure guarded by spirits. Sir Francis Drake, the first English pirate to sail along the Pacific coastline, visited this area, too," said Weston.

After raiding Spanish outposts and ships, Drake, with 26 tons of Spanish silver sailed up the Northwest coast seeking a quick way home through the legendary Northwest Passage with his ship, the Golden Hind. No passage was found.

"We believe in June 1599, Drake and his men stopped in Lahkanea Bay for repairs. Stone carvings discovered by the town's pioneers and the fact that our bay matches the map sketched by the expedition suggest Drake platted his 'Nova Albion' right here," said Weston.

Old coins and chunks of washed up beeswax with Spanish trade symbols used during the 1500's have been collected around the village since the days of Lewis and Clark. Tourists still find small pieces today.

Is there gold or silver treasure on the Oregon Coast or only so much beeswax? Come find out for yourself this weekend in New Halem.

Alive! Will felt alive! The fresh salt air whipped through his hair and slapped him awake. His Fiat Spider hugged the curves of Highway 101. At each turn he shifted down and gunned it, pulling the car low and fast with a throaty growl.

Everything was changing too fast. He felt disconnected. You would think winning a Mega Lottery would have made his life easy. Wrong! He'd tried to keep quiet about it; kept his job reporting for the Oregonian; didn't splurge on anything showy, and pretended nothing had happened. But it only lasted a week.

He wound through a tunnel of tall firs, dark and impenetrable. The road opened to a magnificent vista of ocean, craggy rocks and small coves. He pulled the car off the highway onto a gravel wayside to take it all in.

To the west was open water with piles of cumulus clouds dotting the horizon. With all his winnings he thought his horizon was endless. His first call was to a college friend. Harry had become a successful tax attorney in Lake Oswego. They celebrated and talked, over many beers, of things to do and places to go. It was Harry who called him at the office three days later with a great idea for an investment with a friend of his, Ronald Kingston. Will had to ask who Kingston was. He didn't remember him from their frat house. Why should Kingston be trusted with so much of his winnings? Another reporter overheard the conversation and the next thing Will knew, he was all over the front page: "Oregonian Reporter: Mystery Mega lotto Jackpot Winner." His life had been a whirlwind since.

Looking south, below the face of the mountain, a long hooked jetty formed a quiet bay with a low bar. The village of New Halem nestled around the east and south of it.

Kingston had a new project there, a tourist center financed with economic improvement bonds from the county. With guaranteed payments and plenty of tax incentives from the state, Kingston promised a quick and lucrative return. Harry pushed Will into it saying, since he had quit his job at the Oregonian, he needed something and before he knew it he owned Oak Enterprises which financed Acorn Development for Kingston.

Kingston encouraged Will to visit, see the annual festival and gather additional research for the tourist center. Harry agreed. "Get out of the city. Breathe some salt air and get a new perspective."

Looking over the beautiful vista of the village he asked himself--could this really be Nova Albion? The little bay did look inviting and Captain Drake would think so too.

Will planned to attend a symposium sponsored by the University of Oregon about the area's pirate history. If nothing else, he could sell a travel article to Sunset or Travel Oregon.

Scenic photography would sell the story he thought as he unloaded his camera gear and set up a tripod. He took a variety of mountain vistas, craggy sea coast and quaint fishing village shots before taking off down the road again.

Escaping Portland, even for a weekend, was a great idea. He hadn't realized, until now, how numb his life had become.

Pulling into town Will stopped at the museum to explore and pick up a program of the weekend events. The McFarland Historical Museum sat next to a larger than life bronze casting of the good Captain looking toward the ocean across the fine hamlet he founded. Will thought the old Scott looked quite pleased with himself. How would McFarland feel with Kingston's new center looking down at him?

The museum was housed in a clapboard building, supposedly one of the original homes built on the cove. In the middle of the main room was a large oak and glass display case. The largest item was a round basalt stone with cryptic symbols etched on its face. There were letters, numbers, various lines in several directions, and Roman Numerals. The display claimed some of the markings matched symbols on Captain Drake's map. The stone was found near the turn of the last century, but there was no way of knowing how old the scratches on the stone were. Will knelt to get a closer look. Was the stone part of Drake's platted community? Were the etchings key to finding the hidden ship he left behind somewhere on his trek north? Were they directing those with the secret code to a hidden treasure left by the Spanish? As he turned, a bright blur of soft cotton brushed his cheek and when he looked up, a smiling face looked back at him.

"Oh, pardon me." The docent touched his shoulder. "I didn't see you down there." She continued her story to the family gathered around her. Children pressed next to Will to get a better look.

"As I was saying, treasure hunting is taken quite seriously in New Halem. During the depression, the hills around town were a honeycomb of tunnels and digs made by those seeking fortune. Since then, secret locations have been passed on as family legacies. In the last 80 years, at least five men have died when sandy tunnels collapsed on them. Be sure and visit the waterfront this afternoon before you leave town. There's music, food and lots of pirate activities for the kids all weekend."

As the family headed out the door, she added, "You might want to stay the night; there is a fun treasure hunt in the morning before the tide comes in."

Looking down at Will she said, "I have a large magnifying glass if you would like to take a closer look." She walked toward the battered oak store display case that served as the front counter.

"Well, uh...yes, please. I would like to take a better look at those marks on the rock."

She was already standing next to him holding out the old round glass. His hand touched hers when he took the glass. She asked, "Are you here for the university symposium? It's actually being held a few miles south at the high school in Rockaway."

"I am, actually, I stopped to pick up a schedule. My name's Will, William Cooke, and I'm a travel writer. A local pirate's tale makes a great story. Would you mind if I take a few photos? I thought I read the museum was the host."

"Welcome to New Halem, Will. I'm Maggie. The museum was host in the beginning but I'm afraid the academics from the university consider us another petty tourist attraction and moved it to the school. I think I have a copy of their agenda with directions. Let me see if I can find it." As she walked back to the counter and shuffled through the drawer Will couldn't keep his eyes off her.

"The museum board won't mind if you take pictures, they want all the publicity they can get. They are focused on enticing more people to visit, not on improving their collection. They say tourists will bring economic growth. Personally, I'm happy with things the way they are."

Will remained silent as he focused on his work. After each shot, he looked at the docent. Each time he noticed a bit more of her; the curve of her hip, the shine of her hair, her bright sweater. Whenever their eyes met, he would turn quickly, embarrassed for being caught, but she glanced and had that same small smile. He felt awkward, it had been decades since he dated and over two years since Robyn left without a word; followed by two letters from her attorney. The first was "no fault" divorce papers. The second, six months later and a week after his front page news, demanding half of the prize.

"Don't miss the beeswax display. It's real popular with the tourists," she said pointing to the opposite end of the display. "I have a floodlight in the back if that would help."

"Thanks, but I think I have enough for now. The beeswax will be something to come back for." After he finished packing his gear he handed Maggie the agenda. "You know, I don't feel like sitting through a stuffy symposium. The festival sounds much more fun."

"After you see it, you should stick around. I recommend the Sea & Sky. They serve excellent seafood caught by local fishermen and have a great view of the marina. The owner and his partner escaped Portland to start something new after a personal tragedy. I think you'd like them. You may have much in common." She put the agenda on the counter and reached for his hand. "If you have any other questions, I'll be here till six."

Nelson City Park surged with color and motion. Ocean breakers stretched to reach the boardwalk. Wind-whipped flags snapped along the seawall, drawing attention to the craft booths that lined the sidewalk. There were rings, charms, bracelets, handmade soaps, candles and a bounty of other artistic efforts.

Pirate costumes and accessories popped up everywhere, as did pirates. The crowd was peppered with striped shirts, headbands, torn short black pants, sashes, swords, and eye patches. There was even a booth that specialized in peg legs. Will stopped to examine highly polished black lacquered pegs, rustic moss encrusted wooden stumps, carved and scrimshawed ivory-like and rusty black iron pegs with matching gnarly hooks.

Street performers entertained at every nook and corner. Musicians of all ages played melodies that ranged from Gypsy folk tunes to cowboy ballads with open cases to catch donations. The one with the most cash was a six year old pirate, straight out of Peter Pan, squawking out "Glow Little Glow Worm" on a saxophone he could hardly hold. Will didn't get the pirate-sax connection, but he could not help but reach for his wallet.

A whirl of color and soft fabric caught Will's attention. A troop of belly dancers twisted through to the accompaniment of finger cymbals and a trio of flutists. They wound around the crowd enticing visitors to follow toward the main stage. As they passed, Will looked at his watch; he wanted to get back to the museum before six. He kicked himself for not talking more with Maggie. Her comment about the restaurant was probably a hint to invite her.

Will went back to his car to grab his camera, and was enveloped in the aroma of hickory smoked chicken. A tight line of trees protected the diners from sand-laden wind but it also held down the Lion's Club barbeque smoke. Fifty feet of roasting chickens lined up along the trees. For the more adventuresome, whole turkey legs were proffered as a pirate's favorite meal. Will passed by the food offerings and headed back toward the waterfront. Along the way he noted the Rotary Beer Garden next to the stage. It offered pints of Guinness as a pirate's favorite, at least Irish pirates. Will thought it would be a good place to hang out after shooting a roll or two of film.

He strolled along the boardwalk to the end of the booths soaking up the afternoon sun and salty air. It had been years since he'd been to the beach and he enjoyed a deep breath and slowly exhaled. All these people and no one knew him; no one cared. He could get lost here.

A large group of youngsters chasing a pirate clown jostled and pressed past Will on a beach treasure hunt. Knowing a good photo opportunity when it screamed at him, he grabbed his camera and fired off several shots capturing the exuberance of youth and the bright colored enthusiasm of the clown. He turned and shot more photos of the crowd. He thought this pirate history was about as authentic as the last Renaissance Festival he'd attended outside of Dallas, where a buxom Queen Elizabeth reigned with big hair, big teeth and a Texas drawled cockney accent. Nothing here promised a historic pageant; it was only a quaint coastal village making the most of its quirky spot in history.

"Hey Friend... Can you spare a few pieces of gold for a homeless pirate?" called a young man dressed in an elaborate pirate costume hobbling on a peg leg.

"I don't know," replied Will. "Aren't pirates supposed to be homeless, you know, like wandering around the seven seas, off to loot and plunder?"

"Well, you caught me there. But, you could help me mend my ways if you donate a few pieces of silver to give me some religion. Me crew and I found an old church we wish to purchase. What do you say, kind Sir. Can we count on you for a donation?"

Will inspected the pirate and was intrigued by his enthusiasm. "Thirty pieces of silver to turn a church into a brothel, perhaps? What would a band of pirates do with an old church?"

The young man doffed his hat, bowed low, and dragged the ground with an emerald plume. "Allow me to introduce myself, Sir. I'm the infamous Caribbean legend Blue Beard, or more accurately, Jeffery Roland, the sports editor of the FishWrap Bugle. In my spare and crazier moments I'm the manager of our local theatre troupe, The Lahkanea Players. The old church we desire is presently empty, gathering moss and mice to worship there. It will be a permanent performance home and will certainly bring entertainment and prosperity to our humble hamlet. Please follow me to our booth and I can show you photos of the building and drawings of the stage. Did I mention it has fantastic acoustics?"

As they picked their way through the crowd, Jeffery explained how the troupe had been founded over twenty years earlier and produced three community plays a year. He and a coworker at the paper got involved in last year's play and when the old church building went up for sale, the group decided there had to be a way to buy it and make it their home. Because he was the most vocal, Jeffery became the troupe's manager and headed the drive.

"With encouragement from the newspaper owner and friends in the Lion's Club, which by the way organizes the Beachcombers' Festival every year, we came up with a novel plan. We attracted the interest of the Arts Department of Portland State who proposed summer acting workshops. We hired a handful of professional actors and received a serious review and were promised a grant."

Jeffery pointed to the poster with photos of the old church and a sketch of how the finished theatre would look.

"However... and this is where you, kind and generous sir, are desperately needed. It is a matching grant, so we have to raise $100,000 to get it. Portland State pledged $50,000 and we've raised $30,000." Jeffery stopped to take a deep breath. "We're down to the wire; we're at the end of this state funding period, so if we don't raise the rest of it by the end of the month, we're sunk; forgive the pun. Can we count on you for say....$200? You can even have my photo taken with you. Or better yet... for $300, that is completely tax deductible, I'll round up our entire pirate band for a thankful group photo, with you in the middle. What do you say? See the building here on the poster. Doesn't it just scream great community theatre?"

Jeffery's tale had attracted a crowd. Several dropped a few bucks in the collection box. "I'll tell you what," Will said, as he leaned closer and lowered his voice. "I really don't like to be the center of attention, so I'll write you a check for $300 if you'd come with me to the beer garden. I'd like to know more about this New Halem village you are so enthused about and the newspaper you work for. I'm a reporter and editor and am looking for something new. I've only been here a couple of hours and feel a certain kinship to this place."

"For a pint, I'll spill all the dirt about our little coasty oasis. For a pint and your $300, I'll be honest. Your timing is right if you want to work at the FishWrap. The old man has decided to retire and sell the whole thing, printing presses and all." Jeffery reached out to a stack of papers on the table and handed one to Will. "The idea of new owners frightens most of the staff, especially the editor. He's afraid we're all getting sacked when they bring in their own people."

"What can you tell me about Maggie, the docent at the museum I met on the way in?"

"Oh, it might take a couple of pints to tell you about Maggie. She's a tad quirky even for New Halem standards. Beyond that she's very nice and a real good person. However, the one to watch out for is her daughter, Astra. She's the county sheriff and very protective of her mom."

Double Whammy

by Charles Thompson

Glenda Gadabout

FishWrap's new Publisher-Pooba arrives

by Glenda Cunningham

for The FishWrap Bugle

Recently, Good Reader, Miss Gadabout had the opportunity to visit with The New Halem FishWrap Bugle's new leader and Grand Pooba, William R. Cooke, publisher. We sat through the stuffy stuff about his journalism degree, reporting for big city papers, blah de blah de blah. Even though we are a correspondent and not actually an employee of the paper, he's sort of Miss Gadabout's boss, so even we must be polite.

The interview took a while because Mr. Cooke does go on once he's started. He would make a good party guest with his knowledge of Northwest history, but we digress.

After several "professional" questions, that I won't bore you with, we got to the good stuff. Miss Gadabout asked the big guy what most attracted him to our fair village. We were fishing for something spicy about a certain museum docent, Maggie Billings, he has been seen walking along the waterfront at sunset with. But instead, Mr. Evasive shared that it was the scrumptiously succulent salmon at the Sea and Sky, Drew Delacruz's great eatery, which kept him here.

Like a thousand other tourists he came for the Festival. After spending a dizzyingly delightful day taking in this past spring's Beachcombers' Festival (Cheers to those picturesque pirates in the New Halem Lion's Club!!) and being charmed while photographing our gorgeous little coast line, the future Mr. FishWrap

Publisher enjoyed the most sumptuous salmon meal he'd ever tasted. At that moment he knew he had to join our community.

But the important question was, "Did he dine alone on this momentous occasion?" We utterly failed to pry out the details. All that he would say was the, "company was even more delightful than the meal." Seeing this was going nowhere, Miss Gadabout politely excused herself and headed out to question Mr. Drew as to the identification of the aforementioned delightful company. However, we found our delectable restaurateur ever so abundantly closed lipped and what cute pouty lips those be. Too bad for us girls, it's always the cute ones, but I digress, again. Miss Gadabout worked him over but was unable to get anything of substance with his I-was-too-busy-in-the-kitchen fall de rah.

Not willing to walk away without some hot scoop, we appealed to his community spirit to share his secret savory salmon dish that brought to our humble hamlet such a journalistic giant. Surely, he could see the community service he would serve by providing this gastronomical attraction. He succumbed to Miss Gadabout's seduction.

His secret? Rosemary and Walla Walla Sweet Onions. Whether grilled on a soaked cedar plank or in a broiler pan from the oven, he rests the salmon filets on succulent slabs of Walla Walla Onion topped with sprigs of fresh rosemary, cut fresh from his and Daniel's garden. This keeps the pink perfection out of the pan juices and they flake perfectly. He seasons the filet with the lightest rub of extra virgin olive oil, sea salt and fresh ground black pepper. The filets are grilled or broiled lightly covered with foil for the first 15 minutes and uncovered for the last 5-10 minutes depending on how hot the fire and well done one likes their salmon. As for Miss Gadabout, she likes her salmon like she likes her gossip-- searing, sweet and saucy.

"You're the lucky winner" announced a wrinkled magazine flyer that had settled in the flowers beside the FishWrap Bugle's front door. Every morning Will stopped to pick trash and weeds from the planter as he made his way into the office. Lucky, indeed! New Halem was an opportunity for a new home and an escape from the Portland crowds. Within a month of his visit, Oak Enterprises purchased the paper and he hired himself as its publisher.

Looking through the door he saw Miriam at the front desk. She frowned and wagged her head back and forth like a parrot. As he came through, Will felt her dark eyes follow each step. He wondered what the crisis was this time. Last month the managing editor quit in the middle of the production day. Corporate take-over, Delaware mafia!

Will was anxious to get back to work, but it was becoming more than he wanted. His plan was to enjoy building and coaching a news team. When he could let them loose, he would spend the afternoons with Rotary lunches and golf. But there had been too much building and not enough time to learn to golf.

"If you would have checked your horoscope this morning, you would have stayed in bed. When both your Capricorn and Virgo signs have bad business, you're in for a double whammy bad day and today Sagittarius is going to make it worse," Miriam snorted.

Most mornings, Miriam started her greeting with her own interpretation of his daily horoscope. On his first day in the office Miriam cornered Will for details of his birthday, time and place and she insisted on doing a complete reading for him. A couple of days later she presented him with a 10 page horoscope. Afterward, she counseled that since he'd been born Capricorn, but on the cusp with Sagittarius with Virgo rising, he should read all three daily. His personal inclination for the day would be strongly Capricorn but his heart would be ruled by Virgo and everything would be nudged by Sagittarius, but only slightly.

"Well, good morning to you, too Miriam. Tell me why my bad horoscope has you so upset? It's going to be my bad day, right?"

"Your bad day has already started and it's giving me the fits. Brad

Ruskett, of Ruskett Chevrolet, has been calling every ten minutes since I walked in at 7:30, yelling at me asking why you don't have a pager or something. Tom in advertising has been yelling at Julio and the composing room staff. And, Her Gloriousness Glenda is waiting in your office and she's in tears. I don't think I have ever seen her in tears."

Looking through the glass wall separating his office from the newsroom Will could see the tall thin frame of the paper's immaculately dressed, 63 year-old society columnist. Most papers have a fluffy society column. It's an easy way to add hometown names in print, but not his paper. Glenda Cunningham was so serious, you'd think she was the queen of New Halem, and there in his office Her Majesty paced back and forth, wrung her hands and engaged in quite an animated conversation with herself, waving a copy of the paper like a sword.

"It looks like she's already started the conversation without me, so I'd better see what it is. When Brad calls again put him straight through," Will said as he walked across the newsroom.

"We've never been so humiliated in our life, Mr. Cooke," said Glenda. "We're ruined. This will be the end of us. It was supposed to be the highlight of the social season; the merging of New Halem's finest families, the Rusketts and the Oldhams. Now, you've gone and outed the groom as a cross dresser. At least we showed he has good taste. Nevertheless, we'll never be able to attend a party again. Oh, we'll be invited; we are always invited, but to be laughed at? No No."

"Glenda, take a seat. Explain how we 'outed' young Mr. Ruskett? Are we talking about a business merger or a same-sex union or something else? I seem to remember that the Oldhams have a daughter."

"Oh honestly, don't you read your own paper? We are not amused, dear boy. It was a wedding! THE wedding of the year. Look right here for yourself, we've highlighted it for you. You printed that the groom 'looked ravishing in a torrid taffeta tunic whose bodice hugged every delightful curve'. That is not the way WE wrote it. It was written that the groom's MOTHER looked ravishing. What stupidity. We're finished and will have to move away."

The door burst open and Tom and Julio tumbled through. They jostled each other like a couple of kids to jockey for a position in front of Will's desk

"Mr. Cooke," Tom whined. "Ruskett is pulling his ads. He's as mad as Hell about this stupid composing room mistake and I don't blame him. He says that our stupidity is too much for him to keep supporting us. He's our biggest advertiser. If we lose him, I don't know how we'll make it."

"Wait just a minute," chimed in Julio. "You keep yelling at me and my staff, but this is not composing's fault. Miss Sharp-tongued Society Suffragette has made it abundantly clear to all of the staff that her copy is not to be edited, no matter what. The typesetter only typed what he saw. Nothing more, nothing less. If I would have noticed it, I would have changed it, but she has young Alan completely buffaloed."

"Our copy is always perfect. We're sure of it," responded Glenda.

"Read it for yourselves," Julio said as he thrust a crumpled sheet of typed paper with her original draft into her face. "This is what all of you turned in yesterday morning, after the deadline I might add."

The phone rang and Miriam yelled across the room, "It's Ruskett." The room went dead silent and everyone stopped to look at Will.

"Hey Brad," Will said with a little forced enthusiasm in his voice. "I've seen the mistake and I'm working on it. Sorry, could you hang on for a sec? I've got Glenda, the composing room supervisor and the ad director in my office going over the problems with the wedding column now. Let me get them out of my office." He set the phone receiver on the desk sharply. With his voice raised Will added, "Get back to work everybody, and Julio like I said, this is the last straw. I want the new typesetter, Sam, fired. I want him out of here by the end of the day."

Picking up the phone he continued, "Yes Brad, great way to start the morning isn't it?" Will listened with the receiver about half a foot away from his ear while his biggest client vented.

After ten minutes, 50 I understands and 75 I'm sorrys, Will finally broke in. "You know Brad, the guy's fired, gone. You're right and we'll set this straight. Let me buy you lunch at Rotary today. That will give me a few hours to check things out and we can talk some more. OK? Good, I'll stop by the dealership at noon. Right?" Will put the receiver back on the phone and looked around. No one had moved an inch.

"Come on everybody, lighten up." Will laughed. "I don't like getting yelled at either, but you've got to admit, it's pretty funny. I bet young Ruskett would look right cute in taffeta. They'll have something to chuckle about with their grandchildren. We have work to do.

Glenda, when the new managing editor gets on board, he'll edit your copy like everyone else. Now go over to the florist and pick out an appropriate I'm-sorry-that-I-made-your-event-look-silly bouquet to take to Mrs. Ruskett and tell her that we'll run a half page special photo spread of the 'Wedding of the Year' in next week's edition. Bring us back wedding photos, as many as she will give you. Tom, I want you and Julio to go over them and pick out some real quality family shots." Will picked up the paper to take another look.

Julio added, "I see where you are headed. There should be a couple showing Mrs. Ruskett in the taffeta and we should find a manly man photo of young Ruskett holding his new bride. If there is one with his hand on her butt, that would be perfect."

"Yes." Tom started to smile. "We should find a snappy picture of the happy couple leaving in their brand new Chevy and make sure the car looks good."

Will stood behind his desk. "I want that one run on the front page as a lead in to the big layout. If he still pulls his ad, Tom, put Tillamook Ford in Ruskett's usual spot on the back page and give Ford free color. Got it? Let's get back to work. Julio, give Glenda a prominent byline for the story. "

Julio made a face as he was leaving. Just outside the door, he stopped and turned to Will. "We don't have a new guy named Sam."

"You bet we don't. I just fired him. That's my story and I'm sticking to it."

The phone rang again and Miriam announced through the intercom, "It's a Portland attorney, a Mr. Harris Buffington for you, Mr. Cooke."

Glenda jumped toward Will. "See what I told you. They've already hired an attorney to sue us all for slander."

"Everything will work out, Glenda. Things always do. It's more important than ever to take the flowers to Mrs. Ruskett and get those photos. While you're at it, would you pick up a bottle of fine brandy for me to give to Brad at noon? Thanks." Will waited for her to leave. They stared at each other.

"Oh, very well. A spot of brandy does seem appropriate." She strode out of the office and across the newsroom without looking back.

Will closed his door and picked up the phone. "Harry, I've asked you not to call me here. Someone will catch on; leave a message at my home number. As my attorney you're too close to everything. I don't want people to know about my funding Kingston's development. That's keeping me up nights. Did you know he plans to tear Maggie's house down?"

"Hey Will," Harry replied. "I know you want your secrets kept, but we have a problem, buddy. There is a private dick from Lake Oswego who's been nosing around. He's trying to find out who actually owns Oak Enterprises, the dummy corporation we created to funnel funding for your New Halem projects. He made several calls to the phone numbers we listed as the local contact for the Delaware holding company. He claimed to be selling a directory service but the caller ID listed a Lake Oswego office of a private investigator. I can't tell who hired him."

Harry continued, "I approached Kingston about pulling out of the New Halem project, even though I think you're being foolish. You stand to make some serious cash on this little venture. With the county as a partner and cheap financing using low interest and tax free bonds this should net you about a hundred fifty grand. Are you sure you really want out? Anyway, I asked Kingston how much he would want to terminate the contract. He went ballistic. That little runt got all red in the face and fumed something awful. He said he wouldn't even consider it."

"But Harry, you've got to find a way to get me out of this thing. I don't care about the hundred fifty grand. I thought the project was going to be a nice roadside display building with restrooms for the tourists, not this 60 acre interpretive center extravaganza. I wanted to help the town, not kick someone out on the street. Harry, I want the project stopped!"

"Sorry, buddy. Sure, you can kiss off the cash, but it's going to be more costly. Even if Kingston doesn't sue, you'll have to pay him to cancel the contract and that will take a couple hundred grand."

Will noticed Miriam watching him through the glass door trying to gauge how the conversation was going. She looked worried.

"But this house means everything to Maggie. Her family has lived there since the founding of the town. Maggie and her daughter were born there and it means everything to her. I don't want to take that away, the money isn't that important."

"Can you really afford it? There's one more significant cost to consider. If he sues we can try to settle but if he takes it to court, he'll go for as much of your fortune as he can. He would see you as a fat cash cow and I think settling would be out of the question. Plus, what would your lady friend think of you and your lies to her? Sorry to push you but I need a decision now. If Kingston sues, then the county would probably follow and that would double your costs. Plus you really don't want to face them in court; they'd bring in the state attorney general's office. So what is it, let it ride, or let them expose you? Your secret... your call."

Will stood up and turned his back to the glass wall. "Great choice! I could save her house, but they would take my quiet secluded life. I don't think I could take that. Even if I told her now she could hate me. I'll stick with the project and hope she never finds out. Let Kingston know we're staying in."

"If it's any consolation, I have a thought, but it's a long shot. Remember, how we applied for your little beach bungalow to be put on the national register of historic places? You said her house was old and a meteorite fell through the roof. If you could get it on the national register the county might reconsider and might pull out. Kingston can't pull off the project without their support. It would die and you'd be in the clear."

After the call, Will sat and stared across the newsroom. His stomach churned. He would take Maggie out to dinner and casually suggest the filing. If she balked, he could enlist Roma's help. Maybe, this could work after all. Why did he feel this way about Maggie? If she hated him would it really matter? There were lots of other women out there. Yeah, right.

"Hey, Miriam," Will said into the intercom, "has Matthew called yet? Isn't he supposed to start today?"

"No, Mr. Cooke," Miriam replied, "you told me last week that he was supposed to start next Monday. You know, your horoscope for tomorrow is much better. It's supposed to be a building day for you."

A new managing editor would be a building day for sure, thought Will. He could take care of Ruskett and all of the other little problems around here. Things always work out, don't they? Maybe things could work with Maggie. Will couldn't stop thinking about that.

It All Falls Down

by Charles Thompson

January 4
Business Briefs
House Demolition this Week
The FishWrap Bugle

The 127 year old pioneer home on Skye Ridge, built by William and Hannah Billings in 1889, will be demolished next Wednesday, January 11th at 3 pm. Traffic on Skye Ridge will be restricted beginning at noon on the 10th to make way for the heavy equipment.

The house, owned by William and Hannah's great-great-granddaughter Maggie Billings, was sold to the county under threat of condemnation to make room for the new Lahkanea Interpretative Center and Trail. Billings attempted to have the building placed on the National Register of Historic Places, but the National Trust for Historic Preservation ruled that even though the site was historic, too many significant changes had been made to the structure to warrant historic designation. The New Halem Lions Club has donated funds to erect a bronze monument at the site of the home in the new county park.

The Cedar County Sheriff's Office warns that those interested in watching the demolition must maintain a safe distance and not park within 100 feet of the property.

"I asked her to marry me!" Will stammered. "I don't know what I was thinking. We were sitting on the deck watching the sunset, chatting and sipping wine. I was so taken by how right everything felt when I was with her. The words popped out."

Saying it out loud made Will as nervous as he was on that sunset evening. He stammered so badly Maggie asked him to repeat himself. He said it again and got down on his knee.

Harry was in town to review Kingston's accounting. After the lot was cleared and ready for construction there would be contracts to attend to. "Congratulations. I assume she said yes."

"Actually, the whole business with the house has her so upset she could not say yes, at least not yet anyway. She wants to talk about it after the house is gone and settled." Will walked across the newsroom to his office.

Harry wasn't sure what to say. "After you drove to Portland and got her antiques appraised, didn't you say that she was letting go; even bought a house near yours?"

"I thought so; it came as quite a surprise. I got off my knees feeling pretty silly and wondered if she was only making an excuse."

"So on your trip together last Thanksgiving, did you tell her about your finances? You said you were going to."

"The whole three days I tried, but I could not come up with the words and the time never seemed right. How do you tell someone, someone you love, that you are behind the project that will tear down her family home? How did I get into this? When Kingston said 'Oh by the way, there is an old rundown house that we will need to have the county condemn so we'll have enough room for the project,' I didn't give it a second thought. How could I have known that it was an old family home and that I would meet and fall in love with the owner?"

"Why not tell her the truth, straight up. Clear the air, ask to be forgiven? Tell her what you just told me. How much you love her and blame Kingston for everything."

"I'm afraid to. Maggie hates the 'forgive and forget' storyline.

Things are what they are. She says that you may learn to understand what happened, but you cannot make things as if nothing happened. I don't think she'd want to be near me if I told her." On the trip Will wanted to talk but whenever he spoke of changes in town, Maggie would go off on a rant about the evil corporate owners, so far away and so disconnected with no concern about the result of their financial decisions and how they hurt real people. People powerless to fight back. It certainly was not the right time to discuss his financial position.

"Hey, how about a prenup?" Will brightened. "People are getting them all of the time. She has quite a bit of money now and maybe I can use that as a good reason. Kind of like insurance to protect her assets and make sure it will be Astra's someday. I wouldn't have to say anything about my situation, would I?"

"Sorry Will, you can't have a prenup without first disclosing all of your finances. You have to make a choice. Either tell her now or tell her when she says yes or let her go."

"Let her go? If I tell her she may very well hate me. All I know is that I want to sit on that porch with her until I watch my last sunset. I love her. I really do."

"I guess you have your decision. Now you decide when and go do it. Simple. You can't control how she will feel. Go with your heart," Harry reached to pick up his briefcase. "So are we going up on the ridge to see Kingston tear down the house with the rest of the important businessmen in town?"

"No, I don't want to see him or the stupid project. I've got to figure a way to tell Maggie."

The bell over the paper's front door jangled, startling Will. Now what, he thought.

It was Glenda dressed for an evening out, not a house demolition. "We only popped in for a camera on our way to the scoop of the year!" Glenda beamed. "That generous Mr. Kingston bought drinks last night at the VFW. After six rounds he offered moi an invitation to his motel room, and to answer all our questions of who is behind the mysterious Oak Enterprises."

"He asked you to meet him in his motel room?" Will stared at Glenda and wondered why he ever agreed to do business with Kingston.

"Don't look so surprised. We declined, of course, it's much more exciting to be chased. I kept his attention with an offer of an exclusive interview today. A special get to know the man behind the shovel including a nice portrait of him for the front page."

"Front page? Glenda, you shouldn't promise what you can't deliver."

"We will deliver all right. There is a bottle of Dom Perignon in the car on ice to toast his success. Actually, two of them. We are anything if not resourceful. His little male ego will be stroked like he has never been stroked, in only the way Glenda can. It won't take much to open him up. Have you seen his enormous Hummer? The tires must be 5 feet tall; and you know what the girls always say. 'The taller the tire the smaller the fire,' poor little man. Anyway, with a little flattery, bubbly and our special brand of charm.......oh he'll talk alright and his picture will be on the front page, but not the way he thinks! And WE will out scoop the great investigative reporter and editor of yours." With a quick turn and a flip of her scarf, she was out the door.

Will could not believe it could get worse, but it did. He grabbed his jacket. "Don't just stand there with your mouth gaping. Leave your papers; we're off to the house. I can't let that little letch of a man spill the beans. What Glenda knows the whole world knows, front page or not. I need more time to tell Maggie my way."

By the time he and Harry got to the demolition site, Will could see that Glenda had already started to get Kingston warmed up, plenty warmed up. She was trying to take a photo of the little weasel ready for action in front of the excavator, but instead of standing still, he kept stepping closer to her and leaning in to talk and touch her arm, elbow or shoulder.

"Now Ronald," Glenda said, "the best picture to really bring out your contribution to our fair community would be on the driver's seat, ready for action."

"I think you have taken plenty to choose from. Use a close-up of my face, that's what people like. I'm ready for us to finish off the Champaign you brought and we could enjoy the 20 year old Bourbon I have back at my suite."

Seeing Will puffing his way towards them, Kingston broke off and stepped back from Glenda. "Oh. Oh hi, Will. You look awfully winded; did you run up the hill?"

Will was breathing hard after rushing across the site with Harry several yards behind. "Glenda, I'm glad I ran into you. While you're here why not take photos of the whole scene." He waved his arm around. "From as many angles as you can imagine."

"You know very well Will, WE are here to capture this exciting moment with Ronald; to tell his story on this momentous occasion," Glenda replied, not budging an inch.

"Actually," Kingston chimed in. "We are ready to leave this dump and get out of the way of the construction crew so they can do their job. I really don't care to watch that crazy lady's old shack come tumbling down. I bet there will be a hillside full of rats rushing out when the foundation is crushed."

Will bristled. "There is no need to insult the owner; she was only trying to protect what was hers."

"Insult the owner!" Kingston was feeling the bottle and a half he and Glenda polished off in her car waiting for the crew to arrive. "The owner...the owner is a whack job who should be put away. Far away. She is so whacked; she claims her daughter was fathered by an asteroid. She screwed a freakin' rock and got knocked up?"

"I think you've said enough," Harry said, seeing the red on Will's neck rising and he stepped in-between the two men. "Why don't we focus on the job ahead, I brought a few papers for us to review."

"Everyone in town thinks she's crazy. Even the old men she went to school with didn't care if we tore her place down." Kingston was on a roll.

Will stepped around Harry. "Just shut up and get to work, you moron."

"Oh, that's right. You've gotten to know her very well. So well, maybe you can tell us. Does she really have rocks up in her..."

"I said shut the Hell up!" Will threw the first punch of his life, landing squarely on Kingston's nose.

Kingston put his hand to his face. Blood oozed through his fingers. He squealed as he twisted and turned while Glenda tried to put her handkerchief up to his nose.

"You freakin' bastard. I'll have you arrested for assault. Just because you financed this little shindig, doesn't mean you own me. I'm not your bitch!" Kingston said.

Glenda's head popped up. "What did you say? Will has something to do with this project?"

"That's right, he is Oak Enterprises. He and his millions financed this project from the beginning and guess what...he even owns the newspaper. How's that for a laugh. He could buy most of the town, but he sits in that stinky FishWrap hole to keep his fortune a secret."

The bleeding stopped. Kingston's face was swelling and turning purple.

Will looked at his hand still clinched in a fist and he felt proud. He really hit the jerk; there was blood on his knuckles.

Kingston turned. "Hey Glenda, hand me your cell phone. I'm calling the sheriff."

Glenda didn't reply; she wasn't there.

"You better think about it before you make that call." Harry pulled out a packet of tissues and handed it to Kingston. "You smell like you've been celebrating. Drinking on the worksite and being stinking drunk would carry some serious consequences."

Will stared at his fist. Glenda, he thought. Oh no, Glenda. She got the scoop she wanted and much more. Panic rose in his throat. His fist tightened and he held it. He heard the jaws of the excavator bite into the house.

He loosened his grip and let out a long breath. Will felt free, that's what it was, free. "I don't know how Maggie is going to react to what I've done, but it's over now. I've got to talk to her before Glenda does."

The Parking Lot Prophet

by Catherine Kigerl

Parking Lot 'Prophet' Crusades for Public Beach Rights Around the World

The FishWrap Bugle

The Parking Lot Prophet, local soothsayer and prophet about town, was caught in the parking lot outside The Green Grocer recently. He was rounding up some followers for a public beach-rights walk later that day at Nelson City Park.

He told the FishWrap Bugle about his one-man crusade to free all world beaches from sole ownership by making them public. His crusade apparently involves beaches everywhere. Says the PLP, "I've traveled to all of the world's continents and have walked free beaches and non-free beaches. It doesn't matter what the status is of any particular beach. My point is to make it known that all beaches should be available to the wondrous masses."

He says our New Halem, Oregon beach is his all-time best place to park. Not only are the people friendlier and more open to conversation, but in his own words, "The sand is much easier to remove from one's shoes." He is also extremely grateful that Oregon has made all its beaches public.

Humming to himself, the Parking Lot Prophet pulled his truck and camper off the beach into the lot of the Nelson City Park. It was exactly 7:30am on a Wednesday morning and, as was his customary routine, he was exactly on time. His residence on the park beach at night was an important example for his beach campaign. His campaign was also a perfect supplement to his underlying mission in life, which few, if any, were truly privy to. It all worked out in his favor. There were always early walkers and runners who would greet him each morning; there would usually be at least one whom he would reach in some way. It was all a matter of ears. Ears meant a potential opportunity to clear the clogged tunnel to a ripening soul. He never knew who it would be on any given morning. He laughed to himself about the divine providence of it.

The Parking Lot Prophet, known as the PLP to most locals, peered out, gazed up at a foggy sky, and then looked down at his shoes. They were white canvas cloth and, despite his beach haven at night, he was pleased to see, on yet another fine morning of clarity, they did not have a smudge of dirt on them. A vessel of truth was not to be smattered with dirt. Above them he wore white pants, freshly pressed, and a white business shirt also pressed and spotless. The white business shirt was all that remained of the necessary figure he'd cut when he worked on Wall Street and before that on the Prague Stock Exchange.

It was, in fact, on Wall Street that the guru's call came loud and clear. At precisely 10am on a busy morning three years ago that very day a vision of a vast beach appeared in place of the exchange board. Instead of numbers, a single trail of footsteps wandered into the distance in the sand.

Then a voice said, "Stop!" in English, Czech, Latin and a host of other languages he could not identify. A universal spiritual message followed. Since it was ineffable he interpreted it as, "You mean nothing! The Path is everything!" The PLP stood transfixed. He knew in that instant the multi-purpose of his multi-doctrinal work: to help others remove the roadblocks barring their way to a greater sense of peace.

He walked off the floor to the shock of his colleagues and in one day donated his business suits and his car to the Brooklyn, New York Saint

Vincent de Paul, purchased his truck and camper, carefully packed a small suitcase, leaving the rest for his landlady, and drove to Albany, New York where his cousin Marcus lived. Marcus, an Anglican priest, was the 'white sheep' of the family and the only person in the United States who would understand his career change and his need for temporary parking. A link of beach stops around the world followed, which eventually led the PLP back to his truck and camper in the United States and to New Halem, Oregon.

In the camper, he unfolded a small mirror from behind the door. The PLP examined the close shave he'd given himself that morning. "Amazingly accurate edge around the goatee," he said to himself. Facial hair had always been a necessary part of his professional machismo when a college boy, a stockbroker and now as a guru. His complexion was so soft and so clear without a goatee he could easily pass for a Madonna.

He let out a sigh. To think that, despite his boyish appearance, he was now somewhere in his 60's and still as healthy as a mountain goat. He wouldn't reveal his exact age even to himself. For age meant nothing other than a wrinkle on the vine of time. The more of his old self he dropped the better he was able to serve the masses.

Since it was a cool morning he slipped on a beige wool sweater. It had a rounded collar and the cuffs allowed a quarter of an inch of white shirt to peek in a circle at his wrists. He nodded. "Perfect," he said.

He began to walk toward the trail that spun out to the beach and stopped. The trees were thinning, the sky was peering through the spindly branches of the fall, soon-to-be-winter trees and the squirrels were busy gathering seeds or nut fruits, whichever it was they gathered that time of year. For some odd reason the Parking Lot Prophet could not identify which it was, fruits or seeds. What he could recall was the alto voice of his grade school teacher and her biology lecture on plant development back in what had since become the Czech Republic. He recalled her marching up and down the aisle of the classroom, a hefty Czech gendarme in a tight black skirt and ankle boots, one hand on a broad hip while she recited over and over, “The life cycle of a tree is flowers, fruits and seeds! Flowers, fruits and seeds!” Her heavy fingers, filled with rings, snapped time to the beat, her black eyes skinning the face of each boy like apple peelers as she passed. The PLP clearly saw his own pious face turning to look at her and although he could vividly recall her mouth caked with pomegranate-red lipstick and even more clearly hear his young voice asking how human biology fit into the lesson, he could not recall, here, in the Nelson City Park, which season meant fruits and which seeds. Flowers were beside the point; they gave a high sign that spring was blooming.

The Parking Lot Prophet was tapping his finger on his chin to the beat of ‘flowers, fruits and seeds’ when his mind switched from science to work, religious-spiritual work that is, and his divine purpose for the people of the town.

Just then New Halem Mayor, Alston Bumgartner, appeared at the other end of the parking lot in an oversized t-shirt and baggy shorts. What would he tell the mayor, an A-type personality, when he jogged up to him? Would he stop and listen to the word of the Godhead?

As the mayor huffed and puffed toward him with a big smile on his face, the PLP found himself in dire need of a focus shift. He recited a quick mantra to himself—Om Ma Ne Padme Om. He worked his mouth into a smile, his lips into a careful but cheery, “Mr. Mayor, how are you on this fine morning?”

“Mr. Prophet! A fine morning it is.” The mayor bent down to brush some dirt off his bright new blue and white Nikes. “Humph! Dirt! Can’t keep it off of ourselves out here can we?”

Aha! the PLP thought to himself. I think I’ve touched upon a common vein. “You are aware, Mr. Mayor, that ‘Cleanliness is next to Godliness’ is not just a slogan for cleaning fluid?”

The mayor chuckled. "Well, Ahem! It does pay to always present the best appearances."

"The best appearances are the only appearances," the PLP replied, his face frozen in serious concentration, his eyes trained not too indelicately on the mayor's pudgy face, which had very deep bowls under the eyes in a tragic shade of grey. This told him the mayor was losing way too much sleep over some unwarranted trivia having to do with...an event he was planning that was extremely significant to his image by the populace of the town! He nodded to himself. I must be especially savvy this time. The mayor, as representative of a capitalist community of comfortable means, was indeed feeling the weight of his age and the professional A-type American ego was one of the most sensitive on earth.

The mayor fiddled for a few seconds with his mustache. "Yes, of course. But what are you onto anyway?" He glanced nervously at his watch.

"The body, Mr. Mayor, inside and out, is a vessel by which we receive the truth. If we do not take care of it we may find we are not only subject to its rapid decline, but also subject to losing out on the wisdom it takes to know how to do our true work in this world."

The mayor looked at the PLP a little apprehensively as though he wanted to hide something. "As a proper, church-going Christian I do know a little about the truth, my friend." He lifted his right eyebrow. "And as the mayor of this town, I also know quite a bit about my work in this world."

The PLP nodded. "You certainly do!" He continued to nod while he heard the mayor think: Of course, if things keep going the way they have, this job is going to kill me unless I...

"Unless you take a break, Mr. Mayor. Fly to the South Pacific. You've always wanted to go to Vanuatu," the PLP said.

The mayor's mouth dropped. An incredulous look crossed his

face. "How did you know? I...I was just thinking, I mean this morning that well, before breakfast anyway, that I needed a little vacation." He peered at the PLP and stepped sideways away from him. "I hadn't even told my wife about it, about Vanuatu I mean."

The PLP saw the mayor, a tropical Martini in one hand, his wife innocently sipping a ginger ale by his side, the mayor's eyes discreetly focused on the behind of a bikini-clad young woman as she bounced down the beach.

"A-ha," the PLP uttered. "I see."

"I trust you won't spill the beans. I want to make the vacation a... little surprise...for my wife."

The PLP saluted the mayor, his chin thrust up as he clicked his heels together. "On my honor." He paused. "And how are those gold mining stocks coming along?"

The mayor nodded. "I can't complain. Thanks for the tip-off." He tilted his head to one side as though considering the potential of a new employee. "You know, Mr. Prophet, I'm making plans for next year's Beachcombers' Festival. How about you take a booth for your beach-combers' campaign?"

"You mean my public beach-rights campaign, Mr. Mayor, informing people that beaches everywhere in the world, from Seychelles to Valparaiso, Chili, should be public?"

The mayor grinned. "Of course. That one! We'll give you a choice spot near the water to make it well, most effective."

"Sounds wonderful." The PLP beamed.

The mayor glanced at his watch again. "Well, gotta go jog now! Work is waiting!"

"Have a pleasant and Godly day, Mr. Mayor."

"And a good day to you, Mr. Prophet!" The mayor trotted down the trail to the beach.

The PLP watched the mayor disappear into the trees. A most productive conversation, he thought. Exposure for his beach campaign and thus for his higher purpose had dropped into his lap. He had a sinking feeling. The mayor's 'little vacation' was going to prove as unsatisfying as last year's 'little vacation.' But a feeling of euphoria followed. He saw the mayor strolling down the beach in Cape York, Australia his arm around his wife. Next year's vacation would provide a fresh new outlook for the mayor's 35-year marriage. "Spiritual development sometimes takes unusual turns," he said out loud.

At that instant something dropped on his head, bounced off and landed near his feet. It was a very big pine cone loaded with seeds that spilled to one side on the ground.

He grabbed it, jumped up and held it before him like a religious vessel. "I've got it! Seeds! Fall and Winter mean seeds!" He laughed out loud.

Those Demon Denims!

by Catherine Kigerl

Early Autumn Garden Tour!
The FishWrap Bugle

Jones Flower Farm at 4100 Old Pacific Ridge Highway will be open for an Early Autumn Garden Tour this Sunday from 1pm to 4pm. The flower of the season is the Dahlia and there will be many on display in vibrant colors. Linny Jones, owner of the farm, will also give a short lecture on Dahlia growing and cutting and will offer a raffle for several flower bouquets in association with Sows Garden Shop and with florist, Manny Baker, of The Green Grocer.

With one hand in the crook of an elbow, the other hand scratching his chin, the Parking Lot Prophet stared at an old robin-egg-blue flatbed truck as it puttered into the Nelson City Park lot. He continued to stare as the truck was brought to a stop. A gangly woman quickly jumped out of the driver's door. It was Linny Jones, the flower farm lady. She turned around and started fussing with something in the front seat.

She was one difficult ear to penetrate, and what in the world was she doing here anyway at 7am? He nodded slowly to himself as he watched her. It must be a sign. He continued to scratch his chin and stare at her as he fished into his shirt pocket and pulled out a cigarette. It was the one 'dirty' vice he refused to part with, for parting with a morning cigarette would be parting permanently with...what? A small voice with a Czech accent inside him said, "It is a stubborn attachment to the old country!" He sucked in his breath as though in shock, then soon after calmed himself. He had no time to analyze his attachments this morning. He stuffed the thought back into his brain, puffed on his cigarette and watched as Linny Jones strapped a satchel over her shoulder, slammed her door shut and slowly started to make her way toward the park office. She ignored him as she took long, giraffe-like steps. But there was something in the way she'd taken her time getting out of her truck and in the way she was slowly walking. It was something he knew well. It meant that a normally reticent resident of a small town like New Halem—which Miss Linny was—had anticipated his greeting and a chance at his confidentiality.

"Good morning to you, Miss Linny Jones," he called politely with a nod. He moved toward her with grace and confidence.

Linny glanced at him suspiciously. "Now look here Mr. Prophet-guy. Don't expect to lasso me into one of them consciousness-raising talks 'bout the importance of beach rights. It's just another morning." She paused. "You seen Loc Pham, my flower man this morning?"

"I cannot say that I have, Madam," came the polite but firm reply.

"Well, if you do, tell him I'm looking for him." Linny continued on her long-loped way.

"Just one moment, Miss Linny," the PLP said in a forceful voice.

Linny wore the same suspicious look but this time she stared straight-on into his eyes. She stood quiet as though expecting something.

The PLP tilted his head to one side and a little grin traced his lips. "Miss Linny, if I'm not mistaken I would say you have a question for me this morning."

She glanced around. "Well...there's a pair of pants back at my house. Found 'em out in one of my dahlia fields yesterday." She blushed and chuckled nervously.

"And..." The PLP scratched his chin. The fact that he felt calmer than a seagull bobbing on a slack tide had obviously ignited an anxious strain in Miss Linny. Or was it the fact that she was talking to a man about a pair of pants? Despite her masculine garb—baggy old bib overalls under a brown leather motorcycle jacket—she had a distinctly feminine way about her. Even when she popped a self-rolled cigarette into her mouth and chewed on it like it was cud it was a dainty chewing, more like a lamb's than a bull's. He extracted a lighter and lit her cigarette to which she did not thank him. Then she puffed absently for a few minutes staring at the ground as though he'd disappeared. Startled, the PLP imagined he'd become an abandoned flower on the farthest corner of her last acre. Miss Linny wasn't used to engaging other people in conversation, he thought. No, she wasn't. There was a strong hint that Miss Linny had always felt more comfortable with flowers than she had with human beings.

"These aren't just any ordinary pants," she finally went on. "It was like they fell right out of the sky." She peered at him intently as though anticipating a ripple in his calm. "But that's not the most unusual thing about this pair." Her voice trailed off.

The PLP took a puff of his cigarette. "Why don't you start...from the beginning, Miss Jones."

She hesitated, nodded, then began. "Well, it was a day like any other. Or so it seemed. I was turning over the soil in one of the rows of my farm. The sky was so blue that I leaned over my hoe, tilted my head up and simply marveled. In fact the sky was as blue as any denim I've ever seen, fresh-washed. I'm not a woman to just stand there and dream over the color of the sky. Work is work and I have a huge stretch of a flower farm that during the fall dahlia season—which it is—takes eight hours of labor each day to tend. I have Loc, my Vietnamese flower-growing expert, but he only comes by to help on Saturdays. So there I was, taking a breather right in the middle of one of my fields, just gazing up at the blue sky."

The Parking Lot Prophet pictured her standing there like one of her dahlias but without a lot of the color. Miss Linny had slate-grey hair and a pale complexion with pond-brown eyes.

"I'm ahead of the growing season this year," she continued. "My mind was traveling to that new dining set I might be able to buy if my profits exceed the usual at the city markets. I'd relaxed into the handle of my hoe and closed my eyes so that the sun could lay its sweet, warm breath on my eyelids. But I flipped them open pretty fast when I heard it!"

"Heard what?" The PLP was on the edge of his breath. Then he let it out slowly; it was important to stay centered with this woman.

"It was a heavy thump like something solid had dropped on a patch of my dahlias nearby."

The PLP lifted an eyebrow but remained quiet.

"I got into a defensive position and tipped my hoe up like a spear." Linny bent over and gestured as though she were holding her hoe. "'Who's there?' I called and slowly turned around. I carefully eyed the perimeter of my farm. It was as quiet as my house is when I get up to check the woodstove in the middle of the night. Not a single sound was heard, not even a breeze; there wasn't any sign of human or animal life for a quarter-mile around."

"I see." She would know, the PLP thought, for at over six feet tall she towered over her domain. If it weren't for his command she would surely tower over him. "Could someone have been hiding, in the trees for instance?"

"The only trees on my property that would shelter a voyeur are around my house. This sound was close! I wasn't going to let up until I found the culprit. So, still jutting my hoe spear-like, I began to walk between a row of red dahlias and a row of pink scanning the ground. Then I spotted a telltale blue object lying amongst five or six of my precious flowers. 'What the heck?' I asked myself. I picked my way toward the object. As I approached, it looked more and more like a pair of denim jeans. That's exactly what they turned out to be too, a pair of denim jeans all crumpled up and squashed down on top of six of my favored red dahlias." Miss Linny's face had turned almost as red.

"What did you do with the derelict piece of cloth, Miss Linny?"

"Well I abandoned my hoe and examined it." She sucked in her breath, threw her head back and looked up at the sky. "No planes ever pass over my property. There certainly had been none in the last five to ten minutes." She blew out her confusion in a puff of air. "And I knew those pants weren't there a few minutes before. I'd just hoed that row. And I know I didn't hear a peep of anything except for that sound." Linny hesitated.

"I believe you," the PLP said.

"So I picked them up and held 'em out in front of me." She gestured as though she were holding the pants with the ends of her thumbs and forefingers. "I searched around the waist for the size. It said 38. I got a little more commanding, took them in both hands and pulled them open so I might see the shape that had filled them. The person was long and tall. Probably a man," she said.

"Hmmm. Yes, I'd agree." The PLP unconsciously pulled at the goatee on his chin. He had a funny feeling that she could have been lying on a psychiatrist's couch instead of standing before him.

"They'd been washed a few times," she was saying. "They certainly didn't belong to me, or to Loc, who is as tiny as a leaf and never wears jeans anyway. I flipped them around again and saw a little red brand tag sewn into the back inseam. "Suitor," it said. "I've never heard of that one."

The PLP shook his head. "Neither have I..." his voice drifted off as he tried vainly to see what it all might mean. "And what did you do next?"

"Well, I rolled the jeans up and set them on the ground so that I could tend to the flowers that were crushed by the impact. A few of them had to be picked for their stems had been broken. I had to mound the dirt back up around others so they would stand again."

"Of course." He scrutinized her face while Miss Linny puffed on her cigarette, which was now nearly burned down to her fingers. She was a sensible enough woman. No inclination for fantasy there; nor did he see any delusional behavior. "To create such a pit of destruction on a small circle of dahlias, the jeans would have had to be assisted by the forces of gravity." She kept silent. He delved into her absent, cigarette-inhaling stare. He knew she was a single woman. But had she been that way all her life? He had a strong inkling the answer was no. "Could it be a former suitor deposited the pants, Miss Linny? Someone who...wanted to get back in touch with you?"

"Ha!" she spouted. "My last suitor? He was as cold as on old bottom-fish and just as slow." She pointed at her chest. "I'm 65 now. Men my age are getting too old to be worth their weight in top soil and I don't care to babysit the younger ones." She turned and puffed on her cigarette vehemently. "As for chance meetings with any man, that doesn't go further than the Sow's Garden Shop where I pick up my mulch and flower bulbs. There's usually some man curious to know what week I first planted or what I do to keep the bugs off." Miss Linny shot him a skeptical look.

"I see." The PLP dropped his gaze not wanting to intentionally interrogate Miss Linny about men any longer. They were definitely a sore subject. No wonder the pants were so...mysterious to her. This certainly was an intriguing case. "And what did you do next, Miss Linny? With the pants?"

"I snatched the pants up and stuffed them under my arm." She looked up at the sky again then at the PLP. "It's like they fell right out of the sky." Her voice trailed on, "Right out of the sky."

"The sky can speak in mysterious ways, Miss Linny. And then what did you do?"

"Well, I took 'em back to my house and went straight to my shed and hung 'em in a wooden closet where I keep my coveralls. When I entered my office off the kitchen the phone was ringing and I was hooked onto a long trail of telephone calls from urgent marketers who wanted to know about the dahlia crop that year, whether they might be able to receive their first load in a few days time. There were several orders for wedding and funeral flowers and I was swamped by huge orders from buyers who wouldn't need my dahlias for a month! In fact there were so many calls that afternoon I completely forgot about the pants until I had to dart over to my shed to grab the cigarettes I'd rolled that morning from the pocket of my coveralls." She dropped the stub of her cigarette on the ground, stamped it out and pulled out another.

"Amazing, simply amazing," the PLP cooed and carefully lit her cigarette. He pulled out his own, caught up in the intensity of her extraordinary tale, and anxiously lit it.

"Well, you can imagine. By that time I was flying high on a carpet of red, pink, yellow and lavender dahlia orders. My flower farm has barely provided for my needs for three years and last year I gave away a third of my extra crop to hospitals and nursing homes after selling a fair number well under cost. It's not the quality of my dahlias. They've won awards at the New Halem Garden Club for the last five years straight. It's a cross between the competition—two farms around here have doubled in size—and the fall buyer's fancy for the chrysanthemum in recent years."

"You don't say."

"This year was my last hold-out. It was going to be sell 'em or sorrowfully leave my farm."

"I imagine that smelled as bad as a compost pile."

"Yep, it was certainly a thing I hoped to plow under." She chuckled.

"But things are turning around. Fast. In one afternoon I became an enterprising floral farmer again." She tossed her head like a wild horse and flung her hands up in the air. "Thank...somebody!" she shouted and let out the first laugh the PLP had ever heard erupt from her throat.

The PLP gaily laughed with her, tipping his cigarette and letting the soft ash drop to the ground. He sensed the best part of the story had not yet emerged. "And the pants...?" he urged.

"Well inside the shed I made a beeline for the wooden closet and threw the door open. The pants were still there, right where I'd left 'em hanging. But they were different."

The PLP cocked one eyebrow. "In what way, Miss Linny?"

She eyed him suspiciously again.

"You can trust me Miss Linny." He made a cross over his chest with one hand.

Miss Linny folded her arms and shifted her feet. "Well, it was as though I expected a voice to burst out from between the seams. I leaned over and gave one of the empty pant legs a slap to see if anything was there. Then, well I found myself talking to 'em. 'This is going to be an amazing year for my dahlias,' I said. 'More orders in one afternoon than I've filled in a whole season.' I paused and wondered for a minute who I was talking to. I've never talked to myself let alone a pair of pants in my life!" Linny let out a huge sigh. She turned abruptly away from the PLP sucking on her cigarette nervously. "Next thing I slammed that closet closed, fixed the padlock on the door and ran back to the house. "Talking to pants. Now, what the heck," she muttered to herself. "When I got back inside the telephone was ringing again."

The PLP boldly stepped into her line of vision so she couldn't avoid his face. "They have an unusual appeal don't they Miss Linny. Like that of a handsome stranger." His words rolled off his tongue quick, fountain-like. He puffed from his cigarette nonchalantly.

Linny took a long step backward. "What the...How'd you know? I mean, what are you on to?" Her eyes narrowed.

The PLP looked apologetic, innocent. "I don't know, Miss Linny. It's only a whim, a thought that attached itself to my brain as you completed your story."

"Attached itself? From where?" Linny glanced at her watch. "You seen Loc this morning?"

"I haven't seen Loc in an epoch," the PLP replied with a smile. "He's off to do his park duty while I'm still meditating each morning." She'd forgotten she'd asked him about Loc already. His talk made her nervous. The paranormal was obviously not her subject but she would have to warm up to it if his suspicions proved true.

She glanced around the parking lot nervously. "That's why I'm here at Loc's full-time job, to give him his paycheck. He's due to pick it up tonight but I decided, well its best he have it this morning." Her mind drifted.

"Despite what common sense and science often tell us, there are other dimensions," the PLP said loud and clear. "Other dimensions where information travels." He pointed at her head then tapped his. "My brain to yours. I might hear what you think. The pants might still harbor...whoever was in them once. Or still is. Get it?"

Linny looked at him as though he were a quack. "Are you saying these pants came from another dimension? If that's right, then why are they so much like this one?"

The Parking Lot Prophet laughed. "That's the mystery! They're like something we've both never experienced. They are like this dimension in that they are a piece of clothing and they're not in that you're compelled to confide in them." His eyes widened, he pointed his finger at her. "They are the Truth, those pants. They are there to show you something, my dear. Treat them carefully." His face dropped as he read her thoughts: This man is as crazy as an old bat flying out of a frog swamp. He certainly isn't making my sanity any more sound.

"Well, enough of this talk," she said in a huff. "I've got to find my employee." But before she stepped away, she turned one last time toward her confessee. "I assume I'll have your confidence about this story. All I need is to lose my clientele over a silly pair of pants."

"Silly! I would say not. But you do have my confidence, Miss Linny." The PLP's eyes widened. "I must come around and see those pants, soon."

"Let's let it go for now. If I need your...powers, I'll be sure and let you know." She started toward the park office. Then she stopped and turned to face him. "How about you come around day after tomorrow," she called out. "Let's say 11 in the morning?"

"Yes, Ma'am, I'll be there. Jones Flower Farm at 11am sharp. And don't wash them!" The Parking Lot Prophet gave her a little wave when he saw her nod. He continued to stare after her as she entered the park office. The Truth comes in many forms, he thought. But a pair of denim jeans? Hmmm. That was a first.

That evening Loc Pham knew Miss Linny wouldn't be out with the flowers so late in the day. So he was starting to get worried when he knocked and knocked at her front door and she didn't answer. Through the soft mesh curtains he saw a light was still on in the kitchen. He knew she wouldn't leave a light on unless she was inside. She was too careful with her money for that. He also caught the smell of cooking dinner as it slipped onto the veranda from an open window. But Miss Linny was not in sight. She'd come by the park office that morning but he'd already left to weed another part of the grounds. Had she forgotten that he was coming around that evening before dinner to pick up his pay check? Funny she would. They'd kept the same Tuesday evening payday routine for two years. He knocked again and this time he let his voice get a few octaves higher although it was still within the polite range. "Miss Linny," he called. But there was no answer. He'd have to come back later. His wife was waiting with dinner at home. He sighed, turned around and was slowly plodding back to his old Toyota in the driveway when he caught a whiff of his bosses cigarette smoke. It seemed to be coming from the shed just beyond the back porch where Miss Linny kept some of her small garden tools. Loc smiled. Ms. Linny hadn't let his family down that week after all.

When he approached the shed he stopped abruptly before the door. It was ajar and he heard voices. His boss was meeting with someone inside. But in the garden shed? He shrugged. Miss Linny was a funny woman. He decided he would just stand there and wait until the conversation ended. As he waited Loc ground his heel into the dirt. He couldn't make out any of the words but the voice was that of a man and the conversation was completely one-sided. Miss Linny was not getting a word in. There was something strange about that. Some Americans had a hard time stopping when they got to talking. Miss Linny, on the other hand, had always been a lot more like a Vietnamese than an American. She got right to the point and was quiet about it, never loud and commanding. This was one of the reasons he liked working for her. But she had no patience for people who talked a lot. Most people in town wouldn't believe that Miss Linny was passing so much time listening instead of turning her head and walking away. He'd seen her do that many times at the garden shop in town.

Loc scratched his head and watched the light coming in through the door. Maybe, he thought, it wasn't even Miss Linny in there. Maybe it was two different people. He could be standing there waiting for nothing. He decided he'd better try to get a look inside to make sure. Loc crept quietly over to the open door and peered in. He spotted some movement next to a big brown wardrobe and folded himself a little around the edge of the door so he could see better. He was glad he was short. Then his eyes widened. It was Miss Linny all right and she was standing there saying nothing...to no one at all. In fact she was facing her open closet and the clothing that hung inside. Loc sucked in his breath. So where was that other voice coming from? Just then Miss Linny turned away from the closet and Loc got a direct view of a pair of denim jeans that looked like they were filled with...a body or at least the spirit of a body. The voice kept talking but Miss Linny's mouth was closed and she was nodding as though talking to a pair of denim jeans was as usual as talking to Loc himself! Loc's hands started shaking. He peered all around the room to see if there was anyone else. There was nobody. He quickly stepped back outside and rubbed his eyes. He cautiously crept to his car and jumped inside; his legs felt like mush. His hands still shaking, he started his car and drove slowly home.

It must be a ghost looking for something from Miss Linny, he thought. In Vietnam this would call for a Buddhist ritual. But where would he find a priest here? And would this jeans-clad ghost respond? Loc steadied his hands on the wheel as he turned down his street. He must be calm he told himself; he must not worry his wife.

Vietnamese Buddhist Priest visits New Halem

The FishWrap Bugle

Thich Quang Dô, a Vietnamese Buddhist monk and teacher from Portland's Three Treasures Buddhist Temple is visiting New Halem until this Sunday. He is also meeting with Reverend Charles Semple of our New Halem United Methodist Church to discuss Christian and Buddhist common faith issues and plan a Buddhist spring ceremony to take place at Nelson City Park next year. Thich Quang Dô (Thich in Vietnamese is synonymous with Buddhist Master) practices in the same tradition as the renowned Buddhist monk and teacher, Thich Nhat Hahn.

According to Master Dô many people in the west still believe that meditation, which is an important part of a Buddhist's practice, is an escape from reality, from the real world. Says Master Dô, "Thich Nhat Hahn once likened people to flowers when he said that

> meditation practice actually helps people who are uprooted become rooted again to society. So [meditation] is not an escape at all. At least it shouldn't be; it depends upon the flower."
>
> Master Dô became a Buddhist monk twenty-five years ago when he was twenty-two years old. He emigrated from Vietnam to Portland in 1998. In addition to his work with the temple and within the religious community of Oregon at large, he also is a regular lecturer at Portland State University and at Southern Oregon University in Ashland.
>
> You can hear Thich Quang Dộ speak at 4pm this Saturday on "Socially Engaged Buddhism" at the New Halem Library. We welcome Master Dô to our community.

The decision to move the pants into the house was without question. It just made perfect sense. So Linny wasted no time carrying them in the next morning. She folded them over a big wooden hanger and hung them inside a spare-room closet. Why did he say not to wash them? She was on the fastidious side and the PLP's order had been a hard one to follow. Would something be removed with a washing? Yes, that must be it no matter how foolish it seemed.

The most important thing now was to keep all this to herself, to herself and that crazy prophet that is. He had an uncanny sincerity about him that made her inclined to believe him. Linny stole one more look at where the pants hung silently. She shut the closet and the door to the spare room. She turned down the stairs feeling a little wary of the pants. At the same time she was confident in her flower farm's success. She made her way to the kitchen.

It was Saturday and Loc was due anytime. They'd agreed that he would work the whole day helping with cutting and preparing dahlias for the first of the big orders. She had a couple of high school kids joining in too. The coffee was brewing and the scones were baking in the oven. On days like this she liked to offer her help a nice treat.

She heard a car pull into the drive. Linny peeked through the curtain to see who it was. It was Loc. But he wasn't alone. There was a man, also Vietnamese and about the same size and stature as Loc, getting out of the passenger seat. But that's where the likeness stopped. This man was wearing a long, brown-colored robe with sandals and his head was completely shaven. He was carrying a bundle of something wrapped in a cloth and he tossed an old packsack over one shoulder.

"Now, what the..." Linny said to herself. "He's brought one of his Buddhist priests with him!" Then she remembered. Loc had called earlier and said he wanted to do what he called a 'flower blessing' prior to the major cutting. This must be the priest who would conduct it. She stepped out on her front porch, waited for the two to join her and thought to herself: I wonder if he likes scones.

Loc nodded at Linny, a grin masking his anxiety. It had come as a surprise that there was a ghost hanging about Miss Linny's place. It was such a peaceful farm without a hint of bad omen in the air. But he'd heard the ghost's voice with his own ears, and after discussing it with his brother, Danh back in Saigon and then his cousin, Minh in Portland, it was decided that a ritual must be conducted. So he'd contacted a priest at the Buddhist temple in Portland where his family went once a month. He knew Thich Quang Dô personally and respected him. Luckily Master Dô was already coming to New Halem for other duties. He would put this hungry ghost to rest. Depending upon how and where they died, these ghosts could wander across an entire continent and terrorize whole villages for decades. What would happen to the quiet town of New Halem if such a ghost were loose here? This one had obviously been out wandering for a while for it to appear in Miss Linny's shed. It also must have had a horrible death if all it manifested into was a pair of pants. As for Miss Linny's response to the ghost the other night, he still couldn't quite figure that out. She was such a practical woman. His brother's explanation about Miss Linny being too lonely made the most sense.

"Good Morning, Miss Linny," he called then gestured to his priest. "This is Buddhist Master, Thich Quang Dô. He is here to do the flower blessing." It made sense to call it a flower blessing for the matter was delicate. He wanted to save Miss Linny the embarrassment of telling her outright that she had a ghost on her property, which needed to be settled. A blessing was the most sensible way of saying what Thich Quang Dô was about to do. By cleansing the house and making an offering of food to lure the ghost they hoped it would come to peace and stop wandering.

Linny nodded. "So pleased to meet you."

Master Dô put his hands together at his chest in a prayer-like position, bowed to her and smiled generously. "Pleased to meet you, Ma'am," he said with only a trace of an accent.

Linny nodded again in return. "Please come in." She stepped aside and the two men entered and stood in the foyer. "Well, ah, would you both like some coffee and scones?" she offered a little nervously.

"Thank you, Miss Linny, but it is best we do the blessing first," Loc replied. He stood a little behind and to the left of Master Dô and glanced down the hall as though he expected someone else to be there.

"Oh, well, then I won't stand in your way," Linny said.

Master Dô handed the bundle he was holding to Loc who unraveled the cloth revealing some incense sticks wrapped in cellophane, a brass bell and a little clay pot.

Suddenly a siren went off in the kitchen. Linny darted through the swinging door to her oven clock. She yanked it to 'off,' grabbed a kitchen mitt, pulled the scones out of the oven, and tossed them onto her wooden cutting board. "Thank goodness, they're not burnt," she sighed and covered them with a cotton dishcloth. Then she dashed back into the hallway. She sure didn't want to miss this for anything; her first chance to see a Buddhist blessing and in her own house! She didn't know too much about the religion but had been acclimated to it a little through Loc and his family. Master Dô had few words for a priest and there was a hush about the whole thing. She'd expected more pomp. Maybe even something a little like Easter Sunday services. This was, after all, a flower blessing. Linny watched as Master Dô closed his eyes, his lips formed in a half-smile. Then he said a prayer that only Loc, still standing a little behind and to his left, seemed to hear. Yes, this was definitely quiet compared with the New Faith Baptist church services back in Norfolk, Virginia where she was raised.

"If you don't mind, Miss Linny," Loc turned to address her, "Master Dô will first bless this house and then we will move outside and into the fields."

"By all means," Linny replied and backed behind Loc and the smiling Master Dô so they could pass her and start up the stairs. Loc was holding the bell. Master Dô lit a stick of incense while he uttered indiscernible words. She noticed he had placed three incense sticks in a fan-like shape on her small mail table next to the door. The little clay pot was also placed there and had sand in it. Well, I'll be, she thought.

There was a knock at the door. When she opened it there were two youthful faces peering at her, one a girl's with a red ponytail and the other a boy's with a dark, buzz cut. "Hello, Miss Jones. We're here to help today with the flowers," the boy said.

"Oh, of course! Come on in, kids." She glanced up the stairway, but the two men were already down the hall. The light jasmine smell of incense hung in the air and the muted ring of a bell was heard. "My flower man, Loc Pham, is having one of his Buddhist priests bless the crop today," she announced as she showed the two youngsters into her kitchen. These kids certainly did arrive at an inopportune time, she thought; so much for seeing an in-house Buddhist blessing.

"Cool," the boy piped. "By the way, I'm Justin Bates and this is my girlfriend, Anna Raymond."

"Well, I'll be...you're Dirk's boy, aren't you?" She'd seen a picture of this handsome young offspring of the owner of Sows Garden Shop. But he'd looked less cherubic in his football picture. "How about some scones and coffee to start your day?" She grabbed plates from the cupboard and coffee mugs.

"Oh thank you, Ms. Linny," came Justin's grateful reply. His girlfriend laughed heartily. She was a tall, good-looking girl who put away scones and coffee as fast as her boyfriend.

While they devoured the scones like a couple of park squirrels onto a sack of peanuts, Linny filled them in on the day's work. Then she excused herself anxiously, "Well, you help yourselves to more. I'll meet you outside when you're ready."

She slipped through the kitchen door just as Master Dô and Loc were descending the stairs. They stopped at her mail table by the door and Loc turned to her. Master Dô placed the incense stick he was carrying—now burned down to three-quarters its original size—in the little clay pot that held sand. "We hope you don't mind, Miss Linny, that we use this table as an altar. We just need to leave this incense burning and these incense sticks here for you to burn later. Oh, and if you have a plate with perhaps a little food to place on it, we would be grateful."

Master Dô nodded. "Yes, we would be grateful."

"I can place a scone on a plate. Or ah, a couple of them," Linny offered.

"That would be wonderful, Miss Linny," Loc said.

In her kitchen Linny put three scones on a plate and added an orange, and before the teenagers wolfed down the rest, she grabbed two more scones to give to Master Dô and Loc and wrapped them in a fresh cloth.

Master Dô bowed when she handed him the plate. "I am grateful, very grateful," he said after placing the plate with the offering on the table. He picked up the orange and placed it beside the plate separately.

Linny noticed a tiny little brass Buddha statue had also been set on the table. She supposed a Buddhist altar was not an altar without one, just like a church was not a church without a cross.

"Now we will go out to the fields," Master Dô announced and he followed Loc onto the porch and down the steps. Just then Anna and Justin emerged from the kitchen and were on the porch with the priest and Loc before Linny could say "Jack Robinson." Soon after, Master Dô, with Loc and the two teens in tow, were moving down the first row of dahlias. Linny dashed into the kitchen for a gulp of coffee before she ran out the door to follow behind them.

That evening Linny got up from her easy chair where she'd plopped a half hour before with a cup of tea. It had been a long, ten-hour day cutting and preparing flowers for shipment. She went out to the hallway and turned off the porch light before climbing the stairs to her bedroom. Glancing at the altar where the scone and orange offering still sat, she shrugged. "I'm ready to accept anything now that I'm harvesting one of my best crops ever." She lit an incense stick, stuck it in the clay pot then bowed to the little table like she'd seen Loc and Master Dô do. She turned up the stairs and to bed.

The next morning Linny sat up, stretched and rolled her stiff shoulders. Early morning sunlight had squeezed through the slits in her blinds and patterned her moss-green bedspread in stark, yellow lines. Thank goodness she only had a half-day's work left to do. Sunday was the day of rest her Papa had always said and she thought of how he would scorn her in his after-Sunday-services-voice if she was even thinking of working instead of praying. Wouldn't he just roll in his grave right now if he knew she had a Buddhist altar in her house? Linny got out of bed chuckling.

She absently pattered on bare feet to her bedroom door and was surprised to see that it was wide open. She backed up. "Now I know I closed that darn thing last night." She never left the door open, never.

Ever since she was a child, she'd been unable to sleep with a wide-open door and there it was wide open.

"Maybe I'm getting a little senile," she muttered as she walked down the hall to the bathroom. On the way she passed the spare room and again, the door was wide open. She shook her head and pulled it shut. "Maybe it was that blessing yesterday. They might have opened that one for some reason." She was still too tired and was willing to give all of it the benefit of the doubt. Until, that is, she descended the stairs after showering and she looked at the altar.

Linny folded her arms across her chest and stood staring at the plate, empty save for a neat pile of orange rinds. "What the heck..." she said out loud. Her gaze turned slowly back up the stairs.

The phone rang startling Miss Linny. She darted to her office off the kitchen.

"Hello, Linny. It's Astra Billings."

The Sheriff! Of all people to call! "Well Hello, Sheriff Astra. How are you today?"

"Good, I thought I'd stop by. I heard you had a big cutting yesterday. Lots of orders coming in."

"Plenty. Am I busy!" Stop by? How could the Sheriff be persuaded not to stop by?

"I'll be around in about fifteen."

On the other hand, Linny had a soft spot for Astra. If she'd had a daughter, Astra Billings was exactly the type of woman she'd want. She was no-nonsense about everything including her mother's oddities. Not being a woman's woman, Linny didn't take to the others in town. Astra was the only exception. She usually looked forward to the regular cups of coffee the Sheriff shared with her. They never disclosed anything real personal; she especially liked that about Astra.

"Okay! I'll see you then."

Linny readied another pot of coffee and fussed around in the kitchen for a few minutes. She'd decided to hand the Sheriff a cup of coffee on the porch and ask that they walk the farm. It was best Astra not enter the house right now. It was too risky.

An hour later Astra and Linny were walking slowly around the farm sipping coffee, the Sheriff's dogs darting ahead. Well-trained, not a single dog's paw came close to a single dahlia.

"You really have been busy, Linny." Astra pointed toward a section of Linny's dahlia field. "The last time I was here all these rows were full."

"Yep, busy is not the word. I can't hardly keep up with the orders. Fine thing after all this time."

"I call it a good streak of luck." Astra took a sip of her coffee.

Linny hadn't thought of it that way. "It's like it kinda fell right out of the sky." She glanced at Astra nervously.

Astra put her hand on Linny's and patted it. "And I hope it lasts for a long time. You deserve it. Your farm is not only the most beautiful farm in the county but you're a business woman this town can be proud of."

Linny shook her head. "Now don't start filling my head. I do what I do because it's what I'm called to do. Just like you!"

Astra laughed.

"What color's your favorite?" Linny asked.

Astra looked around. "I've always liked the red...and the white."

They happened to be standing right next to a row of red and Linny bent down, took a pair of clippers out of her pocket and carefully selected some red dahlias. She walked a few rows over and cut some white. "I've a little paper to wrap them with back at the house," she called over her shoulder. She inserted the white dahlias into the red and handed the bouquet to Astra.

"For me?" Astra looked perplexed but took the flowers. She called her dogs that were sniffing around the compost pile and they all walked toward the house.

"Just because we're women to be reckoned with doesn't mean we forego a woman's touch from time to time." Linny winked at Astra. "You don't need to put them on your Sheriff's office desk—I sure wouldn't! Drop 'em off at your house and enjoy them there."

"I like that idea. You sure do think a lot like me, Linny. Now if I could only get my mother..." her voice drifted off.

When they reached the porch, Linny paused. "I'll go in and get some paper. You'll have to excuse me today Sheriff Astra, for not inviting you in but it's ah, kind of a mess in there right now. We had a big day yesterday."

"I understand, Linny. I've got to head back to town anyway. I'll wait here." She handed Linny her coffee cup.

After waving at Linny who stood on her porch waving back, Astra drove slowly down the drive and away from the farm. She realized how much she appreciated these little chats with Linny Jones, no matter how short. They had an unspoken understanding, the two of them, an understanding that made Astra acutely aware of subtle differences in the other's behavior. Linny had seemed more nervous than usual today. With her farm's sudden success, it was to be expected. But she'd keep an eye on her friend and make sure everybody had the Jones Farm's best interests in mind.

Alien Loses His Pants!
The World Enquirer

United States. According to local sources, an Oregon State flower farmer was standing in one of her fields one sunny day recently when a pair of jeans fell out of the sky. The jeans are believed to be those worn by a Connecticut man who was abducted by a space ship last year on the opposite US coast. Both the flower farmer and the abducted man refuse to disclose their names. But the man swears he was taken aboard the ship and asked to remove his jeans after which he saw one of the aliens try them on. He can't recall what happened afterward for the next thing he remembers is standing in his bathroom shaving the next morning.

The flower farmer in Oregon says the jeans "Definitely belonged to a man" and had an odd brand name: "Suitor." The abducted man did not recall the brand name of the jeans he lost except that he says he almost always buys Levis.

Of further news is that this particular pair of jeans is believed to be inhabited by an alien who is undoubtedly heterosexual in nature and has a very big appetite according to other undisclosed local Oregon sources.

While he drove, the Parking Lot Prophet hummed the same little tune he'd picked up on a sailing yacht the year before where he'd served as a crew member and private guru. The sail took him all the way to Hawaii and back with a cattle-rich Texas man who'd repeatedly sang the tune while he drank martinis. Via a quirk of something likened to luck, he'd run into the man on a Southern California beach a few weeks before the sail; it was at a rally for his public beach-rights campaign. The tune had a catchy mid-ocean wave-like lift to it that the PLP found similar to a mantra. After humming it every day for six weeks while he let out the sails or fastened them, it had become a mantra.

As he pulled into Miss Linny's drive the PLP noticed two things: one was that several rows of dahlias had been dug up; the other was that the central view from her farm was the sky. It was a big bowl of a sky stretching in an oblong over a voraciously colorful stretch of dahlias that Van Gogh would have donated his other ear for. The PLP parked his truck, slid out and stood beside it. He bowed to the floral multitudes accented by a heavenly open sky. He heard a door slam closed and he turned to Miss Linny who stood on her porch watching him, her arms folded. A smile was attempting to curl her lips but was pressured by a frown. He jogged up to the porch and took the few stairs in one leap. "How, may I ask, are you on this fine morning, Miss Linny?"

"Good morning, Mr. Prophet," Linny said. She ignored his question. "I've got something to show you. This isn't what you came for, but...it's related I think." She nodded toward the door then opened it.

"Like a cup of coffee?" she called over her shoulder.

The PLP followed her into a foyer, through a swinging door and into the kitchen. "I do not indulge, Miss Linny, but I thank you for the offer." He made a little bow toward her.

Linny sipped from a mug of coffee as she leaned with one hip against the counter. "You don't happen to know a Master Quang Dô do you? He was here yesterday with Loc doing a flower blessing." She set down her cup. Before the PLP could reply they were out in the foyer again looking at a small corner table next to the door. A white plate sat there with orange rinds gracing its center.

The PLP noticed the little Buddha statue and an incense stick that had burned down to a stub inside a cup of sand. "It looks like an altar, Miss Linny." He peered at the orange rinds. "And perhaps a very hungry Buddha."

"That's exactly what it is," Linny barked. "But not a Buddha..." She paused. "My knowledge of the religion is pretty limited...so who am I to tell the difference between a Buddha and a ghost?" She bent down, her shoulders sloping, so she could look the PLP right in the face. "You tell me."

The PLP stepped back to see beyond her fired-up brown eyes and smiled at her candidly. "I assume you're referring to the pants, madam." With a chivalrous swoop he waved a hand toward the stairs. "Please, take us to thy leader."

Shaking her head, Linny cast him a glance that doubted his sanity. "Leader, hmmph. I wouldn't declare that sort of thing." Before taking the first stair she stopped him. "And how did you know they were upstairs anyway?"

Putting his hands together the same way Master Dô and Loc had done the day before, the PLP purred, "It was a premonition, Miss Linny."

"I see," she said slowly then quickly climbed the stairs with the PLP following. She went to her spare room door, opened it wide and waltzed up to the closet. Throwing it open she exposed a pair of blue denim jeans folded neatly, if a little tightly, on a wooden hanger. "May I introduce you, Mr. Prophet, to the pants?" Linny gestured gallantly toward the pair mocking his earlier movement.

The phone rang as though on cue and Linny darted out the door, down the stairs and to the kitchen leaving the PLP looking at the pants.

"Well, well, what have we here," the PLP said out loud. His voice echoed in the high-ceilinged room. He moved closer to the denim enigma and felt some type of presence but it was muted by—what? He tilted his head sideways like a retriever eyeing a stick. He nodded. "Yes, that must be it." Carefully he reached for the pants, pulled them gently from their folded leg-to-leg position, swung them out of the hanger and hung them by the waist on a hook inside the door. Then he sat cross-legged on the hardwood floor and quietly waited.

The Parking Lot Prophet woke up. At least he thought he'd woken up. He couldn't tell what realm he was in. His head felt like a boat anchor lodged into a sand spit. His left cheek rested on his shoulder and he couldn't lift it. He managed to get his eyes halfway open and realized he was sitting on the floor in Miss Linny's spare bedroom. There was a blanket over his shoulders and the afternoon sun was filtering through a slot in the blinds across the room. He heard voices somewhere out in the hallway, but the words were muffled. One of them was clearly Miss Linny. The other was the voice of a man, the very deep voice of a man.

He tried to screw his neck around to look but it felt like a brick of cement. Then he tried lifting himself from the ground but he might as well have been sitting in quicksand. The forces of gravity would simply not free him enough to undo his legs. They were still in a cross-legged position but numbed. He felt like a soft, New York City pretzel that had been sitting out on the counter too long. The PLP stopped trying to move, gave in to the resistance of his mummified body and let his eyes close again. The muffled voices continued. His mind drifted and he started to dream that he was a child again and he was running to school back in the old country. He dodged into the room as the clock ticked to one minute after eight and the stinging voice of the schoolmaster sang out, "You're late again! You shameful boy!"

The closet door slammed shut and he flipped his eyes open. Miss Linny was staring down at him with a shocked look on her face as though he'd just bulldozed an acre of her farm without consent. He jumped up from his seated position catching the blanket that slipped off his shoulders with one hand. He couldn't believe how clear his head was now and how strong his legs felt. "Miss Linny. What happened? And where are the pants?" were his first words, which were not necessarily his first thoughts.

She stood there like a foregone conclusion. "I don't know where they've gone. I thought they were here with you. You've been in here practically all afternoon." She continued to stand with her hands on her hips.

"What were you doing while I was in here, Miss Linny?"

"I had my tea then I fell asleep in my chair downstairs. Kind'a unusual for me, but—"

"So, you weren't talking to anyone?"

"No. Who would I talk to? You're telling me the pants are gone?" Her voice was almost a moan and instead of the usual affront she looked dejected and sad. Then out of nowhere—out of any known character trait she'd exposed to the town of New Halem—she started to weep. They were slow tears at first, but soon poured down her face while the PLP watched with amazement. He rested a hand on her shoulder. "Now, now Miss Linny. Why don't you take a seat here and we'll look into this." He led her to a rocking chair and sat her down. Her hands cupping her face, Miss Linny continued to sob.

He began to think out loud and paced in front of her. "I assume they're Levi's since Levi Strauss and Company is the most famous manufacturer of American jeans with a long history of success in the apparel industry. In fact men in America's civil war wore them when they fought against slavery. Levi stock was pretty strong up to the 1990's. I don't understand that label Suitor though. But then, who said this particular pair of jeans hails from the United States. They could have emigrated from another country into your dahlia field, Miss Linny. In fact that theory makes complete sense." The PLP looked at Miss Linny.

She was staring at him with an odd, hopeful look. "You mean he might still be here...with me?"

"He?" The PLP gasped while he was at the same time transfixed. She was absolutely enchanted by whatever inhabited the pants. Then he remembered he had a role to play here, that of counselor as well as seer.

At that moment Miss Linny moved her hand to her eyes and began to wipe her tears. Through her mind's eye, the PLP caught a glimpse of a man's body. The man was tall, very tall, was probably around 60ish, but since he did not clearly have a face, the PLP wasn't treated to his facial features. He had a big mop of dark hair, was shirtless, in fact clothing-less except for the jeans, and had back and arm muscles up the yin and yang. Pretty fine specimen for a paranormal being, a non-being, a superhuman being or whatever type of being he is, the PLP thought. No wonder Miss Linny is so choked up. She's probably been waiting her entire life for a suitor like him. "Suitor! Good Godhead! Why didn't I think of it!" he whispered, although it may have sounded like a loud exclamation.

"What?" Miss Linny said.

"Oh, nothing, nothing I was just thinking." He put his hand to his chin. "I have a feeling they're back in the last acre of your lower ten where you first found them." He gave her one of his intense guru on-the-mark looks. He motioned to the door. "After you, madam?"

She continued to move forward and backward in the rocking chair while she wiped the last rivulets from her face. Then she closed her eyes and worked her jaw a little before she set her mouth into a familiar tense line. She rolled her shoulders back and with that, got up. "You sure you have time for this?" she asked.

"Miss Linny, I wouldn't miss this for all the beaches in the world." She followed him out the door and he turned down the stairs. "I mean for at least most. I might make an exception of the beaches on the island of Skiathos in the Aegean Sea and a Rainforest-coast beach in Queensland, Australia and a beach south of—" he went on as he marched down the steps to the front door.

There was only one thought on Miss Linny's mind as the Parking Lot Prophet continued to chatter about beaches: she had to get rid of the pants. Just what had set her to bawling? All she knew was she hadn't bawled like that since she was a baby. Such a bout of cry-babying had no backbone to it. She vowed she never would cry like that again for the rest of her life. It certainly wouldn't suit her now that she was coming into the most productive flower season of her life. To be thought of as dimwitted or, worse yet, given to bouts of female hysteria was unpardonable to her. She knew hysteria was an old-fashioned term but she'd always agreed with Papa: a woman who gave in to fits of crying was not suited to take on anything more than darning and yarning. Such a woman certainly wasn't suitable to be the owner of a successful farm, Linny added to Papa's tried and true advice. She'd make this guru-guy vow he wouldn't repeat what he just saw. You'd think she'd turned into another woman back there by the look of his eyes. Had she become another woman? When she thought of how he'd stood there staring at her like a wound-up clock ready to strike midnight, she knew she had to rid of whatever it was that had set her to bawling, and fast.

Dahlia Season the best in years
Jones Flower Farm Prospers
The FishWrap Bugle

Linny Jones, owner of Jones Flower Farm at 4100 Old Pacific Ridge Highway is experiencing the best dahlia season she's ever had. "I first came to New Halem to farm some 15 years ago and have never seen such a strong crop," Jones says. "My first year here was good. But back then it was because the soil hadn't been planted before and was rich with never having been plowed." She hasn't put her finger on why the current dahlia crop is so bountiful. But she does say that the perfect, early fall days and "no sign of frost just yet" must have a lot to do with it. Meanwhile buyers from as far away as Maine have asked for shipments.

Jones, originally from Norfolk, Virginia, learned all about flower farming in her youth as part of the Jones Family Flower Farm. When her parents died and her brother moved to Florida and switched to alligator farming, Jones decided to settle in Oregon and carry on her own version of the Jones family tradition. She grows tulips in the spring, a short crop of carnations in the summer, and dahlia's in the fall. "I like to focus on one crop a season," says Jones, "because this allows me to give everything I've got to that one special flower. Flowers are like children you see. You have to give them your whole attention and unconditional love." She mentioned plans for an addition to her two-story Tudor home. For some reason it's become a little too small. "We'll see what the next planting season brings," was all Jones supplied when probed about those plans.

They stood side-by-side gazing at a peaceful patch of field. A few rows of dahlias had been cut for orders, but the rest created a rich plaid of red, pink, purple and yellow. Linny pointed to a row. "See that line over there, the red. That's where I found the pants."

The PLP followed her pointing finger and carefully stepped over several rows until he was on the path to the red dahlias. There were the pants, folded up as though nature herself had placed them there after a wash. He walked up to them, Miss Linny following. "Is this the exact spot you first found the pants, Miss Linny?"

"Yep it is." She scrunched her mouth up as she peered down at the jeans. "But these aren't the same pair. They're folded too neatly. They look too innocent. It must be some trick!"

Nodding slowly the PLP agreed. "Let's take a look." He stepped into the dahlia aisle to retrieve the pants.

Linny jumped forward as though to stop him.

"Trust me," he said as he got down on his haunches. "Then again...I think you should pick them up yourself, Miss Linny."

She looked relieved and bent down amidst her beloved dahlias. Then she placed the jeans carefully over her right arm. She gingerly stepped back trying hard not to step on any flowers. The pants dropped from her arm as though they'd sprung loose. She began to stoop to pick them up again. "I guess I—" she started.

The PLP put his hand up. "Wait," he whispered gently not wanting to alarm her. "Let's leave them for a minute."

Linny got down on her haunches next to the PLP. Then they waited. For what, he wasn't quite sure. But he was certain something was going to happen.

Right before their eyes the pants took form. The legs bulged into human-like limbs even though the body inside was completely invisible. Miss Linny's face contorted in horror as her dahlias were bent under the weight. Out of the corner of his left eye the PLP saw the pants moving toward Miss Linny. He protectively shielded her. The pants turned toward the PLP. He pushed Miss Linny out of harm's way and scrambled backward like a crab on his hands and feet crumbling a line of purple dahlias in his path. Then something hit him over the head and he toppled over. Shaking his head and blinking, he sat upright. The pants lay crumpled at his side.

He looked at the flattened pants, which gave no indication that a being had inhabited them. Miss Linny was getting up from the ground, brushing dirt off her legs and muttering to herself, "...those damned demon..."

"I agree, Miss Linny. But did I hear you say, those darling demon denims?"

Before he could stand up on shaky legs she charged over, scooped up the pants and strode away.

"Miss Linny!" he cried. "What you are about to do is abominable! Do you realize, folded over your arm are a pair of jeans, Levi's if you will, that are worn by the most extraordinary being that inhabits this earth at this particular point in time?"

"Mr. Prophet," she shouted back to him, "it is my understanding that these pants are possessed by some sort of demon who has no intention but to bring me ruin. I therefore have every right to save myself and my farm from whatever may come out of them."

She was running to a burn pile. The PLP nearly gagged on his racing thoughts. He ran alongside her and placed his right hand on the jeans. "But, Miss Linny. You have no idea. These pants are not possessed, at least not in the way you think. Since you found them hasn't your farm met with the most profitable yield in all the years you've owned it?"

"That has nothing to do with these pants," she snapped back. "Purely coincidence that I found 'em out there in the field when they happened to fall right out of—" Her voice trailed off and she stopped.

They were now standing in front of the burn pile. Heaps of dried-up weeds, grass, and blackberry vines formed a ready sacrificial pyre for the jeans. It was a cool day, obviously one that hadn't been declared 'no burning.' The PLP stood on the precipice of what Miss Linny would or wouldn't do. He was prepared to snatch the jeans from the pile and make a fast run to his truck where he would start it up and take off to only Buddha knew where. He must save those pants at all costs. But a second thought sidled out of the first and was more urgent: he must save Miss Linny.

He cupped his hands at his chest in a gentle gesture of good will. Slowly, calmly he spoke to her. "Miss Linny, those pants were brought to you here in your own dahlia field for a divine purpose. Are you going to just burn it all away?" He snapped his fingers. "Like that!"

With the haunted pants hanging over her arm like a limp rutabaga plant and the PLP standing next to her with his hands folded in prayer fashion like a saint, Miss Linny wondered if there might be a holier meaning to these crazy shenanigans after all. He did have a point about the farm profits. What if she burned the pants and the profits took a dive? She'd allowed Loc's Master to do his blessing on her land hadn't she? Even though she hadn't been sure what it involved, she'd still allowed it thinking it might keep the orders coming. "Okay. I won't burn 'em." She turned quickly. "But I'm not keeping them on this property!"

The PLP was fast on her trail again as she strode onward like a tall woman determined. "Miss Linny," he called to her backside. "Miss Linny, you must understand! This pair of jeans is a very unusual specimen. As you know, a superior being inhabits them. It is not out to harm you! It was just experiencing...a little healthy male rivalry with me!"

Without a backward glance, Linny strode right up to her truck, threw the door open and handed the pants to the PLP. "Get into the passenger seat...please. You're coming with me to the Salvation Army."

"But there is no Salvation Army in New Halem!" he retorted.

"I know that!" she barked. "We're going right on into Portland with 'em. I'll be damned if I drive with those things alone. Here's another chance for you to use your protective powers." She ushered him around the truck and fitted him and the jeans into the passenger seat. Then she slammed the door and darted back around and into the driver's seat. She was starting up the truck before he could even chant a mantra. The PLP closed his eyes. "May she come to her senses before we leave the New Halem town boundary line," he whispered to the greater will.

Just as they were pulling away from the house, the truck died. Miss Linny cursed, and cranked the engine over and over, but nothing happened. She glanced at the Parking Lot Prophet who sat with the pants folded trimly on his lap. "I guess we'll have to take your rig," she announced.

The PLP got dutifully out of her truck, closed the door carefully and waltzed over to his. He had a premonition about how things would go but only smiled. He let Miss Linny into the passenger's seat after agreeing to place the pants in his camper. He carefully strapped on his seat belt and adjusted his rearview mirror, relaxing into his second favorite seat after the meditation seat.

"Are we ready yet?" came the impatient voice to his right.

"Here we go." He turned the key in the ignition and heard the expected cranking then nothing. He undid his seat belt and placed his arm on Miss Linny's shoulder. "I'm afraid someone doesn't want to go, madam."

Miss Linny crumpled as though she was caving in to something beyond her control. The PLP got out, ran around, opened her door and retrieved the pants from his camper. He placed the folded pants in her arms. "You're safe with them, Miss Linny," he said. She looked down at the jeans and he saw a faint blush of relief cross her face like a wife whose traveling husband has finally agreed to retire and stay home.

He watched her mount her steps. Before slipping inside she turned around and called out to him, "Thanks for your help."

He bowed his head to her, hands folded at his chest. "I think you've made a wise decision, Miss Linny. You know where to find me." But he knew there wouldn't be a need. He heard her door click shut and in his mind he saw her climb the stairs to the spare bedroom where she placed the pants on the same hanger. She'd just closed the closet door when the phone rang and she was running down the stairs to answer it. "Another dahlia order," the PLP said to himself. He stood beside his truck for fifteen minutes smoking a cigarette. He would have to assure Loc that this entity was no longer a threat, that its wandering had met an end. That, in fact, it offered his boss companionship and peace. The Parking Lot Prophet nodded to himself, got into his truck and wasn't surprised when the engine started up. He drove away.

Do Your Dream

by Catherine Kigerl

The Parking Lot Prophet had just arrived at the Sea Sprite Café. Miraculously enough, for a Saturday morning, the best table in the house had been free. It had a prime view of the water and was right in the middle of the room where patrons would most likely be snagged for a good spiritually-based discussion. He adjusted himself in his chair and flattened an article on the table that he'd cut out of the Pacific Rim Dharma News that morning. It was titled, "The Dharma and the Emboldened Mink." He wondered what in the cosmos it could be about. He had at least five minutes before the first unsuspecting patron would slide into the chair opposite, so he began to read in earnest. There suddenly appeared before his nose a dark-skinned hand that placed—right on top of the title of the article—a little card that simply stated: "Do your Dream."

He stared at the card for several minutes. He examined each carefully calligraphically-painted letter drawn in indigo blue watercolor on a faint, light blue background. The card was evenly cut on the edges. A second sense told him the person who'd made the card was inclined toward folksy creations and beliefs.

He finally began to absorb the message "Do your Dream." Only he was doing his dream or more correctly, his vision. What did this charlatan think he, the PLP, was doing sitting here in the middle of the café waiting for his first unsuspecting patron of the day? With the advent of winter, fewer New Halem residents were running and walking the beach in the early mornings because of the darkness and rains. Yet more were sitting in this café so the Sea Sprite had become his morning 'client office.' He leaned forward examining the letters on the card more closely. Okay, maybe there was a dream pointing its finger at him from beyond that faint blue sky or within the magic of those indigo letters. But what? He shifted uncomfortably in his chair. Finally he, slowly and gradually, rested his eyes upon the human being who stood to the right side of his table.

She was a tall, thin black woman. She wore a red jean jacket and a flowery cloth skirt with a paisley design in purple, blue and red. Her dark copper hair was pulled back by a matching paisley band from her oval face which was the color of coffee with milk. Her brown eyes were rimmed with little brown freckles that scattered in an even pattern around her nose. She peered down at him with the intensity of polished gold. There was a little diamond pierced into her right nostril and he wondered why the right side instead of the left. "What do you mean, do my dream?" he asked and gestured to the chair opposite him at the table. "Please excuse my impolite indiscretion, madam," he added.

She smiled, revealing a missing tooth on the right side of her mouth. Could this be why the diamond was placed on that side, the PLP thought, to offset the vacancy? He made a mental note of it. He placed his hands in the usual fashion on the table before him, folded and ready for conference.

But when she sat down, she simply stared at him and didn't say a thing. Then she burst into words like a robin that'd been waiting for the first song of spring.

"And whom do I have the pleasure of sharing a table this morning?" Her voice had a sing-song quality as though it was already tuned. In fact it was like she'd been singing not only in the shower that morning but ever since she'd woken up. She continued to smile and finally she said, "My name is Felicia, Dr. Felicia Douglass. It certainly is a beautiful day in this little seaside town isn't it?" She held out a hand. He took it. Hers was the strongest hand he'd shook since he'd left the Czech Republic fifteen years before. A flood of respect flowed through him toward this woman. He grinned from ear-to-ear.

"I do agree," she said. "Most people in this country don't know how to shake a hand anymore." She nodded her head vigorously. "And whom do I have the pleasure of speaking with this morning?" she asked again, returning an ear-to-ear grin.

The PLP sat mute. How did she know he'd thought that? What was she trying to do, turn his tables around? Those were his tables! He was the one who read minds. He stared at her, trying to read her thoughts. But all he could see was her smile and that little diamond winking at him from the side of her nose. He sucked in a deep breath and let it out slowly. His calm returned. "My name in these parts is the Parking Lot Prophet," he offered.

"And in other parts?" she asked.

"Those parts no longer exist," he replied.

"I see," came her answer.

Thank goodness, the PLP thought, she doesn't know my old name. His guru's command returned and he even sat back in his chair comfortably anticipating a most memorable discussion.

But Felicia got up, nodded at him and said, "It was a pleasure, Mr. Parking Lot Prophet. But I must get on to my business here."

He jumped up from the table. "And what, may I ask, might that be, Miss Felicia Douglass?"

She winced. "Well, I have all my moving-in to do."

"Moving in here? Where?"

She laughed out loud, a hearty laugh chock full of the sing-song. "Just off Parsnip Road." She turned and elegantly strolled toward the door. Before she exited the café, she turned to him, "Later, neighbor."

She smiled, another all-but-one-tooth smile.

The door shut behind her.

To his left Sir Roberts, the janitor at the local high school, was muttering to himself. He looked up and handed the PLP the card Felicia had given him. The card was exactly the same except the colors were different. Sir Roberts' was written in red letters on a faint, pink background.

"You must have a dream to do, Sir Roberts."

Sir Roberts blinked under his wire-rimmed glasses as though he had just cleaned an especially dusty school room. "What dream?" was clearly written on his face although he remained mute. Sir Roberts wasn't inclined to speech.

The PLP nodded. "I'll be working on that answer, Sir Roberts," he replied and handed the man his card. He looked down at the Pacific Rim Dharma News, his interest in the article he'd intended to read now permanently on hold.

New Halem Professional Services
Psychic Healer

Specialty: Energy blockages, physical and emotional for transformative change. Individual sessions at my home office. Will do house, clinic or in-hospital calls.

Contact Felicia Douglass, MD.

Felicia sucked in a long breath of sea air. "Ahhh." She continued to inhale and exhale, her shoulders relaxing, her arms at her sides. "Just what the Dum dee-dum ordered." She gazed at a lip of wave that curled onto the sand below the bank where she stood. She stretched her shoulders and arms over her head. "So grateful to those who have brought me to this shore." She gazed up at the sky. "I've been blessed." She walked the grassy path toward her house that sat on a knoll. It appeared to be a small house because Felicia was approaching it from the front. In reality it was a large house, built in a traditional shotgun style—long and rectangular—like her grandmother's house back in St Louis.

As anyone in St. Louis would know, if a person stood on the porch steps and shot a gun through the doorway of such a house the projectile would most certainly fly out the back door. Unless an unlucky soul happened to be in the hallway. Or an unlucky dog like Grandmother's poor dog Cecil years ago when he'd run down the hall in anticipation of the mailman. Instead of grabbing letters in his mouth, Cecil had caught the bullet shot by a rogue suitor Grandmother had once jilted and hadn't seen in years and whom had gone right back to jail.

The steps were so solid Felicia couldn't hear a creak as she climbed the five leading to her door. Of course with that wind rustling the maple tree in the yard and those waves curling on the beach below, she wouldn't hear a creak if there was one. After stepping inside, and tossing her jean jacket on a chair, she went to the picture window overlooking the yard and the horizon where the sky met the sea. It was a view not only for the aesthetic-minded but quite rightly for the alien-minded. Tonight would be the first night of her watch. "Just think," she sighed, "they'll soon be with us and nobody in this town, except for maybe that Parking Lot Prophet, will have even a clue."

Her mind rested for a while on the Parking Lot Prophet. She had to admit, he'd been hard to read, very hard to read. He kept himself under a tight wrap. But she'd out-clued him. Years of living in St. Louis, of working as a pediatrician in a county hospital for fifteen years and then as a general practitioner in a bourgeois section of St. Louis for the next ten had fine-tuned her psychic intuitions. Through it all she'd clung to her personal beliefs in the unbelievable, like alien visitors and she'd created a dense camouflage. Of- course it didn't hurt to be a black woman who had early in life assumed an unreadable countenance. Stereotypes about black women rarely included belief in aliens. She chuckled to herself. “So, you will never figure me out, Mr. Parking Lot daddy-o!” Still, she had an inkling the little man would prove to be a challenge. He’d been parked here for a while and she had just pulled in. But just how established was he? He had the feel about him of not owning very much, let alone a house or property. “Poof!” she spouted, for she knew damn well home ownership meant diddley when it came to spiritual work. Felicia strolled into the kitchen absently humming her old favorite Miles Davis tune, ‘Freddie Freeloader.’

Tea time had arrived even though most of the kitchen was a blur of unpacked crates. Felicia removed her tea kettle from the stove, added water from the tap and slipped the plastic wrapping off a box of mint tea. She gravitated back to the picture window in the living room. Yes, Grandmother’s death, God bless her old tired soul, had been somewhat of a godsend. Granny’s death had released her from the need to be a doctor any longer. A nephew, Dontay, had sealed the deal. He had just finished medical school and would carry the physician family lineage. There had always been at least one physician for four generations—if you counted her great grandfather, who due to racism, had to practice underground without an official degree. She had proudly carried the title even after things got vinegary. Now she’d finally flown the coop for something sweeter.

“Ha!” Felicia laughed out loud, scaring a pigeon that was peeking at her from the eaves above the picture window. She waved to it, but it flapped away. Yes, she was done with the charity lunches, the catty nurses, the meaner-every-year children—one of which had taken out her front tooth in a state of shot-induced terror. Was that ever the last straw! All of it was left in the wake of her dust when she jumped into her pale blue BMW sedan and landed in New Halem. Here she could do all the alien-watching she chose and from the comfort of her own living room. She was also setting up an entirely different type of practice in this town: that of the psychic healer. Her grandmother had trained her well in that ancient art and she'd practiced it on the side most of her life. Now she was finally going to be able to apply herself to it wholly and legitimately. As for her youthful, medical intern's dream of opening a clinic that combined the art of psychic healing with the science of standard medicine, that was a dream of the past.

Felicia grabbed her binoculars from the couch and trained them on the pale white line at the ocean horizon. Due west. That's where they would come from all right. This window, the ocean, this house, everything was like her dream. It was nothing short of amazing. She'd seen it and now here it was. "Can you imagine that?" She glanced around the room expecting to see her cat, Milky Way, returning a silent agreement with her yellow eyes. But the feline hadn't yet returned from scoping the outdoors for tasty, skittering things. She returned to the kitchen where the tea kettle was whistling. After all these years, Felicia thought, I'm still one amazed and whole-heartedly grateful woman when I live what I've dreamed.

And there had been many times in her life when she had.

When the PLP went into meditation early the next day he struggled against drowsiness. He finally got up from his pillow five minutes early. He grabbed a cigarette and stood on the landing of his camper staring at the horizon where the sea and sky met and became one. His hair was still ruffled, his chin was coated with stubbles. On any other morning he wouldn't let a seagull see him in this state. But today was different. It was not only an unseasonably warm and spring-like day but he had a funny feeling something was coming even though there were no physical signs. The PLP puffed away on his cigarette. Was it extraterrestrials? No, the world's masses weren't yet ready. Despite their ability to elude the eye, even his, with inter-dimensional aeronautics, extraterrestrials were not on the agenda today.

He continued to scrutinize the horizon. The anticipatory feeling became almost tangible. He backed into his camper, took a shower, shaved and dressed. He paused briefly at his camper window and pulled aside the two cotton curtains with white daisy designs etched along the ridges. The sun was not yet refracting a pale pink light upon the beach. The waves were calmer than he'd ever seen them. After slipping on his shoes, the anticipatory feeling lured him outside. It was a still morning, the sky a pastel blue. The sand pipers were jogging at the edges of the waves; foam glided in and out with the lapping sea water.

Breathing slowly he kept walking, farther and farther down the shoreline. No other joggers were out yet that morning. To be alone was something he'd normally relish. But today it made him nervous. He finished a cigarette and put it out in the sand. He picked up the butt with a piece of tissue and examined it. He brought it to his nose and the noxious smell startled him. "Why do I need these?" he asked himself out loud. Then he pocketed the offensive butt.

Placing his hands on his hips, he faced the horizon. His mouth dropped.

From her perch at her telescope, Felicia yawned. She'd gotten up early for her morning watch. The telescope had just arrived yesterday and man, it was a powerful one. She was sure to not miss an alien ship with this instrument. She took a sip of her now cold tea and trained her eyes once again on the horizon for another ten minutes before she took a break. She pressed her eyes to the telescope lens and scanned the flat line of water at the horizon then back to the sand and shrubs below. Something was moving up the hillside to her house. What was it? She jumped up just in time to hear, "Hurry! Get upland! It's coming!"

Felicia got up from her chair, ran out the open door, down the steps and stood with her arms folded at her chest as the Parking Lot Prophet's face bobbed into view. "Now what's he up to?" she muttered to herself.

The PLP climbed the trail to her steps panting. "Did you see it? The wave of water?"

"What? Where?" she asked puzzled. He was holding his hand on his chest like he was about to have a heart attack. "Are you okay?"

The PLP turned around and stared at the beach, a puzzled expression on his face. Then he turned to her and bowed. "I'm wonderful, my lady. I have just seen something quite other-dimensional. Not quite in the line of your extraterrestrial 'do your dream.' But we're really in for it here, I think. Either here or on some other vulnerable coastline."

Felicia frowned and peered into his eyes. She didn't care how impolite it was. She had to determine if he was telling the truth or if he was simply crazy. Her heart fell when she realized he was telling the truth. "In for what? I didn't see anything." She tried to disguise her acute disappointment but "And I've been at my watch for the past hour," slipped out with a jealous twang.

Damn it! She thought. Why didn't I see what he saw? She unfolded her arms and gestured to the house, forcing a genuine smile. "Why don't you come on in and tell me all about it over a nice cup of tea?"

He grinned. "Sorry, madam. I have my usual office hours at the café this morning. Good day to you!" He sauntered back down the trail, soon disappearing into the trees.

"That man is really prickling my skin! How did he know about my alien watch?" Felicia walked back inside and to her telescope. Through her lens the shoreline was as quiet and peaceful as Baltimore at four o 'clock on a Sunday morning. So was the horizon. So was the sky. "I'll be forced to return to standard medicine in this town if he is some type of mystic-seer." She shook her head and let out a little growl. "What did he see that I didn't?"

University of Oregon
Department of Geological Sciences
For The FishWrap Bugle

The US Geological Survey reported today that mild to moderate earthquake activity has been recorded throughout the Pacific Rim Region. Tsunami standby alerts have been issued to several islands in the South Pacific including the Figi Islands, Tonga and the Cook Islands.

On his way to town, two thoughts were on the PLP's mind: how perfectly serene the day was and what he'd seen earlier on the beach must have been a mirage. He looked at the still horizon where water met sky and walked on. Then he looked at it again. Nothing.

Another thought popped up like a marmot pops its head from a den: Can a day truly be this calm? He shoved the marmot-thought back down. The water was lapping too kindly, the morning sun lifting its golden-rayed head too majestically, the shorebirds rising and falling above the waves too acrobatically.

Reluctantly, as the sun continued to ascend, the PLP contemplated how the day's apparent perfection could change with a whiff of the wind...or water. Change. One of the veiled wonders of the Path. He'd seen much change in this lifetime including an intercontinental move from the Czech Republic to the United States and a change of metaphorical 'hats' from broker to guru. Yet sudden change still jolted him.

He forced his canvas shoe-clad feet in the direction of town. He rounded a corner and the Sea Sprite Café signage loomed in the distance. All of a sudden a vessel of acceptance poured through his body. His mind stilled. He felt his heart open and his resistance to what might happen next dissipated like a morning mist. He practically floated the last twenty yards.

At the café he found Felicia Douglass standing at the counter gritting her teeth. The waitress handed her a large cup of coffee and she turned to the PLP.

"Something's up." Her mouth was turned up at one corner; her brow creased.

"Of course something's up." The PLP made a giant circle with his arm. "The world is right today."

She nodded, openly drilling for his thoughts with a doubtful look. "Sorry to spoil your parade, but something is not right today."

"Too perfect is it?"

"Right...I mean no," she said nervously. "It isn't perfect."

He put his hands together at his chest and bowed to her. "It is all perfect, madam. Right or not right."

Felicia rolled her eyes and turned toward the door. Before it closed behind her she poked her head back in. "Yeah, it's all perfect but that doesn't mean something isn't right." The door fell closed.

The PLP shook his head and thought of the many people in the world, Felicia included, who insisted on raining on a sublimely perfect day's parade. An hour later, as he read the New York Times, a shadow crossed over the newsprint. He looked out the window. The sun was shrouded by a dark cloud. He stared at it, willing it to move away. But it wouldn't. In fact it soon developed into a darker and more menacing cloud. Then in a miraculous state of decomposition, it simply evaporated. The PLP laughed out loud as the sun shined supreme once again. He turned to Sir Roberts who was, as usual, muttering to himself at the next table. The two made eye contact. Then a piercing scream rose up from the street outside followed by the sound of a pack of running elephants or kangaroos depending upon what country the likeness was based upon. The PLP watched as a mob of townspeople ran past the café. In the blur of people, he identified William R. Cooke, newspaper mogul-publisher, pointing in the direction of the beach.

Sir Roberts and the PLP dashed to the café entrance and then ran outside.

"What's happening?" the PLP shouted through the din of running feet.

"A wave, a wave..." Cooke cried.

"What?" he heard Sir Roberts mutter. But the PLP was already running. Only instead of following the others he was running toward Nelson City Park and to his truck and camper that he'd forgotten to move off the beach that morning.

He was just past the New Halem Supermarket when he saw it: a giant layer of water that could only make Paul Bunyan drool, if he was a surfer. The next split-second the PLP was running for his life toward anything that could protect him, could serve as a raft or as a coffin if the need called. He spotted the flag pole in front of the New Halem Library and prayed that his feet would make it up that slick, skinny tree before the water engulfed the street.

The PLP scratched his nose. Then he felt himself sliding down, down a slimy pole into a great pool of water. He grabbed the pole with both hands, climbed up a few feet and clung on, his eyes now wide open. What in a guru's nightmare had happened? He looked up at the sky. It was as clear as trout in a mid-winter stream. Above his head, the stars and stripes of the United States flag were flapping with a mild breeze. "My gads, you saved my life!" he shouted up to the strip of cloth and slowly nodded in gratitude, careful not to put his hands together in a bow. He sneezed into one hand then re-grabbed the pole. He looked up and down the flooded streets below. What had happened to the town? Not a person was in sight. Cooke's dog, Rusty Nails, was sitting on top of a picnic table that floated in front of the library entrance. Then he remembered: a tsunami had swept in and he had tried to make a run for his truck and camper.

"Oh, no! It must be...gone! My truck, my camper, my home...argh!" He leaned his forehead into the pole and tried to pray but all that would come out was "Damn it! Damn nature...!" then he looked up at the flag again, reminded that he was still alive. And he prayed.

He was still praying when a voice whispered into his ear, "It's time."

"Time for what?" The Parking Lot Prophet looked around. Up the street a small boat with a churning little motor in back was slowly weaving toward him amidst a bevy of boards, a child's stuffed lion and a collection of plastic bag flotsam. "Hey, partner! You need a hand?" a man called.

The absurdity of the question! "Well, since I only have two hands and they're wrapped around this flag pole at the moment, a third would be appreciated," the PLP mumbled then blurted out, "Oh ah, yes, so grateful you found me." He grinned.

"Then here I come," the man replied.

When the PLP looked closer he realized it was Sir Roberts himself whom he'd last seen at the café. Since he'd never really heard Sir Roberts speak louder than a mutter, he was astounded at how operatic was his vapory smooth, tenor voice. "Sir Roberts! Am I ever glad to see your handsome...voice!"

The little boat slowed almost to a standstill. Sir Roberts stopped the motor and grabbed a paddle from the inside. When he paddled to where the PLP was clinging he gently unfastened the stiff white hands and helped the drenched and shaking prophet into the boat. He wrapped a wool blanket around his shoulders. The PLP sat numbed, staring at his savior. He shook his head back and forth. "You know, Sir Roberts, I should have known it."

Sir Roberts started up the motor again and slid the paddle along the floorboard. He was a short man but had long, muscular arms and a barrel chest. His balding head was hidden under a black beret and he was wearing grey army fatigues and a pair of solid army boots.

Must be the military is already on the scene, the PLP thought.

"Should have known what, Mr. Prophet?" Sir Roberts handed a thermos to the PLP.

After unscrewing the top with shaking hands, the PLP inhaled the scent of hot chocolate. He took several gulps followed by "Ahhhh. Jumping Jehovah's Fax, if this isn't the finest day of my life." Then he glanced over his shoulder at the flag receding behind them. He drew his hand to his forehead in military fashion and saluted to it.

"Should have known what, Mr. Prophet?" Sir Roberts repeated as he steered the boat up the flooded street toward the hill.

The PLP faced Sir Roberts after another gulp of hot chocolate. He beamed at the poised male figure. "That you, Sir Roberts sir, would one day be...a hero."

Sir Roberts smiled and kept smiling as he steered the boat down a side-street.

The PLP raised an eyebrow in alarm and grabbed the side of the boat. "But, but, what're you doing? Shouldn't we be heading uptown? I mean uphill?"

Sir Roberts paid no heed and continued to steer the boat around New Halem Savings Bank—now sitting in four feet of water—until he stopped the motor again and pointed to what used to be the adjacent sports field.

There, grounded on the only spot of dry land in the middle of a newly formed lake, was the PLP's truck and camper. He stood in the small hull of the boat, nearly tipping it over, put his hands together in prayer fashion, and bowed to Sir Roberts. "With this little camper home, you and I will help save the world...at least a part of it." He winked.

Sir Roberts tipped his head to one side. "You'd better set yourself down Mr. Prophet or you'll throw us both into that muddy water."

The PLP dropped onto the boat seat reached over and shook Sir

Roberts' hand. "I am indebted to you, my friend."

"I don't believe it!" a voice cried. "I don't believe it. It's you! Mr. Parking Lot!"

He cupped a hand over his eyes to block the strong sunrays and searched for the body that held that familiar, yet alarmed female voice. "Now madam, if you'd just reveal yourself on this fine but watery day, I'd be forever thankful."

A woman leaned forward from the roof of his camper. She was sitting cross-legged, a straw hat hiding her features, her left hand self-righteously planted on the side of her hip. One intuitive glimpse of her was enough. It was that new woman in town, she of the 'do your dream' cards.

"Why, Miss, I mean Dr. Felicia Douglass! Do I have the pleasure of meeting you once again?"

"You certainly do and I don't know whether to thank you or strangle you!"

Sir Roberts nosed the boat onto ground, jumped out and pulled it onto the bank. Then he ran over to where Felicia was beginning to dangle both legs over the side of the PLP's camper. "Let me help you, Ma'am." She took Sir Roberts' hand and Felicia carefully slid off. As soon as she did she strutted over to the PLP who was still sitting inside the boat a broad smile on his face.

"You saw that wave coming didn't you? You saw it and you said nothing to me or anyone about what you saw. How could you? My new house....is destroyed!" She stomped one foot on the ground.

The PLP got up slowly and gingerly stepped onto land. "But Miss, er Dr. Douglass, would you have truly believed me? Would anyone have in this town?" He paused just enough for her to absorb that for a few seconds. "And do I have the right—" he waved his arm at the flooded streets, "to try to reverse the life lessons this act of nature has brought forth to the citizens of this town? Including yourself?"

"Life lessons?" She was clearly fuming but managed to calm herself.

Sir Roberts was walking around the truck and camper measuring its circumference with a tape measure.

The PLP turned to him then looked at Felicia. "Sir Roberts. Dr. Douglass. We three have been blessed."

"By what may I ask?" Felicia blurted.

"By the presence of this truck and camper. We...have been called to help our stranded, flooded-out and very hungry neighbors."

"You mean you have been called. I have heard no call since the call of the tsunami took down this town...and my house!" Felicia glared at him. "Just what are you talking about?"

"A mobile burrito canteen, Ma'am."

"A burrito canteen? What! Are you insane?"

"Well, depending upon what we can salvage at the restaurants around town, we might also offer rice, fish tacos and coffee!"

She shook her head. "You are insane." She turned away from him shaking her head and began to push the boat off the bank.

"Dr. Douglass, where's your sense of altruism?"

She looked back at him. "It drowned with my brand new telescope, my grandmother's favorite china and my photograph albums containing four generations of Douglasses," she said sourly. Then she jumped inside the boat and paddled down the street.

"You're always welcome to come back and lend your expert tea-making hand," he called. "We don't have to just offer coffee!"

But Felicia didn't turn her head. "My skills as a physician would be better put to use elsewhere in town, Mr. Parking Lot!" she shouted.

"Yes, and indeed they will!" The PLP swung his attention to Sir Roberts. "Well, it's just you and me, dude."

Sir Roberts extended a hand and shook the PLP's vigorously. "I'm with you, Mr. Prophet!"

"Goodness and philanthropy will be yours, Sir Roberts." The PLP paused, once again taken by the man's operatic voice. "How about singing some scales for me."

Not hesitating Sir Roberts started in the key of C, "La-la-la-laaa, la-la-laaaaa!" Then he crept up the scale and sang the notes several octaves higher and after that dropped several octaves lower displaying his incredible range.

Impressed, the PLP folded his arms and nodded slowly. He kissed his hand and lifted it to the air above his head. "Bravo! You are...a singer!" He looked through the wire-rimmed lenses and he saw Sir Roberts' lifelong opera-singing dream in his cobalt-blue eyes. "Do you happen to know how to sing one of those Mexican ballads that tells a story? Or better yet! Let's make one up! We'll call it, 'La Onda!' That's 'the wave' in Spanish! It'll tell the story of your heroic efforts to save the town." He clapped Sir Robert's shoulder. The latter just smiled.

BREAKING NEWS
The FishWrap Bugle

The State of Oregon continues to be impacted by extreme budget cuts in public K-12 education. Small town and rural schools are to be especially hit hard in the months ahead. Faculty and administrators are gearing up for additional reductions in work force and after-school programs.

Someone was pounding on his door. The PLP blinked several times and pulled his legs out of the lotus position. One foot was asleep, the other tingling. The pounding continued. He limped to the door and called, "Who's there, please," in his least irritated voice. He rubbed his sleeping foot.

"It's me, Mr. Prophet. Sir Roberts!"

Drawing the door open slowly the PLP peeked outside. All looked normal on the Nelson City Park beach, not a sign of tsunami damage anywhere. He sucked in his breath. Could he have been...dreaming? "You didn't happen to see a wave did you? A big wave?"

"No, not today," Sir Roberts replied in that exquisite tenor voice. Day-old stubble dotted his normally clean-shaven chin and his eyes were red like he hadn't slept for 24 hours. Instead of army fatigues and boots and a black beret he had on a wool field jacket and navy slacks with a pair of cross-country walking shoes. A tweed cap covered his balding head. He looked more like an agitated British gent than a military hero.

"So, Sir Roberts, my friend! What brings you to my abode on this fine...morning."

"I just lost my job. The school laid me off, Mr. Prophet. They said the budget won't allow them to carry a full-time janitor anymore. A high school kid took my job." Sir Robert's voice drifted off. He folded his arms at his barrel chest.

"Ahem! You don't say. I'm very sorry to hear that." The PLP tapped his chin. "I always say when one door closes another usually opens. Would you mind waiting a minute while I shower, shave and dress?"

"Of course not."

Once inside his camper, the PLP pulled the door closed and let out a huge sigh. What a dream! He'd committed a major act of meditation insubordination—falling asleep on the pillow—but what a dream he'd had! Only it was much more than a sleep dream. It was what Buddhist's called an entering the stream-dream. The PLP blessed the Buddha, all prophets, gods, saviors and saints that the town of New Halem was still intact.

His mind ticked with a new plan as he quickly showered and gave himself a careful shave. He reached for his white pants, slid them on and then reached for his white shirt. He pulled his arms through the sleeves, put on his canvas shoes and stepped outside. "How are you at rolling burritos? And have you ever tried opera singing?"

Sir Roberts just stared at him for a long minute. "I've never tried either," he finally blurted. "I mean—" He looked down at his shoes and, with a sheepish grin, looked back at the PLP.

"What is it, Sir Roberts?"

"I've never told anyone but...I listen to Pavarotti when I'm working, with my earphones," he said nervously. "Nobody knows. Who would suspect?"

"Nobody but me! And...is there something else, Sir Roberts?"

"I try to sing like him at home. Me! I live alone you know."

"Maybe it's high time you tried out your vocals in public," the PLP said. "And rolling burritos is as easy as pie...depending upon the pie of-course. Pumpkin is a little easier than say, mincemeat." He paused. "I hope you're ready to do some traveling. You see, what I have in mind for you is a mobile burrito canteen, with singer."

"Traveling? A mobile canteen? So you mean I'll need to buy one?" Sir Roberts gestured toward the PLP's truck and camper.

"Sir Roberts, I've been called to take the next step on my Path. To not only offer my help as a beach-rights activist and, well, a prophet but to help you set up a business serving natural disaster victims with some deliciously savory grub. Earthquake, tsunami, tornado, hurricane, fire, flood, and landslide survivors will be your priority. Your food mission will be a natural disaster mission. Get it?"

"Ah, I think I do," Sir Roberts replied. "But I can't afford a mobile canteen. I just got laid off."

The PLP placed his arm on Sir Roberts' back. "Don't worry. I'll take care of it. I'm going to help you launch your business. I'm seeing a motor home for you, my friend. A bigger rig than mine. We'll do it a little more bourgeois since you'll be singing Pavarotti while you dish up the entree. There will be plenty of room for you and for a good-sized burrito kitchen too."

"Really?" Sir Roberts looked at the PLP sheepishly again. "And ah, what would you like me to start refining, 'O Sole Mio' or 'Amore?' I prefer the former but I can also sing the latter."

Pavarotti was a stretch from a Mexican balladeer. Yet the PLP knew that the details of a sleep dream, such as what kind of food Sir Roberts would serve and what songs he would sing, were not important. "Go with 'O Sole Mio!' We might even add pizza to your menu or ah, start with it, or let's see. Hmmm. A pizza canteen. I suppose that could work. Who says it has to be burritos? Shall we move my truck and camper then walk and talk over the plans?"

It was Sir Roberts' turn to pause. "Wait a minute." He got into the passenger seat as the PLP took the wheel and they drove up to the Nelson City Park lot. "You said a wave, a big wave. I just heard at the café that a tsunami hit the coast of Argentina this morning."

"You don't say!" The PLP turned off the engine. "Did it do major damage. I mean how strong was it?" The PLP's heart bumped into third gear.

"It was strong. Took out a whole town. But it's only going to create some good surfing waves down south in San Diego. No warning's been issued here on our coast."

The PLP sighed. He got out of his truck, turned south and bowed in the direction of Argentina. "May they be at peace and free from suffering," he said. At the same time he felt a great sense of relief that the watery repercussions of this particular southern hemisphere quake wouldn't be tapping the toes of New Halem beach-walkers.

Sir Roberts came around the truck and stood next to him.

"Unfortunately, Sir Roberts, you aren't geared up yet to take your food mission that far. You'll have to start with the North American continent. I'll help you do a trial run here in New Halem. After the Mayor's Beachcombers Festival in May, you'll be ready to shove off." He tapped his chin again. "The more I think of it in the moment, the more I see you serving pizza. You'll want a vegetarian option as well as pepperoni."

"But won't I need a pizza financier, someone who'll back up my supplies of ingredients like tomato sauce, cheese and—"

"I'll take care of it, Sir Roberts." The PLP absently pulled at his goatee. His mind shifted to his cousin Marcus in Albany, New York, who was in charge of his bank holdings. When the PLP left Wall Street the two had decided to create a trust fund he could dip into to do his work. His expenses were minimal so he'd barely tapped it. He recalled the voice in his dream that had whispered 'It's time,' as he'd clung to the flag pole.

"So...you will take care of it?" Sir Roberts sounded uncertain.

He turned to Sir Roberts. "Yes, me," the PLP assured him. "Yes, me."

"Thank you, Mr. Prophet." Sir Roberts put his hand to his mouth. "But how will I...repay you?

"By singing, serving tasty pizza and helping the struggling masses."

"I see." Sir Roberts was obviously struggling with the new idea but at the same time seemed excited about it. "I do a real nice pizza dough," he offered. "I'm kind of partial to anchovies though."

"Anchovies, yes! You must have anchovies!"

Together they took the trail to the beach. The water was lapping the shore quietly and there were lots of joggers and walkers at that hour. The Parking Lot Prophet waved at the lovely Miss Maggie Billings as she approached him at a steady clip. In his younger, pre-guru days he would have been envious that this fellow activist's heart was turning in the direction of Mr. William R. Cooke. There may have even been a check into Cooke's financial portfolio to see if it rivaled his. Instead, at this juncture in his post-Wall Street life, he felt glad for them both, although his gladness was weighted a little more on her behalf than his. To be sanctified by a meteorite on a mission that ended in one's own home was nothing short of a miracle.

"Miss Billings. I am as always honored." As he bowed before her he removed an invisible hat and waved it away from his chest.

"Mr. Parking Lot Prophet. Things are looking up today!"

"And I assume that will be further than your roof, madam?"

She smiled and shook a finger. "If I have my way it will."

"May the powers that be, be with you." He allowed himself a wink.

She just laughed and with a "Ta-ta!" went on with her walk.

About a mile down the beach the PLP stopped.

"What, Mr. Prophet?" Sir Roberts asked.

The PLP patted his shirt pocket. It was empty. "Ha!" he shouted and clapped his hands. "It appears, my dear friend, I have given up smoking!"

Sir Roberts slapped him on the back. "Way to go, Mr. Prophet."

He took a long, slow inhalation of air and let it out. "Such good air. We are so fortunate to have good...air." They continued on.

"Mr. Parking Lot...Prophet!" called a sing-song voice to his right.

He turned and saw Felicia Douglass standing there, one hand on a hip. She was breathing heavily as though she'd been jogging.

"Ah! Miss...ah Dr. Douglass. How are you today?"

She shook her head then smiled. "Very well and yourself?"

"I could not be better." He thought of asking how her new telescope was working out but decided against it. Instead he queried, "And are you all moved in now?"

She nodded. "Everything and the kitchen sink. I brought way too much with me."

"A standard American woe. But you've plenty of land there on Parsnip Road."

Felicia looked puzzled. "Land? A house was all I needed to get my psychic healing business off the ground." She paused and looked thoughtful.

"There is a need for another clinic in this town...if you were wondering." He continued to stare at her unabashedly.

She looked at her watch nervously. "My run time's about to expire. We'll have to continue this conversation later," she nodded to Sir Roberts and began to jog down the beach.

"Yes, later, Dr. Douglass," the PLP called.

But in his mind's eye, the PLP saw a medical clinic next to a house on a bluff, a clinic that combined standard medicine with psychic-healing. In the house, Felicia Douglass sat comfortably at her telescope, her family photographs lined up on her bureau, her grandmother's china intact in her china cabinet. All this, he thought and without the help of a single wave.

In Which Relationships Are Key

by Gwendolyn Van Hout Knechtel

Come One, Come All!

By the Book owner, Adele Donley Delacruz, invites you to a pre-holiday sale November 3rd – 5th. Selected titles are 10% - 15% off. Enjoy a cup of hot cider and browse our newly expanded children's section or wander our Internet aisles at: www.bythebook.com

We're open Tuesday – Saturday 10AM – 5PM

Support Our Community Theater

Enjoy wonderful wine and tantalizing tapas Saturday, November 25th, 7 – 9 pm at Sea & Sky. Tickets are $20 apiece and benefit New Halem's Community Theater. Come join the fun as Chef Drew Delacruz introduces the flavors of sunny Spain. Tickets available at The FishWrap Bugle and By the Book.

Art with a Heart!

Lahkanea Art Studio is the place for photographs, painting, pottery and tasty edible art.

Winter Hours: Wednesday through Saturday 10AM – 5PM. For that hard to buy person give "Art with a Heart". Watch for the new culinary classes starting in January! For more information check our web page at: www.lahkaneaart.com.

Coffee. The smell of it was enough to make him weep. Too many hours on the road and too few caffeine breaks. The source seemed to be the bookstore. The rich aroma wafted through the door as he entered and his eyes fastened on a cart where a coffeemaker streamed strong dark brew into a glass carafe.

"May I help you?" inquired the young woman behind the counter.

"Ah...would you mind if I had a cup of coffee? I'm quite desperate."

She smiled. "Help yourself."

"Bless you my child." The tall man poured a cup and sipped gratefully then returned to the counter. "Nothing like a shot of java after a long drive. I'm Kevin McLeod. May I know to whom I owe my eternal salvation?"

"Verity Haydn. And a simple thank you will do. I only dole out eternal salvation every third Wednesday. But if you'd like information, we do carry many books on the subject."

"Ah – an educated woman of spirit." Kevin took her hand, kissed it. "I look forward to our acquaintance."

Verity withdrew her fingers gingerly. "Are you vacationing in our lovely seaside town, Mr. McLeod?"

"Actually, I'm here for a job. I heard about your well known theater and signed on for the next two productions."

Verity sighed inwardly. An actor – she should have known. "Well, welcome to the neighborhood, Mr. McLeod."

"It's Kevin..."

"Not until we know each other longer." At twenty, she'd learned a few things about handsome charming men. "Now, is there anything else I can help you with?"

He set his cup down. "Directions to Bishop's Playhouse."

"Well, since it's open only on specific days off-season, I doubt you'll find anyone there. But the sports editor of our local newspaper, Jeffery Roland, may be able to help you. He's the gentlemen in charge."

"Excellent. And where will I find the honorable Mr. Roland?"

"Working in his office. Take a right on Bayview Road; it's the next street over. Then take another right on New Halem Drive. The Fish-

Wrap Bugle will be on your left."

"Thank you, Ms. Haydn, for the coffee, the conversation and directions. I look forward to future conversations with you." Kevin took his cup and neatly disposed it in the trash can. He doffed an imaginary hat, bowed and executed a precise about face and was out the door when he nearly mowed down a woman.

"I'm terribly sorry – didn't mean to run you over." He steadied the auburn haired lady.

"No harm done," she assured him.

"That's a relief! Don't want to start my first day in New Halem getting arrested for assault."

The woman laughed. "I'm sure Sheriff Billings has better things to do than to harass tourists."

"But I'm not a tourist. I'm a thespian come to join the Bishop's Playhouse – Kevin McLeod."

"Welcome to New Halem, Mr. McLeod. I'm Adele Donley Delacruz, owner of By The Book."

"Great store! You have a very helpful employee and excellent coffee."

"Thank you. Drop by any time. We're open off-season, Tuesday through Saturday from ten to five."

"Thanks for the invitation. Well, time to find Mr. Roland. Good to meet you." He gave her a courtly bow.

"We'll look forward to seeing you soon." Adele resisted the urge to curtsy. "See you around town."

"I'll look forward to it," the young man said then walked briskly to his destination.

Adele entered her place of business convinced that Kevin McLeod should be crowned New Halem's Ham of the Year.

From the window of his restaurant, Sea & Sky, Drew Delacruz observed his sister-in-law smack into a tall dark haired man. Interesting way to meet someone, Drew thought, though the guy looked too young. Had Allan lived, he wouldn't be thinking about a man for Adele. Still, it was six years since his fraternal twin's death. Time to move on.

Drew recalled the long ago conversation that brought him and his life partner, Daniel Benson, to the Oregon coast. Adele, widowed just a year, returned from a vacation and surprised him with her news.

"I bought a bookstore, Drew, in a small seaside town. The building was recently renovated. It has a two bedroom apartment above the store where Alona and I can live. You know how I feel about the Oregon coast – being near the ocean brings me solace and strength. And thanks to what Allan left us, well, I figure it's the best place for my daughter and me to make a new start."

"Darling girl, it's only been a bit over a year..." Drew squeezed Adele's hand. "Are you sure you want to leave Seattle?"

Her hazel eyes sparkled. "You and Daniel will love New Halem! And there's a restaurant for sale a few doors down. Here's your chance of having a place of your own. You told me Allan left you enough to dream big. Time to do it, Drew. Talk it over with Daniel. I know the two of you love the city. Bet you could buy a house with plenty of room for out of town guests. And if you want a weekend away, Alona and I would feed your cats."

"Interesting you should mention moving. Daniel's decided to try his hand at consulting. He says the firm isn't the same since Allan died. And he can take his expertise anywhere as long as he has Internet access and isn't too far from an airport. Daniel's been talking about a home office; the commute is getting to him."

"Is that a yes?"

"It is indeed my beautiful outlaw."

Remembering the moment, Drew smiled. He wondered where the

years had gone. Alona (who now preferred to be called Lonny) was nine and in fourth grade. Adele's bookstore was doing well. Daniel's consulting business prospered and the restaurant earned a great review in the Oregonian. Now if he could get Adele a good man, another chapter of the Delacruz family adventures could begin. This would take considerable thought and planning – along with bribery and trickery. But Drew knew he was up for the challenge. He'd think about it while he prepped the dinner menu.

Drew slid an omelet filled with chorizo and cheese onto a warm plate. He topped his creation with fresh chunky salsa, added a side of crisp hash browns and placed it in front of his longtime partner.

"I'm glad you don't get tired of cooking." Daniel took a bite of the golden eggs. "Mm... this is superb, sweetheart."

"Glad you like it." Drew stood behind the Vulcan gas range and started his omelet. Soon he was enjoying his handiwork.

"I do like Sundays," Daniel remarked. "Especially when we don't have a long list of things to get done!"

"Well, Adele and Lonny are coming for dinner today. I've decided on a good autumn meal, stuffed pork chops with roasted vegetables and for dessert, a pear and apple tart drizzled with caramel sauce."

"Sounds perfect."

"You know, love, I've been thinking it's time for Adele to start dating."

Daniel cocked an eyebrow. "Really? Don't you think she'll have something to say about it?"

"Well, I thought with a bit of strategy, that part won't come up."

"And what strategy would that be?"

"It's called 'Let me introduce you to the next love of your life'."

"I take it you have someone in mind."

Drew smiled. "Of course. Aiden Campbell. His family operates Campbell Estate Winery in the Willamette Valley and he's their local representative. Sea & Sky has a fine pinot noir and chardonnay from there. And you know how Adele loves a good pinot noir. We're negotiating a deal to use a few Campbell Estate wines for the Bishop's Playhouse fundraiser. If it goes forward I'm sure Aiden will be there – a perfect way to introduce our favorite outlaw."

"And if the deal falls through?"

"He'll receive an engraved invitation to the Benson and Delacruz annual Winter Solstice Soiree."

Daniel shook his head. "You are a hopeless romantic, Drew."

"Nope – I'm a hopeful one."

Adele stared at the blank page of her journal. An evening peace, warm and quiet, flowed through her as pen touched paper.

Lonny and I had a wonderful autumn dinner with Drew and Daniel this evening. The dessert was especially delicious. My brother-in-law has the culinary magic touch and we enjoyed the benefits.

Lonny is finally asleep after begging for one more chapter of A Wrinkle in Time. The book has fantasy elements, but for me, the heart of Madeleine L'Engle's story is family love and how it strengthens each character. The relationships in this timeless classic are very real. Like these storybook people, we all want to be understood, to fit in and do what we can to find our way through the challenges of life. Some of us do this by self-reflection and grow in mind and spirit. Others of us forget to do the homework piece and that can be problematic.

After Allan died, a grief counselor suggested that writing would help me move through the pain. Well, it did help – though some days the pages got wet from tears and made the ink smudge. Sometimes it still happens. I will always miss Allan for our love was strong and good. From it came our beautiful Alona. And what a blessing she has been!

Every day at 5pm, I close the bookstore and climb the stairs to our apartment. Usually Lonny is doing homework, or checking contents of the crock pot. My nine year old daughter is an insightful fourth grader. Her creative gifts can be a blessing and a bane. Some days I wonder if it would have been easier to stay in the city where educational choices were plentiful. Perhaps I was selfish moving us away from the energy of Seattle to a small town by the ocean shore. But at the time, I needed to walk sandy beaches in fair weather or foul. Allow the ocean to soothe and strengthen; the wind and waves to restore dreams. Hold dear memories of the wonder, the power of love. And to heal.

Love. It can bring joy, comfort and peace and it can bring pain, sorrow and uncertainty.

My young employee, Verity Haydn, is definitely in the hurt and sad stage. She's told me a bit of her story of heartache. Currently, all men are suspect. When I mentioned I ran into (literally) the new actor in town, she sniffed. Further comments of him being a friendly sort were greeted with eye rolls. Verity pointed out he was an actor and probably was playing the part of a charming new-to-town guy.

Had to agree the latest addition to the Bishop's Playhouse cast could easily win a Ham of the Year award. Still, there was something genuine about his easy manner and infectious charm. Kevin McLeod made me smile.

Today I found my way to Drew's restaurant; the Sea and Sky is one of my favorite places to eat. The menu changes frequently and is farmer's market fresh. I'm partial to the spinach and feta pizza, Caribbean salad and pico de gallo tortilla soup. Actually, I'm a huge fan of the entire menu as my figure can attest! My only complaint is that off season hours are at the whim of the chef and proprietor. Not that I can blame my brother-in-law; it's pretty quiet weekdays in New Halem during the colder months.

Of course, I could hassle Drew about this, but then he might say he'll only be open for fewer hours. Since I enjoy lunch at the Sea & Sky at least once a week, mum's the word, otherwise no more onion soup or pear, Stilton and toasted walnut salad. And I can say farewell to flaky croissants and irresistible chocolate caramel cream puffs. Better stop – I'm beginning to sound like Glenda Gadabout waxing poetic in one of her food reviews!

Still, Sea and Sky cuisine is worthy of such words – just ask my bathroom scale. Every week, after I weigh in, I'm ready to use a very old fashioned hammer to help change its mind. I rarely agree with the scale's unbiased opinion – even though it is the height of modern digital technology.

Meanwhile, I'll walk a few extra miles so I can be ready for the Bishop's Playhouse fundraiser. With Drew at the culinary helm, should be an evening of fabulous food and wine. Guess I'd best get the old hammer ready for the bad news the scale will certainly deliver. Ah well, it's all for a good cause. New Halem's community theater is tops!

When Allan and I were first married, we had season tickets to the Seattle Rep. Now I buy tickets for plays that use local talent. If it's not a production my daughter would enjoy (Lonny's rather particular) I usually treat Drew and Daniel. It's always good to spend time with family celebrating the arts.

Sometimes I still wonder what my life would be like had Allan lived. Would I be in New Halem running By the Book and enjoying lunches at Sea & Sky? Probably not. My former life was all about identifying then selecting worthy causes as part of my husband's dreams. He made money and was all about sharing it.

Allan will always be part of my life. If I ever meet another man, I hope he would understand. A new love doesn't replace an old one - it's just what it is - different and special to the two people involved. And life does go on...

With the holidays around the corner, time to start displaying the extra inventory. The shoppers are coming! By the Book will be ready with the latest novels by favorite authors as well as fun items like CDs, cards and stationery. I'm thinking of adding additional candles to the Warm & Cozy Corner. Last season, flavored tea, coffee and hot chocolate sold well so plan to stock them alongside decorative mugs.

Being a small business owner is hard work; however, it has it perks. I've always wanted to put together a personal favorites list. Every morning when I open my store, I see the titles on a specially designed "Adele's Favorites" poster. Never fails to warm the cockles of my heart.

The ocean's lullaby is calling me to bed - a soothing song this time of year. Fall is my favorite season; I love the wonderful colors, the feeling of new beginnings and especially, the autumn air which gives me a peaceful night's rest...

Hard as she tried, Lonny could not find passage to dreamland. A Wrinkle in Time, made a wrinkle in the nightly visit with the Sandman. When her mother had checked to see if Lonny was asleep, she did her best impression of a possum. Then the possum turned into a squirrel skittering inside her mind not allowing the Sandman to enter.

She tried to recall ways to induce sleep and remembered her Uncle Drew sharing he liked to work on new recipes. Uncle Daniel preferred multiplication tables and her Mom, journal writing.

Lonny swung out of bed, enveloped herself in a warm robe and slipped behind her desk. Her journal was on the shelf above hidden behind several books; she grabbed it, found a pen and started to scribble.

Tonight I can't sleep. All I can think of is kicking Ellen Ferguson for asking if Uncle Drew and Uncle Daniel got married which one would be the bride. Maybe Ellen will move to another school. Another state. Another planet. Why do I have to be stuck in the same class with this ignoramus for another year? And now, Ellen's mom is PTO president. Ugh - one Ferguson in the building is enough!

Not everyone is like Ellen of course. But one of her is one too many. That's what I think anyway. And thinking can get you in trouble. Or is it talking about what you think that really does it? However it works, it landed me in a pullout class for gifted kids. Might as well tattoo "different" on my forehead. Okay - we did some pretty cool stuff like putting the Big Bad Wolf on trial for threatening bodily harm to the Three Little Pigs. I played the lawyer and got to be dramatic and verbose. Night of the Notables project was awesome too; I gave my report dressed as Amelia Earhart.

Ellen claims I'm a snob and that her mom says the gifted class is just a bunch of show offs. Mrs. F and her daughter need to ask the Great and Powerful Oz for brains! If I told Ellen that she'd probably be clueless - unless she saw the movie.

I don't want to worry Mom about all this stuff. So for now, I'll keep my problems with Ellen Ferguson and her wicked witch of a mother, my secret.

Adele flipped the sign to OPEN. She started the coffee and hot water for tea then booted up the computer. Grabbing a cup, she poured some fragrant java and checked online orders. Insistent meows led Adele back to the second floor to open the door for Frodo, her daughter's rescue kitty. "Hey cat, ready to curl up with a good book?"

Frodo's gold flecked eyes regarded her briefly; then with a swish of orange and white-striped tail, headed down the stairs. Adele followed him slowly and pondered the daily To Do List. Her part-time employee, Verity Haydn, would be in after her community college classes to work on the Cozy Corner. With Thanksgiving and Christmas arriving soon, it was time to mix autumn leaves with a few holiday items.

As Frodo jumped onto an overstuffed chair near the Children's section, Adele surveyed her small book-filled kingdom where all seemed in order. If it were only so in her personal life! Something was up with Lonny. Last night her mother radar noted her child's pretend sleep. Having once been a fourth grade girl, she knew the routine. Something was bothering her daughter. Adele hoped Lonny would share what was troubling her. An upsetting secret, kept silent, could cut deeply into the tender heart of a young girl.

A mixed blessing, that's what Lahkanea Studio was, thought Emma Invelt Bauer. Just what a forty-five year old woman and her forty-eight year old husband needed. The idea of running a studio that offered classes was a dream they never thought would happen. It took Aunt Aggy's death to make it come true. Emma smiled and silently thanked the woman that had always said, "If I ever win the Lotto – my business will be to finance dreams."

Her Aunt Aggy hadn't won the Lotto, but her wise investments gleaned a healthy bank account. Since she never had children, her wealth was willed to her sister's only child. Ten years ago the Bauer family moved to New Halem. Jeremy was seven and Elise four when she and Jonathan bought the studio. They'd both been thinner then with hair not yet streaked with gray. (Oh why didn't she remember to color it more often?) People in the small seaside town accepted them – a brown-skinned woman of Asian and European extraction and her sandy haired, blue-eyed husband.

Lahkanea Studio had become the place to purchase a variety of art and attend classes. Pottery, paintings and photography were main attractions, but after a recent exceptional dinner at the Sea & Sky, Jonathan had convinced the chef to teach a class. They would hold it at their home where last spring a dream remodel had expanded the kitchen and added new appliances. It was the perfect place to prepare great food and have a party.

With the holidays fast approaching, Emma and Jonathan's quiet off-season would turn into several weeks of shopping frenzy. She wondered what her husband of twenty years thought of designer chocolates as edible art. The studio needed more holiday inventory and chocolate always soothed the soul. Who could resist dark, delectable truffles all dressed up for Santa Claus?

Emma looked at the ordering catalog, glossy with sweet delights. Something chocolate sounded mighty good...she'd just dash into the bakery, grab a coffee and brownie. Or better yet, she'd send Jonathan. More than one brownie would be bagged since his resistance was even lower than hers.

She located him in the small office, checking online orders. "Jonathan, what do you think about carrying designer chocolates for the holidays? Something local we could bill as edible art?"

He looked up from the computer. "Sounds good."

"Actually, what sounds good is some coffee with a side of brownies from the bakery."

"Didn't we just have lunch?" Jonathan eyed his wife warily. The last time he visited the bakery he returned with a lot more than ordered. His spouse loved the selections until after eating an éclair and a cream puff, she moaned about never being able to lose weight and why had he brought so many goodies to tempt her? Then he became the culprit.

"That was hours ago, sweetheart!"

Jonathan dropped his eyes to the screen, quickly typed a word.

Without a doubt this was a no-win situation and would require the utmost diplomacy. "Double fudge or regular?"

Jeremy Bauer pocketed the keys of his silver Saturn SL2. The thrill of having a ride hadn't quite worn off, though he'd had his driver's license for a year. He bounded up the front porch steps where his trim fourteen year old sister, Elise, greeted him.

"That you Galaxy Boy?"

"None other."

"I need a ride to McFarland Square."

"Like that will happen! I just got home from drum line practice, Listless. I'm starved."

"Don't call me that!"

"Well, don't call me Galaxy Boy. Galaxy Man maybe."

Elise snorted. "Yeah, right." She had given her brother the nickname when he'd inherited the Saturn sedan last February for his seventeenth birthday and it fit him perfectly. Too often he was in outer space and flying blind.

Jeremy stuck his head into the fridge. "Any leftover pizza?"

"You ate yours before we went to school this morning after breakfast."

"Well, I see two pieces in here."

"Better check if it belongs to one of the parental units. Last time Mom taped TOUCH THIS AT YOUR OWN PERIL, on her stuff."

"Yeah, she's a real comedienne. Don't see any warnings though – so it's mine."

"Wait a sec. Note the ELISE in permanent ink. They're my leftovers. But I'd be willing to trade for a ride."

"Fine." Jeremy grabbed the pepperoni pizza, shook it onto a paper towel and warmed it in the microwave. "You also have to make me a p and j."

"Honestly, you're like a garbage disposal." Elise watched her brother inhale the pizza.

"Hey, like Dad says, 'It takes a heap of vittles to feed a growing boy'."

"Okay, I'll make you the stupid sandwich, but then you have to give Jenna a ride too."

"Man, I am not gonna be a chauffeur for your loser friends, Listless."

"Come on big brother – I'll even get you a glass of milk to go with the p&j."

Jeremy guffawed. "Throw in an apple and dinner clean up and maybe I'll consider it."

"Okay, deal."

"And don't forget to cut up the apple. I don't get these damn braces off for another two months."

"Poor Galaxy Boy. Bet it makes kissing Aubrey Bellamont a challenge."

"A lot you know."

"Jenna said she saw you in a lip lock with Aubrey the other day."

Jeremy glared at his sister. "Tell Jenna to quit spying on me."

Elise grinned, her voice dripped saccharine. "Of course, maybe it was Azule not Aubrey. How do you tell them apart?"

"Shut up and get with the food prep. It's your night to cook dinner so better be back before Mom and Dad get home from the studio."

Elise grabbed the peanut butter from the cupboard. "I already have dinner planned. I'm using a recipe from Mr. Delacruz that was in the FishWrap."

"A little upscale for you – actual cooking is usually Dad's and my department."

"I can do an easy and elegant dish," Elise said primly. She found two pieces of bread and spread them with peanut butter. “But maybe I'll have you taste test before I serve it. Better you die than us.”

“Hurry up before I die of starvation,” Jeremy retorted. “Then you and Jenna will have to walk to town.”

The calico cat licked its paw with great concentration.

“Come on CC, I can't spend my entire evening waiting for you to come in.”

Green eyes rimmed in gold stared at Emma then CC started on her other paw.

“You're as difficult as a teenager! Fine. Ignore me you wretched feline. No treats for you!”

At the word “treat”, CC abandoned her toilette and entered the Bauer kitchen.

“And they say cats don't understand words. Ha. You know ‘treat’ just fine.” Emma scooped up the pet and hugged her. The cat meowed, wriggled, meowed.

“You torturing CC again, Mom?” Jeremy headed straight for the cookie jar, dug out several snickerdoodles and disposed of them in record time.

“No, I'm not. Now that my children regard hugs as suspect, I have to pass them along to this member of the family.”

“Well, it sounds like CC isn't interested. Man, that cat can yowl! Here, I'll get something to quiet her down.”

Emma watched her son grab the pouch of Kitty Delights from the top shelf of the pantry and wondered how he got to be as tall as his father. It wasn't too long ago when Jeremy used the step stool to reach high places. Where had the time gone?

“Here ya go, Calico Critter.” Jeremy dropped a few treats into the cat's empty dish. “Enjoy.”

"Thanks, Son."

"No problem, Mom. Always glad to assist my wonderful mother."

"Hmm. So, what is it this time, Jeremy?"

"Why is it when I'm trying to be helpful, you think I want something?" He pulled a hurt face.

"Oh, I don't know – maybe that gleam of desperation in your eye..."

"Fun-nee, Mom."

"We do our best."

"Well, actually, there is something." Jeremy grinned, draped an arm over his mother's shoulder. "I could use a little extra cash."

"And why is that?"

"You know payday isn't until next week and I promised Aubrey I'd take her out for a latte after our study date."

"I suppose a can of pop from home isn't going to cut it." Emma tried to hide a smile.

"Aubrey would think I was a total loser!"

"Gracious – we couldn't have that happen! Why the world would stop and everyone think Jeremy Bauer was a cheapskate."

"So that's a yes, right?"

Emma found her purse, took out two fives and handed them to her son. "Don't forget where they came from on payday."

Jeremy gave Emma a quick hug. "Not a chance, Mom. Thanks. Well – I'm off to meet Aubrey at the library. I'll be home by ten."

"Eww – CC's shedding again." Elise picked cat hair from her morning orange juice.

"Great observation, Listless. Just close your eyes and finish it. I'm meeting Aubrey before homeroom today and we've gotta go."

"You just saw her last night; what's the deal? I've got to hurry because it's been too long since you've been in a lip lock?"

"Zip it or you don't get a ride."

Emma prayed for patience. "Jeremy, remember who pays the car insurance. And Elise, CC had her shots. A little cat hair won't hurt you. Now put your dishes in the sink before you go."

"Okay, okay – we're out of here." Elise scrunched her nose, drained the glass, and whisked it to the sink. "Come on brother dear."

"I'm way ahead of you, sister dearest." Jeremy followed his sibling and dumped the bowl with a clatter. "Last one out has to clean CC's litter box!"

They raced for the door; Elise barely managed to squeeze out before him.

Emma sighed as her spouse entered the kitchen. "Why is it you always miss the morning drama, Jonathan?"

"Excellent timing." He poured coffee in his cup, added cream. "So what's on the agenda at the studio today?"

"The usual and one unusual."

"Really? And what would that be?"

"An interview with the FishWrap Bugle's social events reporter."

Jonathan took a sip from his mug. "Hmm. I think I have lots of things that will keep me busy in the back office today."

Emma sighed. "You don't know how much I wish I could help you out!"

A swirl of purple and red blew in. Glenda Gadabout had arrived.

Emma Bauer could have kicked herself. What possessed her to say "yes" to an interview with a woman who fancied herself New Halem's elite society columnist? Emma decided it must have been temporary insanity. Certainly it would be good publicity, but at what price?

"Oh Emma, how perfecto!"

"Excuse me?"

"The cunning way you've arranged the display case. Tray-man-u-feek! Just in time for the shivery delights of All Hallows Eve."

"Would you like to sample some of the chocolates, Mrs. Cunningham? The Dark & Stormy Night has been popular."

"Oh please – you know better than that - call me Glenda. Mrs. Cunningham always makes me feel like Ritchie's mother in Happy Days." Decked in Red Hat Society splendor the columnist waved her feathered boa. "And yes, we would simply adore a taste."

Emma reached into the display case and handed her the sweet. "It's a locally made dark chocolate with caramel and sprinkled with gray sea salt."

"Wonderful – perfect for dark and stormy delights! We Red Hatters need all the help we can get - especially the ones who still have husbands. Why even as a widow... Well, we won't get into that now. I'm sure you and your handsome husband don't have a thing to worry about in that category."

Emma was rendered speechless – a rare occurrence. Had she just seen Glenda coyly bat her baby blues before she bit into the sample?

"Simply luscious!" trilled the tall lady towering over the petite proprietress. "We must have some to share at the Red Hat Society meeting this evening."

"Will a dozen be enough?"

"Man-u-feek! The ladies will love this! You must come to one of our meetings dear Emma."

"I don't think I quite qualify."

"Those under fifty may wear lavender and pink." Glenda's enthusiasm set the large lipstick red orb on her head bobbing and purple plume shedding. "Do drop by, m'dear."

"Thank you for your kind invitation, Glenda, but for now, my life is pretty full with family responsibilities and being here. Speaking of work – you might have seen our ad that Chef Drew is offering a cooking class through Lahkanea Studio. We'd appreciate another plug for this."

Glenda's eyes gleamed as she whipped out a pad and pencil. "We did see the advertisement. My Red Hat Society patronizes The Sea & Sky so we would be delighted to place additional information in my column. Do tell me everything! We find Chef Drew so skilled in the kitchen. We're fans of whatever he creates."

Emma shared details and a short time later, the tinkling of the bell signaled the slender reporter's exit.

"Gone at last?" Jonathan Bauer stepped cautiously into the studio's display area.

"You're safe enough, though derelict in your duties."

"I didn't think you needed me around, champ. You can do several rounds with anyone on your own."

"That may be, Jonathan, but it might have been easier with your input."

With an engaging grin, he embraced his wife. "Dance with me, Love of my Life!"

"Stop it! Someone might come in." A bubble of laughter surfaced.

"As long as it's not anyone from the FishWrap Bugle or Sheriff's office we're safe." Jonathan released Emma and took her hand. "So – care to dance?"

"Nice deflection technique, husband. But don't think for a moment, I'll let you forget your tactical error of not being around for the interview."

"As I recall, you were the one that said, 'yes' not I."

"Do you remember the part in our marriage vows that said we'd be 'together through all life's challenges'?"

"Come on, Em. Glenda wasn't that much of a challenge. From what I could hear, you had her eating out of your hand - especially when you mentioned the handsome and talented chef of the Sea & Sky."

"Well, you'd better hope someone doesn't cancel their cooking lesson or you'll be enjoying the class held in our kitchen with the infamous society columnist. She was fishing for an invitation to 'experience' Drew's class for another article."

"Glenda must have seen our ad in the paper. She could have signed up."

"Oh she saw it alright and called. It was one of the days Jeremy was here. Our son told her the class was full and offered to put Mrs. C on the wait list in case of a cancellation."

Jonathan laughed and twirled Emma again. "Remind me to give Jeremy a raise."

It was time for a warm drink by a blazing fire. As the day closed, the Bauers gave thanks for retirees who enjoyed autumn by the ocean. They came with open pocketbooks and helped the studio survive the slow season. A seaside business was dependent on tourism and each season had its own rhythm. The holidays ushered in families visiting relatives on the coast and New Halem would bustle as shoppers came in to purchase items on wish lists. The New Year brought in winter storm watchers who would come to town for a good browse and a hearty meal. By late spring temperatures would rise along with sales. When happy summer vacationers returned, business would be booming.

"Not a bad day for off season," remarked Emma. "I'm glad the Kendrick's came by after Glenda left or her presence may have discouraged them from buying the copperleaf fountain."

"Doubtful. They've had their eyes on it for a while." Jonathan shrugged into his coat. "Got everything, Em?"

"Almost – just need my purse." She grabbed the colorful handbag.

Jonathan armed the alarm and they quickly stepped outside. The ocean air mingled with aroma of autumn leaves. It had been a good day at Lahkanea Studio.

"So Listless, any big weekend plans?" Jeremy grabbed an apple from the bowl on the kitchen table, sliced it in braces-acceptable-pieces and crunched away.

"Like you cared!" Elise didn't look up from her magazine.

"Well, you got a point. Anyway, I need a favor."

"Don't talk with your mouth full! Geez, bro, how do the girls at Ocean Crest High School stand to be around you?"

Jeremy swallowed. "I'm on my best behavior around them." He bit into another slice.

"Must you make those disgusting sounds while you're eating?" Elise scowled.

Her brother grinned, all apple pieces. "Yup."

"God must be testing my faith 'cause he gave me a big bother like you!"

"Ha ha." Jeremy slid in the seat across from his sister. "Now about that favor..."

"Like I'd be interested."

"You may be when you hear it has to do with pirate treasure."

Elise rolled her eyes. "Don't tell me you're buying into one of the old legends where you find gold and jewels 'in the shadow of the great mountain'. Come on, bro, get a life!"

"Wait before you judge, Listless. I found a key. And it's ancient." From the pocket of his jeans came a rusty object which he placed on the table. "Take a look and tell me what you think."

"You're deranged." But there was no heat in the comment. Somehow it had been sucked away as she carefully picked up the key. Dull colors spoke of history now silenced.

"Well?"

"Where did you find it?"

"Near the entrance of Lahkanea Mountain trail. A bunch of us went hiking a few weekends ago and we hadn't gone far when I got a rock in my boot so went to take care of it. That's when I noticed something by this nurse log. So I checked it out. And there was the key."

"Why are you telling me this now?"

"The key is weird, Elise. Sometimes I think I hear it kind of hum. I don't know...could be my imagination. Anyway, totally creeps me out. So I had to tell someone my secret. And believe it or not, I trust you."

"You're kidding, right? How many of your pals – not to mention the lovely Aubrey – know about this?"

"Actually, no one. Except you."

"Your imagination is working overtime again. You and your goony friends always find something. It's like you all have testosterone poisoning." Her eyes flashed. "Last spring it was beach glass you all insisted was a crystal ball. "Now it's a woo-woo key."

"I'm telling you, no one knows about this except me. And now you. Strange as it seems, sis, I know I can trust you to keep your mouth shut. And the key has to be kept secret."

Jeremy had sworn her to silence then asked his favor - to find information about the key. Elise's fingers flew across the keyboard. She was good at research – more like excellent. The technology teacher said her aptitude for negotiating the internet was first class. Well, she'd see if it was true. First a check of collector's websites; someone would surely have historic keys to sell. Then an in depth review of tales of lost treasure so popular around seaside towns. Stories of storms sinking ships laden with riches; legends of pirate booty hidden in the coastal range.

That her brother trusted her with his secret made Elise feel the guy wasn't as stupid as he seemed. Maybe Jeremy had some redeeming qualities after all, though they could probably be counted on one hand.

"Elise." Emma knocked lightly on her daughter's door.

The teen continued to scroll down a collectors list of keys absorbed in the different sizes and shapes.

"ELISE!"

"Yes, Mom."

"May I come in?"

"Okay – but will this take long?"

"Not at all; I just wondered if you'd like some chicken pot pie."

"I thought Friday was scrounge night."

"Officially it is, but I found some hidden in the freezer from our last Costco visit. So I baked them."

"Thanks. Maybe I'll grab one later. I'm in the middle of doing some research."

"Another paper? From everything your teachers say you do a great job with your projects. Still – homework on a Friday night? That's not like you."

"Well, ah, I'm um – doing some stuff for a friend whose computer died."

Emma went on Mom Alert. "Really, so what 'stuff' are you researching?"

"Oh you know – just stuff. You wouldn't be interested."

"Actually, I am."

Elise sighed. "It's nothing. If you must know, a kid in my history class brought in this antique key from his grandmother. I'm just checking it out. I'm pretty sure he lied about how much it was worth."

"Why would he do that?"

"Because he's a loser, Mom; it's his way of getting attention without being sent to the principal's office."

"Oh... well, guess things in high school haven't changed that much since I was there."

Elise rolled her eyes. "Right – so – I'd better get to it. I promised Jenna the 411 ASAP."

"Okay – I get the hint. If you want a bite later, you know where to find it." Emma gave her daughter's shoulder a light squeeze.

"Thanks, Mom."

As Elise returned to her research, she heard the bedroom door quietly close. Mothers, she thought, were estimable creatures. You had to make sure to share just enough truth so they would be satisfied or all hell would break loose! Right now she couldn't afford distractions. If the antique key unlocked treasure, Elise Bauer would be the one to find it.

In Which the Best Defense is a Good Offense

by Gwendolyn Van Hout Knechtel

FishWrap Bugle Events Calendar:

Ocean Crest High School
Homecoming Festivities
All Alumni Welcome!

Please join us on Friday, November 5th at 1:30pm for the annual Homecoming Spirit Day Assembly in the school gym. The Homecoming Game kick off is 7:00pm at Stadium by the Sea. Be sure to wear your Blue & Green!

After, come celebrate the Ocean Crest Orcas' victory over the Shoreline Pirates at the Homecoming Dance, Saturday, November 6th from 8pm – 11pm. Held at Ocean Crest High School in The Commons, this semi-formal event is open to students and alumni. Tickets are $5 with ASB Card, $10 general admission.

For details call: 509-798-2054.

New Halem K-8 School
Invites You to a Winter Wonderlands Concert!

Mark your calendars for Thursday, December 9th at 7pm for the Winter Wonderlands Concert at New Halem K-8 School. Holiday favorites from around the world will be performed by choirs, bands and orchestras. The PTO will also sponsor a fundraiser for new school computers. Chef Drew from Sea & Sky will provide Culinary Creations to tantalize your taste buds!

It's That Time of Year!

New Halem merchants invite you to "shop local" during this festive season. Special holiday hours begin Friday after Thanksgiving and continue until Christmas Eve. For merchant hour listings and their Holiday Hoopla events please check www.newhalemholidays.net or The FishWrap Bugle's special Thanksgiving circular.

Fourth grade sucked. Why did Mr. Elliott have to assign a writing topic around "Something that changed your life in some way"? Lonny sighed as the young enthusiastic gifted pullout program teacher continued the lesson.

"So, writers, this can be an event that altered your viewpoint. For example – changing breakfast cereals because one has more natural ingredients and you want to eat more healthfully." His pen streaked across the paper projected on the screen above. "Or it might be about a community service project and how it feels to help others."

The small group of fourth and fifth graders groaned.

"I'm passing out a graphic organizer for structuring ideas. Once you've got some things down, start thinking about how a state required learning objective – writing a 5 paragraph essay - can be presented in imaginative ways."

"Like what ways?" A fifth grade boy wanted to know.

"Let's ask your fellow writers, mathematicians, artists and friends, Joseph."

Lonny raised her hand with a few other students. Moments ago the assignment seemed boring - teachers always harped on fulfilling state required academic objectives. You could always count on Mr. Elliott to look at it differently, make it thoughtful and fun.

"Lonny."

"You could do almost anything! Digital photos in a PowerPoint, build a model, create a sculpture or – "

"A knitting project!" An excited voice interrupted. "My Mom's teaching me to knit and it helps calm me down when I get too hyper."

"Great idea, Marilee. Now next time, please wait your turn. Lonny wasn't quite finished."

"Oh... Sorry, Lonny. I just got a little hyper."

Lonny smiled her understanding. Everyone in class knew Marilee Anderson had a major case of hyperactivity. "I was going to add - making a collage."

"Excellent ideas. Would anyone else like to share?" He waited for students to offer comments. "No takers? Okay then, let's get started."

As Mr. Elliott passed out the forms Lonny already had a project in mind. With a little help from Uncle Drew, she would cook something unforgettable. He had taught her that sharing food brought comfort and joy into daily life. Creating a memorable meal could help people get through the most difficult things - even the loss of a dear father.

She had impressions of tears and laughter, of dishes passed around a table crowded with family and friends. Mom told her often about the memorial dinner menu: hearty pasta in pesto accompanied by perfectly browned Italian sausages; a crisp green Caesar salad and rustic loaves to dip in olive oil and balsamic vinegar. With it grownups drank deep red wines and sparkling gold ones while the kids had fizzy lemonade or cider. Her Dad's favorite sweets found their way to the dessert offerings: fresh raspberry and lemon gelato, crunchy biscotti and tiramisu with cups of hot aromatic espresso or café au lait.

Uncle Drew said sharing this menu brought back the best memories of his twin. And every time he gathered around a communal table for a meal, or cooked one for appreciative appetites, he knew his brother lived on.

Lonny located the area on the form for topic sentences. Her pencil flowed across the paper. "I lost my Dad when I was 3 ½ years old and it changed my life..."

Lunch time was never a peaceful half-hour. Lonny managed to get through it and opted for a visit to the library instead of outdoor recess. Other than Mr. Elliott's class, being surrounded by books was the best thing about a school day. And the library was a quiet place to think. Usually the librarian's assistant, Mrs. Wakefield, could be found behind the counter during lunch recess. She was a kind grandmotherly woman with amazing computer skills. When Lonny walked in she was greeted by a parent volunteer – one she'd hoped to avoid.

"Good afternoon, Mrs. Ferguson."

"Lonny - how are you?"

"Okay."

"Anything I can help you with?"

"No thanks, just looking for some books for a GATE project." Lonny winced. She should not have mentioned her gifted class. This information would find its way to Ellen Ferguson who would gleefully trash the GATE program and all involved - especially Lonny - using finely honed mean girl skills.

"Is Mr. Elliott assigning more projects for another Parent Night?"

"Ah, I don't think so..." Lonny moved cautiously towards the nonfiction section.

"Last time he had an after school parent event he applied to PTO for some assistance. Hope he knows we try to share the wealth, so to speak."

"Ah-ha, well, it really was great of PTO to help with Night of the Notables." Never hurt to thank those holding the purse strings, Lonny thought, even though they were not fans of gifted programs.

"Glad it was appreciated."

Lonny sidled to the book shelves, quickly pulled out a title and paged through it. From the corner of her eye she saw Mrs. Ferguson log off the computer and come her way. Not good.

"What book do you have there?"

"It's a kid's international cookbook. Shows different countries and a few sample menus."

"Are you helping your Mom with meals these days?"

"Sort of. But this is for my project."

"Hmm. Is everyone doing a cooking project?"

"No, Mrs. Ferguson – we're choosing what interests us personally."

"I see."

Lonny dared not comment. She knew the old bat did not "see" except with large blinders. It seemed today was not the day to find peace and quiet in the library.

"Well, guess I'd better go out to recess. I'll come back another time." Lonny carefully shelved the book.

"You do that, dear. And if I'm here again, I'll be more than happy to help you."

"Thanks." Lonny quickly walked out the door. Some days you just couldn't win.

"Appreciate the recommendation, Adele. I'm sure my great-niece will love Where is Spot? It's so much fun to pull up the pages and see what's hidden."

"When Lonny was a toddler it was a favorite." The By the Book owner handed her friend the bagged purchase. "Thank you for your business, Emma. Have fun reading with Amy!"

"I always enjoy browsing your bookstore. Well – better get back to the studio. I'm way over my break time."

"See you soon." Adele saluted her petite pal and wandered to the Cozy Corner where several holiday items were displayed. Halloween figurines shared space with orange and yellow taper candles, pumpkin printed napkins and autumn leaf dishes. Soon New Halem's children (and those young at heart) would celebrate the high holiday of costumes and candy. Ghosts and goblins, pirates and princesses would collect their share of goodies and celebrate.

Long ago Adele decided Halloween was the start of the holiday season. Thanksgiving quickly followed and the buying frenzy would begin - a crucial time for retail businesses big and small. She smiled as the bell jangled, ready to greet a new customer.

It was her daughter in tears.

"Lonny, what's the matter?" Adele closed the space between them.

"Just something in my eye – wind's strong today."

Adele knew the breeze was nominal. She took her daughter's hands. They were cold. "Honey, why don't I get some hot cider and you can tell me what happened."

"Some customer may walk in, Mom. I'll tell you later," Lonny said glumly.

"Verity should be back shortly – we can go upstairs and you can tell me about your day."

"It sucked."

Adele gave her daughter a quick hug and gently let go. "I gathered that. The Mom radar went off when you came in."

"Did it?" Lonny looked up into her mother's worried eyes. "Does it mean I get a ticket?"

"That depends. Radar is good for initial detection. After that it needs some assistance."

"Which means I should tell you what's bugging me."

"Only when you're ready, Lonny. Unless it's a safety issue."

"Well, it may become one for Ellen Ferguson."

Adele sighed. "It's no secret you and Ellen don't exactly see eye to eye."

Lonny snorted. "No it isn't. What is a secret is she's a bully, but the kind that isn't obvious. She makes vicious remarks then laughs and says she doesn't mean it. But she does."

"Okay. Have you spoken to your teacher or school counselor about this?"

"They may not understand. It has to do with -"

The doorbell jangled and two middle aged women walked in.

"Hold that thought, Lonny. We'll get back to it. Right now I have customers."

Out of the corner of her eye, Adele saw her daughter open the employees' only door that lead to their upstairs apartment. When her part-time employee returned from the post office, she'd continue the interrupted conversation.

Adele knew her almost ten year old was a sensitive soul - and being well advanced intellectually didn't help matters. Contrary to what the general public thought, parenting a gifted youngster was not easy. Alona was mature beyond her years, concerned about environmental and social justice issues. Most of her peers did not "get" her. Their interests were closer to home like what to wear for Halloween.

Lonny wanted to make a difference not just in New Halem, but in many places for the greater good. She volunteered at the local food bank, worked with special needs pre-school children and with her uncles, participated every year in Portland's PFLAG Parade. Lonnie "walked her talk" and difficulties arose when peers did not understand.

Adele sighed. She had a feeling her daughter had walked her talk and run straight into a brick wall.

Drew hung up the phone. "That was Adele."

Daniel looked up from his book as his partner sat next to him on the small sofa. "Kind of late for her to call. What's up?"

"It's Lonny. She's had a run in with a girl from school. The nasty bit of goods, Ellen Ferguson, wanted to know who would be the bride if you and I married."

"We could toss for it - though I think you've got the better figure."

Drew looked at his partner. Shook his head.

"Okay – not funny. What can we do to help Lonny?"

"Other than injecting some sensitivity and compassion into specific people in this town?"

"We could put it in the water like fluoride." Daniel took his partner's hand. "Might work."

"She's been keeping it a secret since school started. You know our Lonny; she didn't want to worry Adele and ..."

"She didn't want to hurt us."

"Yeah," Drew agreed. "Sometimes I wonder if we did the right thing moving to New Halem."

"No question - Adele and Lonny needed us and we needed them. Besides, some gay couple has to be the poster children for marriage equality."

"But will it ever happen, Daniel?"

"It will. Just takes time for people to dig deep in their hearts and figure it out."

"Right – when someone they love decides to come out of the closet."

"Well, that's often the way it happens."

"And it can take a long time before the damn closet door opens."

"It can." Daniel nodded. "And in this case the adage 'Sticks and stones may break my bones, but words will never hurt me' is definitely not true for Lonny."

"Okay then, I counter with, 'The best defense is a good offense'.

Maybe it's time to bake some of my awesome cupcakes and bring them to the next PTO meeting. Chat up the president, who happens to be Ellen's mom, and offer to help with some fundraising."

"Geez, sweetie, you just did an event for The Bishop's Playhouse."

"Nothing like being philanthropic. Lonny's school does a holiday concert. What if I bake some savory and sweet goodies for a price and donate the proceeds to PTO? I could have several conversations with Madame President. Maybe slip in a word on PFLAG and raise some awareness."

"Education usually is beneficial."

"At least I can straighten her out about gay marriage etiquette."

Daniel laughed. "Is there such an animal?"

"Doubt the subject will come up, but we can begin the conversation. After all it will be the season of peace."

"And what about Lonny?"

"No more secrets! Once I win over the PTO with my cupcake strategy, I'll have our niece invite Ellen to help sell them at the concert." Drew gave his partner's hand a squeeze. "And subject to Lonny's approval – the nasty bit of goods can even help bake."

Not a bad turn out, Adele observed, for a rainy evening in November. PTO meetings were not usually well attended, but word got out that Chef Delacruz was contributing refreshments.

Crisp colorful vegetables and garlic laced crackers surrounded a salmon dip and a spinach one. Flanking the coffee and tea were three choices of cupcakes – a rich chocolate topped with mocha, a pumpkin spice with caramel icing and a vanilla with strawberry butter cream.

Adele poured a cup of decaf coffee and mingled. It didn't take Pauline Ferguson long to find her.

"Your brother-in-law makes the best cupcakes," she exclaimed. "It was very generous of him to bring the food."

"Drew has a kind heart and a willingness to share his gifts with others."

Pauline nodded. "New Halem was fortunate when he landed in town. Sea & Sky is great for tourism and the community."

"You really think so?"

"I've always thought so."

"And what about what his partner brings to our town?"

Pauline's lips formed a half smile. "I attended a Rotary Club presentation where Daniel Benson gave a talk on Teens and Technology. He's very knowledgeable. And seemed to be – well – just a nice guy."

"That's exactly what Daniel is. He and Drew make a great couple and bring their considerable talents to New Halem."

"I have to agree, though...well, you don't mind me speaking frankly Adele..." Her voice dropped to a whisper. "The gay couple thing is a bit uncomfortable."

"Pauline, will you have time to meet for coffee later this week? You have a meeting to run in a few minutes and I'd like to discuss this with you in more depth."

"I'll have to check my calendar, but sure, I can do that. And while we're at it we can talk about Chef Drew helping with a PTO fundraiser."

Adele laughed. "Absolutely. Let's put it on the agenda."

Drew's plan of infiltration by way of tasty treats seemed successful. Pauline had given him a public thank you that was met with enthusiastic applause. Now the ball rested in Adele's court - coffee with Pauline and honest conversation about her gay brother-in-law and partner. Not exactly the usual topic when enjoying a cuppa.

Adele flipped her journal to an empty page and put pen to paper.

How does one begin a conversation about the love between two gay men living in a small coastal town in America? What is it about the homosexual minority that the heterosexual majority fears? If you believe love is for all, why is there controversy if a man and man or a woman and woman have a romantic relationship?

Perhaps I should begin with what is key – LOVE. With Pauline's conservative religious roots, that's the word to emphasize. It is the common denominator. We all seek it in our lives no matter what our culture, color or social class. Humans want to experience all aspects from love of family and friends to spiritual and sexual awakening. While it is easier to understand the former, humans continue to search for the latter.

Through the years I've observed society has a problem with sex whether gay or straight. The topic makes us uncomfortable and is rarely talked about sensibly. Instead it either becomes something to joke about or censor. Add in religious beliefs and how one was raised, sex can be a volatile subject whether hetero or homo sexual. Yet love – that four letter word can be a beautiful part of a committed relationship. For love matters.

I remember over a dozen years ago when I first met Andrew. It was at Allan's and my engagement party. My recall gets hazy about most things that happened long ago, but the memory of our introduction remains clear as that winter night…

Adele closed her journal; in her mind's eye she saw again Allan and herself standing in front of the fieldstone fireplace, warmed by the bright hot flames. It was the first Saturday in December; scents of cinnamon and cloves mingled with fresh evergreen boughs. Holiday lights and candles twinkled and glowed as guests left the cold dark of near winter to enter the spacious home overlooking Puget Sound.

"Drew should be here any minute," Allan announced. "Haven't

seen my brother since last Christmas. You and I had just gotten together, but you never met him because of that holiday trip your family took to Hawaii."

"Well, I feel I know him. I hope he can verify some of your Mom and Dad's stories. You two give new meaning to trouble! Okay, let's see what I remember. Andrew graduated from the New York Culinary Arts Institute, decided to practice his trade on the East Coast, then Spain and France and won some awards along the way. Looks like this will be more than an engagement celebration."

Allan gave Adele a quick kiss. "I hope you don't mind sharing a bit of the limelight. I haven't seen my brother for a year. I intend to ask him to be my Best Man."

"Sharing is fine as long as there are lots of champagne toasts! Do you think Drew will bring a date to the wedding?"

"Who knows? Maybe his Plus One will be some handsome Spaniard who plays Flamenco guitar."

"He's welcome to invite him." She looked up at Allan. "The thing is - I really want your brother to like me."

"He will. My emails to him starred Adele Donley. I bet Drew will say he feels he knows you. Especially after I shared your response when I told you he was gay..."

"All I asked was did it matter to you? And you answered, other than your concerns about his safety and how society would treat him, it didn't. And I agreed. Andrew is the same person he was before he came out - the brother you loved then and now."

"One of the many reasons I love you, Addy. You get to the heart of things. Love is what matters."

"Yes it does. And look who just walked in...You may not be identical twins, but the Delacruz boys sure are a handsome pair!"

Allan grabbed Adele's hand and pulled her towards his brother. "Andrew – great to see you!"

The two embraced, laughing. "Hey, Lan, you look good. Happy. And I bet this lovely lady has something to do with it."

"She does. This is Adele Donley – the woman who holds my heart. And this is my younger brother, Andrew."

"Younger by a mere ten minutes; guess Lan was more eager to see the world than me." Drew shot a smile her way. "Okay if I give my almost sister-in-law a hug?"

Adele nodded. "More than okay."

And it had been. She felt an immediate connection to Allan's twin. As they hugged she knew she'd found the brother she'd always wanted.

Adele felt grateful that Drew and Daniel lived in New Halem. They were the closest family she and Lonny had in the area. They helped setup By the Book, provided childcare, brotherly support and many delicious meals. Though the Delacruz and Benson family were not traditional, they had the key elements.

And that's where she would begin the conversation with Pauline. "Love matters..." From there she'd share memories of meeting Andrew that December evening long ago. And when on her and Allan's autumn wedding day, he was introduced to LanDre Tech's lead software designer, Daniel Benson.

Adele smiled, satisfied. She'd call Pauline in the morning and find a time for that cuppa.

The usually excellent coffee from the Sea Sprite Bakery tasted bitter on Pauline's tongue. Perhaps it was due to the story Adele was sharing, the tale of two gay men that loved one another. She added cream and sugar – just in case.

"Without Drew and Daniel, I would have never managed my move to New Halem. They supported me through losing Allan and helped start my new life."

"Okay, so these guys are good people. But why did they choose to be gay?"

"It's not a choice, Pauline. They were born that way."

"Can't buy that."

"So you wake up each morning and make a decision to be heterosexual."

Pauline's eyes widened. "Of course not, I just know I am..."

"Then you have that in common with Drew and Daniel. They know who they are too."

"I guess I haven't given this enough thought. I was raised in a strict Christian home and the Bible was the absolute Word of God."

"And it was Hellenized, Romanized, Germanized, and Anglicized. Lots of translations. And while there are specific passages in the Old Testament used against homosexuality, I don't recall Jesus saying anything. What I do recall Him saying is 'Love one another'."

Pauline sighed. "There is that. Well, you've given me a lot to think about, Adele. I'm still uncomfortable with the whole gay thing. But as a twenty first century woman, I can agree that what consenting adults do in the privacy of their bedrooms is none of my business. And I can work on following the Golden Rule. We all want to be treated with respect and consideration, gay or not."

"That's a good start, Pauline, a very good start."

Drew placed the last tray of crostini topped with chevre, sun dried tomatoes and pesto on the refreshment table. Concert intermission would begin shortly and he'd be ready to receive the hungry hordes.

Pauline had requested a menu with a taste from different countries to go along with PTO's 'Winter Wonderlands' theme. It had been thoroughly enjoyable to create appetizers and desserts from around the world. His offerings were fresh and colorful. As he adjusted a garnish, staccato beats of high heeled shoes drew his attention.

Enter Pauline Ferguson, Lady in Red.

"They'll be done with the first part of the program in a few minutes."

"Everything's ready - just waiting for your volunteers to help serve food and beverages."

"That would be Adele, Janie and Rachel. Hope you kept a bit back for the help; I bet there won't be a crumb left."

"That's the idea."

Pauline bit her lip. "Ah, speaking of ideas...and it being the season of peace and goodwill, I'd like to apologize for any unkind comments I've made." She cleared her throat. "About you and your partner."

Drew waited quietly for her to continue.

"Adele probably told you we had coffee last month and had quite a discussion. Though I am still working on understanding this gay thing, I wanted you to know I am trying. You and Daniel Benson have been nothing but exemplary citizens. I need to focus on that."

"I'm glad you're trying, Mrs. Ferguson. And when we have more time, if you ever want to talk, I'd be happy to. For now, let's focus on making PTO's fundraiser a success."

"I can get behind that, Chef Delacruz!" Pauline smiled, put out her hand.

Drew shook it and returned the smile. He hoped her trying would spill over to other family members – especially Ellen. Perhaps after a time, the Ferguson's would be more comfortable with the LGBT community. Meanwhile, he mentally congratulated himself. Infiltration by tasty treats worked!

"So Research Rat, found anything yet?"

Elise scowled. "You always expect miracles, Jeremiah, for no pay."

She grabbed the car door handle, gave it a jerk.

Jeremy grimaced, pressed unlock on the key fob. "Don't call me that Listless or you and your putrid pals won't get freebie rides."

"Putrid. Geez. Is that on your new vocabulary list?" Elise tossed her pack in the backseat then slid into the front. "Just get in and drive. I'll tell you on the way to school."

"You did find something!" Jeremy got behind the wheel and fastened his seatbelt.

"Maybe."

"All right!" He started the engine, looked sideways at his dark haired sister. "Got your belt on?"

She rolled her eyes. "I'd like to belt you! It's on – now let's go."

"So what did you find out?" Jeremy eased the car out of the driveway and swung on to the road.

"It's not as old as it looks."

"You're kidding."

"I do not kid, brother. And don't sound so disappointed. With a bit more time, I'm sure to find an explanation."

"How much more time?"

"Don't know yet. It'll depend on how long it takes to get a response to the ad."

"What ad?"

"The one I intend to place in the school newspaper."

"No way! I told you it has to be secret. If the whole damn school knows about it half of them will claim it's theirs and the other half will say they know who lost it."

"You don't have to yell."

"Yeah, I do. No ads – it's just stupid."

"Are you calling me stupid?"

"Well if the shoe fits..." Jeremy braked for a stop sign. "Come on, Elise, think of something else."

"Fine. But you aren't making this easy. Someone may know about the key's origin. Give us info. Then you can obsess about something else - like washing your car." She gave him a sly smile. "Or maybe the adorable Aubrey."

He smirked. "A lot you know."

"I know plenty. Now would you get us to school? I want to check something in the library. Ms. Stenson has a whole section on Oregon coast history and lore. If I'm lucky, maybe I'll find stuff on treasure chest keys."

"So it could be a key to some pirate's treasure?"

"Or to someone's clothing trunk or a ship's storage cabinet. Lots of possibilities."

"I bet this is something big, Lis. Something that might make us famous."

She grinned. "Or infamous. We'll just have to see where the research leads us."

The lunch time exodus to the girl's restroom was in full swing. The place was filled with chattering females using the facilities, freshening make-up, gossiping. Elise grabbed a paper towel from the dispenser, slowly dried her hands and eavesdropped on Aubrey Bellamont and her friend Jennifer Bolin.

"You won't believe this, Aub. Mark Knowles told me Jeremy found something that's going to make him rich."

"I doubt it." Aubrey streaked on pale pink lip gloss. "He would have told me."

"Well, maybe he was going to surprise you. You know how guys are."

"Not my guy. He couldn't keep a secret to save his life." She noticed Elise at the far end of the sinks. "Right, Lis?"

"Maybe." Elise tossed the paper towel into the wastebasket. "What deets did Mark give?"

Jennifer's mouth curved into a sly smile. "Well, he said it happened on a hike. That Jer had something in his boot so he told everyone to go ahead. Mark went back to check on him cause he was taking so long. And that's when he saw Jer put something in his pack."

Elise shrugged. "Could have been anything. My brother's a garbage gut. Probably was trail mix."

"Yeah, he sure can eat," Aubrey agreed. "I baked him some chocolate chip cookies once and he ate at least a dozen and drank a half a gallon of milk!"

"That's my bro."

"Okay – if you two want to discuss Jeremy's eating habits, fine. I'm more interested in what he might have found."

"Or not found," Elise said.

Aubrey put her make up back in a small purse. "Guess I'll have to ask him. Well – there's the bell. See you..." And the two girls were out the door.

As Elise headed to her technology class she wondered about Jennifer Bolin's sly smile. Why had Mark mentioned to the gossipy Jen, that Jeremy might be hiding something? Was he trying to get into the girl's good graces? Mark was hopeless around females like Rollin' Bolin who could easily crush him to bits. Jennifer and him – eew – what was he thinking! It would be best to get information from the source. After school, she'd track the guy down.

Jeremy was angry. This could not be happening. If only Elise was wrong. But he doubted it. If there was a crown for Ms. Research Girl USA, she'd be wearing it. Jeremy blew out a breath. "You're sure?"

His sister bit her lip, nodded. "You could always get Mark to fess up yourself, but I weaseled the whole sad story out of him. The key is part of his uncle's collection; even has a woo-woo legend attached so might actually be valuable."

"I'm gonna kick his ass!"

"Yeah, like that will fix it. Mom and Dad would be thrilled."

"This totally sucks! He set me up so he could get Jennifer interested enough in him to go to Homecoming. I know Mark has a hard time talking to girls, but dropping one of his uncle's collector keys and using me as the fall guy – not what you do to a buddy."

"No argument here." Elise grabbed a treat from the jar on the kitchen counter and offered one to her brother. "Maybe instead of kicking his ass, you should ransom the key."

Jeremy took the cookie, laughed. "Only you would think of something like that! And it's not half bad. But the better idea might be to give him tips on how to get a young lady's attention."

Elise snorted. "Lady? This is Rollin' Bolin we're talking about - the one who's tried to get her claws into every male along the coast! As I recall, she even made a play for you."

"Would never happen, sis." He chewed the oatmeal raisin bar thoughtfully. "Aubrey's the lady for me."

"And I suppose you're her knight in shining armor. We live in New Halem not in Camelot."

Jeremy's eyes narrowed. "Don't go there Listless."

"Fine. Guess this puts an end to my career as your research assistant."

"For now. You never know when I'll need help again." Jeremy lightly punched his sister's arm. "If Mark doesn't take my advice, I might have to bury a body."

Elise grinned. "I'll find the shovel and the best place to dump the corpse."

"Before you do – grab some more cookies and sit a minute. I need your expertise on how to give my pal a special thank you for giving me the starring role as the fall guy. Seems Mark wants the key back ASAP. Guess his uncle thinks he's borrowed it long enough. So I'd like to return it in the spirit it was found. Bet we could come up with a great way to do that – like maybe at the Homecoming dance."

"I like the way you think, bro." Her eyes gleamed. "I'm sure between the two of us we'll think of something."

Grinning, brother and sister slapped hands in a celebration high five.

The Cave

by L. C. Mcgee

Hemlock Washed Away

By Carmella Williams, Reporter,
The FishWrap Bugle

The relentless rains of the last two weeks have finally claimed its victims. The town of Hemlock was completely destroyed.

Fortunately, before the Cedar River crested six feet beyond flood stage, our ever-ready Cedar County Disaster Brigade provided early warning and assistance to the town's people. The evacuation was made in the nick of time. Evacuees fled to the houses of family and friends throughout the valley.

The only lives lost may be that of Marvin Peter's prize Buff Orpington Layers. Anyone who spots his chickens, please call Marvin at 436-5625. A reward is offered.

The battered road sign pointed to the town of Hemlock. My stomach muscles tightened. I heard of the disaster on the evening news. Probably everything was changed, forever. Oh hell. I'd see for myself. Why not? The acting job in New Halem could wait. After all, the theatre group wasn't expecting me until Wednesday.

I slowed down, ground the gears and turned my pickup onto the old road. The aroma of pine, mixed with cedar, floated into the cab. The blend of scents brought it all back. I was sixteen miles out of my way and years into my past.

The jolting of the truck conjured up memories of the old farm roads. I wanted to see it again, Emily's house, the barn and the cornfield next to it.

I was surprised; familiar landmarks still existed. There was Gilmore's Garage with windows boarded up and the antique gas pump rusting away in front. I spotted the ancient cedar tree that Mr. Playfair, the town crank, said was obscene. I smiled. He'd always threatened to split the snag into fence rails. He claimed it was the work of the devil; after all it had been hit by lightning, twice. And if that wasn't the worst of it, the old-time loggers called the tree, "that thar school marm".

I carefully shifted into low and looked down the steep sides of the canyon road. The Hemlock River was running high.

In the Portland Oregonian, the flood was front-page news. The article was about Main Street that'd washed away and the few houses that remained. It said that the leak in the dam had been detected early and many valley folk had taken refuge in New Halem and other nearby towns. The mudslides, the real town destroyers, came later.

I hit the brakes just in time. Around the curve the pavement beyond was gone. Four Jersey barriers blocked the road. Yellow warning-tape fluttered in the wind from the canyon below. Dad always gave me a bad time about daydreaming and driving. Cripes! Why was he always right?

My heart thumped wildly as I restarted the engine and carefully maneuvered next to a fern covered bank. I wrenched on the handbrake, put the gears into reverse, shoved the rest of my lunch into the glove box, slid over the seat and opened the passenger door.

Leaning on the barrier I surveyed the river. It thundered in a new channel. I broke into goose bumps at the ominous sound of boulders clunking along the river bottom then plunging over the falls into Green Valley below. Nothing was familiar. Emily's house, the cornfield, the gigantic barn, all were gone. In their place a huge sandbank was awash with red mud and gravel.

After three weeks of cold and torrential rainstorms, the entire month of October had strangely heated up. I'd left Seattle, wearing only a tank top, shorts and my lucky sandals. When I crossed over the Columbia River into Oregon, the weather was even hotter. I took my time to wander down the roads of the wine country. The heat was an excellent reason to work on my dream of becoming a budding oenophile.

Disconsolate at the destruction, I walked back to the truck, thrust my hands into the pockets of my shorts, slouched against the battered fender of my old Dodge truck, and... remembered.

Ten years ago a very peculiar experience happened to me here. I've had different ones before and since, but not as wild. I never tell anyone about them. Each weird event is touched off by some kind of innocuous object.

I glanced again toward the river. The breeze rushing up from Green Valley was hot. It rippled sensuously under the front of my shirt. The soft caressing air felt the same as it had on that Halloween evening.

Emily was in fall quarter at college when her mom died after a long illness. At the funeral, Emily decided to stay with her dad through the holidays. On the last day of October I called her. She said she had to pick up a prescription and we'd meet at the drug store connected to Mabel's Soda Fountain.

When Emily paused by the luncheon counter all my friends stopped talking. I casually finished my milkshake, pretended I hadn't noticed anything, but quickly left a generous tip when Emily nodded her head in the direction of the pharmacy. With all eyes on me I sauntered through the connecting arch to the Drug Emporium and chatted with the beautiful and sophisticated Emily at the prescription window.

While the pharmacist filled her order, we talked in subdued tones. Emily had told her father, that tonight he'd have to greet the trick-ortreaters, as she would be finishing up business at her part-time job in town. Afterward she'd take their dog for a long, long walk. She winked at me, paused then whispered that tonight was special, the old barn was too stuffy and we would meet at the edge of the cornfield, near the gnarly Gravenstein apple tree. I grinned. She always named the place. The weather was warm, like a mid-summer evening, and there would be a full moon.

At dusk I ran down to the cornfield. I could hear the occasional barking of Emily's dog, Black Bart. He was off-leash and rustling in the corn for rats and mice and things that hunted in the night. Emily's dad was wary of the dog and kept him penned up in their small backyard. But, the Labrador was smart. He could easily figure a way out, over or under the fence. Once free, Bart was gone for days, but he always came back, exhausted and grinning, his glossy coat covered with mud and debris. Locals claimed that no bitch was safe in Cedar County, even if she was spayed.

"Black Bart! Here boy. Heel!" Emily shouted several times. There was a distant wild woof; Bart ignored her and made his escape to freedom and adventure.

I turned quickly as the leaves and corn stalks moved stealthily behind me.

"Why Kevin R. McLeod you're extremely early. No wonder your middle name is Race!"

I faked a grimace. My grandfather's first name was Race. Emily never missed an opportunity to tease me about it.

Her smile was bewitching as she brushed a strand of raven hair from her face. Her wild green eyes locked with mine. Tonight they glowed with the same intense seduction as they did the first time she dared me to kiss her. It was on a Halloween night, too. I was dressed as a sheriff. I remember she looked up at me, took off my hat and rumpled my thick hair, then moved me into the dark part of the porch. I tripped over my candy sack and crushed it under my boots. First I was embarrassed, but what followed quickly made up for it. We met at her old man's old barn every week after that.

Emily twisted a thick, large corncob between her strong and graceful fingers. She caressed the silky tassels over and over, then stood back and laughed softly at the effect it had on me.

"It's Samhain tonight, aren't you afraid?" Her deep throaty voice always carried a challenge. It made my jeans immediately uncomfortable and necessary to adjust.

"No! I'm not afraid," I blurted out.

A huge harvest moon slowly broke through the trees above Green Valley. The cornfield began to glow with a gold-white light. All my senses tuned into the sounds of the insects murmuring in the sepia-tinged shadows, the stealthy movement of mice, and the strong pulse-beat at the side of my throat. I caressed Emily's arm then hesitated. Dangling pieces of what seemed to be a charm bracelet brushed my hand. My fingers tingled when I clasped it.

"Where did you get this? It feels... strange."

She smiled. "Father gave it to me. He bought it for my mother on their tour in Turkey." Moonlight shimmered off the pieces as she turned her arm. "A few of these charms are very old."

Feelings, odd and indefinable came over me. A presence seemed near.

Light-headed and too excited to pay attention, I cupped my hands over her loose top. Her nipples pushed into my palms. She tossed the corn ear aside, grabbed the front of my jeans and shoved me backwards. We slid into the rustling stalks. Earth and dry leaves ground into the back of my new cotton shirt, but I didn't care. Our tongues and fingers had found each other.

Hastily we shed our clothes and shoved them around and beneath me. It was at that moment the feeling of something peculiar, something watching, became even stronger.

As I buried my face in the smooth warmth of her breasts, I was disoriented. Strange sensations told me we weren't in the cornfield anymore, but in some kind of cave. We were together, feeling, moving, but at the same time I was floating above, watching.

The cavern opened around us. Its sides of towering rock twisted into impenetrable blackness above. Rock slabs had fallen from the ceiling long ago. They roughly bordered a floor of sand. In the middle, a roaring wood fire shot flames into the dark above. Stone oil-lamps glittered in crudely hewn niches. The fire and lamplight flickered and bobbed creating grotesque and eerie shadow-shapes that danced everywhere.

It was no longer rumpled clothes that pressed beneath my body, but thick layers of animal pelts. The furs, soft and sensual, caressed my back and legs as we moved together. I was transformed. My body was large and hard with muscle, my hair a burnished auburn. I could feel it moving long and thick around my torso. Emily too, was sinewy and strong, her hair, dark and silky, and as long as mine. The delicious curves of her brown body glistened with scented oils and the fluids of our lovemaking.

We growled and shouted in a strange communication. The sounds of the cave joined with our voices and echoed back. After we collapsed in one ecstasy, we nuzzled, dried our faces and limbs on the furs, and then began again. The licking and biting reached crescendo after crescendo as we coupled in new and more convoluted ways.

I recall vividly the orange-gold of the fire. At times, the shooting flames revealed paintings of people and animals on the rock walls. The drawings were charged with spiritual meaning and the multiple figures writhed in the firelight, further encouraging our primal abandon.

Buried deep in each other the last ecstasy came. Her legs wrapped around my back. We keened in unison.

We lay panting. The aroma of burning pitch and the scent of our lovemaking surrounded us. Slowly, I raised myself onto my elbows, the taste of her hair and skin still in my mouth. We gazed into each other's half-lidded eyes.

It was then the walls of rock slowly dissolved around us.

"Emily, Emily," I whispered. "I had the strangest vision. It was real. We weren't here...we, we were in a giant cave...and it was a long... very long time ago. We were different people." The corn rustled in the warm night breeze as I raved on. "You were, I was..." She drew the tips of her fingers across my lips.

"Hush," Emily murmured and rolled over until her green eyes danced above me. Her hair held shards of silver moonlight. She traced the outline of my swollen mouth. I could smell the cave's lingering scents.

"I know," she said with a slow smile. "I was there too."

In the year that followed my father took a new job and moved our family to Seattle. For the first two years, I sent letters to Emily, but she never wrote back, or returned my calls. My mother, who kept up with old friends in the town, said that Emily's father remarried and when Emily graduated from college, she hadn't returned to the farm. Soon I began to forget her. I focused on acting school and became totally immersed in student life.

I sighed, opened the truck door and slid across to the driver's seat. The engine started on first try. I hung my head out the side window and carefully backed to where there was room to turn around. At the main road, I paused with the motor running.

Several years ago Juanita, my last girlfriend, ran into Emily at a medieval arts fair in Canada. Emily was teaching English in a rural community on Vancouver Island and was thrilled with her new life.

Then, with a knowing wink, Juanita said that Emily was the leader in a fight to prevent a local nudist beach from closing. No surprise, she said, Emily had always been an activist. I asked Juanita, if Emily ever mentioned my name, or enquired about me, but sadly she said no.

I turned on a western music station and tapped listlessly on the steering wheel. I was glad Emily was happy and hoped she hadn't heard of the flood. But, I was certain that even if she had, she'd never come back to Hemlock, to see the devastation, or to remember...like me. I shook my head. Most of the time men are plagued with a more romantic nature than women.

I pulled onto the main highway, and focused on the journey ahead.

Sure the river had taken away material places, just things. I vowed this part of me, the memories of Hemlock, Emily and the cave, would never be washed away by the inevitable stream of time.

Streams of Connections

by L. C. Mcgee

Rumor Has It!
By Carmella Williams, Reporter
for The FishWrap Bugle

It's true. The first play of the season, in fact the first ever-legitimate theatre in New Halem, opens this December 2nd for the holiday season. The Bishop's Playhouse debuts with Neil Simon's hilarious, "Rumors".

Mr. Jeffery Roland assured this reporter that the remodeled church, with carpeted foyer, elevated stage and new restrooms would be ready for action by November 30.

Roland hired two new thespians to hit the boards with the local cast. One, Kevin McLeod who heralds from Seattle and Emily Saunders fresh from a successful two seasons in Ashland, Oregon (see photo section page four).

The Seer

The Hair of the Dog tavern was dark and almost deserted. I drew my fingers down the cool wet sides of the empty beer schooner. Typical small town they roll up the streets at midnight. I looked at Casey. "Guess I'd better go, Case. Acting workshop starts tomorrow, 8:00 am sharp."

In a cloud of beery breath, my college friend, Case, leaned over on his barstool. "Take my cap and windbreaker." He put down his glass and tousled my hair. "The wanabee star mustn't get even a wee head cold." Case winked, took a long pull on his beer, and continued, "I've only got a block to walk and there's a storm coming, a real Sou'Wester. You'll be soaked by the time you make it back to the church. And that basement room you've rented is one torture- rack short of a dungeon. Course, I don't have to tell you that," he said then took another gulp from his pint, smacked his lips, removed his hat and coat and handed them to me with a flourish.

I crammed on his sweat-stained cap and shrugged into the windbreaker. Enough space for two, I thought. The roominess reminded me of his former amateur wrestling days. I gave him a high-five, said, "See ya, Case," and swaggered out the bar door. I paused and weaved a bit as I looked at the sky. Whoops. I was hammered. Have to pick my way, very carefully.

The temperature took a serious drop. Damn and it was starting to rain. "Damn again!" I exclaimed aloud and stumbled forward. The wind pushed hard and now ice-pellets rattled against Case's ill-fitting hat. A sheet of lightening illuminated the entire street, followed simultaneously by an ear-splitting explosion. The ground shook and the streetlights went out. I leapt into the shelter of a brick-lined entryway. "Shit!" I peered out at the slanting rain. Nothing was familiar. I was lost.

How did I get so turned around? I thought I'd just come around a corner. Cripes. Big city fella lost in New Halem and the place wasn't much larger than a Super-Mall. I wrapped my arms around myself and shivered in Case's light jacket. "It's gotta stop soon." I muttered through chattering teeth and looked up into the darkening sky.

I huddled in a doorway while a rain-streaked sign creaked in the wind. The writing was in Gothic script. Curious, I stumbled out and craned my neck. Even in the darkness the white letters stood out. "Madame Des Lisieux," I read aloud. Then below, in smaller letters: 'Reader of palms', then below that, 'Sees-all, Knows-all, Tells-all.' "Hah." I shouted into the night, "A seer with an unforeseen sense of humor... or a ghastly mistake." I congratulated myself on my terribly witty observation and retreated back into the entryway.

I felt something soft under foot followed by an unearthly screech. Claws sunk into my left ankle and a gigantic ball of fur leapt hissing into the night. "Goddamn cat." I yelled and kicked out as the beast tore down the rain-slicked street. I was shaking. The thing was the size of a small dog.

I leaned against a door to examine my throbbing ankle. I couldn't see anything and the pain was incredible. I shifted my weight to pull my sock down, the door swung open. Staggering backwards I hit the floor with a yelp.

A phosphorous glow emanated from a star-studded ceiling. My eyes were not focusing, was that the Big Dipper and was I passing out?

Jangling bracelets signaled a curtain hastily shoved aside. A flicker of dim candlelight illuminated the alcove. I sniffed; there was the pleasant odor of sandalwood. The strong miasma of beer and pizza that clung to me faded slightly.

"My. What a dramatic entrance." The voice barely contained its laughter. "I'd just let Brutus out for his nightly carousing. And look what I find on my threshold, another carouser. You startled poor kitty. He's usually quite the gentleman."

Indignant, I sat up and turned to look at the apparition behind me.

"Kitty? Gentle? With a name like Brutus!" I snarled. "That damn cat razored half my leg." I rubbed my ankle. "And look." I thrust out the palm of my hand. "I'm bleeding," I shook my head and wiped the blood on Case's jacket, "and it stings like hell." I shot her my best woebegone look. "It could even get infected."

She touched her lips. "Oh. I am sorry, but Brutus does take umbrage at being stepped on. Stay there. I'll find some Band-Aids and disinfectant." In a tinkling of bracelets and coin necklaces, she shut the open door firmly and disappeared behind the curtain.

"I think it'll require major surgery!" I shouted at her retreating back. Damn. Her voiced irritated me. Umbrage? She wasn't at all sympathetic and never once lost her slightly amused attitude.

Minutes later she returned clutching an ancient candle lamp, a suspicious looking blue bottle, and a cardboard container of bandages.

"Here, let me do it," I growled and took the open box from her. I paused. "My God, these Band-Aids saw action in World War I." I shook the box. "They're collector's items." With a dramatic gesture, I pushed the box toward her. "Don't waste these on my account. I'm sure you'd garner a small fortune by offering them on E-bay, or possibly the next Antiques Road Show, or..." Oops overboard. She looked a bit put out. Dramatically I swept my bloody hand across my damp forehead. "It must be the beer, what am I saying?" I swallowed and made a longer pause. "Actually... I want to thank you. It would be stupid of me to risk infection." I rolled up my pant leg. "Would you mind doing it? Usually, if I see blood, white and black tennis balls start bouncing in front of my eyes."

"This is so cool," she said and knelt down and put the lamp on the floor. "I'm in the nursing program at Manzanita Junior College."

I jumped as antiseptic soaked cotton hit my wounds. I grabbed my knees and rolled back and forth with my eyes closed. "Righty-ho, keep a stiff upper lip and all that rot," I muttered through clenched teeth.

"Well now, that looks better," she said and finished bandaging my wounds. She sat back on her heels and cupped her chin. "After your misadventure I think the least I can do is to offer you a cup of restorative tea."

"I'm sorry, er Madame Des Lisieux I don't want to take up any more of your time." I attempted to stand then immediately sat down.

For the first time I'd had a good look at her. She was a knockout. "I think you'll need to help me," I said weakly and bit my lower lip. "I've, er lost my balance."

With much heavy leaning, on my part, she helped me behind the curtain and into a tall ladder-back chair. Gracefully she moved to a sideboard and poured something steaming into what appeared to be not a cup, but a bowl. She placed it on the table.

I found myself gazing into a voluminous container of hot tea. The odor of mint and citrus assaulted my nostrils. Holding it in both hands, I managed to stifle a beery burp and took a hesitant sip. "Um, er delicious," I mumbled around a rather large bubble in my mouth. It tasted not unlike mouthwash.

The girl leaned over the dimly lit table. She was an indulgent Florence Nightingale. "That's better, isn't it? By the way, my name is Sybil, not Madame Des Lisieux, that's my mother. I'm helping her out while she's in Portland." She took a lengthy pause and frowned at me. "But, I think I know who you are. You're that Kevin McLeod person. I saw your picture in the FishWrap. You're one of the thespians hired for this year's plays."

"Yes. I um." I smiled and made myself comfortable. "I'm one of those." I felt it imperative that I expand on my credentials. Not to impress her of course, but to illuminate this corner of her sheltered world.

After a few moments she politely stifled a yawn and abruptly stood up. "What you're saying is absolutely fascinating, but if you will excuse me for a moment. I'm not sure that I locked the street door." She walked briskly away.

I frowned. Well maybe she wasn't all that interested, but I sure was. She was the quintessential, gypsy beauty. Dark hair, graceful moves, tinkling baubles, complete with deep, penetrating glances...wow, what she could do for a production. I'll ask her if she'd like to take a shot at acting and suggest an interview. I smiled. Case would congratulate me on my talent-scout abilities.

Sybil returned shortly. Great name too, I reflected as she drew the curtain and sat down. Her dark eyes studied me carefully. "You know, I feel I should give you a free reading. Do you have any objections?"

It was odd. My mouth was dry and I still felt woozy, but I nodded an ascent. I could talk to her about the stage thingy later, when my head cleared up.

Slowly rallying I put on a face of exaggerated dignity and groped for my wallet. "I'm no piker, I can pay," I said and opened my wallet with an audible snap. Whoops, real dismay, all I had was a few hastily written notes on debts owed, nothing more. I summoned up a shred of dignity. "I'm, very sorry. Um, do you take credit cards?"

She laughed and touched my wrist. "Don't be silly. I think it may have been Dorothy Parker who said, 'most young men's wallets are as flat as their stomachs,' or something like that. Besides, this is a free reading," she paused, "Consider your bleeding ankle as ample payment... that's if you want to."

"No reading," I said hastily then blushed and sat back in my chair. "Okay, sure, why not? I've nothing to lose."

Sybil cocked a pretty eye at me. "Oh, I wouldn't be too sure of that. It depends on what I see. Doesn't it?" She gently clasped my fingers, I again felt light headed, at least she's holding my hand, I thought.

Sybil studied my open palm. "Ah ha," she exclaimed with that irritating hint of mirth in her voice. "I see you regard yourself rather highly and you're quite the ladies man."

Jeez! I almost yanked my hand away.

"Ah. And you will have a long life and oh," she said faintly then cleared her throat and leaned forward.

"Wha, what do you see?"

She dropped my hand like it was hot. "Nothing ... palm reading is obviously not my specialty." She hastily turned to the sideboard behind her. "I'm much better at cards. Here," she said and expertly fanned them out.

The card deck was very large, very old and very queer looking. I snorted. The tacky things looked hand-made.

Sybil stared at me; all humor left her voice. "These are very special cards. My mother inherited them from a great aunt. At present, Mom's teaching me how to use them."

I got goose bumps. Could she read my mind?

She nodded slowly. "Besides, I really do feel more comfortable with these. Now, select nine cards and keep them face down."

I circled my hand like a hawk and pounced on the farthest card. It had the desired response. She jumped; I looked at her with half-lidded eyes and slid the cards in front of me, slowly, one at a time. She gestured for me to turn over the first one. Cool. A large snake entwined around the body of a voluptuous and very naked lady. Laughing skeletons decorated the four corners. A long border of what appeared to be snake skin connected them. Sybil inhaled sharply.

"I don't believe it!" She stared at the card. "Your totem, or guardian spirit if you will, is the snake." Sybil ran her finger down the palm of my hand. "And, related to this lined matrix, it is ... very unusual. Uh, turn over the next card."

Oh jolly. This one depicted a skeleton with two skulls growing out of a single neck, one head was white, the other black. It clutched an ancient hourglass in its bony fingers and sand seeped out of a crack at the side of the glass. In the four corners of this card were roses. Each depicted the different stages of life from glorious bud, to flush beauty, to brown petal and finally, the black of death.

Sybil gasped and leaned back in her chair. The sudden pallor of her complexion surprised me, and the skin tingled at the nape of my neck. "Is everything still all right?" I asked nervously.

"Um, yes...taken together the pair would suggest that you have the nature of your totem, able to grow, then when ready, shed your skin. It's a sign of self-renewal, sort of." She tapped the first card. "This one implies that you actually shed, or alter time, or are obsessed by history, or you're quite potent, or you're able to skillfully wriggle out of difficult situations, or..."

Wide eyed I held up my hand. "Whoa, whoa, you've covered all possible bases here." I looked down my nose and employed my best stagey, father superior voice. "Nor does this appear to be like any normal card reading that I've ever been party to, past, present or future." I paused, why had I said future?

Sybil made a noise of exasperation. "I'm still a novice, but I do know that this deck is based on those used by; well the best modern term is 'sacred readers'. They're a small group whose lineage and training go far back in time, actually to a group of men and women with special powers of observation. Today, they might be referred to as a 'coven'. Even certain Neolithic cave paintings indicate their presence. The first historical evidence appears near Mohenjo-Daro, India. Eventually some of the 'sacred readers' wound up, via Spain, in the Caribbean, had contact with, oh...oh. I see I'm boring you. It is rather involved."

"Mo, Mohan, who?" I asked.

Her arm gesture took in the entire room. "Look, let's ground things here. No more lectures from either side. Regard this reading as essentially 'entertainment'. Usually people want to explore the so-called, mysteries, or universal questions of life, contact dead relatives, pets, etc. They feel they have some control over their destiny when they do. But, one can't take things too seriously. Most readings are nebulous and capricious at best. The energy can travel in diverse directions, or occur unexpectedly at the same time, at any other time, or at no time at all. And most, if not all readings, are subject to a multitude of interpretations, depending of course, on the methods used and the nature of the Seer and..."

I nodded. My mouth open, my eyes glazed. "Wow, wasn't that just a lecture?" I asked, but thought, what a smoke screen artist. Really the best, did she have any idea what she was saying? I doubted it and I certainly didn't have a clue.

Sybil smiled indulgently, and rubbed her hands together. "Sorry, anyway this is great practice for me." She reshuffled the cards. "Go ahead. Select any three cards this time. I'm really excited about this, the chance of order is important. What? Oh!" Her eyes turned darker as she flipped each card over. Her laughter, for the first time, had a nervous edge.

Surprise! Oh surprise. The new cards had more skulls and bones in their corners. In the center of the first was a large white crow. It pecked at the eye sockets of a jawless head. The next card had two skeletons holding hands and dancing. The first was headless; the second bore a jeweled dagger piercing its ribcage. Under their shuffling feet glinted gold coins, an ornate goblet and a peculiar necklace. On the last card, a skeleton in a black-hooded robe pointed to a post with four directional signs painted in elaborate symbols. Amused, I moved the cards closer to study them.

Oops, I was feeling strange and having difficulty swallowing. Was it the weird cards? Faintly I heard the cry of seabirds then the room began dissolving into a fog. 'Curses, it's happening again', was my last thought.

I gazed at my feet in wonder. Both ankles were awash in the icy cold of a sudden wave. The water sucked at my legs, which were as dark and well-oiled as cherry wood. I ran my tongue over my lips. They were crusty and tasted of salt. Wow! I was standing on the deck of a wrecked ship. I clung to a stair railing that led into the dark below. Rain raged around me; oddly, the violent gusts of wind were warm. The foundering ship was tilted, bow up and pointed toward the beach. I shivered as the aft end of the wooden hull ground against the rock reef beneath the keel.

Above, canvas sails and loose rigging flapped like useless wings of a giant bird. Three quarters of the length of the foremast lay splintered on the deck. Broken spars, tangled in a morass of shrouds, moved in the water behind me.

Inhaling deeply of the salt-tinged air, I held fast to the rail and scanned the boulder-strewn beach. At the foot of the reef tall cliffs loomed above a long stretch of sand and debris. Men, ropes circling their waists, clung to the rocky face. Wind and rain tore at them as they crawled spider-like up the wall of stone. Their connecting line was taut with the combination of their weight and the heavy loads lashed to their backs.

Above the crew, I could see Juan in the lead, his slight body searching for precious hand and toeholds. Juan intermittently paused, then with his sinewy hands he threaded the rope through iron guides, pounded into the cliff the week before. Ten feet above him a small crevasse hid the entrance to a cave. Juan was the best of men, for some reason I knew him well and hoped fervently that he would make it.

My head throbbed, particularly at the back. I reached up, a large bump swelled at the base. Whoever I was, my memory was returning in selected bits.

I remembered that I had lowered my mate, Mikos, over the starboard side. But Mikos would be safe only for a short while, he was lashed to a makeshift raft. Evidently I'd tied it amidships, away from the grinding stern.

If the ship held together, we would escape from the whole damned lot of them. I looked up again at what I had come to call, with the exception of Juan, 'the crew of greed.' I smiled then grimaced. I knew they would have a helluva time trying to stow the last remnants of the treasure in the cave.

"Ahmad! Well now. Ye still alive? Thought the cosh took care of ye, below."

Christian, sword at the ready, waded up the steps.

Anger and adrenalin flooded my body. Instinctively I crouched in a fighting stance. His voice was grating and loaded with arrogance. I was shocked at my thoughts; I would have to kill this bloody fool.

"Ye Turks are tough, I'll give ye credit." Christian thrust his grizzled chin towards the men on the cliff. "Do I gut ye now Ahmad? Or when ye try to squirm away?" In his meaty left fist he gripped his favorite snee. "Sa no matter to me."

What? My name is Ahmad? I looked at my hands. They were callused and gigantic, my forearms corded with muscle and under multiple tattoos my skin, dark brown, like my legs.

Christian waved the deadly knife at me. Then he grinned and jabbed in an upward movement followed by a vicious twist. I'd seen this skilled and deadly dance kill many a man. With his other hand Christian possessively patted a red-leather girdle at his waist. Immediately I recognized it. The large belt had once belonged to Mikos. Mikos had thought he'd lost it in a brothel in Chittagong.

Christian's smile was a sneer, large and deadly. "Yor kind are sneaky. Ye won get fur this time; now will ye?" Behind him a section of mast snapped and crashed to the deck. Christian didn't flinch. I tried to focus on what I must do, but Ahmad's thoughts were stronger.

"Ye otter gone with yon mateys, instead of tend'n to your friend. E's gone direct to hell fire anyway. The fever'll get im, like tothers, or," he nodded toward the beach, "them rocks... 'tsall the same."

Vivid scenes flashed in my mind. I saw why Ahmad hated Christian. The man relished his role as a tormentor. He was vicious, unpredictable, and unrelenting.

A shade of puzzlement crossed Christian's scar-riddled face. "Wha's matter ye? Yor all cum over weird-like!" He then crouched, ready to spring. "One of em sore spells? Won't save ye none. Ye a dead man." Christian nodded toward the cliff. "I be damn sure ye make crow meat wit the rest up yon cave." He hooted at the look of shock on my face. "Oh yeh. I plan keep'n it all to meself!" Then he lunged.

I could only yield to Ahmad's control. With a twist and a quick spring-like movement we dove over the starboard rail and with a few powerful strokes emerged on the protected leeward side of the ship. Ahmad grabbed onto the raft that held the feverish Mikos; he made sure the young man was covered and still breathing, then his eyes raked the beach. I could hear Ahmad's thoughts, calculating the distance from the ship, through the debris, to the rocks and then the shore. Ahmad was certain he could make it. I wasn't at all sure.

"Kevin! Kevin, wake up!" Sybil vigorously shook my shoulder. I groaned. My entire body ached. With one eye I located the concerned face that loomed above me.

"What happened?" Sybil asked eagerly. Then said: "Here, drink this." Sybil shoved another cup of that dreadful tea in my face. Thank the gods it was smaller. She stroked my hand. "You were in some sort of trance. You kept moaning that you had to save Mikos. I wanted to wake you, but Mom insists that a client who is in the, er... 'experience' must run their course. You were away a long time; at least ten minutes."

I rubbed my eyes and sat up. My hands smelt of the sea, the back of my head throbbed. "Away? Away is a good description... I think."

"You kept saying the name Ahmad, too. Are they friends of yours? Are they in some sort of trouble?"

I grimaced; my thoughts were still foggy. "You could say that." My eyes fell on the scattered deck of cards. I touched them gently, as if they were tired too, and sighed. "I shouldn't have mocked these you know." I looked up at her. "Be careful, treat them with care, they're far more powerful than you think."

Sybil looked exasperated and then smiled slowly. "I assure you, I'm quite aware of their powers. At a very young age I learned to treat them with respect, but at the same time to be cautious about interpreting how they fell. 'Remember,' my Aunt would always say, 'these cards are like life. If you take them too seriously, they will take you seriously and then you're in deep kaka.'"

Shakily I laughed and shrugged my shoulders. "Yeah man, whatever the Seer says." I quickly looked away from her piercing stare. Then she grabbed both my hands firmly. "Tell me. Tell me what happened while you... well, while your mind wasn't here."

"I'm not sure. I don't like to talk about these things that happen to me." I reflected for a while. "Oh, I guess I can, at least with you, but please, keep it to yourself." I looked away. "I've had peculiar experiences before. But this was way weirder, way intense." I shrugged. "Sometimes I space out, go places that are really quite impossible. It's strange; I become part of the surroundings ... and the people. And it's like it happened before and I know it is real." I squeezed her hands to reassure her. "Nothing bad occurred this time. At least I don't think so." I felt lopsided. "But... oh, I'll tell you more, later. I need some space to sort it all out."

"Anyway, rehearsals start tomorrow and I have to be at my best." I smiled and straightened my spine. "At least try to be the best I can... or act like it." I raised her hands to my lips and kissed them. "You're the most beautiful and unusual girl I've ever met," I whispered. She blushed and looked away.

I fended off further questions as she led me to the door, but I hesitated in the entryway. The rain bucketed down but thankfully the wild wind had gone. I turned to her. "You must have a business card or something with your phone number and address. I don't think I could find you by... er, just dead reckoning."

"Well. You did tonight," Sybil said while searching the many folds of her voluminous skirt. "Here, this also has our website on it."

I smiled and fingered the grubby and crumpled card. "Yeah, thanks for the, ah... ah rather unusual evening. My friend, Case, rescued an old computer from a dumpster. He's going to give it to me, after he fixes it. But I'll contact you before that." I touched the bill of Case's cap and bowed deeply. "Thanks again mademoiselle," I paused, "er ah, by the way, my digs are at the Bishop's playhouse, you know, the converted church. Can you tell me how to get to there from here?"

Sybil's directions were surprisingly concise. With an excellent mind map of the streets and corners, I toddled into the night. But a slight queasiness returned and the pavement pulled and swayed like the deck of a ship. I stopped and listened. I distinctly heard a cat howling somewhere.

Ah, the Actor's Life
By Carmella Williams, Reporter for the FishWrap Bugle

'Rumors' by Neil Simon is the premier opening production at the Bishop's Playhouse. The building was once an abandoned church and now has been remodeled and reborn into New Halem's rising star. One of our newest actors, imported from out of town, is the elusive Kevin McLeod.

Heralding from Seattle, Washington, Kevin is a graduate of the U of W acting school and starred in several productions at the 'Children's Theater' and the famous 'Theater in the Round'. Does he have aspirations for the Ashland Theater's milieu? It's this reporter's job to find out and also uncover new and juicy items on everyone who is acting or involved in this production of firsts.

At present Kevin lives a monk-like existence in the basement of the Playhouse and... more to come later.

Digs and Delusions?

Yawning mightily, Kevin swung his feet over the edge of the bed and swept a mop of hair out of his eyes. His entire body ached from the bones outward. No doubt from balancing on that wretched deck, then swimming like an Olympian athlete afterwards.

Ahmad and Mikos must have made it. They had to have made it. His intense feelings surprised Kevin.

Fumbling along the wall he covered his eyes and opened the one window. The sunlight blinded, but he needed air, great gulps of it. It was not only the bar bash with Case the night before, but the experience at Sybil's was the topper.

Case called his place a dungeon. He was right. The dank room smelled moldy and the ancient wallpaper was peeling around the edges. Remodeling had not reached here. Not good. He made a mental note: find an electric fan, hopefully at the local thrift shop.

Last night he'd stripped off his wet clothes, they smelt of the sea, then hung them in the drafty hall to dry. Exhausted, he wrapped himself in several blankets and dropped shivering onto the mattress. There were no sheets; something more to add to his 'to-do' list.

The unusually warm ocean air felt terrific washing over his skin, but his head still throbbed. Was there really treasure buried in that mountain? Again he thought of Mikos and Ahmad. The last thing he remembered was Mikos' unconscious body on the raft, and the vivid image of a strange necklace that glowed against his dark skin. He was sure he'd seen it somewhere before and recalled that it was made of carved beads, and some other kinds of stone. Taken together the pieces weren't gaudy, but intricate and beautiful. For some reason he felt that the necklace was an artifact of luck and power. He'd seen it before on one of Sybil's cards.

Kevin shook his head. It was really weird, inhabiting another person's thoughts, let alone a body. It was almost like acting, but with the significant difference of vividly recalling another person's memories.

Reflections could wait, he was ravenous. He padded over to the small kitchen alcove and filled the teakettle with cold water. A single, ancient tap stirred up a rattling and banging throughout the building. The racket couldn't disturb anyone; besides the scrabbling mice in the walls (at least he hoped they were mice) he was the only living creature in the church.

Kevin switched on the two-burner hotplate that Case so generously had provided. Stooping over he took a carton of cream from the bar fridge and froze. A garbage truck shook the floor as it rumbled down the lane. He swore. Accompanying the truck's noise was a group of crows, squawking mightily. And damn, they were in the willow tree, right outside his window. The cacophony increased his headache, and he imagined a lump of pain at the base of his skull.

The birds reached a crescendo of condemnation, then out of the corner of one squinting eye, Kevin spotted movement on the window ledge. Swishing a humungous tail, a black cat, a very large black cat, sat itself on the sill and studied him coolly. Its unusual amber eyes seemed to peer into his very being. Egad, it was that infernal Brutus!

Displaying a huge mouth, replete with sharp, healthy teeth, the monster yawned and stretched; then in one muscular leap, landed in the middle of his bed. Brutus shot Kevin a defiant look, made three turns, and settled into a convenient nest on one of the rumpled blankets.

What was Sybil's cat doing here... and...and... acting like he owned the place? Kevin's eyes, still swollen slits, warily regarded the interloper. He thrust a used teabag in the battered kettle of boiling water. But he was amused, for some odd reason the title of a series of pictures, called 'The Rake's Progress' came to mind. He slowly moved closer to the behemoth, hesitated and glanced at his bandaged ankle. Then he heard a scrabbling in the walls and taking a sip of tea, Kevin grinned evilly. The image of church mice, clutching each other in terror, was a delightful vision.

Oh hell. Feed a cat and you've a freeloading friend for life. But maybe, if he was lucky, Brutus was a good mouser. Kevin put a dollop of cream into his cup, removed a saucer from the cupboard, filled it with cream, and placed it on the wobbly bedside stand.

Brutus leisurely got up, stretched his dog-like frame, frowned sideways at Kevin and sniffed the contents. Then, with purring that suggested the power of a motorboat, he lapped up the proffered libation. After all, it was his due.

In the under-the-counter fridge, Kevin replaced the carton of cream and extracted a quart of non-fat milk. On a narrow shelf above stood a large box of organic cereal, he shook plenty into a chipped red mixing-bowl. Stirring the contents, he carried it over to a round, metal garden-table beneath the window and plopped down in the plastic lawn chair. He shot up with a yell. Christ! The thing was a block of ice.

Brutus looked up. He appeared disgusted with the interruption then resumed lapping his breakfast. Kevin grabbed the blanket off the bed, threw it over the offending chair, and gingerly sat down. With vivid remembrances of the night before, he eyed Brutus and slowly chewed his breakfast.

The cat lapped his milk delicately; in contrast, Kevin felt he was a cow munching its hay. He paused, chopped one overripe banana into his bowl and stirred in a container of yogurt. "Well, at last I can tell Mom I'm eating right."

Doubting the veracity of that statement, Brutus sat back, carefully washed his face, and regarded Kevin with a suspicious look.

Deciding to run the gauntlet and hoping he would not retract a bloody stump; Kevin got up and cautiously scratched the thick patch of fur between the cat's ears. It wasn't possible, the purring became louder. Although the sound was calming, Kevin felt agitated and got up. Vigorously scratching his own head, he began to pace the room.

"Okay fellah, I've got to talk to somebody." Brutus cocked a curious eye.

"Last night the whole enchilada happened. And it was more real than any of the other times, even the damned cave. Not dreamlike at all, it lasted longer and I've never had to swim for it before, either." Kevin shivered. "The water was damn cold." Brutus yawned and stretched, but both eyes remained on Kevin.

"I'm really scared, and keep this under your furry hat. I don't want Sybil or Case to know...not yet. Anyway, it seems I'm experiencing things that happened in the past. And I have a suspicion they're somehow connected." He paused. "But, I don't feel that pre-determination of events, or for that matter, freedoms of choice are realities. However, I do believe in what appears to be chaotic patterns and crossing webs of energy." Kevin crossed his arms. "I think we repeat some things that have happened to us in the past and the now. Maybe we should call any time 'the now'... we're just following threads of energy that connect, er randomly."

Arms akimbo, Kevin shrugged then sat down again. Brutus appeared to be intrigued; his ears cocked and turned in Kevin's direction.

"Ya know, now that I'm older, when things suddenly happen I'm not frightened, but when I was a kid I was real scared. Now I feel I'm an observer, just going along for the ride. At times though it gets real hairy, and I wonder if I'm in physical danger; like when that Christian fellow was going to cut my guts out." Kevin shook his head. "Maybe I'm picking up on some sort of ancient memes," he brightened, "or stumbling over some crossed strings in the universe. I haven't had any real injuries...so far." Kevin felt flummoxed and spread his hands. Brutus got up and moved to the edge of the bed. He peered at Kevin, an intent look on his face.

"Woof!" exclaimed Kevin. "You're giving me the willies." He leaned over and again scratched between the cat's ears; Brutus closed his eyes in ecstasy.

"I wonder Brutus; do other animals, besides the human animal of course, experience similar weird things too?" Brutus's eyes flew open; he slowly backed away from Kevin and sat down. His gigantic plume of a tail swished back and forth. He glared at Kevin. He was not happy.

"Hah buddy, that got you thinking. But be like me, you gotta enjoy the ride if it happens, eh Brutus?"

"Oh well, memes deal mainly with cultural transmissions that somehow stick. So I could gear my thoughts to string theory, and as a last resort there is 'woo-woo' science, not good enough though," he said and crossed his arms. "Case argues with me about the 'woo-woo' bit. He majored in Physics and his mantra is 'everything is better explored through science'. But my question is where do all life's energies go?

What are their natures and how do we tap into them? If indeed we do, and is it by accident?" He jumped up.

"Wow, could I be wandering around the edges of pre-determination here? Actually Brutus; my entire existence is a series of stumbling into things," Kevin chuckled, "like a cork tossed into the river, traveling willy-nilly, wherever the stream of life takes me." He spread his hands. "It could be that the lives I flash into are my ancestor's lives. Or, I wonder, does our DNA somewhere store recollections of memories of what things were? Man, I am getting into extremes again...maybe experiencing things from long ago. Say events that happen to us along the continuum, of human history." He pointed at Brutus. "Now I'm not giving you felines short shrift, but my personal concern is with mankind, as I'm the great ape experiencing these forces."

Kevin screwed up his face. "Something smaller could be in our DNA, something not yet discovered, like energy aggregates, say a living computer chip." Kevin smiled. "We could call them 'Humemes' for the sake of the discussion." He scratched his chin. "Or humbug might be more appropriate?"

Dramatically he threw up his hands and briefly closed his eyes. "Alas philosophy, I do not want my brains to fry, for acting is my métier, do or die."

He looked at the wide eyed Brutus. "Thanks my good fellow for letting me vent, you've been a big help." Brutus walked to the edge of the bed, stretched up, and placed a comforting paw on Kevin's chin and the other on his chest. His large eyes were dilated with worry, his attitude serious. What kind of human friend had he made? The intimate moment was broken by the sound of a heavy thud.

Startled, Kevin and Brutus glanced at the ceiling. Someone was clunking about.

"Hey old man, time to be on stage and up and at 'em. Remember, rehearsals start in an hour." Case's voice echoed throughout the empty theatre.

"Give me ten minutes," Kevin shouted back and stroked Brutus's fur. "My dear chap, I've got to get my butt up to rehearsals. Fortunately, they're only upstairs."

"The plan is, we finish breakfast, I dig up something dry to wear, and you sleep off your carousing." Brutus sat down and gazed at Kevin. "Then, when I get back, we'll visit Sybil. I'm sure she'll highly approve of...our... bonding." Again he ruffled the cat's fur. I hanker to see that sweet lady again, et tu, Brutus?"

The response was a weary yawn as Brutus made a nesting circle on the bed, laid his magnificent head on crossed paws, and began to snore.

Treasures Galore!

(Advertisement in the FishWrap Bugle)

Tourists and locals, while you're enjoying the natural beauty of Lahkanea Mountain and New Halem's own special view of the Mighty Pacific, take time to check out Tony Brack's Harbor Antiques, located at the corner of New Halem Drive and Sea Sprite Street.

Tony Brack has made it his life's ambition to locate valuable furniture and collectables from all over the world, including right here in little old New Halem.

From turn of the century farmhouses to Manses, Tony scours estate sales throughout Cedar County. His motto is, "If I don't have it, give me time and I'll get it." Tony also says....

The Necklace

Kevin hit his pace. His new running shoes were cool. He'd bought them at the Second Chance Thrift Shop in Tillamook – they'd hardly been used. Kevin glanced sideways at Case, who was sweating heavily, but his wind was better than last week.

At first it had been Kevin's idea to start running every other afternoon. And now Case was showing up after teaching his last Math-Physics class at the high school and before they went to rehearsals. Kevin ran to keep in shape for the play and he liked the high it gave him. Though long-legged and lanky, he was surprised. He was putting plenty of effort in keeping up with Case. In fact, he thought, by next week he'd be running the ass off of me.

Case was muscular and stocky. While at college he'd held a part-time job in cement work and was on the wrestling team. He ran to stay in shape, period.

"There's that crazy cat again!" Case said as he glanced behind them.

"Brutus, where?" Kevin slowed to look back. They were jogging past the library when a black ball dashed across the street toward them.

"Someday he's going to get hit," Kevin said and waved ineffectually as the cat bounded ahead of them. "Shoo Brutus, go home!"

Case slowed down. "He's your baby now. Since you fed him, he follows you everywhere." He snorted and ran a bandana across his face. "I bet your friend Sybil is somewhere around here too."

Kevin nodded. "Yeah, she has tea and pastry at the Sea Sprite right about this time. I guess the palm reading shtick peters off in the afternoon."

Case smirked. "You got that right. There's her bike in the rack. Go ahead, check out the bakery and take a chick break. I have to cut it short anyway; got to check out some stuff at Nelson's Drugs."

"Ha!" Kevin exclaimed. "It wouldn't be that you're checking out a certain guy who just may be stocking shelves at this time?"

"You're not supposed to know that."

Kevin laughed. "Come on, this is a small town, remember?"

They rapidly approached the Sea Sprite. Brutus sat on the lowest step of the bakery casually licking his paw. Case gestured toward the cat. "I think we should enter him in the New Halem to Tillamook Fun Run. He'd win paws down."

Kevin laughed. "Amen," he said, halted and shaded his eyes to gaze between the goodies displayed in the bakery window. He waved and smiled. "She's there alright."

While jogging in place, Case rested his hand on Kevin's shoulder. "Good luck old man, maybe I'll get lucky too." With that he yelled "Yahoo Eros!" and hung a right.

The bakery doorbell jangled as Kevin walked in.

"Hey, no mangy runners, or cats allowed, state Health Code." The portly woman shook a knife at Kevin, grinned broadly and continued cutting thick sections of cinnamon buns. Kevin inhaled the wonderful aromas and winked at the knife-wielding Agnes Mulhoun.

"I can't stay away, you have the nicest buns in town," he shouted.

"I'm flattered you noticed," Agnes replied demurely.

Brutus ducked under Sybil's table as Kevin plunked himself into the chair opposite her. Both Sybil and her plate of various goodies looked delicious. He winked and took a deep breath. "Oh kind and lovely lady, would you be so gracious as to let a starving actor join you at your bountiful table, and partake of your gentile company?"

Sybil dabbed her lips with a large paper napkin. "Kind sir, it would appear that your appetite and your disreputable sidekick already have." She fluttered her lashes at Kevin, then biscotti in hand, leaned over and waved it near the bottom edge of the tablecloth. A black paw snagged the cookie. Sybil shrugged at Kevin's open-mouthed stare. "It's one of his favorites, with toasted almonds." She smiled at Kevin's pleading eyes and waved a cherry Danish at him. "I believe this is your favorite?"

Kevin plucked it from her hand. "How ever did you know?" he mumbled around a large bite.

Sybil lowered her eyes. "A seer knows many things like; one

shouldn't talk with their mouth full, one should chew thoroughly and," she picked up her coffee cup slowly, "that you and Brutus would be coming by this afternoon." She paused, took a long sip of coffee and regarded Kevin over the rim. "And there's something else, something very important." Sybil lowered her voice. "It's going to happen to you today, it was suggested in my morning tea readings."

Kevin guffawed, letting a few crumbs fly. "I bet it was a strain to read them." Sybil rolled her eyes and pursed her lips.

Agnes, standing by their table, groaned. She had one hand on her ample hip and the other holding a deep saucer of milk. She grunted, and shoved the dish under the table then stood up, brushing a strand of hair from her eyes. "Brutus needs something for 'afters'. He gets quite thirsty," she explained looking around the small dining room. "And as long as customers don't complain," she paused, "and your big feet don't kick over his milk, Brutus will be able to enjoy himself." She continued to appraise Kevin. "I suppose our sweaty lothario will be wanting that wimpy concoction of half-steamed milk and hot coffee."

Sybil nodded. "Kevin doesn't like too much coffee in his milk. I think he's not old enough to come up to full octane."

Ignoring Sybil's jibe, Kevin's eyes lit up. "It would be saving a life Agnes. I've been running miles and need nourishment. And one of those fabulous cinnamon buns wouldn't go amiss either."

A loud purring commenced under the table. Agnes shook her head. "I can't understand why Brutus has taken to you. I can see certain foolish ladies in town being smitten." She gave a nod to Sybil. "Present company excluded, but not this black monster, he hates men. Likes to bite them on the ankles. I know. When Brutus is around about suppertime, he hides under the hedge near the path. I've heard many a scream with a curse, or two, thrown in." She smiled. "But, he's a real gent when it comes to women."

"He's taken away my best friend." Sybil laughed and ran her hand sensuously along Kevin's arm. "This soft-hearted thespian feeds him. And Brutus always did love the taste of ham."

Kevin lolled back in his chair. "Yeah, love at first bite. My ankle still throbs. But seriously, I have to feed him. He earns his meals; he's cleaning up the mouse population at the church. I've not found a single dropping in my cupboards since he started hanging around." He winked as Agnes left the table. "Well, maybe just the occasional mouse foot or two."

Sybil put her coffee down. "This is not appropriate conversation for afternoon tea and on top of everything else, you smell like a gymnasium."

Kevin peered down his long nose. "I'm keeping fit and it takes work, tears, dedication and unfortunately...sweat too."

Agnes returned and carefully placed a large cinnamon roll and cup of café-au-lait before Kevin.

"Oh a thousand thanks Agnes, you are kindness personified."

He lifted the cloth and peeked under the table. "At least Brutus doesn't treat me unkindly anymore." He sniffed noisily, slathered his pastry with butter, and with a shrug cast a hurt look in Sybil's direction.

Agnes shook her head, "I can see you're an actor and a bad one at that," she muttered sotto voce then hastily returned to the counter. A customer was signaling to pay her bill.

Kevin gazed at his fingers and licked them assiduously. "Now, what's this about serious business?"

"I said something important, not serious. Anyway, I don't know what it is, and I don't know its nature."

Kevin frowned as he sipped his cafe-au-lait. "You can do better than that; after all I've seen you in action."

Sybil frowned. "If my memory serves me correctly, at that reading, you were extremely under the weather and listing dangerously to port.

I'm surprised you remember anything."

Kevin shrugged, crumpled up his paper napkin and tossed it in the general direction of the waste container. "Hah! A basket, that means today, it's your treat."

Sybil stood up smiling. "Monsieur, it is always a treat when you're around."

Kevin had a foolish look on his face. "Really?"

"Yes, really. You have very interesting... er, vibrations that surround you. Now, before your ego goes through the roof, let's take a short walk. There's something I think you should see."

"Uh, what about Brutus?"

Agnes, who had been pretending not to listen, looked up from behind the counter. "Don't worry your pretty little heads. Brutus likes to sleep off his indulgences on the back sun porch. I'll see to the little glutton."

Sybil nodded as she took a small beaded purse from her pocket. "Thank you Agnes and I believe this covers the bill, including Brutus, his mooching friend, and the tip too."

Kevin tried to appear offended, but outside the shop he wrung Sybil's hand. "Thank you, thank you, you saved my life."

"It would appear that Agnes has done that, but I'm going to do more than that, and to avoid danger, much more than I wanted to," she murmured mysteriously and steered him up the street.

Kevin looked around as they crossed the intersection at an angle. "And where are we going dear Lady?"

"Right here," Sybil said, and pointed to a display of rings in the corner window of an antique shop.

Kevin looked at the sign above the doorway. "Oh yes, Harbor Antiques."

Oops, oh no, not a ring! Kevin thought. He closed his eyes and prayed to some god, any god. I'm far too young, just starting my career.

And she's too young too. Well, at least...he began to sweat.

Sybil interlaced her fingers into Kevin's right hand. His palm was sticky with icing and sweat. She shook her head. A devilish smile playing across her lips. "Kevin." She looked up and giggled. "Whatever is your problem? I only want to show you that necklace." She pointed to a display stand. It was draped with baubles, chokers and amulets. "See that necklace on the left? It looks like the one you went on about in your vision." She shrugged. "I think the sensible explanation is that you've seen this necklace before ... right here. Maybe when you were walking by, and I..."

Kevin's reply was distant, hollow. "I've never looked in this window before today." His hands were ice cold, his face waxen. The ground began to move, he heard the distant yelling of men. "I've, I've got to sit down."

New Acquisitions
By Carmella Williams, Reporter
for the FishWrap Bugle

The Portland Art Museum is proud to inform this reporter that it has expanded its Northwest Indian collection with amazing donations. Several are from the descendants of a famous pioneer family living in Clatsop County.

One exciting piece is an old Indian hat. The director, Dr. Millicent Mulberry, said that its origin is attributed to the Nootka of Alaska. And the hat is in surprisingly good condition. She said that as far back as the 19th century, Indian hats were prized by traders, sailors and settlers in the Pacific Northwest.

Dr. Mulberry went on to say that most hats provided insulation from all sorts of weather as they were woven together, with an inner and outer layer; essentially two hats in one. The inner layer was a coarse weave of cedar bark; the outer, an intricate twined weave of squaw grass. Due to these unique qualities the hats became important trade items up and down the coast.

Not only did the hats serve the purpose of shedding the continuous coastal rains, but also their designs are infused with color, movement and significant cultural meaning. Ethnographers have documented Indian Spiritual Leaders sporting similar conical cedar hats along with drums and rattles.

Leaving Ceremony

The buzzing and crackling continued. Roma tapped the old-fashioned receiver and held it closer to her ear.

"Hello? Ah. Hello Mary. What? Speak up. I barely can hear you. No, I'm on the phone in the kitchen. Oh yes. The spirits are active tonight."

"Yes. Sybil brought Mr. McLeod and the necklace over here. About an hour ago...how did you know?" Roma asked and glanced over her shoulder. Sybil was spreading a large piece of toast with butter and blueberry jam.

"Oh I see. She called you from the antique shop before they left, good thinking."

Munching her toast, Sybil shrugged her shoulders, left the kitchen, and walked down the hall to the spare bedroom.

Roma chuckled. "Indeed Mary, it is an interesting necklace. Yes. Sybil spotted it in Tony Brack's display window last week. Well today, just the sight of it made Mr. McLeod dizzy. And you know Sybil, she has to experiment; well, it was when she handed it to him that he passed out."

"He's resting now. Brutus is curled up in his arms. That cat seems to have some sort of attraction to him. Oh yes, he's a charmer all right. This is the first time I've met the young man."

"Oh you know Sybil. She has her ways, insisted Tony loan it to her. But Tony's pretty shrewd; he hinted that we could make a guesstimate as to its value. No. He's pretty vague about where he obtained it, but Sybil has a hunch it was locally."

"Yes. I have it here on the table." She picked up the necklace from a tissue-lined box. "Well... it has been restrung, rather recently I'd say. Not a careful job though, and whoever did it used some kind of stretchy string." Roma peered closer.

"This is interesting Mary. Some of the pieces appear to be East Indian. And the Lapis one is definitely Egyptian, a type of scarab. Blazes! I just got an electrical shock. No. Not bad. I touched the two that look Assyrian, or they could be Sumerian, for all that matter. No, I'm not going to touch them again. The energy field is certainly in turmoil. Yes. Well it's not appealing to me. Looks like a dog's lunch," she said then placed the necklace back in the box.

Roma lowered her voice, held the receiver closer. "I gave him one of my special herbal teas, it calmed him immediately." Roma sighed. "I find him just the opposite, quite impressionable and immature. Definitely not Sybil's type," she quietly mouthed above the receiver.

"What? Yes! An actor no less, no I'm not. Oh? So Sybil introduced him to you last week. I see. Yes, he definitely has an impressive Aura. No. I just shook his hand, very unsettling, left me with goose bumps. Well yes, but we all know looks run only skin-deep."

"Humph! I'm not happy about that. Sybil finally got around to telling me about the free reading she gave him...waited until last night though. I'd just got back from my Portland trip. I've already spoken to her about it. It was very unprofessional. Oh, just a moment," Roma said and placed her hand over the receiver as Sybil re-entered the kitchen.

Roma arched an eyebrow and nodded in the direction of the bedroom. Sybil slowly finished her toast, licked her fingers, and mouthed a yes.

"Hello, Mary? Ah good, I haven't lost you. Sybil says he's still resting."

"I think so Mary, it's best that we work together on this." Roma laughed. "I'm sure that we can get the necklace's energy either organized, or exorcised. Oh. Maggie wants to come too? Good. She's a discerning observer and frankly, the more help the better. In twenty-five minutes? I'll get the kitchen ready, toodle." She placed the receiver back in the cradle.

Sybil was at the sink, washing her hands. "If Aunt Mary and Aunt Maggie are coming, why don't I make a pot of that tea you brought back from Portland? Oh, and I'll put together a batch of cranberry pumpkin muffins. Doesn't that sound cool?"

Roma seemed not to have heard her; she was looking nervously down the hall. "Umm, excellent suggestion Syb," she paused, "er... do you think Mr. McLeod is quite all right?"

"His name is Kevin, Mother. And yes, he's completely out of it since he drank two cups of your 'valerian relaxing-tea' and he's snoring his head off. Brutus is too. You'd think you slipped something into his saucer of milk." Sybil shook her head as she concentrated on filling a large stainless kettle. "Gosh. Kev actually liked the tea." She paused to look out the window. "But, you don't like him, do you Mother?"

Roma sighed. "No, it's not that. It's just, well, he seems so... so unworldly and his Chi energy is quite chaotic. I get glimpses of his past, and things that he couldn't possibly have experienced in his short lifetime." Roma tapped her lower jaw. "The other explanation would be that he can experience past lives. But I doubt it. Anyway, if so, it's a jumble." She frowned. "He's as strange as that peculiar necklace you brought home."

"Well, I know you'll sort it all out, eventually." Sybil placed an old, tinned flour-sifter on the counter. "I did get the impression, from the free reading I gave him," she looked sidelong at her Mother, "that he has an ability to channel memories, memories triggered by some object or an event that happens to him, or around him." She reached up into the cupboard. "And I believe that he's able to do some 'mental' form of time traveling." She placed a container of baking powder next to the sifter. "He told me about a few strange things that happened to him, even in grade school. His experiences were so unusual that I've a hunch he'd traveled in time, even back then. Of course, he was too young to have a clue as to what was happening. And now that he's older he's going through a sort of denial stage. Thinks he might be a nutter," she said and shook her head, "he's just not aware that he has this marvelous ability."

Roma moved over to the sink. She gazed out the window at the deepening night. Funny, she was thinking of her estranged husband and son.

"Kevin told you about other things? Well... you'll have to tell me what they were. They'll help me figure him out." She lowered her voice. "He didn't say you couldn't tell me, did he?"

Sybil clunked several wooden mixing bowls on the counter and peered at her mother. "No. Well maybe; that we keep it amongst ourselves. He doesn't want everyone thinking he's some sort of weirdo."

"That's reasonable. Here, let me help you." Roma put on her favorite purple apron. The logo boasted, 'We serve only the finest wines.' Then asked, in smaller print: 'Did you bring any?' She placed the sifter over a large bowl, opened a tin container, and measured the flour out, by hand.

"What is that horrible rumbling noise, an earthquake?" Roma asked, looking up as Sybil shut the oven door on the muffins.

"No," Sybil said glancing out the window and laughing, "it's Aunt Mary and Aunt Maggie and they're in Johnny's muscle car." It became very quiet.

"Amen, thank the mother goddess they've shut the ridiculous thing off." Roma lowered her voice. "It could have awakened Kevin."

Sybil smiled to herself as she moved away from the window. Her mother had actually used his first name.

Roma took a washcloth and wiped the counter top. "Why don't you go and let them in? I'll get things shipshape here. And when the muffins are ready we'll put them in the warming oven. The tea will keep too." She put a bowl of hot soapy water in the sink, rinsed the cloth out and began to wash up. "We can eat when we're through with... whatever...well whatever Tlingit ceremony, Mary has planned," she said. "It wouldn't be traditional, but a combination of rituals that have worked in the past. I know she often consulted with her uncle, Willie Cloudmaker. You remember, he lives on Bradstone Island near Vashon."

Sybil nodded, then with an excited grin on her face, ran down the hall and flung open the front door. The women stood side by side on the porch. A sudden north wind gamboled down the street.

Mary, plump and squat, held on to the side of what looked like a witch's hat. In her other pudgy hand she clutched the handles of a capacious basket made of woven-grass. Maggie, shorter and thinner, wore a wispy dress. It fluttered around her legs and she tightly clutched a multicolored shawl over her head and shoulders.

"Hi Sweetie," Aunt Mary exclaimed as her substantial arms enveloped Sybil. "Oops, be careful of my Nootka topper. It's the wind." There were deep chuckles as she adjusted her cedar hat. On its side, in black and red colors, Sisiutl, a three-headed sea serpent leered menacingly. She shook the bag at Sybil. "I've stuck in a few things that might help."

Maggie, shivering, slowly put her arm around Sybil's shoulder, an ethereal smile on her face. "Hello Honey, you're looking very well. A man in your life, maybe?" Sybil shook her head. Maggie, her eyes half-closed, studied Sybil at arm's length. "I think someone is fooling herself," she said languidly then looked down the hall. "Yum, muffins and we're frozen and hungry." Maggie pecked Sybil on the cheek then floated toward the kitchen.

"Well, the conjuring girls have arrived," Mary said with a smile and made a slight bow. "Here, take my bag and help me get out of this heavy coat. I'm chilled to the bone. Johnny's heater isn't working. Thank the gods; Roma keeps it roasting in here." They paused as they overheard Roma and Maggie whispering excitedly in the kitchen.

"Now Maggie," Roma said, "be patient, the muffins won't be ready for another fifteen minutes."

Maggie whispered a question and Roma's laugh carried down the hall then she lowered her voice. "So far, everything is okay. He's still asleep. Even Johnny's macho mufflers didn't wake him."

"We had to take Johnny's car. Mary's car is at the Gas and Go, some kind of battery problem. Honestly, Honey, I invoked every helping spirit I could think of on the way over. But we almost froze to death."

Roma chuckled. "Well, it's a bit better than broomsticks." Then she turned and waved as Sybil and Mary entered the kitchen.

"What's better than broomsticks?" Mary asked as she took the bag from Sybil and plopped it on the table. She began removing cloth-wrapped objects.

"Johnny's car," Roma answered.

Mary snorted. "Barely better, it's just as drafty and his car seats are as hard as boards. He always tells me, 'Mom, I'm gonna restore that wreck'." Mary shook her head as she unwrapped a cedar rattle, carved on one side was the face of the full moon. "Johnny's such a good boy," she sighed. "But he just doesn't have that much time. He's trying so hard with his new lawn and garden business. I help him out as much as my old body can. But it's a struggle."

"I don't mean to interrupt Aunt Mary," Sybil said excitedly. "But what are you and Mom planning to do?"

Mary's eyes twinkled. "I'm as anxious as you to get started." She peered into the huge bag. "I've decided to do a 'leaving ceremony'. I was taught some of the ritual years ago by my Tlingit mother's granny." She nodded at Roma. "Your mother is familiar with most of the ritual, but I'll need your help too."

Maggie leaned over and whispered, "Mary's going to cast out any evil spirits that have taken over the necklace."

Roma crossed her arms. "Ahem...evil? Now that's an interesting word and no doubt a useful concept for tyrants, religious fanatics, politicians and ignoramuses." Roma took a deep breath and stuck out her chin. "There's no such thing as good, or evil, there's just the 'Is'. A more precise term would be, 'bothersome spirit'." She paused as the women stared at her.

Sybil gestured helplessly. "Mother, we've heard this lecture before. And don't forget Aunt Mary and Aunt Maggie said Johnny will be back to pick them up before 9:00 PM. Shouldn't we get started?"

Roma looked slightly miffed as Mary nodded in agreement, picked up the choker, and began to rub each ornament between her fingers.

"We're going to have to cut this stretchy stuff. Whoever restrung it scrambled the stones. Obviously they had no idea that whoever assembled them did it in a purposeful order and used a specific combination of ancient spells." Mary shook her head. "Hopefully, tonight we'll get them realigned and possibly find out the reasons for the original sequence; and maybe the purpose of the necklace." She gently pulled on the stones.

"I can feel the energy jumping around, umm it's getting warm to the touch." She carefully wrapped a kerchief around it. "I've brought some roots of Goat Rue. They're very strong and quite appropriate for the restringing. But I wish I could find out what the original material was. It may be important."

"May I hold it?" Maggie asked and reached for the necklace. Mary nodded. "Though be careful, it's getting hot."

Maggie ran her fingers over the stones. Her eyes were closed as she touched each piece. She held very still. "Well... that's sad. I get a feeling of loss, and emptiness." She grimaced. "Here Sybil, take it, too intense for me."

"It's never affected me at all," Sybil murmured with a smile as she ran the necklace through her fingers. "But, what I wanted to ask about..." she paused, "Oh!" Her face became still, she closed her eyes.

"What are you seeing dear?" Mary asked with apprehension.

"I think it's a beach. Yes it's a long bay that appears to stretch as far as the horizon. There are people, whispering, like the wind... and crying." Her voice became sad, she shook her head. "I see an orange sunset, there are men rowing large sailboats. High on a hill is a city and everything's on fire." She rubbed her eyes. "It's all moving faster... beads running through calloused fingers. Oh!" Her eyes fluttered open, she hastily handed the necklace back to Mary. "I can't. Aunt Maggie's right. The feeling of loss, fear, desperation; it's too intense."

Mary grimaced and nodded. "Now Sybil dear, find me a pair of scissors. I'm going to cut loose the pieces, and please hold this underneath to catch them?"

After fetching the scissors, Sybil opened the soft, fur-covered pouch. She felt a shiver run up her arms. "It feels alive! What is it?"

"Beaver, I chose beaver skin," Mary replied and delicately snipped the connecting strands of the necklace. "Beaver is a wise creature, a meticulous builder, and a fierce protector of family and home. Beaver is never satisfied until each stick is just so." Mary squinted over the top of her glasses. "Beaver's spirit will aid in realigning the stones correctly."

She paused and reached into the depths of her bag. "This eagle feather will encourage the confused spirits to soar. Maggie, you wave it over the stones. And Sybil, when I tell you to, put the bag in this pine needle basket, and rotate it clockwise. It must face the cardinal points of the compass. I want you to pause a full minute at each position. Roma, you know what to do with the Moon Rattle."

Roma nodded and shook the ancient musical instrument in a 2-3-2 rhythm. The pebbles inside made an odd, clicking noise.

"We must smudge also," Mary said and lit shavings in a well-blackened clay bowl. The contents flared. Next to the bowl she placed a small incense candle and lit it.

Mary stood back, checked the table objects' relative positions. Satisfied, she went over and switched off the kitchen light, then turned and picked up a long crow's feather. Fanning it smoothly over the smoking bowl, Mary closed her eyes and started a soft, melodious chant.

When the song ended, Mary gestured to Sybil. "Now, it is essential you move the basket in this order: To the North for guidance; to the East for the morning light of wisdom; to the South for the warm pull of the sun; then finally to the West to say farewell."

Mary resumed her chant. After eighteen repetitions she opened her eyes. "Sybil, please stand with your back to the North and keep your eyes only on the basket." Mary glanced out the window. "When we came over tonight a north wind was blowing. It's perfect, helps speed spirits on their way."

Sybil moved promptly, her back to the kitchen window. A chill crept over her neck and shoulders. It was as if the sash were open. She steeled herself not to look.

Mary picked up the smudge bowl and waved the crow feather in longer arcs. Tendrils of smoke thickened and the scent of cedar wafted through the room. She carefully placed her feather and bowl on the table. "Now Maggie, gently move the eagle feather over the basket."

Mary closed her eyes and began a more strident chant, this time louder. Roma recognized the song. She heard Mary use it many times to calm disturbing forces.

Mary fiercely clapped her hands three times. "Now... AWAY!" she shouted and flung her arms upward. Everyone jumped.

Needles, that's what they were, very sharp needles. And there was a thrumming sound, and oh, oh, cadaver breath. Kevin's eyes flew open.

Brutus gripped Kevin's rather prominent chin firmly in his mouth and purred away. Recently, he'd adapted this technique to awaken Kevin. Sybil said that the chin grasp was a sign of affection, a love bite. Kevin disagreed, insisting that Brutus was extending his abilities as a control freak. Besides, the sharp teeth made his chin prickle and itch; no love there.

Carefully he stroked Brutus's thick fur. The purring increased, then there was a distant shout. Immediately Brutus released his hold and sprang to the closed door. His tail twitched wildly back and forth. Growling he looked back at Kevin.

"What's up old boy?" Kevin roused himself and rubbed his chin. Strange noises came from the direction of the kitchen. He sniffed. Wood smoke! Holy crap, a fire! He kicked the bed quilt off and stumbled to the door. Cripes. He did smell smoke and a lot of it. He felt the door handle, cold. With adrenalin pumping and Brutus at his heels, he flung open the door and charged down the hall.

There was an eerie silence. A shimmering haze enveloped the kitchen. Brutus shot between Kevin's legs and leapt onto the counter, his eyes large and dilated. Clutching the doorframe for balance, Kevin stared into the room. What in the hell was going on?

Sybil suppressed a giggle. Kevin looked like a wild man, his shirttail hung out, his dark hair stuck out in spikes.

"Are you rehearsing the witch's scene from Macbeth?" His voice cracked, he hastily clapped a hand over his mouth.

Mary brought a finger to her lips. "Shush! We're not through. And uttering that name aloud is supposedly a bad omen for theater people, but not here." She nodded to Sybil, and directed her to turn the basket, once more to the four compass points.

When Sybil finished, Mary picked up the beaver skin and opened it slowly. "There, that should be the correct order." With satisfaction she carefully placed the pouch on the table then paused. "Hmm, I have the feeling that a key piece is missing. Some sort of pendant."

Mary turned her attention to Kevin and regarded him over the rim of her granny glasses. "Do you remember what the missing object looked like? The one I'm talking about?"

He closed his eyes and visualized Mikos and the necklace. Or would it be called a choker? His mind began to wander frivolously. Discipline, discipline, Kevin thought, got to focus.

"Uuh," he croaked, "I'm not sure. It seemed to be... pinkish, round and translucent. I think it was carved...but... there... there was something else actually hanging from it."

"We'll need a test young man, and you appear to be most sensitive to the necklace's power." Mary motioned for him to step forward.

Kevin started to sweat. The figures of the four women formed an eerie tableau; Mary with an abstract smile, beckoning him, her gray hair tumbling out of the conical hat with the funny bulb on the end; Roma mesmerized and rhythmically shaking a carved moon-rattle; Maggie, eyes glittering in the candlelight, gleefully moving a feather over a furry mound on the table. But it was the look on Sybil's face that unnerved him...a mixture of hope, expectation and fear. Brutus, the only calm one sat on the table and licked a huge paw in complete unconcern.

Mary glanced at the ceiling, closed her eyes, and clasped her hands in prayer. Kevin, dry mouthed, swallowed. His legs wobbled as he moved toward the table.

Mary chanted, her voice far away as if from the top of a mountain.

Kevin shivered and closed his eyes. The chill of drifting snow and glacial winds surrounded him

"Yes that's right," Mary said. "Touch the edge of the fur Kevin. Caress it on the edge, a very light caress; but whatever you do, don't disturb the order of the stones inside.

Sybil watched Kevin's long fingers shakily tracing the beaver skin. Her hand flew to her mouth. A dried snake skin and a raven's skull seemed to have materialized at the side of the basket. The bone-white beak pointed directly at Kevin. Mary motioned for Maggie to step back.

Sybil shook her head, there was a rushing sound, growing in intensity. No one else seemed to notice. It became louder then moved swiftly behind her, the beating of gigantic feathered wings, closer then retreating. Brutus let out one very long and loud howl.

Startled, Kevin drew his hand back. Then the chaos was gone. "I, I don't feel anything, I...," he smiled as a wave of happiness and peace washed through his body. His mind floated in this pleasant sensation of release and oneness. He closed his eyes.

Faintly, in the middle of his forehead was a niggling sensation. There, was still something... a movement; people and backgrounds interacting. Behind his eyelids individual frames of an old film ran slowly. He could tell by the clothes and the glimpses of an ancient forest that the events were long ago. There were gnarled hands exchanging, giving, placing. The flash of frames stopped. Kevin's eyes flew open; his voice wavered. "The piece, I think, I think now I could recognize it again. It's a carved dragon eating its tail."

"And the color?" Maggie asked breathlessly.

"Ah, very pale pink; a beautiful paleness, it looked waxy."

Smiling, Mary signaled Maggie and Roma to cease their movements. Her hunch had been confirmed. "It sounds like some sort of jade, and a very rare type too. However the piece is probably lost. So the necklace is as complete as it can be. And it still has its power.

The ceremony worked. I'll restring the necklace in the way the stones are arranged in the beaver fur." She picked up the roots of goat's rue. "Lights, please."

Sybil looked at Kevin's face. His eyes had changed color; unreadable pools of brown-gray, round with astonishment.

She leaned forward. "Kevin? Kevin what is it? There's something else, isn't there?"

"I...I know. I know where I can find it," he mumbled hypnotically.

Sybil was frightened. She shook her head, her lips in a thin line. "You mean the pendant?"

"Ye... yes I do. But it isn't just a jade piece. It's the treasure from the shipwreck. The treasure is there too, in the mountain, it's..."

Maggie looked around the room at all the knowing faces. "Treasure! Shipwreck? What is dear Kevin going on about?"

Roma shot a glare at Sybil, who turned away with a guilty look.

"Er, Aunt Maggie," Sybil whispered, "I'll tell you later. It concerns a free-reading I gave Kevin. Okay?" She paused, a guilty grin on her lips. "Perhaps...after tea?"

The Face That Launched a Thousand Ships
By Carmella Williams, Reporter
for the FishWrap Bugle

Michael Wood, eat your heart out.

Our not nearly as famous, but equally as erudite, Dr. Millicent Mulberry (Curator celeb at the Portland Art Museum) is guest lecturer at our humble New Halem Library this month.

She will lecture on none other than the Trojan Wars and the ancient city mound of Hissarlick (Troy), located in Turkey. Dr. Mulberry told this reporter that a fabulous collection of jade jewelry was recently found, in situ, at Hissarlick. This find confirms that the once great seaport (so far nine layers of habitation have been uncovered) had direct contact with the peoples who travelled the ancient trade routes from east to the west.

Could these jewels have belonged to the famous Helen of Troy? Maybe they did. You'll find that and more about the cake layers of occupation at one of Dr. Mulberry's fascinating lectures.

While you are there, check out the museum's excellent collection of jade and jewelry brought up from the dark catacombs of the museum to display with the lecture.

Brutus go too?

Kevin jogged north on Beach Drive. He was really going at it. Damn that Case, bagged at the last minute. Said he had a shit load of math and physics tests to correct. Kevin hoped it was only tests and Case wouldn't be late for rehearsals. The man's romance life had been getting pretty hot and heavy. And Case had his own unique way of prioritizing the order of things.

Kevin shook the sweat out of his eyes. He was soaked through. Next time, he'd not rush off sans sweatband and jock. He glanced at his watch. Just enough time to take a quick shower, have a talk with Sybil, and then dash upstairs for rehearsals. Kevin picked up speed.

Earlier, Sybil talked to him on the phone, but her voice broke up badly and she sounded out of breath. Said she didn't have time to chat, but would meet him at his room. Probably that damned necklace. He'd satisfy his suspicions shortly.

Behind him, a car tooted its horn. He glanced back. Wow! A strawberry blonde, driving a red convertible with top down, waved at him. Her hair, tied back in a yellow scarf, flew behind her. She smiled, wildly waved again and shouted: "Hey there, Mr. McLeod."

'Be still my heart,' Kevin thought and quickly moved to jogging in place. The car pulled up beside him. The blonde took a while adjusting a pair of gigantic sunglasses. But her gaze was steady while she raked him from head to toe.

"Why, Mr. McLeod. You're more magnificent than your FishWrap photo." She leaned across the passenger's seat, revealing considerable cleavage. Kevin stopped. He casually adjusted his neck towel then let it fall strategically. With a dazzling smile he made a swooping bow. "Madame, you have me at a disadvantage. You appear familiar, but I'd definitely remember if we'd met before."

Her laugh was melodious. "I'm Ms. Carmella Williams, a freshman reporter at the FishWrap Bugle. You may have read a few of my articles." She grinned, removed her sunglasses with a flourish and laughed. "Don't worry. I'm not going to turn you in for indecent exposure."

"Oh thank you," Kevin said and rapidly tried to recall an article, anything she'd written, but no luck. "Ah, I think I remember them, they were very ... er succinct."

"Mm," she murmured and pursed her very red lips. "Mr. McLeod, I've been dying to interview you, ever since you were hired by the Bishop's playhouse." She assumed a more business-like manner.

"I'm particularly interested in your first impressions of New Halem, the play, your part," she made an encompassing motion with her arms, "in general, the actors milieu through the eyes of the professional. It makes great news. I'm taking the slant of the travails of the city lad suddenly cast amidst his country cousins." Her eyes bored into him.

"My editor wants a series of small articles as a build-up to the opening night of the play." She tapped her teeth with her sunglasses. "Gossipy tidbits get the reader's immediate attention. We can start now. It'll take several days for the first interview to gel anyway. I know you won't mind. Every shred of publicity, positive or negative, is beneficial, to the actor and in turn to the Bishop's Playhouse, don't you agree?"

Kevin didn't agree and he did mind. "Er, I'm very sorry; we'll have to do it later... maybe over lunch, or dinner, tomorrow night?" His hormones were far out distancing his brain. He shrugged. "Unfortunately,

I've got to be back at the Bishop's in 15 minutes. I've just enough time to hit the shower, dress, then it's upstairs for rehearsals."

"Well, since I have my handy-dandy recorder with me. I could interview you during your shower. Get a rough idea of your digs, the actor's struggling life, etc," she paused and laughed, "I'll throw in a lot of interesting schmaltz with a few intimate details, our readers will literally inhale it. Then we can schedule a follow-up interview for tomorrow." She patted the seat beside her. "Come on. I'll give you a lift. It'll buy us time." She winked. "Doesn't that sound fabulous?"

"But, I'm too sweaty to sit in your car and..."

Carmella abruptly whipped a beach towel off the backseat. "Now you're not." She patted the blanket. "Sit here. It's been scientifically proven that the scent of the masculine body is a necessary therapeutic for a woman's hormonal system. Not only does it add to her physical well-being, but her psyche as well. Isn't that amazing?" She inhaled deeply and pushed the passenger door open. Kevin slid in.

"Uh thanks. This will save me a little more time, but..." Oh great, he thought, Sybil and Case were already at the playhouse, they'd tease the hell out of him, particularly if they saw him entertaining Ms. VaVa Voom Williams.

As they roared off in the powerful car, Kevin's mind roared too. I've got to tread carefully here, got to focus on the play, and then there's Sybil.

Carmella grinned and gave him knowing nods. Kevin stared straight ahead. Keep your attention on the road woman! Whew, definitely a voracious news hound at the helm.

Near the steps of the Bishop's playhouse Carmella slammed on the brakes. "I'll be just a tick, after I park."

Kevin squirmed around in his seat. He talked rapidly convincing Carmella to interview their director first. He hoped Ms. Emily Saunders would approve of this nosey reporter...and tolerate her interference during rehearsal. But if she didn't, Carmella would be forced to observe all the actors in real time and determine that he wasn't the only talented one in the ensemble. Also, his so called 'apartment' was taboo territory for any interviews. The shower was in the men's room and he smiled.

He leaped out of the car and darted towards the side door.

"I'm sure your Ms. Saunders realizes the publicity impact of my interviews," Carmella shouted after him. "She'll definitely want one for herself. And, my readers must have an intimate glimpse of Kevin McLeod, in his digs, and in action."

He blushed angrily. He hoped Ms. Saunders would point out to Ms. Williams that there were many important support people behind a successful production. He shook his head and shut the side door firmly behind him.

With a hot shower followed by a cold one, Kevin felt fresh and alert. After a quick rub down he grabbed his terrycloth robe and walked down to his room. Sybil was sitting on the edge of his bed. He sat in the plastic chair, and jumped slightly when Brutus's thirty-pound body leaped purring into his lap. Kevin stroked him. Then, with a smile of trepidation, he nodded at Sybil.

"Okay, what's up?"

For a moment she regarded him with that devastating half-smile then spoiled it all when she held the necklace out to him.

"No, no Sybil. It's not a good idea. Rehearsals start shortly. I don't want to be totally gaga when I'm on the stage."

Sybil frowned. "But I told you on the phone, I have to return the necklace to Tony Breck at six o'clock, and that's this evening. Tony has a buyer for it." She shrugged. "It's your last chance to find out what happened to Ahmad and Mikos. And I'd also like to know. Besides everything should work a lot better, now the stones are in the right order." She paused. "And there still is the missing pendant."

Kevin grimaced. "Okay. But if my mind is away too long, you've got to pull me back. Bop me on the head with the tea kettle or, if that fails, Case is upstairs, he can come down and deck me, throw me into a full-nelson, anything to break contact with the hold of that damned necklace."

Sybil smiled and shook her head. "Kev, such dramatic measures are simply not necessary. There are gentler things that I can use." She pulled a carved ivory fetish and a wooden moon-faced rattle out of one of her deep smock pockets. "These should work quite well."

"Hah!" Kevin snorted. "Should, is the operative word here." Gad, he already felt faint. Reluctantly he stood up and placed the grumbling Brutus next to Sybil.

She slid the necklace behind her and ruffled Kevin's wild hair. "You're very brave to do this. I admire your courage and... and, I think the other word is... is forbearance. You're way cool."

Kevin gulped. At least the lady thought well of him. That's a healthy start to any relationship.

Resigned, he returned to his chair. Brutus jumped off the bed and sat by his side. His look was calm and appraising.

Kevin gripped the sides, and nodded assent. Sybil got up and gently placed the necklace over his bowed head.

A rush of wind and the intense odor of smoke and dried fish assailed his nostrils. The last thing he heard was a piercing screech from Brutus.

Kevin's mind blurred then slowly focused. He was inside a large building. It was made of planks and logs, the walls decorated with animal skins. It was somehow familiar. That's it, a long-house. Interiors like this were depicted in his First-Nations art books. Suddenly Kevin's thoughts and senses kicked into high gear. He was warm and dry and best of all he'd been hurled back into Ahmad's mind, not someone else's.

Mikos stood next to Ahmad. They were trussed to a vertical pole. Ahmad, the larger and taller of the two, balanced them both. His right ankle was tied to Mikos's left.

Kevin began picking up Ahmad's thoughts with more ease.

This morning, at their shelter near the beach, Ahmad noticed the men of the tribe cautiously approaching. It took a little time to convince Mikos to let them be taken. Ahmad argued that they had no quarrel with these men and Mikos was still very weak.

Now the headman, the tribal council, and the curiously garbed man, who looked like a spirit-doctor, regarded them fiercely. Ahmad tested his bonds. It was highly probable they would become slaves. Ahmad nodded to himself there were opportunists among the men standing in front of him. These men would employ Ahmad's and Mikos's foreign knowledge and skills to their advantage. This type of man was found in every society, always looking for something to be gained, or exploited.

The use of captives for labor and trade to other tribes was universal. He'd been through this before, in the Aegean. Each time he'd fortunately escaped. But Ahmad was alone then, and knew many of the languages and dialects. Now in this new captivity, he and Mikos' only plan would be to become invaluable through their knowledge; and most advantageous of all, create friendships.

Ahmad grimaced; this vast land with its great trees and endless forests was far different than the Aegean and the accompanying Sea Islands. Exploration was more difficult due to the inaccuracies of earlier mapping expeditions, the hostile actions of contacts on both sides, and the surprising variety of tribes inhabiting the region, not to mention the various languages they spoke.

Picking up languages quickly, focusing intently, and observing like a cat was among the many of Ahmad's talents.

He was pleased he had already acquired some useful pieces of information and expressions. Too, he was hearing a common coastal pidgin, and had learned a few fragments, it would all take time. Escape was extremely doubtful. But, as long as he could keep himself and Mikos in the same settlement or camp, they could talk and plan. Somehow he must convince the council that he and Mikos could be trusted together.

Ahmad determined that the headman was related to the young female who had been spying on them. From the moment they'd taken refuge in the forest he had noticed her. And now, she still watched intently. Ahmad was puzzled. Usually, a woman was not allowed in a male tribal council. Earlier, Mikos had whispered that he felt the headman was her father and had heard her called Xli-tse. Ahmad was aware that, from time to time, the girl had interceded on their behalf and seemed to show a definite interest in Mikos. Ahmad smiled; a budding relationship could definitely be a benefit.

Kevin quietly listened to Ahmad's thoughts. He watched through Ahmad's eyes.

The council members were at logger heads. A few claimed that the two aliens were forest demons; others that they were evil salmon men, cast up by the sea. Some thought they were sorcerers, biding time until they could summon destructive forces. But the tribal members that traveled across the mountains, or traded goods up and down the coast, argued that these two were only men like themselves. One wag commented, "but having the further misfortune of being shipwrecked and lost."

Ahmad glanced at Mikos. Great Caesar's ghost! Kevin exclaimed to himself. Mikos' necklace was in full view and it was complete. Kevin gazed raptly at the pendant. There it was. The opalescent-like object; a dragon eating its tail, the one that Mary said was missing. Kevin tried to study the small carvings and the black pearl-like object attached to it, but Ahmad turned away.

Whenever Kevin was close to the necklace he could always hear a low buzzing sound. But something else whined, a single note, high and irritating. Did Ahmad hear it too? No, his thoughts were distant, planning.

Whoops, harsh feelings of hatred and fear entered Kevin's thoughts. Confused, he searched through Ahmad's mind and eyes. The mental cacophony was emanating from the man in an elaborate dress standing next to the headman. It was a medicine man. The tribe's spiritual leader.

Crap! Kevin could also tune into this man's thoughts, they became clearer. His name was Swaxwa.

The image of the pearl like object spun at the center of Kevin's mind. He focused on the energy radiating from it. Resentment and anger was becoming more evident. Kevin mentally sweated, like a waterfall. The dude was really pissed, Kevin tried to penetrate deeper, but something like a shimmering wall let him read only the surface of Swaxwa's thoughts.

The Spiritual Leader was having a hard time controlling his emotions. He feared and hated all members of the fire-stick men. They killed with poles that shot flame and smoke. With the exception of their deadly sticks, they were like the dreaded Haida from the north. And the fire-stick men were increasing in number. Some had been found and killed as they came over the mountain passes to the south. True, a few had been friendly and helpful to his people, but they usually brought pestilence and death. The council was not being wise. The female upstart, Xli-tse had convinced her father and his retinue of cronies that the men were not a threat.

Swaxwa ground his teeth. After the girl showed the villagers where to collect proper spirit herbs and how to prepare them to combat the great sickness, the council trusted her completely. And, they further reasoned, she was the granddaughter of the once famous Spiritual Elder of their tribe. Swaxwa knew it was really the old woman and not Xli-tse that possessed this great knowledge. The grandmother had no doubt directed the girl where to find the necessary leaves and roots. The old woman still possessed much of her legendary powers, even after Swaxwa had rendered her helpless with his curses and potions. Since he had taken her place her powers were still not nullified. He would have to do more.

In the beginning, Swaxwa greatly feared the two men's magic and planned to steal the younger one's necklace. He was convinced that it was the power of the strange object that helped the two sorcerers survive the wreck.

When Swaxwa watched the giant canoe founder on the rocks he advised that any survivors be killed instantly. They must not have time to summon any harmful demons. But Xli-tse convinced her father and the council elders to allow her to observe the men secretly. And, she reasoned, she had the protection of her legendary grandmother.

Swaxwa smiled to himself. Actually, her daily recognizance had proved useful. The fevered young man was obviously no threat and neither was the larger one. He was occupied with the building of a shelter, gathering herbs, seafood and berries, and tending to his sick friend. Most importantly, he made no weapons or performed strange ceremonies.

Kevin saw more in Swaxwa's mind regarding Xli-tse's powerful grandmother. She had predicted strangers would come by land and some in giant, cloud-like canoes. Evidently, when she was a girl, a giant wanderer from the forest appeared. He had the skin color of obsidian. He surprised her village by easily speaking their inter-tribal language then teaching useful skills to those that listened. Soon he became a valued member of the tribe and eventually a great spirit-doctor. After he married, his red-haired descendants were prized by the Northern tribes and when they couldn't be obtained by bargaining, they made surprise raids on the villages taking the red-hairs by force.

There were also tales of ancient travelers who came from the great ocean. Some appeared in battered wooden canoes with strange carvings of sea monsters and some could call on spirits that possessed great power. The old legends said that the wayfarers had skin color similar to the tribe's people and had strikingly similar facial features.

Many of these ancient ones demonstrated unusual skills in fishing, trapping and in the healing and forecasting arts. Some were taken as slaves and though different, allowed to become working members of the tribe, others even attained high status. When Xli-tse's great-great-grandmother married one of the more powerful spirit-men, rivalry between spiritual leaders of different tribes became more intense.

Swaxwa chuckled; he was the current spirit-doctor and had the skill and cunning of a raven. He had succeeded in casting an evil-spirit possession upon Xli-tse's grandmother. Soon she was hardly able to speak or walk. Then she became too ill to carry on as medicine person to the tribe. Through the help of his cohorts and skillfully staged magic tricks, he convinced the tribal council that he should take the old woman's place.

Kevin sensed that Swaxwa was forcefully clenching his jaw. Before Xli-tse's grandmother had fallen under his curse he'd had a powerful and terrible drug-induced vision. His people and all the tribes he knew became slaves of the fire-stick tribe.

In this vision, Swaxwa saw his own powers become useless and Xli-tse replace him. And helping Xli-tse would be the men from the sea; the tall one with the magic tattoos and the other one with the powerful necklace, and skin of the wet seal. Kevin was startled by Swaxwa's fierce determination to call on all his powers to avert the outcome of his dream. He would marry Xli-tse and use his spies to keep her in his control. Swaxwa smiled secretly. There were ancient spells and spirits that would aid him. He would avert his horrid vision.

Kevin felt drained from the power of Swaxwa's thoughts; then abruptly they were severed from him by a blocking presence. Mentally shaking the chaos of anger from his own mind, he became aware that the council's arguing had ceased.

Above Ahmad and Mikos a great shadow appeared. The sound of powerful wings filled the long-house. Kevin strained to hear and see what was happening. The men in front of him were looking up and began uttering an eerie chant in unison. When Ahmad's eyes widened Kevin could see a giant raven ponderously circling the high ceiling. The bird was searching for something. In its slow, erratic flight it appeared confused and irritated. The raven did not cry out, only the whoosh of the mighty wings marked its path.

All eyes followed and it circled once more. Then, with a low rumbling croak, and great ceremony of wing-flapping the raven, landed on Ahmad's right shoulder. A gasp chorused throughout the room. Ahmad and Kevin froze. This either would be very good omen, or a very bad one. They both grimaced as sharp claws dug into Ahmad's skin.

The bird made a low mewing sound beside his ear then it grumbled with irritation, thrust its head forward and grabbed Ahmad's chin in its vice-like beak.

Up to this point Kevin had remained as passive as possible in Ahmad's body. He was still stunned at the revelations of Swaxwa's thoughts, but very rapidly became aware of what was happening.

'Oh shit!' Kevin exclaimed in Ahmad's mind. 'It's Brutus!'

Ahmad stood stock-still his insides trembled. 'Who's there?' He thought wildly.

'A friend, a friend,' Kevin shouted mentally. His mind raced. 'I'm here to ...to help you.' Instantly the raven made a loud purring sound and took a firmer hold on Ahmad's chin. 'The bird is too,' Kevin added hastily. 'His name is Brutus and I'm called Kevin.'

There was no reply, but Kevin could feel every muscle in Ahmad's gigantic body tense and flex as the sharp beak clutched his chin. 'Hang in there man!' Kevin thought as he surveyed the council through Ahmad's eyes.

'We've got their attention and it will work to our advantage.' Kevin tried to emanate a sense of calm throughout the sudden turmoil in Ahmad's brain.

Ahmad swallowed slowly. 'Friends?' He thought. At least the damned corbie wasn't pecking his eyes out. Then a vague memory came to him. There were tales of such mental whisperings throughout his family's history. Accounts went far back to the ancient legends from Wilsua, a place revered in the oral traditions of his ancestors. Ahmad was sweating. There had been stories about one possession, but never two that could cause insanity. Were the God's helping, or plaguing him?

'Friends of Ahmad, I humbly greet you,' Ahmad thought then paused. 'Where do you herald from?' From his youth he'd been taught that it was prudent to show respect and proper decorum when elders, people of importance, or mental visitors were about.

Kevin began to reply. But for some reason his throat muscles were tight, his mind confused. Oh, oh, peculiar feelings of separation were creeping over him.

'Ahmad, we've got to bag. Though, by the looks of things you won't need us anyway. Tell the... tell them you have an important message from the Raven spirit, and...and... well improvise.' He gasped. 'Brutus, let's scramble!'

By now Kevin was shouting, his thoughts shattering at the same time.

The Raven released Ahmad's chin, let out an ear-piercing scream, and shot up through the smoke hole.

Kevin felt himself collapsing inward. Ahmad could feel it too; he saw vivid lost patches of memories. 'Good journey...friends,' he thought hastily. Good riddance flashed through Ahmad's mind too, but he attempted to suppress this last thought.

Sibyl sounded distant and distraught. "Case, oh Case. What's happened to Brutus? He's as limp as a wet towel."

While Sybil crooned to Brutus, Case shook Kevin's shoulder and tapped him sharply on the cranium. "Anyone in there?" he asked in a voice fraught with worry. Kevin growled and rolled over. "Good riddance, indeed!" he snarled aloud.

Case threw up his hands in panic and turned to Sibyl. "Forget Brutus. We've got to get Kev alert and upstairs and we've only five minutes. What's happened to him, anyway? He's mumbling crazy things."

Sybil paused, her mind spun rapidly. "Oh... ah he'll be okay. We tried a little experiment. You know er... a little mental focusing. He's just too sensitive." Sybil sniffed. "He didn't like what happened."

Too damn right, Kevin thought as Case loomed over him. He coughed. His throat was sore as hell.

"Gosh, sorry about your arm and neck old buddy," Case said, his face flushed with concern. "But you're amazingly strong, really put up a good struggle." Case sounded puzzled. "Have you been working out at the gym on the Q.T.?"

Kevin coughed. "No, but now that you've stopped throttling me, for Crissakes, help me up." Case nodded wildly, grabbed Kevin's arm and jerked him upright.

"I need water." Kevin rasped then stumbled. "Better yet... a shot of that whiskey you brought over the other day." Case smiled primly and shook his head. "Negative. The Director won't like it. She has quite the sniffer."

"To hell with what Emily likes," Kevin choked out. "I've been through a horrible experience. If she wants a live body up there, you'd better get that whiskey. Now," he paused, "and NO chaser!"

After a gulp of the fiery fluid, Kevin wiped his lips across his sleeve and grabbed Case by the shoulder. "Come on. You're my front man," he mumbled and shakily headed for the stairs.

Case glanced back at Sybil then turned to Kevin and lowered his voice. "Guess I'll have to help you fend off the strawberry blonde too. Whenever did you get cozy with that sex maniac?"

"What? Oh no! You mean Carmella Williams? She's still upstairs? Rats! Emily let her stay?"

Case paused and bowed with a flourish. "She swept our tough Emily off her feet; great publicity 'don't you know'. She also said she's an old timey friend of yours. Personally, she strikes me as one glib and sexy reporter. Man, how do you do it?"

Kevin stole a look at Sybil. She was busily shaking her rattle at the groggy Brutus and in general making a great to-do over him.

"She is not a friend," Kevin snarled loudly. "I just met the woman about an hour ago, jogging. She was real pushy about interviewing only me." Kevin looked flustered. "She didn't even mention the rest of the cast or crew. Good god. It's not a one man show."

Case laughed and tweaked Kevin's ear: "Man you're quick, just a babe magnet in tenny-runners. I've got to get some pointers. That is, er of course, with a few modifications," Case rolled his eyes and said more loudly: "Your La Carmella chatted Emily up through the roof. Then she went on and on about your health. Said you were soaked to the skin and was worried that you hadn't dressed appropriately for your run; might have got a serious chill, etc, etc." He guffawed.

Kevin turned to glare back at Sybil. "That woman knows nothing about my health. And Syb," he said loudly, "you pay more attention to Brutus than you do to me and all I've been through. Thanks for your touching concern...and when you've finished 'kvetching' over poor Brutus, you can 'kvetch' me two Aleve and a glass of water. That'll be my chaser."

With a dramatic gesture he pointed at Sybil. "And if I suffer any ill-effects from this fiasco the blame rests entirely on you!" Kevin 'harrumphed' then squinted at Brutus. "And it looks like our mutual friend could use a heavy dose of catnip to calm his nerves." He began to mount the stairs then froze; a stunned look came over him. "Christ," he yelled. "The jade amulet, the 'something else' attached to it, is really weird. It hums." He stared wild-eyed at Sybil then bolted up the stairs.

Sybil picked up the necklace. It was still quite hot to the touch. Why had she pushed him to put it on again? And why was she so inexplicably furious with this Carmella Williams person whoever she may be? And what about Kevin's sudden super macho attitude toward her and the situation... it was totally unlike him. "He wasn't even acting," she exclaimed aloud. "And what was so important about that attachment to the jade piece?" Her voice got higher. She ran over to the stairs and shouted. "You're being a real... real stubborn pig! And you can get your own pills and water!"

A befuddled Brutus with demented tinged eyes and mouth agape was not to be out done. He hurled a piercing screech of outrage at Kevin's retreating back.

OH, A Hiking We Will Go
By Carmella Williams, Reporter
For the FishWrap Bugle

Hi ho theater fans, some of our Bishop Theater's cast lead double lives. We not only can act, but we can rock-climb and possibly spelunk too.

This reporter spied Case Edwards and Kevin McLeod rehearsing on the green behind the Playhouse.

Then, at break-time they were sorting through a Medusa's tangle of ropes, harnesses and helmets (with headlamps no less). Could our acting stalwarts be tempted by the craggy heights of Lahkanea at night? Or are they...

Janus

Kevin pulled on the climbing rope. It was fastened to the trunk of a nearby Douglas fir. Double check everything, Case always told him. Now, where in the hell is that dude? Turning, he frowned at Sybil.

"I can't wait all day for Case. I've got to see what's down there." He jutted his chin toward a fern rimmed opening in the ground. The rope snaked over the lip then disappeared below. He struck what he felt was a dramatic pose. "I'm not going to stand here and argue about it."

Sybil shook her head. "Kevin, you're being ridiculous. Please stop the drama. It's too dangerous to go it alone. Wait for Case." She dug her toes into the plush carpet of the forest floor. "Mary was having a little car trouble, that's all. But they'll be here shortly." She smiled lopsidedly. "Patience is not one of your virtues."

Kevin breathed deeply. The odor of salt air mixed with evergreen boughs filled his lungs. They stood roughly one hundred feet from the edge of a cliff that plunged to the Pacific Ocean, and he was surprised. On their short walk into the forest they couldn't hear the waves crashing on the beach, two hundred feet below.

"Patience!" he exclaimed, adjusted his climbing helmet and walked to the edge of the hole.

"Case and I located this two weeks ago. What with rehearsals and Mary putting things off because the stars weren't right," he gestured helplessly as he looked up into a patch of blue sky, "and then, with last week's relentless rains, part of the edge has already sloughed away. If there's any treasure down there it's probably covered in ten feet of mud."

Sybil patted him on the shoulder. "I don't think two weeks compared to several hundred years is going to make much of a difference."

"Well it's time I found out, isn't it?" He clamped the rope's beaner to his harness, adjusted the small head lantern, checked his flashlight and made the rope taut. "Tell Case, the spoils go to the first." He shot Sybil his best pirate leer. "Avast there matey, play the rope out like I told ye. Hah, tis over the side for me." With the occasional exaggerated grunt, he backed nimbly over the edge.

"Kevin you're not being sensible," she pulled on the tight rope and gritted her teeth. "This is not a play!"

He looked up, a devil may care attitude on his features. "My dear... all the world's a stage, and...WHOOPS!" Kevin's foot slipped. Sybil gripped her hold tighter and let out a squeak. He caught himself.

Kevin looked into the void beneath. "I feel like Alice down the rabbit hole. I'd guess it's about 50 feet, plus or minus a few to the bottom, as Case would say." He looked at her strained face and smiled. "That's of course if there is one...tah, tah." He disappeared from view.

Muscles strained as he slowly descended the rope. The helmet lamp played on snagly roots that hung from the cave roof. The smell was moist and earthy and he could feel a slight updraft. Weeks ago, they'd found the actual cave entrance on the ocean side of the cliff. But, a rock -fall blocked the opening inside. He sniffed. Sea air was still seeping in. Good, plenty of oxygen.

Kevin paused; was that a rustling sound below? He looked up at Sybil's head silhouetted by the hole. He wondered how long ago the original ceiling had begun to open, and why, and if the released material had buried everything beneath it. His head lamp played along the sides. Erk! It reminded him of another cave, but not as inviting.

Slowly he rappelled until his feet touched something solid.

The head lamp revealed a mound of wet dirt and plants. Fairly recent collapse, he thought then unclamped the extra flashlight from his harness. He switched it on. The surface was spongy, but negotiable. He was about six feet above the actual cave floor.

Holding the rope around his waist he carefully edged down the slippery pile of debris. At the base he paused and played the light along the walls. The cave wasn't too large and the mound he descended extended to the north corner. As he swung the lantern around he was able to pick out the rock-fall that blocked the actual entrance.

Kevin could feel the dank air spilling through the rocks. He swept the light along the cave floor. Oh great, bones. He slowly walked over. "Whew!" It was a deer carcass and smaller animal remains, nothing else. Being in Ahmed's mind he knew that Christian had planned to kill the rest of the crew that survived the wreck. Had he managed it? And if so, where were the bodies?

His light beam fell on a pole thrust into the ground; Kevin carefully pulled it out and hefted it. Attached to the other end was a stone spearhead. The shaft was carved. He felt the curious glyphs, and...oh shit; there was that weird feeling again. Kevin tried to drop the spear, but it wouldn't release from his grip.

The cave's odor quickly changed. His body told him he was in somebody else's, and somewhere in the past. He was sitting on a rock strewn floor; the cave entrance was open.

Kevin felt a pain in his side and for some reason stared at his right hand. It was covered in blood. Cripes; he'd been stabbed in the side. And to top it all off that damn medicine man, Swaxwa was standing in front of him. Instantly Kevin knew that his name was Thuiwat, and Thuiwat could see the last of his tribesmen walking out of the entrance. They carried casks and chests.

"Don't call out Thuiwat. You must die honorably." There was a sobering pause. "Why didn't you trust me? You knew that I would have made you my main assistant."

Thuiwat swallowed thickly. "That potion you used, at the purifying ceremony this morning, what did you put in it?"

Swaxwa grinned. "Yours was specially prepared. It will make the journey to your ancestors more pleasant."

Swaxwa raised his spear. "Tell me, before you go. Why did you help the fire-stick men escape? Why did you turn against me? And, why did Xli-tse go with them?"

Thuiwat's tongue was becoming weak and loose. Swaxwa would get all the answers he wanted.

It was difficult for Thuiwat to focus on the threatening spear and Swaxwa's cold, penetrating eyes. Why had he tried to trick Swaxwa? Shaman Swaxwa was very powerful and once a good friend. But, his great ego and whispering sycophants made him blind to many things.

Thuiwat felt sad; it was his love for Xli-tse and his fear for his tribe's people that helped him make his decision. Eventually all would be threatened by Swaxwa's relentless desire for the sacred necklace. Once he possessed the fire-stick man's powerful charm, Swaxwa could rule as he wished.

"Answer me before you die."

Kevin felt Thuiwat's heart pumping. How the hell is he going to get out of this one?

Swaxwa thrust his spear menacingly. "Answer me. I want the necklace. With it, we will become the most powerful of tribes. The Haida, the Tlingit, will be our slaves. And I thought foolishly, you would be at my side."

Thuiwat grimaced. "In the past, Those Leaders possessed by your great greed, have spoiled most everything they've touched. With the power of the necklace you plan to enslave our tribesmen. And you have no respect for our great chief, or his lineage. You've become cruel and vacant; the benevolent spirits have abandoned you. I know of your plans to kill the great chief and make Xli-tse your wife. You will try to destroy her, but she will kill herself first, she understands your nature and detests you."

Swaxwa's body stretched, his face distorted. "How do you know all this?"

"Xli-tse and I followed you to the sacred clearing. We heard you invoke the help of the Dark Spirits. Your sorcery will bring the wrath of the shape-shifter, Sisiutl, upon all of us."

Swaxwa raised his spear. "When I have the necklace, the great sea monster, Sisiutl will help only me. Now, I will take great pleasure in killing you."

Overwhelmed by Thuiwat's fear Kevin panicked. "Stab the dude," he yelled. But it was Kevin's voice that echoed throughout the cave. Kevin gulped audibly. Somehow he'd overrode Thuiwat's vocal chords.

Thuiwat was in shock. He was suddenly possessed by an evil spirit that made him utter powerful and dangerous sounds.

"No, no, I'm a helpful spirit. I'm here to help you destroy this evil person and restore harmony to your tribe." Wow! Where'd that come from; a line in an old movie?

Swaxwa jumped back. His eyes bulged and became wide pools of black. He stumbled further back then froze.

"It will do no good to entreat the fire-stick man's Gods; they are fickle, they will desert you." His voice shook, his waxen face contorted in spasms, then his mouth and tongue moved stiffly.

With a clear and precise English accent, Swaxwa asked: "Who are you? How did you get here? I recognize your voice." Swaxwa clutched his throat, trying to stop the odd sounds that spilled from his lips.

Stunned, Kevin realized at once that Swaxwa was also possessed by a mind traveler. Sybil said this could happen and he would not be the only one with this ability.

As the whirlwind of thoughts caromed through Thuiwat's brain he was sure he had entered the netherworld of evil warriors.

Again Kevin forced Thuiwat's tongue and lips to speak. "My name is Kevin." Oh crap, what must he say...from the future? "I'm from the 21st century. I'm..." he was becoming confused, disoriented, like Thuiwat.

Swaxwa, a horrific look on his face, replied: "It is clear. You've come for the treasure and the necklace too. You're too late. I alone know where they are."

"No, no. I'm not interested in those things. I don't care about them. And I'm not even supposed to be inside Thuiwat's mind. It's all some sort of accident."

Swaxwa's face was forced into a sneer. "Don't think I can be fooled. Men always seek treasure, in any guise; whether corporeal or non-corporeal. It's man's common directive of universal greed that drives him. I'm from your time too. But none of this is significant. It will all be mine, including the powerful necklace." Swaxwa's eyes narrowed.

"Over thousands of years those who knew of its existence, have sought to control the choker and lost. But I have possession of the ancient tablets that tell how it was made and how to direct it. When Xlitse and the others return, the talisman will be with them, and then with me. Of course I will make Swaxwa forget that I have ever possessed his mind. If any remnants of images remain, he will think they are from spirits that favor him. He has an insufferable ego."

"But, how did you get here and how will you get back to your real body?"

"Humph, you are a novice. It would be interesting to talk to such a young mind traveler, but unfortunately, Kevin of the 21st century, I must dispose of you." With that Swaxwa crouched and raised his spear. "Through the heart," his crazed face shouted and he lunged quickly.

"No!" Kevin yelled as Swaxwa leapt. Without thinking he steadied

Thuiwat's spear butt against the ground for leverage, the heavy stone point drove into Swaxwa's abdomen.

Swaxwa's body stopped in motion, a surprised and agonized look on his face. But, paradoxically, his eyes were very much alive and staring intently into Kevin's.

"You've killed my host," the voice panted, "but not me." Swaxwa dropped to his knees; he tried to pull the spear out of his chest then howled and arched backwards. Both hands grasped the weapon, his bare feet kicked up clods of dirt.

"I've killed a man!" Kevin shouted his horror throughout the cavern. Sweating profusely he clutched his side. He felt terrified, desolate; then his thoughts gave way to Thuiwat's.

Thuiwat staggered up. In shock Kevin's thoughts floated somewhere. The light began to fade. "In the movies, it's only a flesh wound," he gasped quietly and felt himself falling.

Near hysteria from the crazy voices swirling in his head, Thuiwat staggered toward the light of the entrance.

Case grumbled to himself and looked down the hole. "You haven't heard from Kev, since a half-hour ago?"

Sybil, wide-eyed, nodded. "He insisted on going it alone." She spread her hands helplessly. "I heard him talking loudly to himself. And just before you got here he was yelling. Now there's only silence. We've got to get down there. I've shouted and shouted and there's no answer."

"Not we, Sybil. You're staying here. I've the strength and the know-how to get him out safely. You'd just be in the way."

"Well thanks Case, I really needed that," she sniffed.

"Sorry Sybil, but I'm really pissed off. At times he's so incredibly foolish. I taught him a lot, and he's good." Case shook his head while he checked his gear. "But he could have waited at least ten minutes, only ten freakin minutes."

"Let's not lament what could have been, hurry!" Sybil said frantically.

"Calm down Sybil," Mary said nervously. "Last night your mother and I read the cards. No death cards were there, but there was an indication that Kevin would be in grave danger. From some...some interfering force. We couldn't pin the origin down, but...."

"Calm down? Grave danger, an interfering force! Those cards are not just alarm bells; they come incredibly close to the truth..."

"Mumbo jumbo and reading cards, ye cats, what am I getting into?" Case snorted as he put his harness on. "You ladies are getting nuttier by the moment."

He approached the hole. "Nutty or not, I'll need everyone's help. Mary, you start the truck engine. This cable that runs from the hood provides power for my floodlight. It might help down there. I'm going to use Kevin's line. If he's incapacitated in some way I'll shoulder him up. Sybil, you handle this white line. I'll tell you in a moment. Everybody in position," he ordered as Mary jogged to the truck.

Case hooked his beaner to the rope. "Don't worry Sybil. Kevin's a strong guy. As I've said. We've climbed a lot and he's smart."

Sybil was crying softly. "Kevin can be an awful ass when he's showing off."

"He can be an awful ass most of the time," Case grumbled and deftly lowered himself over the lip. He sniffed. Good. Fresh air wafted up from the cavern. He moved partially down the rope then looked up.

"Remember, don't turn on that damn light till I signal, and tell Mary not to go too near this edge, it's unstable. Let the light cable out slowly, about fifteen feet." She looked at him questioningly. "Blue tape, it marks the footage. That rope, the one tied to the other tree. You saw me coil it there?" She nodded. "It's only for backup. Toss it down if I yell for it. And you watch the edge too. If we need to, I'll secure the rope to his harness and together we'll work him up the line. It pays to be prepared for any eventuality."

"Now, dry those tears and pay attention Sybil. This white line is for hand signals. It's thin, but strong. I'm taking it down with me. Listen, these are the rope commands I'll use..."

Repelling down, Case shouted Kevin's name. There was no answer.

He flashed his hand light on the floor of the cave. At the edge of the beam appeared a rusty knife blade, some wood debris and what seemed to be the barrel of an old gun. Plenty of fresh footprints, though. And the objects had recently been kicked out of the side of the dirt mound. But where in the hell was Kevin? There was only an empty harness.

He swept the beam along the floor. It played over a pile of fir needles. Odd. He swung it back again. Crikey, a dark brown skull's empty eye sockets starred back. No wonder Kevin was talking to himself. Case grimaced. It looked like more bones against the far wall, but where in the hell was Kevin?

The suspended flood light cast distorted shadows everywhere. It was useless. Overkill on my part, he thought. He'd have to be very methodical.

On a hunch he played the flashlight in the direction of where the cave entrance would have been. Bingo, a body wearing Kevin's boots and moving. "Always a good sign," Case muttered as he rushed over to Kevin.

"Get that damned thing out of my eyes! Crap...oh, it's you Case. Sorry I didn't wait. Whew, got a ferocious headache, feel like throwing up!" Kevin's breath came in short, rapid gulps of air. "And... and where in the... the hell...are we?"

"Man, you're out of it. And point your head away from me, pal." Kevin complied.

"Now, stop hyper-ventilating! That's better. We're on the cave floor near the blocked entrance. It appears you've had a jolly time stomping all around by your lonesome. Cause there ain't no one here but us chickens. What happened?"

Kevin started to sit up.

"Don't Kev. Stay down. You may have broken something. Wiggle your toes... they work? Okay, now your fingers." He gestured toward the cave mound. "Did you fall?"

"No, I didn't," Kevin snarled. "And my muscles are working fine. My side hurts a bit... must have bruised it." He started to stand up and then staggered.

"Whoa buster," Case steadied him. "Just sit down. You're not going anywhere, till you calm down and tell me what happened. Here, take slower, deeper breaths. Phew." He shook his head. "Thank God there's fresh air coming in this cave. That's right, slow it down. Now, why are you in such a snit?"

Kevin shrugged and slowly rubbed his forehead. "Sorry Case, it's just I get these er... spells, occasionally. I feel disoriented and sort of in another place."

"Shit. Your spells are getting more frequent." Case squatted down. "You've got to stay away from Mary and her group of dingbats. Every time Sybil gets something on with them you wind up like this." He shook his head and pointed toward the hole. "I'm not saying Sybil is bad. But, together that coven of ladies gives me the whim whams."

Kevin bowed his head. "No, that's not it; it's not what it seems. They're actually trying to help. You see I've this er...ability that when I touch certain things from the past I..."

"Okay, okay. Just settle down, it'll keep until later. Right now it's damn cold in here." He looked around. "And this cave creeps me out, especially with Sybil yowling down the hole. You can tell me everything topside, preferably over a couple of beers. And for the record, I don't give a tinker's damn about any treasure."

Kevin gave a twisted smile. “There isn’t any treasure. But I would like to tell you about my problem, old buddy; I’ve kept it secret too long and I think it’d really help talking it over with a bro.”

“Oh man, you’re not telling me you’re gay? I wouldn’t believe it anyway.”

Kevin snorted. He was feeling better. “No, no it’s not that.” He staggered up and started swinging his arms. “Hey, let’s start. See, I can get to the top under my own power.” He looked up at the hole. “What a racket, I think Mary’s joined in too. Better signal we’re okay, or Sybil will have our heads.”

Case loped over to the mound, yanked twice on the white line and cupped his hands. “Yahoo! Everything’s A-okay,” he yelled. “And turn off that damned flood light. We’re coming up.”

An exhausted Kevin sat on a tent tarp. His back against a log, his arm around Sybil; the others sat on a larger tarp in an arc. Kevin was the focus.

“I might as well tell everything.” He smiled at Case. “Don’t fret; we’re still going to have those beers at the Hair of The Dog.” He looked at the ground, pausing to gather his thoughts. “It all started when I found an old Indian spear down there.”

After Kevin’s dramatic, but succinct account, Mary sat forward on her log, laced her fingers and stared into them. “How extremely interesting, that’s not precisely what the cards said last night,” she looked up, “although there was that part about tricking death.”

Kevin straightened his spine. “Tricking death? You mean because I panicked and survived? You know I stabbed a man, and he died… I’ll never forget that. It was terrible, unnecessary.”

Case shook his head. “Swaxwa would have lobbed a spear through your guts in a minute.” He glanced at Mary. “But, I’ve just had a thought.

And I regret having to ask the 'woo-woo guru', but... is Kevin himself in physical danger here? Because he really feels the impact of these things when they happen to him?"

Mary squinted at Case and shrugged. "We know his mind travels only. Because of that, he experiences the hosts thoughts, pleasures, and stresses. But, if his body is in an unsafe area when he goes into the mind-travel bit; well then, he is subject to anything dangerous that happens there. For example, if part of that cave below collapsed, then Kevin could have been injured or killed. Of course that depends on where his body was when he went into the trance."

"And I wasn't too worried about Kevin this time," Mary said smugly and turned toward Sybil. "Your mom and I held a card reading last night and although there was indications of a dangerous force that would threaten Kevin, there were no death cards drawn. But we thought it would be a good idea to consult the necklace too." She made a sound of disgust; "Which came out a big zero."

"That doesn't make sense. How could you have consulted the necklace; someone bought it last week."

Mary rolled her eyes. "I'm that someone. I bought it. And that thief of an antiquities dealer charged me the earth. Remember, when I went to all that hocus pocus bother two weeks ago? Well, for some idiotic reason, the necklace's powers wouldn't respond to me."

Case groaned. "Now we're having consultations with necklaces? Save me!"

"So," Kevin exclaimed. "All I had to do was make Thuiwat throw his spear aside and run for it. Then things would've turned out the way they were supposed to?"

"Umm, I don't think you could old buddy. Remember, you couldn't toss the spear away."

Sybil put her hand on Kevin's. "And what do you mean 'supposed to'? We really don't know how things should turn out. And Case is right, you said you couldn't let go of the spear." She squeezed his hand. "Besides it was a mental state you were experiencing, not a physical one. Not for you anyway. So you didn't kill anyone. And Swaxwa intended to kill Thuiwat whether you were there or not. Isn't that so, Mary?"

"Well yes, that's one way to think about it." Mary looked uncomfortable. "But if there are parallel universes and if we consider what took place... happened as a crossover event, one could say..."

Case threw up his hands. "What you're talking about is a parallel singularity of which there are possibly an infinite number. I imagine you're alluding to current arguments in theoretical Physics. But this event really weirds me out. Do you mean that Thuiwat killed the witch-doctor guy, not in our time, but in some parallel space-time? And it would have happened anyway, even if Kevin was not in the guy's head?"

"And let's not forget." Sybil smiled apologetically. "To make matters more complicated, there was someone in Swaxwa's mind too, whoever it was knew Kev, and thought he could do in Kevin and this Thuiwat at the same time."

"Geez, great," Kevin said then nodded. "Yeah, makes sense, the dude thought he would conveniently kill two birds with the toss of one spear."

Case sputtered. "I can't believe I'm actually considering these things. Odd bodkins, I've gone down a real rabbit hole and this Wonderland nonsense is beginning to brush off on me."

Sybil stood up, fists on hips. "Case, it's anything but nonsense. It's no different than a particle being in two or possibly more places at the same time." She shook her finger. "Have you forgotten Schrödinger's cat!"

"Wow Sybil, I didn't think you knew squat-didley about quantum theory. Next, you'll tell me that Brutus had a paw in it too."

She stuck out her jaw. "You have a problem transitioning between Physics and Metaphysics? We can't have one without the other, at least on this planet and in this universe."

"Ah yes madam, the question of entanglement, or the counter intuitiveness of quantum mechanics," he said with a bow of his head and squinted out of one eye to see her response.

"Absolutely," Sybil replied, sticking out her chin.

"Children, children," Kevin shouted, dramatically waving his arms. "In this universe, with every nanosecond we are somewhere or nowhere...and... and I can't see us getting anywhere...except into further infinite confusion. Also, you should be aware that Mary has been trying to say something for the last five minutes."

Mary clapped her hands twice and laughed aloud. Three sets of questioning eyes focused on her. She bowed her head toward Kevin. "Thank you, kind sir. I only want to say there are," she smiled, "in this universe, a few important things we can glean from Kevin's experience. One, a spiritual leader named Swaxwa, was most likely killed by Thuiwat in some past time. Two, Kevin didn't kill anyone. It was his misfortune to be in Thuiwat's mind at the time of the event." She raised her hands to quell any objections. "Three, the treasure's location has changed, it appears to be dispersed and parts probably lost forever. And four, the person who was residing in Swaxwa's mind evidently knows Kevin, and no doubt lives in this curve of time and..."

"Curve of time!" Case yelled, his eyes bulged.

Mary frowned at him. "Please don't interrupt...And five, this person regards Kevin as an adversary." She paused. "As a consequence Kevin may be in real, present-time danger."

"Oh jolly!" Kevin exclaimed. "Now I have to look over my shoulder, every moment I take a breath? Sounds like a ye olde Hitchcockian thriller to me."

Sybil laughed. "Kevin, look on the bright side, you told me that five is your lucky number."

"Excuse me, I don't think drollery is in order here," Mary said with a sniff. Then looked thoughtful. "You'll probably have to move over Kevin."

"What, what do you mean, move over...over where?"

"I'm saying that I'm paddling in the same canoe you are. And it is prudent that I watch my backside too."

Case sneered. "Why's that? Not enough incantations, animal sacrifices and bloody bits to help here?"

"Oh, don't be rude," Mary replied. "Obviously he or she never got the necklace. I have it."

"True, that's true," Kevin said shaking his head with vigorous agreement, then suddenly in shock he looked up. "He or a she!?"

Mary closed her eyes, an angelic look on her face. "I never said that mind travel was gender exclusive, Mon Cher."

"Give me the strength of Hercules!" Case shouted as he got up and stomped off. Alternating between mumbles and wild gestures, he gathered and packed the climbing gear. With a few heaves he stowed the bags of equipment into the bed of the truck, shook his head, and looked back at the others.

"Come on time-curvers. If you want a lift, it's back to New Halem for this normal folk."

Can't Keep a Secret?

by Charles Thompson

Glenda Gadabout

Thousands Turnout forThespian Tapas

by Glenda Cunningham

for The FishWrap Bugle

Over two thousand dollars, Good Readers, were raised for The Lahkanea Players at a successful Spanish soirée of wine tasting and tapas with a fundraising auction hosted by that dreamy Drew Delacruz at his exquisite Sea and Sky Restaurant last Saturday, November 25th. In Spanish, "tapa" means cover and the custom of snacks with drinks comes from an old Madrid tale of the barman covering the glass of wine with a chunk of bread, cheese or meat to keep the flies from drinking along.

Everything was prepared with delicious delicateness, but two of the appetizers were devilishly divine. Almejas a la Marinera (Clams, Fishermen Style), local clams and mussels sautéed in wine, with a bite of spice and Totillita de Camarones which were chickpea flour fritters of Guadalquivir shrimp and onions. Such a delight! Drew was ably assisted throughout the evening by his sister-in-law, Adele Donley Delacruz, owner of By the Book. Nevertheless, the night's hostess with the most-ess was little Alona Delacruz, the nine year old daughter of Adele. She was the perfect Shirley Temple hostess, greeting guests with the sweetest Heidi smile.

The emotional evening on the Spanish Coast was enlivened by the colorful costumed characters from The Lahkanea Players serving samples of sumptuous Spanish wines. Drew's partner Daniel Benson served as sommelier, painting delightful descriptions of each wine. Beautiful, dark-eyed flamenco dancers and hooded Franciscan friars mixed with the crowd sampling the stupendous spread of tempting tapas. A wandering minstrel played a classical twelve-stringed guitar throughout the evening. Miss Gadabout closed her eyes and the stirring sound of the music, the smell of the cuisine and the tickling taste of the wine brought her back to the Spain of her college summer tour of Europe. There are stories to share from that summer, hearts won, innocence lost. Oh, Good Reader, another time...

Emma and Jonathon Bauer, owners of Lahkanea Studio, headed up the auction and donated several locally crafted works of art. That hazel-eyed German hunk was the auctioneer and we delighted in his rich baritone voice, bidding sometimes only to keep him talking.

Anne and William Reid, owners of the Treasure Trove donated several exquisite items from their stupendous shop. Adele donated a small library of books on traveling through Spain from By the Book and even our own William Cooke donated a half page ad with color in the FishWrap. This was quickly snapped up by Brad Ruskett of Ruskett Chevrolet who was there with his immaculately coiffured wife, Cheryl.

A night in Spain wouldn't exist without romance, as Miss Gadabout can attest to. Oh, that stupendous summer of our youth, but I digress. There was plenty to go around that night. It was not too surprising for us to see Publisher Cooke attending his oft-seen friend, Maggie Billings. We called that little cooing as soon as he came to town.

We spied the always beautiful Verity Hayden, from By the Book, talking with Anne Reid. We bet Verity was asking if Anne's son, Nate, would be home for the holidays. We understand that Verity and Nate were quite the item in high school. Jeffery Roland, the FishWrap's Sports Editor and manager of our theatre company, was appropriately dressed as a bull fighter. We witnessed that he waved his cape several times towards Miss Verity but sadly it was always a miss.

The heart breakingly beautiful twins, Azule and Aubrey Bellamont, nieces of Doreen and Phil Bellamont were there with a whole swarm of possible suitors like moths around a flame. One young man that stayed close to the heat was Maisy and Frank Jenkins' visiting nephew from Seattle, Ted.

We also saw that ever-so-handsome scallywag actor, Kevin McLeod, dressed as Don Quixote, flirting shamelessly with Sybil Desilieux; but based on the look we saw on her mother Roma's face he was singing the "Impossible Dream."

Hoping for a bit of romance ourselves, we had a most engaging meeting at the front door with a mysterious man dressed all in white. He is known only as the Parking Lot Prophet. I found that he is actually a former stock broker. I'm afraid the conversation with our PLP, which is how he likes to be addressed, was too one-sided for Miss Gadabout. He was oblivious to our flirtatious attention and too focused on his cause to save the public beaches, but he did have a warm, Czech accent and the brightest hazel eyes.

The sumptuously sweet surprise of the night was the sight of our beloved sheriff, Astra Billings, on the arm of the FishWrap's managing editor, Matthew Charles. They arrived together, ignored almost everyone and left early. We think, at long last, Astra has found a man.

With thoughts of our Spanish summer, we slipped out and went home with a half bottle of La Rioja Alta, a delightful red wine from the Rioja region. It was enough to make our much requested version of Sangria. The half bottle of the hearty Spanish red was poured into a two liter wine carafe with the juices of a fresh squeezed lemon, a lime and an orange. We followed with a splash of two ounces of Brandy, one ounce of Triple Sec and one cup of chilled fresh organic orange juice. We topped it off by gently stirring in 12 ounces of chilled Ginger Ale (we prefer Vernors).

We took our carafe out to the porch where sipping this elixir of the Gods, we fondly thought of sweet Alejandro and wondered what other youthful secrets were being thought of under the stars that night.

The Lahkanea Players Present

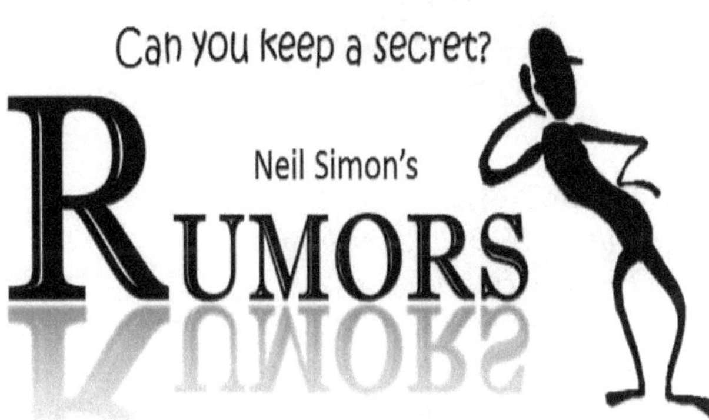

The outrageous "farce of ridiculous consequence" comedy of mistrusted spouses, missing wives, gun toting husbands and the gossip between the best of friends.

December 2- January 21

Friday and Saturday at 8 pm

$32.95 per person for Dinner, Show, Tax and Gratuity

Directed by

Emily Saunders

Featuring: Kevin McLeod, Glenda Cunningham, Case Smith, Verity Haydn, Alicia Gordon, Ernie Benson, Milli Payne, Dave Egan with New Halem Deputy Mayor, Tom Witherspoon and Cedar County Sheriff Deputy, James Conroy

Produced by: Jeffery Roland, Lights and Sound: Ted Jenkins and Stage Crew: Sybil Des Lisieuz, Azule Bellamont, Aubrey Bellamont and Nelly Mulhoun

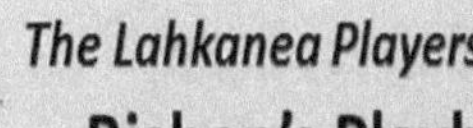

The Lahkanea Players

Bishop's Playhouse in New Halem

Tickets available at The FishWrap Bugle and By the Book

Hannah's Treasure

by Kate E Thompson

Public Notice
William H. Billings, publisher
The New Halem Telegraph

"Married—At three o'clock on Thursday afternoon, June 13, at the residence of James McFarland, by Harrison Miller, Reverend of New Halem Village Methodist Church, Mr. William Hartley Billings and Miss Hannah Margaret Dickerson--both of New Halem Village.

"We congratulate ourselves."

132 years ago in New Halem Village

She was a collector. Each day, after she dismissed the children and finished cleaning the blackboard, she rushed to the sandy shore, a little north of the school house. There she searched for treasures. Hannah considered whatever washed in with the tide as gifts that were meant for her. Every clam shell, periwinkle, pebble, and cormorant feather she placed with care in her apron pockets. At home, she kept her treasures on a special shelf in her bedroom and she dusted every day. If her discovery was especially unique, she wrapped it with something silky out of her sewing basket and placed it inside the little box her father made out of walnut when they lived in London.

Aunt Helen thought Hannah's collections had no place in a civil woman's possession. She was also of the opinion that Hannah was long past marrying age and ought to wed a respectable man, in particular, Mr. William Billings, the wealthy son of the founder of the New York City Tribune. Young Mr. Billings had moved to New Halem Village a year ago and rumor had it that he was looking for a wife.

"It's time for you to settle down and have a family," Aunt Helen said. "I hear Mr. Billings is ready to open his own newspaper. He's shown you more than casual interest. Think it through; he'll build a home for his new wife on Skye Ridge. She'll have a terrace overlooking the great Pacific Ocean and they will host fine parties."

Hannah had an entire classroom of children and she certainly had no desire to be dismissed as their teacher. She loathed the idea of staying home and dressing pretty.

Aunt Helen continued to pester Hannah, but Hannah learned to turn her ear toward the shore, listen for the lapping waves, for the plic-plic-plic of the sanderling.

One day Hannah found someone far more fascinating than Mr. Billings. She found him on the beach on a day of an unusually low tide. He was digging a sizable hole in the sand in a place that was normally under water at the foot of the big mountain called Lahkanea. Even though Hannah had never made his acquaintance, she knew who he was.

Everyone in New Halem Village chattered about Peter Miller, the treasure hunter's son. After his father was buried in a landslide, Peter vowed to find his father's Spanish treasure overflowing with doubloons and silver pieces of eight.

Peter liked Hannah right off. She wasn't afraid of getting her skirts muddy. It wasn't long before she was digging alongside him. She came with her own shovel. They'd work until the sun was ablaze on the horizon and eat the supper she packed atop a rock encrusted with colonies of barnacles, clumps of mussels and Dogwinkle shells. Peter would tell

Hannah tales of the mountain rising above them, the spirits that wove in and out of the cedar branches, the treasures and secrets. When they found the treasure, Peter said it would be theirs. He made Hannah promise not to tell.

Hannah kept their secret and she kept Peter a secret too, or she tried. Secrets were impossible to keep in a place like New Halem Village.

Aunt Helen said Peter was unsuitable as a husband and she insisted that Hannah stop seeing him. She encouraged Mr. Billings to call on Hannah, but Hannah refused to see him.

One overcast day, while Hannah was in school, Peter discovered a large rock buried in the sand. She found him kneeling next to it, his eyes on the mountain. She got down on her knees and he took her hand and with her finger, he traced over a large W etched on the rock. He traced over a cross and the letter E and an arrow.

"This is a map," she said. She was giddy.

"We're close to the treasure," he said in a voice that was proper for church. Then he grinned and he whooped and pulled Hannah off her knees and kissed her. They danced in circles. Her feet didn't touch the ground.

From then on, he and Hannah dug longer and later. They rarely stopped to rest. Or talk. Day after day, they dug, week after week. They uncovered bones and bits of shell. They found rotting rope.

Hannah noted a change. Peter had become like the tides, at times, crashing on the rocks with purpose and others, drawing an uncomfortable distance out to sea. Hannah changed too. When she walked, she kicked at the sand. She thought less of the ocean and more about solid ground.

One day after a particularly rough storm in October, Hannah

found a treasure, no, not a stick, not beach rubble, a real treasure. The sun revealed its hiding place, a silver glint under a slimy ribbon of seaweed. She picked up a coin and held it. Its edges were uneven and imprinted on one side was a great shield like Arthur's and on the other, a thin cross and a fierce lion. She kneeled in the sand and dug with her hands. She found more.

She had to tell Peter, she was quite sure these coins were from their treasure. Could it be buried right under her feet, she wondered, and her heart raced. She lifted her skirts and ran to find him. But she didn't find him that day, or the next.

Aunt Helen said this turn of events was for the best. Men like Peter couldn't be trusted; they tire and wander off. Others believed Peter was buried along-side his father. They were all wrong.

Peter returned after two weeks and he had with him a bride, the granddaughter of a treasure hunter who'd left her more than a dozen rocks engraved with animal heads and peculiar symbols. Rocks, her grandfather was certain, when arranged in the proper sequence, would lead to the lost treasure. But he was one rock short and he spent his last days searching for it. His granddaughter had been looking for over a year. Then she found Peter.

The day Peter returned, Hannah packed up her collections; her feathers, her driftwood, her beach baubles, and she lugged them all, in two battered satchels, to the shore at high tide and she pitched them one by one into the sea. When she finished, she turned her satchels upside-down and the small box her father gave her tumbled out of one.

She opened the box, left the silk inside and picked up one of the coins. She held it between her thumb and finger. She would keep these. She was quite sure they were valuable. No one knew she had them. And she would never tell.

The Asteroid's Daughter and the Serpent Handler's Son

by Kate E Thompson

Rock from Outer Space Strikes Local Woman

by Bob Benson, reporter for the FishWrap Bugle

Local resident, Maggie Billings, was struck last Wednesday night by a rock from outer space when it hurled through the roof of her New Halem two-story home on 21 Skye Ridge, wounding her and prompting an investigation by federal authorities. Billings, who recalls only static on her television and a cloud of dust at impact, suffered injuries to her arm and was in a state of confusion when her neighbor, Ray McFarland, discovered her. She was taken to Bayside General Hospital where she was treated and remains for observation.

The rock left a hole in Billings' roof and caused thousands of dollars of damage. According to McFarland, a concrete like rock the size and shape of a pineapple, was whisked away by federal authorities. There is no comment at this time from either local or federal investigating agencies. Billings is expected to make a complete recovery.

Thirty years ago...

Maggie survived. She didn't actually see an amber globe or winking lights or a crew with green spiky heads, but her forearm was proof of contact, the gash that needed stitches and the gaping hole the aliens left in her roof. Proof enough to make Maggie and the little coastal village of New Halem celebrities. A celebrity, she was thirty years old then. The news traveled over the mountain at light speed and before the medics wheeled Maggie through the emergency room doors, reporters had parked on Highway 101 and made a huge mess of traffic.

People came from all over the country to see firsthand the house the aliens smashed into. Scholars came and vans with initials, psychics showed up and so did priests, the curious came and disbelievers and they all staked camp on Skye Ridge and waited for their own extraterrestrial encounter.

Maggie's encounter was over before her life had time to flash before her eyes, was the story she told Bob, the local FishWrap news reporter, who she promised exclusive rights. Her story began with static on the TV and ended with space dust. There was no middle.

She thought of the light later, after Bob's story went to press, a light that spewed out of the western sky, from Lahkanea Mountain, hissing and humming and blinding white. Yes, a light, and at impact, she recalled no noise, only a quiet like new snow and a force that lifted her out of her seat by the hair.

Maggie's doctors were stymied. Her arm only needed a few stitches at the point of penetration. But an arm hit by a rock, the size of the rock found in her bedroom after the crash, should have been crushed. The doctors called in experts, they hypothesized, and after days of testing, the only interesting thing they found was a new life emerging and this new life was swimming in the dark waters inside of Maggie.

Maggie came home in a cab. Her neighbor, Ray, met her at the curb and he used his body to shield her from the multitude who demanded answers, specifically the day, date and time the next alien craft would fly in. Ray led Maggie by the good arm and guided her up the narrow staircase to the bedroom.

They stopped in the spot Maggie had been sitting when the aliens entered her home. They looked up, Maggie longer than Ray. Hers wasn't the only story of its kind. She'd heard of other alien encounters; stories of lost time, abduction, and invasive procedures. She laid her hand on her stomach and left it there.

She thanked Ray for stapling a tarp over the hole and he offered to repair the roof when she was feeling better.

It had been days since the FBI finished their investigation and left with the rock they dug out of the debris. Ray heard an agent call it an asteroid. A meteorite would be more precise, another interjected, which is a piece off an asteroid. Neither seemed the scientist type. Could have been a chunk of concrete for all Ray knew.

He got a good look at it. Unsure how it could have punched a hole as wide-open as the hole in Maggie's roof. The thing was no bigger than a pineapple. He decided UFO, unidentified flying object, was what the rock ought to be called.

He was interrogated about what he saw that night. In his story, there was no static. There was no dust or light. Just the sound the UFO made on impact, a mess of sound, really, and he thought Maggie's house had been razed.

Ray found a small and curious stone after the FBI men left. Right under their noses and they'd missed it. The green glint under Maggie's side of the bed he wouldn't have spotted if the sun hadn't been shining. He pocketed the stone. He wondered if it had special properties earth rocks didn't have. He'd been carrying it around ever since. He slipped his hand inside his pocket and fingered it.

Maggie was bent over her bed smoothing the quilt. She'd noticed it had been freshly laundered. She thanked Ray. She hugged him and he hugged her back.

Ray's wife was the one who washed the bedding and she hadn't been happy about doing it. She didn't like Ray spending time at Maggie's when he had his own grass to cut and car to wash and walls to paint.

Ray set his wife straight. He didn't want Maggie coming home to a reminder of the otherworldly trauma she'd suffered. He reminded his wife that lending a hand is what good Christians do.

Maggie stepped out of Ray's arms. He wished she hadn't. There was nothing wrong with a hug between friends. He started to say so, but she was looking up at the ceiling again.

Maggie couldn't stop looking up. Chilly air seeped in through the patched roof. She thought of the alien inside of her.

Ray decided to give Maggie the small and curious stone. He hadn't planned to, but it seemed right. He opened her hand and placed it in her palm.

"When the UFO came through your roof, maybe this stone broke off and hit your arm, instead of the UFO itself," Ray said.

Ray hadn't thought of this until now. It made more sense, in relation to the size of Maggie's wound.

She examined the stone for a very long time. The threads of green mixed through ordinary grey. Maggie thought it was the loveliest rock she'd ever seen.

She closed her hand over it. "I want to be alone."

She watched through the window until Ray disappeared into the rolling crowd. She undressed, crawled into bed, and rolled her alien rock back and forth across her pale belly.

FishWrap Welcomes Managing Editor
by William Cooke, Publisher for the FishWrap Bugle

The staff at the FishWrap Bugle is pleased to welcome our new Managing Editor, award winning investigative journalist, Matthew Charles. As Managing Editor, he will be in charge of the day to day news operation of the paper.

Matthew comes to New Halem with 10 years of journalism experience, having begun his career, just out of college, with the Kentucky Gaston Mail. He has worked in various positions, including reporter and photographer and most recently served as City Editor. Matthew holds a BS in Journalism from the University of Kentucky.

When asked why he would move all the way across the country to take a job in our little village, Matthew claimed the job is not only a good fit with his career goals, but having lived in the state of Kentucky his whole life, the move is also an exciting personal growth opportunity.

Chapter 1

He wasn't an Oregonian; she knew that much from his plates. He parked at the opposite end of the wayside. The wind grabbed the door out of his hand and he scrambled for it. He had a camera slung over his shoulder, but he wasn't taking pictures. And the blowy day was perfect for pictures. Those heaving waves. The froth the breakers stirred up.

Not many stopped at Lahkanea Mountain Wayside. The shadow of the ancient mountain looming over it, the ocean vista didn't look like much from the highway. Maggie understood its scope. Sixty years of going there. To get the full impact you had to get out of your car and stand the way he had and look down. He'd been there for a while, his legs pressed against the two-foot tall stone ledge.

Maggie pulled a bright orange scarf out of her jacket pocket and tied it over her hair. She was glad for the distraction. She'd been sitting on the ledge for an hour. She'd gone there to think and to plan, but her thinking went sour before she got to the plan.

That money grubbing financier who was backing Acorn Development's interpretive center project, wouldn't get out of her thoughts. Sheltered in corporate-hood, he didn't have the guts to come out and talk to her face to face. His corporation had a name, it was Oak Enterprises. But he did not. Not one the private investigator could dig up anyway. And the only thing he found on the land developer from Acorn, that weenie Ronald Kingston, was his church going record. He was a Christian. Maggie was disgusted. Kingston was nothing but a crook. Trying to take what was hers. The whole situation made her heart pound red, red, red. She had to stop them from taking her house, but things didn't look so good.

Maggie decided to investigate the out-of-towner who was so enthralled with the view. See who he was and where exactly he came from. She walked slowly his way; she didn't want to scare him. The 1000-foot drop to the sea. The wind tugged at her feet and skirt. She stopped next to his Jetta. Bedding blocked the rear window. Suitcases and boxes stacked in the seat, a meowing cat in a cage, license plate: Kentucky. He was a long way from home. She couldn't imagine leaving hers. Not even for a day. She looked up.

He was watching her. "I haven't taken one picture." He tugged on his camera strap. "I've never seen anything like this. It puts you in your place, doesn't it?"

She liked the sound of his voice. There was a little something in it. Kentucky, she supposed.

"This place does have a way of challenging one's perspective," she said. "I hope once you settle in, you won't take it for granted the way most do. I'm Maggie. Welcome to New Halem."

"Matthew Charles. So Maggie, what makes you think I'm not a tourist passing through?"

She thought he looked like the kind of guy who'd own a dog, not a cat. He wasn't wearing a wedding ring.

"Who would take a cat on vacation?" she asked. "You must have come this far to set your roots down. Perhaps start a new job."

Matthew was close to her daughter's age, Maggie was pretty sure. She'd have to think up a way to introduce them.

He folded his arms and studied her face. "You're very astute. What else did you surmise from snooping around my car?"

Maggie chuckled, sat on the ledge and patted the spot next to her. "I've never talked to anyone from Kentucky."

He glanced in the direction of his car. "I can't stay. I have an appointment."

"There's no need to rush. Oh, you'll learn. People who move out here from the city find our small-town pace a challenge. Try to relax for a moment. Breathe."

A car pulled off the highway and paused on the edge of the wayside. Maggie breathed in and Matthew glanced over his shoulder at the car idling. He understood small towns. He hoped he hadn't made a mistake moving back to one.

He'd written the directions to his new place on a scrap of paper. He tried to think where he put it. Then he heard his name and saw Maggie pointing out to sea.

"You saw them, didn't you?" Her curls were bouncing, the scarf coming undone. "A sighting is rare, and you on your first visit, how fortunate."

He looked where she was pointing. He squinted. He saw waves.

"They're world travelers," she said. "Short-tailed Shearwaters fly over 20,000 miles a year."

"Oh birds. You're a birder then?"

"No not really. Many Shearwaters become partners for life. I think that's lovely, don't you?" She smiled and re-tied her scarf. "Are you married or maybe you have a girlfriend who will be joining you?"

The last thing he wanted to talk about. He shook his head. "Nope, it's me and the cat and no one else."

Suzanne left. He had the whole trip out here to think on it. She left. He was the reason. He was the reason she left.

He looked over at his car. It was filthy. He was dead-tired. He should get going. But he couldn't hear the cat yowling from where he was and that was a relief.

"I think you'll enjoy living here," Maggie said. "You'll have to come to Lahkanea often. Sit on the ledge and be quiet."

He looked over at Maggie. "Is that what you do?"

"I come here to think. Lahkanea gives perspective. Isn't that what you said?"

Was it? He zipped his coat all the way. He wondered if the cat would yowl as long as it was his.

"People see things up here," Maggie said. "My mother did. She saw a ribbon of fire soar across this sky."

"Is that so?"

"I saw a light once. The brightest I'd ever seen."

"What was it?"

She shrugged. "People witness things up here that are of an extraterrestrial nature. They always have. Right here in this sky." She looked up and Matthew did too and he was surprised to see bright blue patches amongst the clouds.

"Who knows," she said. "Maybe you'll have an experience here that will change your world."

"I have enough change in my world. It was nice meeting you, Maggie. I have to check in at work before I go home."

He wondered why he called the bungalow home. He rented it sight unseen. He'd never been in town.

"Didn't your new boss tell you that your office is closed on Sundays?"

"I don't remember him doing it. You seem to have the scoop on me, ma'am. Are you a reporter?"

"No. You're the reporter and a damn good one I hear." She grinned. He didn't.

"Oh, I'm making you nervous," Maggie said. "Will Cooke, the publisher of the FishWrap Bugle is a close friend and you are all he has been talking about. The paper's been without an editor for a while. I think he's fortunate to have an award winning investigative journalist coming on board."

"I hope Mr. Cooke isn't disappointed. All I am is a reporter. The award was minor, really." He shoved his hands into his coat pockets.

"I appreciate modesty, so few possess it these days."

Maggie waited. She could tell he'd slipped deep into thought. She waited one long minute.

"I imagine a successful investigative journalist like you had a good job back home. Better pay, surely. It must be difficult. Leaving your roots, I can't imagine it."

"I'm surprised. You've already imagined so much about me."

Maggie studied his face. "I imagine you left family and friends behind. And I imagine you wonder if you've done the right thing, moving so far away."

He watched a gull flying crooked in the wind. "I prefer to look forward, not back."

She nodded and they watched the gull dip and go out of sight. "Sit for a while. I have a bit of advice."

"You have advice for a stranger?"

The wind howled. The force of it surprised him and he sat down rather quickly on the ledge next to her.

"Oh, these wild October winds. One minute a little breeze and the next, a sudden burst that knocks you off your feet. We lose a tourist about once a year." She peered over the side.

He did too. "Your advice is to hang on?"

Maggie chuckled. "You've already figured that out. My advice is this. The very first thing you do, as soon as you pull into town, is introduce yourself to the county sheriff."

"And why should I meet the sheriff the very first thing?"

"Because that's what a new managing editor ought to do. Just a little insider advice, take it or leave it. Her name is Sheriff Billings."

"Thanks. Do you know Sheriff Billings?"

"Everyone in New Halem knows everyone else. I've lived here all my life. My great-grandfather William and his wife, Hannah, founded the New Halem Telegraph, the first newspaper of its size on the Oregon coast. Yes, the name changed and not for the better, if you ask me. His picture is hanging on the wall at the FishWrap, alongside Hannah's. Great-grandmother Hannah was a woman ahead of her time and was as much about leading and growing the business as he was. She and William built their home up on Skye Ridge 127 years ago. I live there now. My daughter was born there. It's where my roots are. I can't imagine leaving it." Maggie sighed. "But I may be forced out. The county says my home is theirs now."

"I'm sorry to hear. Why is that?"

"Corporate bullies, politics and greed." She stood and then he did. She held out her hand and he shook it.

"I have to open the museum in a half hour," she said. "Stop by sometime and I'll give you a tour. It was very nice meeting you. Oh, and be sure and –"

"Meet the sheriff."

Maggie laughed and walked to her car. She'd found herself an award winning investigative journalist. She liked Matthew Charles. She liked his attitude. Maybe he could help her.

Keep your chin up. Think good thoughts. Her friends Mary and Roma always said. Maybe she wouldn't lose her house after-all. The protest was less than a month away. She'd get started on the flyers.

Chapter 2

The woman on the other side of the window looked in. A red-head. She'd rapped on his window and startled him and he wondered who would come up to a parked car, especially a stranger's, and rap on their window.

She pulled her sunglasses down her nose and peered over the top. Her eyes weren't very friendly. She motioned for him to open his window.

Was she a cop? He didn't see a car or flashing lights. While he powered the window down, he looked her over. She was dressed casual, jeans and sneakers, a tight sweater. He breathed easier.

"Are you lost?" She looked him over, him and everything else inside his car.

"No, I have directions, thanks." He held up what was in his hands and it was a roadmap of the USA.

"New Halem is the end of the line." She nodded toward the map.

He looked at it. The thick red line he drew before he left home.

"Keep going and you'll end up in the Pacific." She pushed a strand of hair out of her face and the wind picked it up.

He began folding the map. "Thanks for the warning." He glanced sideways and saw a little smirk on her face, a dimple right below her lip. He went back to folding the map. "I do have directions that are on a smaller scale."

He'd misplaced them and when he pulled into town and tried to remember where Treasure Cove was, he ended up at the pub he was parked in front of. Grant's Pub and he ate lunch there. After, he felt sluggish and decided a walk on the beach would wake him up. He followed the signs through the park. Thundering waves were barreling in and breaking over the boardwalk, ocean spray on his face. He skipped the walk. When he returned to the car, he found the directions, on the dashboard underneath the map he was folding badly. He shoved it between the seats. "I should get going."

She propped the sunglasses on top of her head and he wondered why he thought she didn't look friendly before.

"I hope you didn't order the Herculean Burger at Grant's," she said.

He wished he hadn't eaten the whole thing. The burger felt like a rock in his gut.

"What makes you think I ate at Grant's?"

She looked over at the pub and back. She was grinning. "You did order the burger, didn't you? A mistake all newbies make."

Her eyes were real pretty. Matthew thought he saw threads of green mixed with ordinary grey, but he was staring and staring was impolite.

"You may want to run next door to Nelson's," she said. "You can pick up antacid if you didn't bring any with you. Next time stick with the micro-beers. Handcrafted and imbued with the ancient secrets of Lahkanea Mountain. So Grant's story goes." She waved it off. "Grant is known around the state for his beer."

"That would explain why the bartender snorted when I ordered a Bud Light."

"You ordered Budweiser from New Halem's primo beer maker?" She laughed and held out her hand. "You have much to learn. I'm Astra. If you're headed to your new place, I can point you in the right direction."

She had a stronger handshake than he would have expected.

"Thanks, but I won't bother you. I'll find my way." He picked up the directions.

"You're younger than I imagined."

"Beg your pardon?"

"I figured an award winning journalist would be older. You are the new managing editor of the FishWrap Bugle, aren't you?"

"I am. My name is Matthew, if you don't already know."

"I didn't know."

"You didn't?"

"I do now." She shrugged. "I hope you don't find our little village boring. We don't have many breaking news stories."

"I hear you have a panty bandit on the loose."

"Impressive, you've done some homework. If you call that breaking news, the culprit has only hit twice. The town's making it into a big deal. If you ask me, it's just a stupid prank."

"I see. If you were one of the victims, would you feel differently?"

She laughed. "Believe me, I won't be."

"I hope you're right about that. Tell me, is the house up on the ridge built by the newspaper's founder and the family about to lose it breaking news?"

She folded her arms and frowned. "Who did you hear that from?"

"Can't say, a journalist doesn't give out their sources."

"Well, Mr. Big-Time Reporter, I have a word of advice."

"I'm not surprised."

She raised an eyebrow and he asked her to go on.

"Don't waste your time on the story. That house is a dilapidated mess and slated to be demolished early next year and a 6,000 square-foot interpretive center built in its place. The homeowner has been fighting it, but the county has the right of eminent domain. The owner will receive a fair and equitable price for the property. More than fair, if you ask me. It's a done deal."

"Let me get this straight. The home owner is fighting the county, yet, it's a done deal and there's not a story here?"

She breathed out her nose. "This battle has been going on way too long and everyone is very tired of hearing about it."

"I see." He wondered why she cared one way or the other about someone else's house. He would check out the story. He smiled. She didn't.

"I stopped at the wayside on my way into town," he said. "You ever go up there?"

"No point, you can see plenty of ocean right here." She pointed toward the park called Nelson's and said the ocean was through the trees and across the street.

He noticed the tips of the trees bending. He heard the ocean roar.

"I saw your beach. I walked over there after lunch," Matthew said. "Y'all have some big waves out here in Oregon."

Astra tilted her head, a slight smile. "I guess we-all do have some big waves."

"Yeah," he said. She had an off-putting manner. Back home they'd call it rude. "To tell you the truth, I'd never been to an ocean until today."

She eyed him like he was a visitor from another galaxy. Then she shrugged it off. "I've lived by this ocean all my life."

"Oh? Tell me then; have you ever seen things up at Lahkanea Wayside?"

"Seen things?"

He nodded.

"What kind of things?"

"Things like winking lights, a silver disc maybe, fire in the sky, you know – encounters of an extraterrestrial nature?"

Astra burst out laughing and doubled over. When she straightened up, she pushed the sunglasses back to where they'd been on top of her head. "You mean have I seen any Martians zipping through the night sky?"

"No. I was serious."

"You were serious." She scowled and clamped her hands over his door. "I'm surprised a reporter would believe in extraterrestrial crap. For the record, I haven't seen anything up at Lahkanea and I'll tell you why. There's nothing up there to see. I truly hope sensationalist reporting isn't the kind of journalism you are famous for."

"I don't recall saying I believed in extraterrestrial crap," he said. "And for the record, I'm not famous."

If only he'd written news stories about Martians and abduction and intergalactic war. Then he wouldn't be moving to a place as far away from home as this one.

"You're not famous? I heard otherwise."

"Then you're getting your information from an unreliable source."

Bartholomew yowled and Astra looked over at the cage. "Your cat doesn't sound very happy."

"You heard that right."

He thought of Suzanne. The cat, the note she left with it. It had never been his cat. Three days driving with the beast.

"Poor little guy," Astra said. "Does kitty have a name?"

"Yep."

Matthew planned on renaming it, but he hadn't thought of a good name yet.

"Well, Astra, it was a pleasure meeting you. Me and this cat have a house to move into." Matthew started powering up his window and stopped. Her hands were still over it and she wasn't removing them.

"We're neighbors," she said. "Wait here and I'll get my car and you can follow me to Treasure Cove."

He hadn't told her where he lived. He said no thank you, he could find the place on his own, but she was already cutting through an alley and was out of hearing range.

"This place is going to take some getting used to," he said and the cat yowled. Matthew opened the last can of tuna and stuck it inside the cage and Bartholomew shoved his face in it.

Matthew tried again to think of a new name. Something masculine, but nothing would come to him.

"Well, cat, no name is better than the one Suzanne gave you."

The cat licked his lips. He looked up at Matthew and meowed. Not a yowl this time, the first meow, and Matthew thought, maybe he and this no name cat could be friends. Matthew reached inside the cage to pet him and No-Name's hair stood on end and he hissed.

Matthew heard a horn and saw an SUV coming around the corner. It pulled up alongside his car and stopped. On the side of the vehicle, he saw the words, Cedar County Sheriff, and in the driver's seat, he saw Astra. Astra. Sheriff Billings.

Chapter 3

I marched into the kitchen with the sign I found on the dining room table. The white poster board Mother had duct-taped to a paint stick, the words on it, 'Say No to Big Money, the Lahkanea Interpretive Center is Baloney'.

"What is this about?" I asked.

"I'm a little behind on dinner, but then, Astra, you're late anyway." She was wearing the yellow and orange sunflower print apron Mary gave her years ago. "Where are Hey Girl and Good Boy?"

"Mrs. Phillips is watching them. I had paperwork this afternoon. Then something came up and she offered to keep them longer. She has the grandkids today. It isn't often the dogs have little kid playmates."

"I'll put their bones in doggy bags to take home." She chuckled and turned to the salad and squirted flax oil all over it. "Did the panty bandit strike again? Is that what came up?"

"No. I was helping someone out."

"Who?"

"No one you know." I waved the protest sign. "Now how about you explain this?"

"Mary made it. I think her block letters are lovely. She and Roma came over this afternoon. I closed the museum early; it was dead in town, the blustery weather. We were going to make flyers, but we got started on signs and well, we had great fun making these. Lost track of time, I guess."

She took the sign out of my hand and told me to bring out the plates she bought from Emma at Lahkanea Studio last weekend.

"Can we stop for a minute and talk?" I asked.

"Go ahead and talk, I'm listening." She left the kitchen and I picked up the bright orange and blue plates and followed her into the dining room.

She was pushing markers and scissors and scraps to one end of the table.

"Tell me you're not planning on protesting at the county hearing," I said.

She pulled out a chair. "We'll put the signs here. I do like Mary's, don't you?" She read the words on it before she stacked it with the others and smiled. "Very clever."

"Money and baloney don't rhyme. You should be packing, not making signs."

Mother pushed an empty wine bottle and three glasses to the side. "This should be enough room for the two of us."

I sighed and set the plates down, one across from the other. "I thought you'd given up. There's nothing more you can do. This old house is coming down and the interpretive center is going to be built here, right here."

"I never gave up. I was just feeling a little discouraged before, but when I was at Lahkanea today, I saw my situation from a whole new perspective. And it changed everything. I'm going to fight for what is mine."

"Your perspective changed? No. Nothing has changed. You can protest all you want, but in the end you'll have to move out and if you refuse, I'm the one who has to evict you. Please don't do this to me."

"I know. We've talked about it before. You're the sheriff, I understand, and evicting people from their homes is what you do. Put out the mugs that match the dishes, will you? I smell the salmon. It must be about done."

"I've never evicted anyone."

She took the salmon out of the oven. Slipped it onto a plate and decorated with parsley. "I used fresh squeezed orange juice to baste it this time. Listen, I know you're upset and I'm sorry, but my fight with these rich corporate bastards has nothing to do with you." She took off the apron. "Bring in the salad and don't forget the mugs."

Mother poured water into the mugs. We sat at the table and began eating. The salmon was perfectly cooked and I said so.

Mother thanked me.

I asked about her job.

She said nothing had changed at the museum.

We ate a bite of salad and then we ate a bite of fish.

"I wasn't thinking about myself," I said. "I was thinking of you."

She looked at me and chewed.

"You're sixty. You shouldn't have to fight. Or worry. Even if you were able to keep the house, you'd be looking at a fortune in repairs you can't afford."

"Will came over and fixed the leak under the sink. Did you notice it wasn't dripping?"

"That was nice of him, but it was a minor repair. The thirty year leak, however, is another story."

"Will's talked about putting on a new roof."

"Even if Mr. Cooke knew how and did it himself, it would still cost more than you have. The settlement the county has offered would buy you a nice little cottage on the beach you could retire in. Think about it."

"I shouldn't be thinking about retirement. That's years away. But you should be thinking about your great-great-grandmother, Hannah."

"Why would I? Great-great grandmother Hannah doesn't have anything to do with this conversation."

"Yes she does. This is her home. She collected every stone in the fireplace. Remember her stories? She put up walls and dug postholes. She was a strong woman."

"And she could wield a shovel as well as any man. I know. I know. But we're talking about you and how it would make sense to stop fighting a losing battle."

"Hannah's home is about the kind of woman she was. Her memory will live on here. Right here." Mother's fists came down on the table and the forks rattled.

"Hannah has been dead for years," I said. "She doesn't need a house and she doesn't care what you do with this one. You could travel."

Mother poured more water into her mug. "Why would I want to travel? My roots are here. Right here." She tapped the table with two fingers. "I would be misplaced without my home."

"You've stayed within a thirty mile radius of this place your entire life. There's a big world out there you've never seen. That's why you want to travel."

She touched the diamond shaped scar on her forearm and regarded it for a moment. The bright white pucker was all that was left from the day the asteroid crashed through the roof, that and the asteroid itself. And me.

She looked up. "You go in the living room and I'll bring out dessert and coffee."

I watched her walk away. The scar and the leaking roof are her roots. Her roots are water stained walls and splintery floors and a rickety gate and that stupid asteroid she props against it.

Matthew was surprised I turned out to be the sheriff. Surprised the woman he met at Lahkanea turned out to be my mother.

He asked if I wanted to get dinner, his treat for helping him unload his car. I said no. Then a mouse scurried across the kitchen floor and Matthew opened the cat cage and his no-name cat wouldn't come out.

"Didn't I say dessert in the living room?" Mother was carrying a tray.

"Uh. Yeah. You did, I guess."

She poured coffee. Dessert was a chocolate pie.

"I wish you'd stop telling men you have a single daughter."

"Oh, he moved quickly." She raised her eyebrows and grinned.

"Not because of you. We bumped into each other. He was lost."

"How serendipitous," Mother said and I waved her off.

I knew who Matthew was before I knocked on his window. He was kind of cute in a bumbling sort of way.

"I wasn't trying to hook you up, if that's what you think," Mother said. "I only told him to meet the sheriff. You're someone he should know. Professionally speaking, that's all."

"Oh come on, getting me married off has been your goal for years. And you had to go and tell him all of your woo-woo lights in the sky, ETs and alien baby stories."

She shook her head. "I didn't share anything personal. I simply told him the truth about sightings at Lahkanea. He seemed interested.

Tell me what you think of him. I thought he was a nice young man, career oriented and a deep thinker."

I picked up my mug. It was too hot to drink. "A deep thinker, huh? He's just another guy."

"Oh come on, in contrast to your Jim Conroy, Matthew Charles is polite and educated. He may not be all muscles like Jim, but he's nice enough to look at, don't you think? Jim won't always have those muscles, you know. One of these days, they'll turn to flab and when they do –"

"Deputy Conroy isn't mine and I don't give a damn about his muscles. Okay?" I ate a piece of the pie.

"You must like Matthew. He's very likable. A little troubled, perhaps." Mother paused and stared out the window for a moment. "I think he needs a friend. And a woman in his life, he isn't married. I checked. Did he ask you out?"

"You're asking questions that are none of your business," I said.

"I hope you say yes next time. I think you and he would make a cute couple. Just don't sleep with him on the first date."

"I wish you'd stop. Aside from that, I'd like to know why you told Mr. Charles about this house and the pending demolition. Now he thinks there's a story where there's not."

"He thinks there's a story?" Mother's eyes sparkled.

"No. No, I told him there wasn't. Does he have anything to do with the whole new perspective you were telling me about?"

"He's a famous investigative journalist. He must be good at what he does or Will wouldn't have hired him. I was thinking."

"No. No way. Acorn Development is legit and within their legal rights. Your private investigator told you."

"The private investigator was a friend of Roma's and he did it as a favor. He didn't seem very good at it. Maybe Matthew could find what Roma's friend missed. Our Mr. Charles may be able to save

Great-grandmother Hannah's home. Wouldn't that be wonderful?"

"No. You stay away from him."

She folded her arms and looked at me. She asked how I liked the pie.

Chapter 4

Matthew finished interviewing Mrs. Bellamont and she was still going on about the panty bandit. He held the Sea Sprite's door open for her.

"We have to get that pervert off the streets before he hurts someone," she said. She stopped on the sidewalk and looked up at the sky, the clouds heavy with rain centering over town.

The bandit hit five times since Sheriff Billings characterized the crime as a simple prank a week ago. Mrs. Bellamont was his sixth and seventh victim. She zipped her bright yellow slicker. "Have I mentioned that my husband is a truck driver?"

Matthew said he didn't think so. He felt a drop of rain on his hand.

"Phil is his name. He's been working long hours to get us through my minor creative slump. I'm a novelist, if you don't already know. I write mysteries. Phil is rarely home. That leaves just me and my nieces, three women alone. No wonder that nasty man hit our home twice. You must understand why I worry."

"I do, ma'am, I do understand."

He thought of his Aunt Vicky. How protective she'd been. He wondered why Mrs. Bellamont's nieces lived with her and not their parents.

"I'm so happy you're taking the panty bandit case seriously," Mrs. Bellamont said. "The Sheriff's Department hasn't done squat." She reached in her pocket and pulled out a floppy brimmed hat.

"If that's the case, I'd better give my department a serious talking to." Sheriff Billings came up from behind and stepped in beside Matthew.

"Hello Sheriff Astra," Mrs. Bellamont said. "Mr. Charles and I have been discussing the panty bandit case."

"Sounds like I walked in at the good part," Sheriff Billings said and she looked at Matthew.

"Morning Sheriff," he said and smiled.

"No offense, Sheriff Astra," Mrs. Bellamont said. "But you and your department need to get off your duffs and catch that fiend before he hits my place a third time."

Matthew thought he would have a chat with the sheriff about the case. He liked talking to her. He wasn't sure why, she was forward and abrupt at times and didn't always seem to care what he thought.

"I'll take the case into my own hands if I have to," Mrs. Bellamont said. "And I'll do whatever it takes to protect my girls."

Matthew wondered if she owned a shotgun. Most folks back home did. He wasn't one of them.

"How about locking up your house?" he asked. "All seven times, the bandit went in through an unlocked door."

"No one locks around here," Mrs. Bellamont said. "We shouldn't have to. New Halem has always been a safe place to live and it's your job, Sheriff, to keep it that way and if you don't –"

"Don't do anything foolish," Sheriff Billings said. "The best way to keep your nieces safe is by being proactive. Have you thought about a security system?"

"I have a better idea. Put Mr. Charles on the case. He's an award winning investigative journalist, have you heard? It was in the newspaper. He'd find our man in no time."

"I don't get involved in police business," Matthew said. "I report the news, that's all I do."

"That's all, huh?" Sheriff Billings asked.

The tone she used. It made him uneasy.

"Yep, I'm a reporter, a mild-mannered one, as a matter of fact," he said and she looked at him. He couldn't read her face.

"Oh, dear." Mrs. Bellamont was checking her watch. "I have to get to the high school and deliver these to the twins before lunchtime." She held up a bag with two bagel sandwiches inside and hurried around the beat-up van she'd parked in front of the café. She gunned it and pulled into the road and then stomped the brakes and waited for a straggly feathered gull that was chasing after a sticky wrapper.

"If you hadn't showed up when you did, Mrs. Bellamont would still be talking. I owe you one," Matthew said.

"It was nothing."

He liked how her face softened. How her nose turned up a bit. He didn't know why he felt uneasy before.

"You got any worries that Mrs. Bellamont might take on the case herself?" he asked.

Astra glared at the squawking gull perched on the Sea Sprite sign. "No, no worries."

"After seven break-ins, do you still believe the perpetrator is pulling a stupid prank?"

She shrugged. "You've interviewed all the victims?"

Matthew said he had.

"In that case, care to guess who victim number eight will be?"

"You're asking my opinion?"

She nodded.

"Sure, I'll give it a stab." He put his finger up to his temple and left it there. "Let's see. I believe victim number eight will be a woman –"

"Pfft –" She waved him off.

"Wait, there's more. Victim number eight doesn't believe in locking her doors. Find her and you'll find yourself a panty bandit."

She laughed. Then he did.

"The whole attitude that our great-great-grandparents never

locked so why should we is a problem we continually deal with in our little village," she said.

"Seems to me New Halem hasn't ever been the peace-loving town folks around here say it is. Y'all have had stabbings, vandalism and plenty of drunk driving, brawls and family disputes, and a few dead bodies washed up on the beaches."

"You've dug up the dirt on us. Seems you are equipped with the super investigative skills people say you have."

Another raindrop hit the back of Matthew's hand. He was tired of this rain. The plink-plink-plink and those noisy seagulls, the rolling waves, foghorns and fishing boats, and he could hear it all with the windows shut. And he'd only lived in New Halem for one week. One long week.

"There seems to be some confusion," he said.

"Confusion?"

Maggie invited him out to lunch yesterday at Angelo's. She had the idea in her head that he was a world acclaimed investigative journalist. She wanted a favor and she leaned over the all-meat, double-cheesy, extra-greasy pizza she ordered and told Matthew he must never speak of their meeting and especially don't tell Astra.

"You said confusion?" Astra asked.

"Yes. Folks are mistaken. I'm not a professional investigator."

Maggie asked him to save her home, She told him about Acorn Development, about pyramid structure and privacy protection. She wanted Matthew to poke around. An investigation would lead to a front page story, she promised him that.

He turned her down. He'd already poked around. The county was within its rights, like Astra said, and he told Maggie. But she wouldn't stop talking about corporate greed and disclosure laws and Delaware and the benefits of incorporating there. About a holding company called Oak Enterprises. "Oak," Maggie said and laughed but did not smile.

"Matthew?" Astra asked and he looked at her. "Didn't I read that you are an award winning investigative journalist?"

"Y'all are reading way too much into that newspaper article. The award wasn't anything and for the record, I don't solve crimes for the police or anyone else."

"I think you're the one who's confused." She tapped him on the arm. His coat sleeve dotted with rain. "Let's move under the awning."

They took cover in front of the liquor store. The sign 'Shop Early' in the window and gift boxes of Kentucky bourbon tied with red and gold ribbon.

"What are you getting at?" he asked.

"Contrary to what you say, you do get involved in police business. I don't know why you'd keep it a big secret and correct me if I'm wrong, back in Kentucky, you were involved in a major police bust."

"You did a background check on me?"

"No, I had no reason to do that. All I did was Google you. The newspaper you came from has an online archive and the award winning story you wrote is there in public space for anyone to see."

He stepped away and folded his arms. "What are you doing snooping around in my business?"

She shrugged like it was no big deal. "I was curious." Then she folded her arms. "And you are a stranger here. And I'm the sheriff, that's why." She glared at him and he glared back.

Her arms fell to her sides and she smiled. "Your investigation played a key role in busting up a ring of animal smugglers. The head honcho, a snake handling pastor, and by the way, I don't know anything about religion, but I would have never equated a pastor with snakes. Crazy, the things you find on the internet, but according to the story which evidently, comes from a reputable source, the pastor was arrested along with a half dozen of his congregants thanks to you. You deserved the award the FishWrap said you got. You were a hero."

"Some folks didn't think so." He left her standing in front of the liquor store.

No-Name yowled when Matthew unlocked the door. The yowl Matthew hated to come home to. All afternoon he'd been thinking about the sheriff and how easy she dug up his story. He hoped she was satisfied with what she found and wasn't as nosy as her mother.

"Boy was I wrong believing a few thousand miles was all I needed between me and the past," Matthew said to No-Name and he bent down to pet him and No-Name scurried behind the hide-a-bed Matthew had taken apart to fix.

The message light was blinking again, no big surprise. He wondered who gave Suzanne his number or if she simply looked it up online.

Matthew reached for a can of tuna. The sound of the can opener and No-Name purred and slinked around and in-between Matthew's legs.

"Half of this tuna fish is mine," Matthew said. "I'll get groceries in the morning before work. Yep, tuna is on the list."

He found a partial bag of chips in the cupboard, picked a fork out of the sink and sat up to the table, the table stained and the name Mel carved into it. Matthew ate a bite. No-Name hopped up on the chair next to his. He ate a bite.

"You would've liked Aunt Vicky's fried catfish. I sure do miss it sometimes."

Matthew finished off the chips and let No-Name have the last of the tuna.

After dinner, they listened to the messages. Matthew deleted them all. Then he went to work on the hide-a-bed. He promised No-Name he could sleep at the foot.

Chapter 5

I bolted out of bed leaving Good Boy and Hey Girl waking up at the foot and taking their sweet time. I'd heard someone banging around in the basement and I knew it was him. The panty bandit and there was no time to call in backup. I wanted that cocky bastard. Did he really think he'd get away with robbing the sheriff?

I stopped at the top of the basement stairs. I'd catch him off guard and handcuff him to the railing before he thought to pull his grimy hands out of my laundry. Then I realized I didn't have the handcuffs. I didn't have my gun. I hadn't worn a robe and I didn't look authoritative at all wearing the baby blue cami and matching bikini panties.

I heard a rustle in the basement. I remembered the emergency flashlight on the kitchen counter and I grabbed it. Authoritative or not, I was going after him. I held the flashlight steady. I'd smack him a good one. Knock him out and tie him up with my dirty sheets. I pounded down the stairs. "You stop right where you are, you son of a bitch."

My dirty laundry, the basket tipped up-side-down, back door wide open. The screen swung on its hinges. He got away.

From the porch, I looked out over the yard. I didn't see the jerk or any sign he'd been here. What would Doreen say now? The pine trees that line the back of my property groaned. My bare feet were freezing. I scurried inside and pulled the door shut. I'd call the station after I put on some clothes.

I started up the stairs. Heard a creak and I whirled around. I didn't see a thing. Because there was nothing to see, the panty bandit was gone, long gone and I knew it. No need to hurry. But I did hurry. I stubbed my toe on the last stair and yelped.

The dogs heard and started barking. I hadn't meant to shut them in the bedroom. I sprinted inside, slammed the door and leaned my back against it. The dogs licked my hands and whined and I called Deputy

Conroy at home.

I had one leg inside my jeans when Good Boy and Hey Girl started nosing my bedroom door and grumbling.

"Is there someone out there?" I asked and the dogs looked at me and drooled.

I envisioned the intruder crouched on the other side of the door. I reached for my revolver. I was the panty bandit's eighth victim. A victim, I was a victim. I shook like a stupid girl, cracked open my door and peered into the hallway.

There were no squinty eyes in the shadows, no silhouette of a man. I saw Good Boy's chewy bone out there on the floor. Good Boy spotted it too and pushed me out of his way and Hey Girl followed and they vied for it.

I laid the gun on the dresser and shoved my other leg inside the jeans. I needed to get a grip.

I zipped and sat on the edge of the bed and put on my socks. I heard a tap-tap-tap on the roof. I laid on my back and listened. The rain was steady. Steady.

Instead of Conroy, I should have called the station. The call he'd take as an invite for a sleepover. What was I thinking?

I wasn't thinking. That was the problem. But no sleepovers, never again, I told him six months ago.

Hey Girl barked and the dogs galloped down the hall. I followed them. Deputy Conroy, I figured, but I took my gun with me.

Good Boy and Hey Girl were barking at the door and Conroy's lights were flashing red and blue through the living room curtains.

My front door banged open and there was Deputy Conroy wielding his gun. The dogs stumbled over each other.

"Are you all right?" he asked and hurried over.

"I'm fine." I laid my gun on the coffee table.

He laid his hands on my shoulders and squeezed. "You must be pretty shook up. The panty bandit has never broken into a house that was occupied, until now."

Those strong hands and he was wearing a flannel shirt, a white tee and he smelled warm and sleepy.

"I'm not shook up. The perpetrator went out –"

Conroy wasn't listening. I'd forgotten to put a shirt over the cami and he was gazing down there and getting an eye-full. I stepped back the same time he tried pulling me into a full on hug.

My dogs foiled his effort. They pushed their way between me and him. They looked up at Conroy and barked.

"You'd think those mutts would know me by now. Can't you get them to shut up?"

"I beg your pardon, they aren't mutts. They have names and Deputy, rest assured, they do know you."

I hugged their necks and asked them to stop barking and they did, but they held their ground and I praised them for it.

"You may as well go home," I said. "I'll get on the police report. Thanks for coming so quickly."

"This case warrants our highest priority. These aren't pranks. I never believed they were, especially not when the bandit stole Mrs. Jenkins' size 22's right out of her washer, all soapy wet and smelling of borax. This panty bandit could be dangerous. You stay put while I secure the premises. Did he come in through the basement?"

"I don't know. He went out that way and now he's gone."

Conroy was skulking toward the basement like a cartoon cop. He was making this into a big drama. But a second look-over wouldn't hurt, I figured, so I let him do it.

I pulled back the living room curtain. The stupid bandit got away. I wondered who he would hit next.

Conroy's lights flashed in my neighbor's windows and spread out down the gravel road. My Explorer was parked under the street light, my title, Cedar County Sheriff, on the side in neon glow-in-the-dark letters. The bandit knew whose house he had chosen.

Good Boy and Hey Girl nudged me and licked my hands.

"The bad guy's all gone." I squatted between them and they licked my face. "I'm all right, don't worry. Like I told Mrs. Bellamont, I'm on top of this case."

Hey Girl woofed and knocked me over.

"Okay. Okay. I'm lying. I'm not on top of anything. I'd better get off my duff and get on with business, huh?" I kissed them on the ears and got back on my feet. "I'm going down to the basement to see what's keeping that dumbass Conroy."

They followed me to the top of the stairs and I told them to wait and keep an eye on things. I found Conroy holding my new, bright blue, push-up bra by the strap.

"I told you to stay upstairs," he said.

"Is this what you call securing the premises?" I yanked my bra out of his hand.

"That pervert has ramped up his game; it's time to get serious."

"You're pawing through my underwear telling me to be serious? Deputy, you get off your duff and go outside and see if he left any evidence. And when you finish, go into the station and file a report and while you're there, go through the other reports and find something that will get this guy off the street."

"Will do, Astra."

I flipped my laundry basket right side up and chucked in the bra. "That's Sheriff Billings to you."

"Sheriff Billings, will do. You and I are going to catch this bastard. We're a team, a damn good team. We'll make him sorry he ever messed with the Cedar County Sheriff's Department." He gave me a nod, smiled out of the corner of his mouth and left. The screen door slammed behind him.

I picked up my dirty clothes and slammed them into the basket. Since I hadn't done my laundry for a week, the pervert found what he was looking for. My new, bright blue, thong was gone, that and six other panties. "Dammit!"

Good Boy barked once. He was at the top of the stairs looking down, those soulful eyes and his tongue lolling out. I told him he was a good boy and I'd be up in a minute and his expression stayed the same.

I was setting the basket on top of the washer when I heard both dogs bark and their giant paws come down on the hardwood. Now what does Conroy want? I grabbed the flashlight and hurried upstairs.

The front door was wide open and in the shadowy entryway, I saw someone crouched down. And he was petting my dogs?

I pointed the flashlight and turned it on the same time I yelled at the intruder. "One move and my watchdogs will be all over your sorry ass."

The flashlight gave off a wimpy glow.

"Matthew Charles, Sheriff." He was laughing. "You have the nicest watchdogs I've ever met. If that's your emergency light, you ought to change the batteries occasionally."

I turned on the lamp and tossed the flashlight on the couch. "Thanks for the advice."

The dogs were licking his face and he wasn't pushing them away.

I tried not to smile. "Why don't you tell me what you're doing here? You didn't pick up a call on your police scanner, because I didn't make one. And why did you enter my home without knocking?"

"I saw the light show from my place and walked over to investigate."

He wiped his face with the back of his hand. "These are some slobbery dogs you have." He parked himself on the floor between the two and rested his back against the wall. They licked him and let him ruffle their fur.

"Your door was wide open," he said. "I hollered before I came inside. Are you okay?"

"We're fine and it turns out you were right. Victim number eight didn't lock her house and victim number eight knew better."

"Are you saying the panty bandit broke into your place?"

"That's what I'm saying."

"I'm real glad you're okay."

Hey Girl nudged his hand. He'd stopped petting her and he started again.

"Newfs," I said and Matthew looked at me. "My dogs are Newfoundlands, you heard of the breed?"

"Nope."

I squatted down and formally introduced him.

"They're fine dogs," he said.

"Thank you. Loyal and sweet, it's their nature. Brother and sister, I rescued them three years ago. They like you. I'm a little surprised; I thought you were a cat person."

"You got that wrong. Just ask my cat."

"I would if I knew his name."

He petted the dogs.

"All right, I'll take a guess. Is your cat named Rumpelstiltskin?"

"Now that's a mighty good guess, but you're wrong. Back home, I have a dog named Samson, a Bluetick Coonhound. He's a great companion, intelligent and loyal, like your dogs. I sure do miss him. I bet he'd take a liking to you." He looked over at me. The corner of his mouth turned up.

I felt my cheeks getting warm. "Well, I've never met a Bluetick Coonhound. Will he be joining you?"

"Soon as he's up for travel. Just days before I came out here, he ran out in the road and got hit by a pickup."

"Oh, I'm so sorry. He's going to be okay, isn't he?"

"He's on the mend. Soon as he's up for travel, I'll fly him out here. For now, I got a friend looking after him. Samson's not very street smart. No sense of boundaries. I'm lucky he's alive."

"It must have been hard leaving him behind."

"Yep, sure was."

"Why did you move so far away from home?" I asked.

"Seemed like a good idea." He stood. Hey Girl and Good Boy followed. "Your house is chilling off. Sorry about leaving the door open." He shut it and walked over to the couch, the dogs at his heels. He grabbed the throw that was draped over the back and placed it around my shoulders.

I experienced a tingly, panting moment. Pulled the blanket tight under my chin and thanked him.

The front door flung open and the dogs started barking. Conroy tracked in wet leaves. I'd forgotten about him. He bragged he left no stone unturned and all was clear and would I call off my yapping dogs. Then he noticed Matthew.

Matthew said hello.

Conroy didn't. "I'll move the squad car around back," he said. "Get it out of sight and when the bandit returns, I'll be here waiting for him."

"That's ridiculous. He's not coming back."

"I'm going to stick around. Keep an eye on things."

"No. You're dismissed."

He stepped closer and lowered his voice. "I don't think it's a good idea for you to be alone."

I spoke softly back. "Get the hell out of my house, Deputy."

He sped off with the lights flashing, the tires spitting gravel.

Matthew left after he wrote his cell number on a business card and Hey Girl licked his hand. I locked the door and turned off the lamp and watched through the window, him walking away. He cut through the alley and disappeared.

Chapter 6

Deputy Conroy reached for his handcuffs. Mother didn't notice. She was too busy waving her neon orange sign, 'Acorn's CEO Is a Robber Baron & Kingston Is His Bitch', in Ronald Kingston's face and shouting that she never agreed to hand her property over to him and he'd have to demolish it with her in it. Which I'm pretty sure, Kingston wouldn't have minded doing. The American flag and that jerk standing alongside it.

Mother had been sitting in the front row, her and Roma and Mary and a few other women friends, the same who marched outside earlier protesting the Lahkanea Interpretive Center project. They came inside when the meeting started and sat with their signs face down in their laps. Conroy stood off to the side and kept his eye on them.

It wasn't until Kingston unfurled the blueprints and proposed a larger parking lot that Mother flew out of her seat.

"This is my home here, not your parking lot." She stabbed her finger on the blueprints. Then she addressed the men who were seated around the table. "Mr. Kingston believes that taking my home by force isn't breaking the law, but that doesn't make what he's doing right. I grew up with most of you. You know my home is my roots. You can stop this."

The men folded their hands and exchanged glances.

"It's too late," Kingston said. "The discussion is over. Case closed. Ms. Billings, if you don't go sit down, and this goes for your little band of women too, all of you will be asked to leave the premises."

Mr. Finagle broke in. "One minute, Ron. Maggie, we understand. We do. But this isn't about one house, this is about our community and what's best for the whole. The interpretive center will celebrate the builders of New Halem, many of whom we're related to, like your own great grandfather, William Billings. It will pay homage to them and their pioneer spirit and is a way to share their stories with families from all over the country." He fingered the edge of the blueprints and leaned across the table. "Besides, Maggie, we're paying you more than market value for the property, which considering the shape it's in, is more than fair."

Mother flipped up her sign. "What you're most concerned about, is the money visitors will spend at Finagles. This may be all about money for you, but it's not for me. And don't you insult me, John, by saying you understand."

That was when Mother and her sign got in Kingston's face and Deputy Conroy marched up to stop her.

"This woman is a nut job!" Kingston said. "Sheriff." Kingston thrust his hand toward the back of the room where I was sitting. "Get your lunatic mother out of here."

Kingston, that red-faced monkey, his arms were spinning and his spit was flying.

I stood and my chair made a racket. The front of the room looked miles away.

I wasn't supposed to be at the meeting. Conroy had volunteered to work it, since I was related to the head troublemaker, but I went anyway. In case trouble ensued.

I straightened my posture and took a breath and started up the aisle. This is my job, I thought. Arresting my mother is my job, my mother, who I begged not to attend this meeting.

Conroy had Mother cuffed by the time I got up there and she was yelling about injustice and right to assemble. Carmella from the Fish-Wrap snapped pictures. And Mother's women stood in solidarity, holding their signs high above their heads and each carried their own little flag they waved in the parade last 4th of July.

"Get those cuffs off my mother, Deputy. And Mother, you be still."

"I have my rights," she said.

"If you don't mind, Sheriff Billings," Deputy Conroy said, standing the way he does and towering over me. "I'm the officer on duty here and I have the situation under control."

"You handcuffed a sixty year old woman who is only 5 feet tall and 120 pounds. Did you really believe she was a threat?"

"What the hell," Kingston said. "You're going to let this crazy lady loose?"

"Mother. You do have rights and you practiced them before the meeting when you peacefully protested out front." I stabbed my finger toward Kingston. "But this, Mother, is getting you nowhere. I'm asking you to stop."

Mother snarled at Kingston and Conroy set her free.

"I can't believe you small town cops," Kingston said. "This woman, your mother, is trespassing. Clearly conflict of interest, Sheriff, I could sue you and your whole goddamned department."

I walked up to Kingston and looked the little beast in his puny washed out eyes. "Look, Kingston, there was no trespassing, because this is a public meeting. And calling a private citizen a lunatic, nut job, crazy woman can get you sued for slander. So I suggest that you shut up or you'll be the one who gets cuffed and I'd be happy to do it."

He opened his mouth and before one more moronic word escaped, I turned my back on him and looped my arm through Mother's.

"Let's get out of here," I said and we started down the aisle. The door seemed miles away.

"You're just doing your job," Mother said. "Don't feel bad." She patted my hand. "I'm proud of you."

I flung open the door. Outside the air was calm. And clean and crisp.

Mother's little band of women were circling around her and I stepped out of the way.

Chapter 7

He dabbed his mouth on a paper napkin left over from last Christmas. “Oh. Officer,” he said when he saw me. “Officer. Uh. Hello.”

A pencil moustache. The most perfect nose I’d ever seen. A ridiculous purple and white, striped bow tie. He sat across the dining room table from Mother, a plate of cookies, a pot of tea.

I’d dropped by to see if Mother was all right after last night’s meeting and Conroy cuffing her. And to see if maybe she was ready to let her house go, although I doubted it.

She raised a hand and waved her fingers. “Come in Astra and join us. This is Chauncey.” She topped off his teacup.

Mother hadn’t mentioned a Chauncey before and this was the first time I’d laid eyes on the guy.

He wadded up his napkin.

“So Chauncey, you’re new around here, where do you come from?” I asked and folded my arms.

He tapped his napkin against his lips and dropped it onto his plate.

How polite of him.

“I come from Lemuel, Utah.”

“Never heard of it.”

“I’m not surprised, you could miss it if you –”

“Blinked?”

“Yes, Astra, if you blinked,” he said and turned to Mother. “I have to be going, thank you for your hospitality.”

“Come back any day and bring your little boy next time. He can play with Astra’s old toys. They’re in a box somewhere. I’ll look for them.”

Chauncey stood and thanked her again and then he looked me up and down. He grinned. “Goodbye, Officer. A pleasure meeting you.”

I unzipped my jacket so he’d get a good look at my holster. He didn’t seem fazed by it.

Mother sent me to get a teacup while she walked him out. In the kitchen, a bright orange folded paper caught my attention. Over by the fridge, on the floor and I picked it up and was about to toss it into the recycle when I got curious and unfolded it. A handwritten flyer and it said: 'Today is your lucky day. You've won a month's subscription to Handsome Home'.

Handsome Home? Subscription? Had Mother given that guy her credit card number? I bolted out of the kitchen, but Mother was already in the dining room asking where my teacup was.

"Did you give that guy your credit card?"

I didn't wait for her answer. Maybe he was still out front.

From the porch, I looked up and down the street. It was empty, except for my Mustang parked in front of the house. Cars zoomed up and down the highway. The sky was blue for a change but fat rain clouds loomed over the water. Had I seen Chauncey's car when I arrived? I couldn't recall.

"What are you so excited about?" Mother opened the screen door and held it. "I don't give out my credit card. I use cash; it's much safer these days. Come back inside."

I did and I handed her the flyer. "You gave him cash for this?"

"It was a free month, like the paper says. I only paid him for eleven. It was a small thing to do; he's down on his luck. His wife recently died and he lost the farm. He and his two year old son are living at the Pink Flamingo. I wanted to help."

"Did he look anything like a farmer? Besides, no one is named Chauncey."

Mother turned and walked into the dining room.

"Are you listening?" I asked.

She picked up the teapot and I followed her into the kitchen.

"That guy was no farmer and he isn't grieving either, especially after you gave him your money. Didn't you get anything out of the Community Safety Meeting we held last week?"

"I think everyone who came to your meeting enjoyed themselves. I know you and that nice Mr. Charles did. I saw you two talking. He's more than interested in you, I can tell. Have you gone out on a date yet?"

I sighed loudly. The answer was no, not a real date. I met him for coffee a few times and I'd been thinking up business reasons to call him or go into his office. I thought about him more than I should.

"Well, have you?" Mother asked.

"Have I what?"

She grinned. "Gone on a date?"

"We aren't talking about my personal life. Your farm boy scammed you and you'll never get the magazine you paid for."

"Selling magazines isn't scamming. You did it in junior high."

"Yeah, I was twelve. Grown men don't sell magazines."

"We'll have tea in the living room. The sun is out. Did you notice?" She chose two teacups and handed them to me. "You'd be happier if you weren't so distrustful of others."

"I am happy and I don't give my money to scammers."

She poured tea and we sat on the couch and stared out the window.

"Isn't the sky beautiful this morning?" Mother asked. "The sun through the stained glass panels reminds me of when you were a little girl and you'd drag me out of bed on sunny mornings to see the diamonds the magical windows painted on our walls. And I'd tell you the story about your great-great-grandmother, Hannah. Remember?"

"Uh-huh." She was going to tell the story again. I wondered how many times she'd told it.

"Hannah drove her horse and buggy alone through the worst blizzard of the century," Mother said. I nodded and she continued. "The new stained glass windows she ordered months before were ready and she wasn't about to wait on the weather. She made it through that blizzard, and it wasn't easy, believe me, she could have frozen to death. She loaded the windows into the wagon and on the way home, there was a landslide –"

"So the story goes. All right, I have to go to work. I want you to promise you'll call if Chauncey or whatever the hell his name is comes back."

"He's harmless. I can take care of myself."

"Then you're locking your doors?"

Mother sipped her tea.

"Please, please lock up. The panty bandit hit again. Last night he broke into Verity Haydn's home. She's the twelfth victim."

"Oh that poor girl, is she all right? Did she see him?"

"She's fine. She described a guy who was between 5'7 – 6 foot, wearing an ill-fitting suit, an ugly tie and polished dress shoes."

"The panty bandit dresses up to steal panties? That's funny. Finally, a description, you must be encouraged."

"Not really, she described half the businessmen in town."

"Oh. Well, something will break soon and you'll find him. You're a good sheriff and you know what you're doing. Why don't you finish your tea before you leave?"

She nodded toward my cup on the coffee table. Next to it was the newspaper.

"I almost forgot." She picked up the paper and handed it to me. "You and I are celebrities."

Chapter 8

Astra held the newspaper tight in her fist. The front door of the FishWrap office shut behind her and the bell jangled. Miriam looked up and put on a tight-lipped smile. Astra looked around Miriam to see if Matthew was at his desk. He was.

"How may I help you, Sheriff Billings?" Miriam asked before Astra had a chance to slip past.

"I'm here to see Mr. Charles, I'll just go back." Astra pointed toward his desk with the rolled up paper.

"I'll let him know you're here."

"No need." Astra thought Miriam was ridiculous. "I'll just walk right over there and tell him myself."

"No one passes reception without checking in. You're well aware of protocol, Sheriff."

Miriam picked up the phone and Astra waited, tapped the newspaper on the counter, and watched Matthew reach for his phone.

He turned and smiled and waved Astra back. Astra didn't return the greeting. She tapped the newspaper in her palm.

Matthew woke up this morning thinking about her. They'd become friends, casual friends. He'd go to her office, on business, of course, and they'd get to talking. A whole morning could slip by before they realized it. He looked forward to those times. They were friends. That was all they were and that was all he wanted. But then he'd laid in bed thinking about her in a way that was more than friendly. Until No-Name jumped on his head and yowled.

"He'll see you now, Sheriff."

Astra didn't hear. She'd already walked back to his desk. Already called him Mr. Charles, not Matthew, and popped him in the chest with the rolled up paper. "What the hell is this?"

He asked her to sit down and he laid the paper flat on his desk. He looked at the photo he'd sized and placed on the front page just above the fold, the photo of Astra's mother cuffed and Astra, looking down on her, the American flag in the background. Matthew wasn't surprised Astra came in to yell at him.

"Please, sit down. Let's talk about this."

"All right, let's start with why you would put a close-up, giant-sized photo of me cuffing my own mother on the front page of your newspaper?" Astra sat in the chair next to his desk.

He was quiet for a moment. Then he touched the photo. "Is that what you're doing here?"

She folded her arms and breathed out her nose. "There must have been a photo of my mother without cuffs. Your reporter was snapping pictures all night."

"This is the photo she turned in with her story. I give my reporters latitude. Had it been sensational or if it twisted the truth, I would have asked for one that was more fair and balanced."

"You could have talked to me first."

Astra felt hurt that he hadn't. She'd been thinking they were friends. Not best friends, but the kind who would bury a picture like this one in the middle of the newspaper on a page, say, the public service announcement page. Friends or not, the least he could have done was warn her.

"My job is to report the news. A community has to trust they're getting the truth when they read their local paper, not a story spun out of town politics or money or greed."

"But this isn't news. It's my crazy mother making another scene. Thinking if she holds out, someone will drop out of the sky and save her house."

Matthew felt bad for Maggie. He couldn't save her house. But still. He knew how it was to be pushed out when you never intended to leave.

"Mother has to move out of fantasyland into reality and get out of that house." Astra stood and her hand came down, smack, on top of the paper. "And you had to go and run this on the front page. It only encouraged her."

"Why are you so upset?" Matthew laid his hand firmly over hers and she sat down, on the edge of the chair.

Miriam was watching from her desk, her head back and forth and her ears perked.

Matthew leaned closer to Astra and spoke softly. "Your mom is fighting to keep the family home, the home you grew up in."

Astra tried pulling her hand out from under his.

"Tell me," he said. "Why are you fighting against your mother and not with her?"

"Because. Because I don't want to see her hurt, that's why. I'm her daughter, don't you see?"

"I don't think I do." He left his hand on top of hers, but he let up on the pressure.

She noticed the same photo of her and her mother up on his computer in the web edition of the FishWrap. The new website he'd designed and had been telling her about. Astra looked down at their hands. What didn't he understand?

"Mother and her band of women are fighting a losing battle."

"She's not going down without a fight, nothing wrong with that. What's she got to lose?"

"Her dignity?"

He lifted Astra's hand off the paper. "Is this a woman who has lost her dignity?"

She studied the woman in the photo. The jaw set, the eyes. The woman glowed.

Astra remembered. Back to when she was a kid and in the principal's office again for bloodying someone's nose, and all because of her mother.

"She's from Mars," Astra said.

"What?"

"Mother. Mother is from Mars." Astra felt pressure building behind her eyes. "All the kids at school said so." Her face was scrunching up. Matthew squeezed her hand.

"Know what they called me?" she asked and he shook his head. "They called me Astra the Asteroid. That's not my name."

Matthew laid his hands over her shoulders. "Those kids were mean."

The stupid tears backed off and Astra nodded. She'd never talked to anyone about this.

"I want Mother's house gone," she said and waited to see if he'd pull away in disgust. He didn't, instead, he pulled her into a huddle.

"It's true, I want it gone," she said. "That house with its thirty-year leak, I can't wait to see it demolished. That house, I can't wait until it's gone and the interpretive center is up in its place. Until there is nothing alien about Skye Ridge. Or anything alien about me."

Chapter 9

Doreen Bellamont was a saint. The wooden post she wielded, the glow the porch light cast and the man in the suit and bowtie who knelt at her feet.

"Put down the post, Mrs. Bellamont and move aside," Deputy Conroy said.

Doreen seemed to be made of marble.

The man in the suit raised his head. I held my gun on him. "Don't make a move." His head wobbled, like a baby bird.

"Doreen," I said. "Drop the wood and go inside."

"Do what the sheriff says." Conroy, his eyes locked on the perpetrator, gun drawn and steady.

I was relieved when she dropped the wood. "All right. This son-of-a-bitch won't be coming around your house anymore."

Doreen's eyes hadn't moved off him.

"He's all yours, Deputy. Get the medics out here, he doesn't look so good."

Conroy reached for his cuffs and clambered over some scrap lumber.

"Let's go inside, Doreen," I said.

Doreen wasn't hearing. I skirted around a tree stump. I had to get to her fast before she did something stupid. "Better check on the twins." I jogged around the burning barrel. "Where are they? Are the girls all right?"

I was too late. She'd already reared back like a mad bull. She kicked the wobbly-headed guy square in the face. His head flew back, ribbons of blood unfurled and he collapsed in on himself.

"What the hell?" I had Doreen by the arm and I was marching her through the long wet grass to the house. "We had him subdued. What were you thinking?"

"He's a pervert and by God, I have the right to protect my nieces. He was trespassing."

"Aunt Doreen!" Aubrey and Azule leaned out of their upstairs window and cheered. "You nailed that bastard!"

Doreen admonished them for their language. Then she waved triumphantly and announced that the whole ordeal was over.

The girls clapped and hooted and I felt like I was on a demented reality show. I took Doreen by the arm again and started walking.

"Wait! Aunt Doreen, wait." One of the twins was still in the window. "What about that other guy?"

"Oh no." Doreen slapped her cheeks.

"Other guy?" I yelled in Doreen's face. "Other guy Doreen? What other guy?"

"Over there!" Her niece screeched and pointed. "Behind you."

I stepped in front of Doreen and drew my gun.

"I forgot all about poor Mr. Charles," Doreen said. She was coming out from behind me. Pointing and she sprinted off in that direction.

Then I saw Matthew, on his knees, in the grass near Doreen's front door.

I ran over and pushed Doreen out of the way, dropped to the ground and held him by the shoulders.

"What happened to you?"

His cheeks cool and damp to touch and he was shivering. His hand pressed to his forehead and didn't seem to know he was bleeding. I started going through my jacket to find something to stop it.

"Matthew, look at me. Can you tell me what happened?"

"I don't know. I'm fine, really, just feeling a little cold. I'd better go home."

"How about you stick around for a bit? I need to brush up on my first aid skills. Let me have a look." I pulled his hand away from his head and pressed a pile of pocket sized tissues against the wound and he winced.

"Tender, I know, to be expected." I placed his hand over the tissues and told him to press.

"Does it hurt anywhere else?" I asked.

"No." He leaned into me and I laid my hand on the back of his head and he groaned. There was a good sized lump back there and he didn't know how he got it.

"You're going to be okay. Let's get out of this wet grass and get you inside."

Doreen and I were helping him to his feet. "I'm so sorry," she said. "I hope you're going to be all right. I'm so terribly sorry. Astra, I didn't mean to hurt Mr. Charles."

"You did this to him?"

Deputy Conroy waved a plastic bag over the perpetrator. He had the guy's feet propped up on a piece of wood, a blanket over him. "The evidence is in the bag. Look at all these panties. I found them stuffed inside this creeper's clothes."

He handed me the bag and glared at the prisoner and when he looked back at me, he was grinning. "We got him. I knew you and I would. We're a damn good team." He held up his palm and I did not slap it.

"I fixed the prisoner up the best I could," he said. "Got the bleeding stopped. The medics are in route."

"After they stabilize him, send them inside to look at Mr. Charles. Mrs. Bellamont is patching him up, but I think he may have a concussion."

"Will do. I've been telling Mr. FishWrap to get rid of his police scanner, stay away from crime scenes and let us do our job. But he didn't listen and now look at him."

"He's a reporter and he has his rights. Now if you don't mind." The prisoner was groaning. "Who is this guy?"

"From the great state of Utah, this is Mr. Chauncey Williams and get this –"

"Chauncey?" I yanked the flashlight out of Conroy's hand and shined it in the guy's purple puffy eyes. He squinted and moaned.

"I believe we've already met," I said.

Big baby tears were rolling down his cheeks and I was surprised his little pencil moustache hadn't washed off.

"You must remember me? Sheriff Billings? We met at my mother's. You might recall it was her lucky day?"

He whimpered.

"I thought as much. A woman alone and you waltzed into her home and took her tea and her cookies and hospitality and sympathy and then you went and scammed her. Shame on you. There were others too, right? Other trusting elderly residents who won't receive their one free magazine or the other eleven they paid you for, you jerk. But then, scamming the good people of New Halem was the least of our problems. Tell me, what were you doing going through this nice family's laundry for the third time?"

"We caught him with his hands in the laundry basket," Deputy Conroy said and chuckled. "But that's not all. Michigan has a warrant out on a Tim Rainey. Rainey's last reported address, a hoity-toity suburb out of Detroit and he matches our prisoner's description all the way down to that wimpy moustache and stupid bowtie." Conroy looked down at Rainey and snarled.

I picked up a pink thong Conroy missed and I bounced it up and down in the prisoner's face. "Tim Rainy, farm boy Chauncey, whoever the hell you are. My mother trusted you. And you lied to her. Don't you just hate when people lie to you?"

He made a gurgling sound in his throat.

"You understand, glad to hear. Maybe you've learned something. And FYI, in case you haven't been keeping a tally, this was your thirteenth break-in. My mother believes thirteen is an unlucky number. This has certainly proven true in your case. Don't get me wrong though, I don't believe in all that woo-woo crap, but it seems our little village had a bit of luck tonight."

I found Matthew lying on Doreen's couch under a hot-pink and lime-green blanket pulled up to his chin, and a puffy pillow under his head. I touched his leg and he opened his eyes.

"Hi," I said and he said hi back.

I grabbed a couch cushion. "This ought to make you comfy until the medics arrive." I lifted his feet and slipped it under.

"I don't need that. I'm ready to go." He started pushing off the blanket.

"Oh no, you aren't." Doreen laid her royal purple knitting down in her lap and sat forward in the rocking chair. "He needs to see a doctor, Sheriff Astra. He says he doesn't. If he won't cooperate, you'll have to cuff him."

"Wanting to go home isn't against the law," Matthew said. "Thank you, Mrs. Bellamont, for bandaging my head. Astra, I'm fine."

I crouched beside him. "You took some serious blows to the head tonight; do you really think you're okay enough to go home?"

"He has a concussion." Aubrey butted in. Sitting cross-legged in a straight-backed chair, flipping magazine pages and she didn't look up. "Aunt Doreen said so. His eyes don't look right."

"No duh." Azule came out of the kitchen texting on her phone. "The way Aunt Doreen swung that board, no one's eyes would look right after that. I saw the whole thing, if you need a statement, Sheriff Astra."

"It was a simple case of mistaken identity," Doreen said. "I thought he was the panty bandit. Who else would be creeping through my yard?"

"Going to your front door to see if y'all are all right isn't creeping," Matthew said.

"I hear the ambulance," Azule said and ran over to the window.

"I don't need the medics." Matthew tried to sit up.

He groaned and sank back into the pillow.

"Dizzy?" I asked.

He shut his eyes and said to give him a minute.

"You must have an awful headache."

"I'll take something for it at home."

"That may help some. Headache and dizziness can be indicators of concussion. Of course, we have no way of knowing. The medics could probably tell you. I highly recommend them."

He opened his eyes, but didn't move his head. "You aren't about to give up are you?" He stared at Doreen's ceiling, cobwebs sticking to the texture.

"You're quite astute." I laid my hand on his chest, leaned closer and whispered. "I want to make sure you're okay, because I care about you. And I like you. A lot. More than a lot. Very much, I like you very much." I kissed his cheek and gave him a careful hug.

"Okay, I'll see the medics." He tried to smile, but it looked more like a wince. "I like you a lot and very much too. Will you have dinner with me this week?"

I whispered yes in his ear.

"I'm glad you came to your senses, Mr. Charles. I would hate to be the cause of your demise," Doreen said. "I hope you understand. I had to protect my nieces, I had a feeling the bandit would strike again. Bad things come in threes, you know. So I made a plan. Are you listening, Mr. Charles? Astra, you're not supposed to let someone with a concussion fall asleep."

"Let him rest. The medics will be in as soon as they talk to my deputy. You said you made a plan?"

"Yes, I did. I went to Finagles and bought all the sexy panties Mr. Finagle had priced bargain basement."

"What for?" I asked.

"They were for him, for the panty bandit to steal. Then I came home and made the booby trap."

"Booby-trap?" I asked.

"Mr. William's nose will never be the same," the doctor said.

I walked into the conversation. He wanted to keep our prisoner for the next twenty-four hours in case of complications. After the blow Doreen gave him, I was relieved to hear he was alive.

I'd been hovering near the nurse's station waiting for word on Matthew and I'd asked a second time if I could go in and see him and they wouldn't let me, since I'm not related and they know it. I argued and got nowhere, rules are for sheriffs too, one of them said.

"His nose will heal," the doctor said. "But it will never be the same."

The most perfect nose I'd ever seen.

The doctor touched the side of his own nose and left.

"Deputy McGuire is on watch and the paperwork's complete," Conroy said.

I thanked him and told him to go home.

He shook his head and laughed. "Mrs. Bellamont sure did a number on that pervert and after we had him subdued. I saw you tried to stop her, but the dumbass panty bandit had it coming. He had the whole town scared, at least the panty wearing part of it."

I glanced over at the nurse's station. No one there and I thought about sneaking in to see Matthew.

Conroy chuckled. "That booby-trap of Mrs. Bellamont's sounded like something from Saturday morning cartoons. Can you believe it? Classic, you got to admit, a trip wire, a crash, the clothesline and all those sexy panties blowing in the wind and Mrs. Bellamont with that club stalking him like she was a goddamn bear hunter." He burst out laughing and an old man on oxygen turned and stared.

"Deputy Conroy, you're off duty now. Go home."

"Too bad for your Mr. Charles, getting caught in the middle the way he did. He took quite a blow, but it serves him right. Maybe he'll stop snooping around."

"Getting bashed over the head didn't serve him right. He was never out of line. But you are for saying he's mine."

A kid was howling. His pajamas hanging down around his knees and he yanked at his stinking diaper.

"Let's get out of here," Conroy said. "There's no reason either of us have to stay. I'll treat you to breakfast, what do you say?"

"I say no."

"Why not? Six months ago we –"

“Made a big terrible mistake and I don’t want you to Ever. Bring it up. Again.”

“Come on, we’ve known each other our whole lives. You and me together, we’re a team, like today. Always have been, you and me are in the cards, don’t you know?”

“No.” I stepped back. “There is no destiny, if that’s what you’re getting at.”

“You want to take our relationship slow, I respect that.” He stepped toward me. “I’m willing to wait. I’ve waited this long. I’ve always been here for you. Remember our junior prom? How about before then, in seventh grade, and that jerkoff, Bob Bowers, said he made out with you and found tentacles, uh, down there. I stood up for you. I told everyone you were not an alien like Bob said.”

“I don’t need you to stand up for me. I never did. It’s time you understood, Deputy, there is nothing to wait for. There is no relationship. No team and there is no love. There are no cards. There’s nothing, nothing at all.”

I sounded like a beast and he just looked at me with his big stupid face.

“You broke hospital rules to see me?” Matthew asked. His eyes only half open and he sounded like he had marbles in his mouth.

“I woke you up. I guess I’m not so good at sneaking in. I’ll just sneak back out,” I whispered.

“Don’t go.”

“All right, I won’t if you go back to sleep.”

He said okay and I rolled the table out of the way and reached through the bars for his hand. “If it helps, the panty bandit looks way worse than you.”

He cleared his throat. “Maybe that’s because Mrs. Bellamont

kicked him in the face, and not me. Baiting and assault is illegal."

"I'm not here to discuss the case. Are they taking good care of you?"

"I have a concussion."

"Well, what do you know? Arriving first on the scene has its risks. Doreen could have killed you with that board. What if the panty bandit was armed?"

"We aren't discussing the case, remember?"

"Fair enough."

He tried to put the side of the bed down and I helped.

"Thanks to you, the panty bandit is off the street," he said.

"No thanks to me. Without Doreen's, uh, inventiveness, the pervert would still be on the loose."

"Inventiveness? Well, she is a mystery writer."

"I bet the panty bandit shows up in her next novel. Maybe you'll be in it too."

"Getting bashed over the head? I hope my character isn't recognizable."

"But a character who acts in a noble and heroic way is always endearing."

"Noble and heroic can get a guy killed off, especially if there's an irrational woman in the story."

"Which often leads to a tragic, yet, romantic demise. Look, I know you see what Doreen did as illegal. But you don't know the Bellamont family. If you were from around here and knew their history, you might see this differently."

He dozed off. Thirty seconds later he jerked awake and asked if I'd tell him what happened to the family.

"Maybe Doreen will tell you their story someday. As for what happened tonight, I see extenuating circumstances and I'll write my report accordingly, with the facts as I see them. And you'll run your news story reporting the facts as you see them. I understand. Now, I think you should get some sleep. We can talk later."

"I understand Mrs. Bellamont better than you think. I know how far a caregiver will go to protect a child, especially one who has suffered a trauma."

"How do you know?" I asked.

His eyes shut and he slept.

I knew his aunt raised him. He never mentioned parents. Maybe he had a traumatic experience when he was a kid. That would explain why he speaks so little about his past.

A nurse whipped through the curtains and startled Matthew. She set Jell-O and sporks and apple juices on the table and took his vitals. He thanked her and asked when he could go home.

Not until the doctor had seen him, and she didn't know when that would be. He groaned. She told him to eat something and she raised the bed and left.

"Wait up here with me." He patted the bed and smiled.

His face bruised and stitches in his head. The way he smiled. I wondered. Had I ever felt like this about anyone?

I took off my shoes and slipped off my holster and set it on the table, laid my jacket over it and climbed up on the bed.

"How many stitches?" I was peeling the foil lid off the Jell-O.

"Three or four."

I stuck the spork in the middle of the Jell-O and gave it to him.

"This is a staple back home," he said and stared at it. The spork wobbled.

"How do you know?" I asked. I'd thought of our earlier conversation.

"Uh, Jell-O was cheap and fed lots of folks, I guess."

"No, I mean what you said before about understanding Doreen, and knowing how far a caregiver would go to protect a child. How do you know?"

"Oh." He finished his Jell-O and I gave him mine. Then he shrugged. "What caregiver wouldn't go to any means to protect a kid?"

"Yeah...who wouldn't," I said. "So, three or four stitches?" I moved his hair to the side to get a better look. "The doctor did a tidy job. You shouldn't have much of a scar." Then I noticed an extensive scar from an earlier injury. "What happened here? This isn't very old."

He pushed my hand away and combed his hair back in place with his fingers.

"It's nothing."

"That scar is a pretty big nothing."

He shrugged and looked away.

I waited.

"All right. The scar was a warning."

"A warning?"

"Yep, you know the award winning news article everyone's been talking about, well, the folks who did this didn't want it going to press."

"You're talking about the pastor and his people."

He nodded.

"Where were the police when they did this to you?"

"The police didn't know about them. They didn't know about any of it until after."

"So you took the law into your own hands. No wonder you understand Doreen."

"No, all I was doing was collecting facts. Soon as I had enough for a story, I planned on turning it over to the cops. But I slipped up, before I had a chance."

He sucked the last bit of apple juice up through the straw. I held out my hand and he gave me the juice container and I tossed it into the trash can.

"Want to tell me about it?"

"You read the story online."

"The part about you slipping up wasn't in the story." I smiled and waited.

"All right, if you have to know, I started out investigating some small time exotic pet traffickers. One night I followed them. Into the hills, nearby where I grew up, to an elementary school that had been condemned. I parked down the road a bit. The school was lit up in the back. I sneaked around. I couldn't believe what I saw inside." He stopped and sighed heavy.

I felt a little bad for pressing. He was wounded, after-all. "You can tell me another time if you want."

"I got it started, I may as well finish. I saw hundreds of animals, all penned up in cages so small I don't know how they fit the poor little guys inside. The place was filthy. There were bear cubs and baby tigers, blue-headed parrots and scarlet macaws, and more, many more and they were all squawking and squealing and crying and a guy was screaming shut up. There were dozens of crates too, all bolted shut. That's where they kept the gators and snakes. There were diamondback rattlers, copperheads and corals, pythons and adders. The men I followed paid in cash and left with their purchases in taped up cardboard boxes. That was when I got a good look at the dealers."

"So this is when you should have left the scene and called the police, but you didn't, right?"

"Right. I knew them. The dealers, I knew them and I knew them well."

"How would you know a snake handling pastor?"

"Uh. I come from a little place like New Halem, where people know people. I had no idea the pastor and the others were dealing in wildlife trafficking. They were church going folks."

"And the church going folks gave you this scar?"

He nodded. "I hunkered low that night and wondered what I should do. Forget about the story, forget what I saw? How could I turn in people I knew? I don't know how long I'd been hiding there thinking what to do, before I noticed they were locking up and shutting off lights and I hadn't had sense enough to leave. Somebody opened a car door and a dog leaped out and took off. They hollered for him to come back. He didn't, he led them right to me."

"Why would someone you knew hurt you like that?"

"Simple, I got in the way. I was lucky they didn't kill me. Instead, they beat the holy crap out of me. Said to forget about the story and don't go to the cops or they'd be forced to do something permanent. One of the men stayed back. He drove me into town and dropped me off a half block from the hospital. Gave me a story, I was jumped from behind and I didn't see a thing."

"But you went straight to the police."

"No. At first I told the story he told me to tell."

"But a death threat gave you plenty of reason to turn those people in."

"Seems an easy choice, considering everything, but you got to understand, I had a lot at stake. It wasn't easy turning them in, I owed them loyalty."

"Owed them? Why would you be loyal to people like that? What was at stake?"

He sighed. "Let's have dinner at the Sea and Sky."

Chapter 10

Astra held a long legged doll by her bare ankle. The spiked heels got lost a long time ago, when the doll was still new. Astra remembered. She was lying on her stomach on top of her mother's bed, her head hanging over the side. "Why did you keep all this crap?" She smoothed the doll's wedding gown, the outfit the doll was wearing when she was new out of the box and blond and stupid.

Maggie was kneeling over the carpet and sopping up water with a sponge. The carpet water-stained from the thirty year drip and the bucket had overflowed again.

"I kept your doll because you'll have a little girl someday."

Good Boy and Hey Girl were nosing in the box of old toys Maggie dragged out of storage a week ago. She phoned Astra that day, chatty and excited and she wanted Astra to come right over and see them and another thing she found, but wouldn't say what it was. Probably baby pictures, Astra had thought; embarrassing ones she didn't want her mother showing to Matthew. Astra was too busy to come that day, but she promised she would the next. Then Matthew got hurt and Astra forgot all about the promise.

Maggie sniffed the air. "I'm really sick of this perpetual leak and this stinking carpet."

"You are?"

"Yes. Every year the mildew gets worse."

This fall, with the onslaught of rain, Maggie had started smelling it and not just in her bedroom carpet, but in the kitchen, the entryway and closets too. That earthy dank odor she expected in the forest behind her home, not inside it.

"Does this mean you're thinking of moving into a house that smells like new carpet?"

Maggie didn't look up. She squeezed more water out of the sponge. "New carpet smell goes away pretty quick I hear."

"I know."

"Okay. So what does my hypothetical little girl have to do with this old doll?" Astra asked. She checked under the doll's gown to see if it was wearing panties and it was; red panties she didn't remember. The doll's hair Astra remembered cutting close to the head and coloring black with permanent marker, the tattoos she drew on and heavy mascara.

"All little girls want to see the dolls their mommies played with," Maggie said.

Astra wagged the doll at her mother. "This would give any little girl nightmares. I don't want a kid, I've told you."

Maggie sat back on her heels and smiled. "You'll change your mind someday and the baby will be a girl, I feel it in my bones. Yes, a girl and she'll have your beautiful grey eyes."

Maggie held her sponge over the faded plastic bucket and squeezed.

"I wish you and your bones would mind their own business. What if they're wrong and your granddaughter's eyes turn out to be red orbs?"

Maggie ignored that. But the word granddaughter caught her attention. A granddaughter would make Maggie a grandmother. Maggie thought through the implications. Grandmother, Maggie thought and she stared into the bucket.

Astra thought of Matthew's eyes. She had trouble pinning down a solid color. When she thought of them, she thought of summer and sea and the end of the day. She liked the way he looked at her with those eyes.

"Maybe you're right," Maggie said. "I'll be a grandmother soon enough. You need a good man first. By the way, how's Matthew?"

"He got the stitches out today and the bruises are fading."

"You two have been spending a lot of time together."

"He was seriously wounded, you know. I couldn't just leave him home all by himself."

"Oh, no, of course you couldn't." Maggie grinned. "You're starting to have feelings for him, aren't you?"

"We've only known each other two months."

"So?"

"So we're friends. That's all. Friends help friends out, you know. Like friends do, I care about him like a friend. Really, that's all."

Maggie tucked a piece of Astra's hair behind her ear. "It's good to have friends. You seem happier."

Hey Girl woofed and Astra smiled. When her mother wasn't looking, she raised the wedding doll's arms up over her head. Hooray!

Astra had been thinking recently, about her and Matthew, thoughts that were more heated than friendly.

The wedding doll didn't come with a boyfriend, he cost extra. But she came with a name. Astra did the doll a favor and before she took her out of the box, she renamed her. Zetty McKay. The name Astra would have named herself if she had a say.

"Zetty McKay," Astra said and she made the doll do cartwheels on the bed.

Maggie burst out laughing. "I wasn't surprised when you gave Zetty a makeover." Maggie opened the bedroom window and tossed out the water she'd collected.

She gave the doll to Astra on her eighth birthday. Bought with the tips she earned at Rictor's and had been saving in a jar to pay for a replacement window pane in the basement. All the little girls at school had pretty dolls; but what Astra really wanted was one of those robots that looked like an ordinary wristwatch when folded and unfolded, a warmonger beast. Jim Conroy got one for his birthday.

The window pane never did get replaced. Maggie put up new cardboard every year, except this year and it was already November.

Maggie reached into the toy box and pulled out a yellow bear and hugged it. "I was thinking Chauncey's little boy would like this. Well, before we found out Mr. Chauncey wasn't who he said he was. It's really too bad." She rubbed the bear's sunshine belly.

"Mr. Chauncey was a liar and he took your money. I was happy to send him and his creepy panty fetish back to Michigan. His face isn't nearly as pretty as when he arrived in New Halem, you know, the nose, well, it served him right and now he's in jail."

"He certainly made poor choices, but we don't know what the boy has been through, his life or the reasons he did what he did. He's on a journey like the rest of us. We shouldn't judge or rejoice when another fails." She dropped the bear into the box and Good Boy took it out and trotted across the room.

Astra shook her head. She was sorry she got her mother started with the life journey crap.

"I have something to show you." Maggie walked over to her dresser. Smiling and stepping lighter.

"Okay. Oh, wait, is it my baby pictures? I don't want you showing Matthew."

"Baby pictures? No, I haven't come across those. No worries, they're in one of the storage boxes, I'll keep my eyes open for it. But that's for later. I have something else to show you. I found a treasure."

"A treasure? What kind of treasure?"

Maggie was pulling panties and bras and stockings out of the dresser drawer.

Astra was surprised how lacey and little and sheer.

"A buried treasure," Maggie said. "Buried right here in the house and I found it."

Buried treasure? Astra rolled over, swung her legs off the bed and sat on the edge. All the drama, what would a life be without it? She shoved the doll Zetty headfirst in with the other toys.

The small box was made of walnut and on the lid, a piece of curly maple with the initials H. M. D. carved in it. Maggie's hands were shaking the way they were when she found the box in the storage room in a nook she didn't know existed. She handed the box to Astra.

Astra held it in her lap and fingered the details, the wood hewn uneven, a chip out of the lid, and the top of the brass closure missing.

Maggie sat next to Astra on the bed. "Open it; this is your treasure too."

Astra guessed she'd find shiny rocks inside along with one of her mother's stories, but she didn't say so. She opened the lid and took out a bundle of coins wrapped in a tattered piece of cloth.

"Money?" Astra spread the coins out on the bed. She walked over to the lamp and held one in the light. A dull grey, and thicker and heavier than a quarter and worn and crusted. "Is this real?"

"Didn't I say I found a treasure? Will came right over when I told him. He's quite knowledgeable about coins. He believes these are genuine and maybe worth something and the one you're holding and a few of the others could be rare."

Astra examined the coin; the faint impression left of a shield and a crown, or was it a castle.

"I think I'll have the coins appraised," Maggie said.

"It wouldn't hurt, I guess."

"Will knows an appraiser in Portland."

"You think you might take a trip over to Portland with Mr. Cooke?"

Maggie shrugged. "Maybe."

"Maybe?"

Astra didn't believe for a minute that her mother would go.

Maggie started thinking about Will. He said he'd cook tonight, a couple of steaks at his place. Maggie liked his place, the little beachside 1910 Arts and Crafts home painted lemon-yellow and enclosed by wind blasted shrubs and a charming fence. All new inside and nothing leaked or smelled like mildew. Will would be over later to pick her up. She would shower after Astra left. Change into the new panties Will hadn't seen.

Astra was turning the coin over in her hand. "Does Mr. Cooke have any idea where these came from?"

"I do. I've done a bit of research this week."

"And?"

"You've heard of the Spanish galleon that shipwrecked on Lahkanea Spit back in the 1700s, a chest laden with treasure and the band of marauders who stole it from a church?"

"They buried their chest in the mountain and never came back for it and no one has ever found it. Yeah, yeah, it's just a story."

"These coins are old enough."

"You think these are from the lost treasure of Lahkanea?"

"They could be. Isn't this exciting?"

Astra was picking through the coins. "These tarnished ones are different." She dropped a few into her palm.

"Silver pieces of eight," Maggie said. "And the gold are doubloons."

"Doubloons? Pieces of eight?" Astra laughed and plopped into the middle of the bed. "This is pirate money, it can't be real. Any kid can get it at the arcade."

Maggie shook her head. "Treasure hunters have been looking for the Lahkanea treasure for decades."

Astra knew about treasure hunters. Since she became sheriff, she'd arrested several who were digging on the beaches and in the steep mountain side, dangerous business and illegal and stupid.

"Treasure hunters don't make the story real." Astra tipped her hand and the coins fell onto the bed. "If these are part of the treasure, how did they get in this box and why are they in your house?"

"H. M. D." Maggie nodded toward the box.

Astra shut the lid. She'd forgotten about the initials carved on it. "Who is H. M. D.?"

"Look inside."

Astra did and found a photograph. She picked it up by the edges. A photo of a woman a long time ago, black dress and a feathered bonnet, a painted landscape of beach and a boardwalk.

The woman was lovely and sophisticated. Astra looked closer. The woman's nose turned up a little. Astra touched the end of her own nose.

Her nose turned up a little, a trait she never liked much, but one that suited the woman. The woman's ears were small like Astra's. Princess ears, Maggie called them.

Astra turned the photo over and Maggie pointed to the name. Hannah Margaret Dickerson. "This is your great-great-grandmother, Hannah. I've told you her stories."

"Yes, you certainly have."

"You look very much like her, right down to this lovely dimple." Maggie reached out and touched the spot under Astra's lip and Astra pushed her hand away.

Astra held the photo next to her mother's face. "Hannah has dark hair same as you. Looks like you inherited her pointy chin. You and I both have her traits. I guess this means I have a branch of humans on my family tree. Proof I'm not 100% alien, I suppose."

Maggie ignored that and tapped the edge of the photo. "This was taken a few months before she married William. You can tell from the date. She was thirty years old. You know, back in those days, a woman was considered a spinster if they were unmarried at twenty."

"And you do know that was then, not now."

Maggie laughed. "Hannah waited for the right man to come along. They had a good life together."

"Are there more family pictures?" Astra asked.

"I don't know of any, except of course, Hannah and William's portraits hanging at the FishWrap office. Who needs pictures when there are stories to tell? My mother told me all she knew, stories that had been remembered and re-told and passed on."

Maggie started thinking about her own father. She remembered the day he wandered off. What dress she wore, the last thing he said, what she ate for lunch. The weather. The story of her father certainly wasn't worth passing on.

Astra was bundling up the coins. "Was Hannah a treasure hunter?"

Maggie looked at Astra. “I never heard that story. If she was, she kept it a secret.”

Astra wondered why Hannah would keep something like that a secret. She put the coins inside and closed the box.

“Will you tell me my story?” Astra asked. “Not the ridiculous alien baby story where I came to you, via the asteroid, but a true story about who gave me red hair and grey eyes and threads of green through the grey.”

Chapter 11

They shimmered, barrettes Astra thought at first, and the little one called Emma, whose mop of hair they adorned, stomped through the yard and bawled for her mommy.

Astra didn’t see Emma’s mommy anywhere. She’d come outside earlier with two walking babies hanging onto her hem and joined her husband, Spence, the new hire at the FishWrap, on their front porch. Spence adjusted his bent wire-framed glasses and hooked his arm around her neck. There was a group of volunteers from their church and Matthew and Astra stood off to the side. Spence thanked them for coming out to unload the trucks on their holiday. He said dinner invites for all.

Astra smelled the family’s turkey roasting. She’d never cooked one. She looked at Matthew and smiled. She hoped he didn’t think she was too presumptuous, inviting herself to come along. Matthew reached for her hand. Spence said let’s get busy.

The group made quick work of their task and went home to NFL football and turkeys to carve. Leaving Astra and Matthew, two pock-faced guys dressed in suits and Spence to unload the super-sized hide-a-bed couch. Spence pushed Astra aside and took her end.

She shut the tailgate and leaned against the truck and watched. Let him, she thought. His face was sweating already. Matthew was stuck walking backwards alongside Spence and Spence was letting his side list. Matthew took up the slack. He was stronger than he looked. He glanced over at Astra and stumbled. She chuckled. She was glad she'd been presumptuous, if that was what she'd been. She'd never felt this way about anyone.

The men stopped on the porch and set the couch down and waited while Spence assessed the size of it in relationship to the size of the door.

"Mommy, Mommy! Get these out," Emma hollered. She was yanking at her barrettes. She ran up the front steps and tried climbing over the couch to get inside. Spence shooed her off. She cried for a while and stopped when Spence ignored her. Astra wondered if Emma ever shut up.

"You can't tell Mommy." Emma's sister, a ripped tutu over her jeans, grabbed onto Emma's wrist and dragged her down the steps.

"Let go of me!"

Astra winced and started thinking about the little girl her mother's bones had predicted. Emma and Tutu were good reminders of why she shouldn't have a little girl.

Matthew and the others were trying to wrestle the couch through the door. "We can do this, men," Spence said.

They were going about it all wrong. Spence, talking more than lifting, and the two suits, minus jackets, tipped instead of turned and pinned Matthew between the couch and the doorjamb. "Go back," he said and they pushed forward. Matthew ended up inside, the couch wedged in the door behind him.

He'd never spent Thanksgiving alone. That was why he volunteered his afternoon hefting furniture. Better than missing home and the smell of chocolate walnut pies baking.

He walked over to the pier this morning. He took his coffee and a book. Sat on the pier and leaned against a post. Not a cloud and this lifted his spirit. He thought about driving up to Lahkanea Wayside. Then he saw Astra. She'd walked her dogs to the water and let them off-leash. She shaded her eyes and he waved her over. She left the dogs swimming and walked out onto the pier and sat beside him. Her leg pressed against his, the sun on their faces.

He was glad Astra invited herself along. When he was with her, he never wished for home. He didn't think about rolling back time.

Matthew was afraid he was falling in love with her.

He heard his name and Spence shouting, pull, pull. The couch moved a half inch.

Astra heard Spence grunting.

Before they left for Spence's, she made Matthew feel her biceps. Rather than reciprocating, he kissed her. No one ever kissed her the way he did.

She thought this was turning out to be the best Thanksgiving ever. She'd never spent Thanksgiving by herself. Her mother gave little notice. She stopped by Astra's late last night to tell her. She and Mr. Cooke were on their way to Portland for the long weekend. It was a shock and Astra didn't think she heard right and asked for clarification. Her mother was going away, yes, and she was about to venture outside of her thirty mile zone. Astra never thought she'd do it. She was still reeling from the news.

When she saw Matthew on the pier this morning, her day took a right turn and she stopped thinking about her mother.

Astra was pretty sure she was falling in love with Matthew.

She heard a whoop. The couch was no longer stuck. Spence slapped Matthew across the back.

Matthew broke into a smile when he saw Astra. He walked over to join her.

Emma plowed into Astra's leg, Tutu attached.

"What the hell is going on?" Astra asked.

The girls huddled together and looked up at Astra, wide-eyed.

Astra sighed. She would make a terrible mother.

A boy slid in the grass and tackled Emma. His head, a buzz cut gone wrong. "You're in big fat trouble," he said. "You got into Dad's fishing box."

"Someone's been in my fishing box?" Spence walked out of the garage.

Astra took a closer look at Emma's hair. Buzz was right; the barrettes weren't barrettes at all. They were fishing lures and the barbed frogs and drunk-eyed fish and Emma's mop of hair were all tangled up together.

Spence kneeled beside Emma and touched a happy polka-dotted minnow. "Son of a biscuit, Emma, what have you done?"

"Why do we get in trouble for swearing when you swear all the time?" Buzz asked.

"What I said was not swearing." Spence tried to untangle the lure and Emma screamed.

"These fishing lures are antiques," Spence said.

"She put them in my hair." Emma stabbed her finger at Tutu.

"She made me," Tutu said and pointed back.

"They belonged to your great grandfather, Heber," Spence said. "Someday, they will belong to your brothers. You have no business getting into things that aren't yours. Damage it, Emma, hold still."

"You're hurting me!"

"Ouch!" Spence examined his thumb. "God bless it, the barbs on these things are frickin' sharp." He shoved his thumb in his mouth.

"Mommy says all that God-bless-it, frickin' talk is just candy coated evil," Tutu said and sneered at her father.

Astra burst out laughing. She couldn't help it. It was all so ridiculous. She glanced at Matthew. She hoped she hadn't embarrassed him.

He slipped his hands around her waist. "God bless it, Astra. You're going to get us in trouble." They leaned into each other and laughed.

Matthew knew he should pull away. These feelings he had. He'd only known her two months. He had loose ends.

His forehead touched hers. He felt her heart beating.

"All right, kids, we're moving the couch downstairs into the family room where the wife wants it," Spence said.

He'd sent his kids inside to see their mother. Emma with the lures still stuck in her hair.

"Why don't you give us a hand, Astra, and we'll make quick work of this," Spence said.

"I wouldn't want to get in anyone's way."

Matthew winked at her and Astra took Spence's end. Spence's wife directed them down a flight of stairs and announced dinner would be served as soon as they set up all the beds.

Astra kneeled on the nursery floor. She was tightening the last bolt. "One crib down."

"And two to go," Matthew said. "This seems like a lot of babies for one room."

"Wall to wall babies. Did you catch how many kids they have?"

Matthew was attaching the railings to the next crib. "I couldn't get a head count. There were more in the backyard. Kids all over the place."

"Like puppies." Astra handed him the screwdriver.

"You want kids someday?" He didn't look up from his task.

She wondered why he asked. "I already have two giant, hairy, slobbery babies."

He looked over at her and smiled.

"How about you? Do you want a kid?"

"I don't know anything about babies. I'm the youngest in my family."

"You have siblings?" She was searching for a missing washer.

"I haven't talked to them for years. Here's that washer." He dropped it into her palm. "My dad died when I was nine. My sisters were grown by then and I went to live with Naomi, the youngest."

"Oh I'm sorry."

"Thanks." Matthew picked up a mattress and put it into a crib.

"I don't think the toy soldier mattress goes in the pink crib." Astra exchanged it with a pink and yellow bear mattress. "Why didn't you stay with your mom?"

When he thought of his mom, he remembered the old-fashioned braid, not her face. He remembered the taxi was yellow.

"She dropped me off at my sister's. Naomi was eighteen, expecting a kid any day and had been married for a whole week. They lived out in the sticks, where her husband's Mamaw June lived before she passed the year before, in a house about to fall down. My aunt came for me a few weeks later and that's pretty much it."

"That's a lot for a little boy." Astra reached out and touched his shoulder. "Seeing all the bad stuff kids are put through is the worst part of my job. Loss and change is hardest on them. The adults in their lives usually aren't coping any better. It's messed up. Why didn't you stay with your sister?"

"Didn't work out, but all for the better, my aunt raised me right."

There wasn't a blue crib so Matthew put the toy soldiers in the white one, clowns in the yellow. "If the mattresses are mixed up, the babies will sort it out by which one cries the loudest."

"Maybe you know more about babies than you think."

"I think it's cruel to bring a baby into a world where there are no guarantees."

Astra thought of her mother, thirty years old, unmarried and pregnant with an alien baby. Matthew hadn't asked about her alien-ness or

Mother from Mars since she told him that day at the newspaper office. He was thoughtful, a quality she'd never seen in any man she'd been with. Someday, maybe she'd tell Matthew the whole ridiculous story her mother made up.

"Imagine if life came with a guarantee against loss, damage, and acts of God," Astra said.

"Guarantees don't normally cover acts of God." Matthew walked around the cribs and shook them to see if they wobbled.

"Nothing, short of a tsunami, will bring these baby beds down."

"Do y'all get those tsunamis in New Halem? Uh, I mean –. No one in New Halem says, y'all."

"Just you."

"I've been trying to stop. I keep slipping up."

"Why stop? It's a good word, one we don't have an equivalent of. Besides, it's who you are." Astra didn't think she'd ever known anyone as genuine. "And I like you very much just the way you are."

He smiled. If life came without loss, he wouldn't be here. He wouldn't have met Astra.

"I see a bolt we missed." She walked over to the window and scooped it up.

She'd been thinking maybe two months wasn't too fast to fall in love with the right person.

"Matthew, look." She'd noticed the view from the window.

He came up behind her. He saw a slice of the ocean through a sparse forest of windblown trees. A golden sky.

"Isn't this incredible?" she asked.

"It is." Matthew slipped his arms around her waist. "Incredible."

The two stepped apart when Spence pounded on the door and barged in. "In five, kids. We'll pray and then we'll carve the turkey. We have a ton of food down there. What a blessed day this is." He left the door open.

Matthew watched him leave. Then he turned to Astra. "I saw a back exit."

"I saw five Jell-O salads on their counter."

"That's tempting, but dining with an army of little kids is not."

"You're right. How about this; we'll make Thanksgiving dinner at my house, just you and me. I have turkey hot dogs in the freezer."

"I have beer in my fridge."

"Budweiser?"

"Yep."

"Perfect. You don't think Spence will be offended if we slip out?"

"He won't even notice." Matthew grabbed her hand. "It's now or never."

They hurried down the stairs and sneaked out the back. They were laughing when they got to his car. Breathing in the crisp air.

Chapter 12

Astra showed Matthew the picture of the pecan pie on the lid. "Does this look good?"

He eyed it. "Sure does."

"They don't have chocolate walnut pies. I don't think I've ever seen one."

"This pie is perfect for our Thanksgiving feast." He took it out of her hand and tossed it in the cart.

"Did you see all the food those church ladies brought over to Spence's?" Astra asked. "A popcorn bowl full of mashed potatoes, big bags of rolls, five pies. Not good for Spence. He has a bit of a gut. His wife must make him goodies, too." Astra shut the freezer. "Did you catch his wife's name?"

Matthew shrugged. "Mommy-Mommy, I guess."

Astra laughed. "Those church women mistook me for her. Do I

look like a Mommy-Mommy?" Astra raised her eyebrows and pointed to herself.

He stopped and regarded her. "Not to me."

Astra felt herself blushing. She opened the freezer and grabbed a bag of vegetables.

"They called me sister," Astra said. "Those church women did. Strange, I thought, seeing that I'm not a nun."

Matthew put a value tub of frozen whipped topping in the cart. "Sister Astra. Hmm, it has a ring to it."

"Oh you think?" She struck a pious pose.

He was laughing. "Seriously, it's common for church folk to call one another brother and sister."

"You know about church folk?"

"It's not Thanksgiving without potatoes." Matthew chose a bag of extra crispy fries. "Will these do?"

Astra nodded and pushed the cart around the corner into the bread section. "Last on the list: hotdog buns. Mother says Spence's church is full of crazy people. But who is she to talk, right?"

Matthew saw an assortment of buns on the other side of the French bread and went after them.

Astra remembered the snake handling pastor Matthew turned in to the police. Talk about crazy church people, she thought.

A package of hotdog buns hit her in the chest and fell on the floor. She looked up and saw Matthew walking toward her, a lopsided grin.

"Hey, I wasn't ready," she said.

"Sorry about that," he said, but he was laughing. He bent over to pick up the package the same time she did.

He held one side. She held the other. "I'm glad we bumped into each other out on the pier this morning," Astra said.

He nodded. "I was feeling a little homesick, but this is turning out to be the best Thanksgiving."

"Mine too." Astra kissed him and they leaned into each other.

Mr. Finagle came around the corner pushing a cart loaded with boxes of stuffing and cans of pie filling and other items that had been marked down and he stopped and said hello to Sheriff Astra and she and Matthew stopped and greeted him.

There was one checkout line open and the clerk had gone after cigarettes for the woman who was first in line. Astra took the last item out of their cart, the hot dog buns they accidently squished, and put the bag on the conveyor. Mr. Finagle was behind them. She felt a little ridiculous when he barged into her private moment in the bread section, but she didn't care and this surprised her.

Matthew had noticed a newspaper next to the gum, and the lead article, "Exclusive Satellite Photos Reveal Image of Jesus on Five-acre Parcel in Kansas".

"Back home, folks say Spence's church is a cult," Matthew said and Astra looked at him, unsure why he'd brought up Spence's church again. Matthew went on. "But I figure he and anyone else ought to be free to believe what they believe."

"Huh. Even if what they believe in is illegal?"

"Well, Spence may be a little different, but I don't think what he believes is illegal."

"I was thinking about those snake handling churches. They're pretty crazy, right? And illegal. Should they be free to practice?"

"Snake handlers aren't necessarily crazy." Matthew picked up a package of sugarless gum and tossed it onto the conveyor. "Those folks who take up serpents are just practicing what they believe. The law can't stop them from believing."

"It's against the law for a reason. Who in their right mind would go to a church like that?"

"My family."

As soon as he said it, he wished he hadn't. What was he thinking?

He didn't want to talk about his family, especially not that aspect of it.

Astra's mouth had fallen open. He'd never seen her as befuddled. She asked him to repeat what he said.

"You heard me."

"Your family goes to church with snakes? Venomous killer snakes? Are you kidding me?"

The woman in line had turned completely around to listen. The clerk was trying to give her the cigarettes.

"Nope, I'm not kidding you. Naomi and my other sisters are in The Church of Believers With Signs Following. My parents took up serpents, my grandparents did. I come from a long line of believers."

Chapter 13

Matthew picked up the rock that was in the middle of Astra's coffee table. It was heavier than it appeared. He didn't remember seeing it the last time he was over. The rock didn't look like much, the size of a football, grey and chunky like concrete.

It hadn't been an hour, since he and Astra ate the whole pecan pie out of the foil pan it came in. He was right about the best Thanksgiving. In fact, this was the best day he'd had in a long time.

Astra came out of the kitchen carrying two crystal glasses. Good Boy and Hey Girl vying for a position beside her. She raised the glasses and the ice inside tinkled. Then she nodded toward the rock. "Ugly thing, isn't it?"

"People don't usually decorate with things they think are ugly." He set the rock on the table. Took the glasses and dumped the ice into the potted asparagus fern. "Bourbon is best drunk neat."

She would have preferred on the rocks, she never really liked bourbon. Matthew brought it over to serve after dinner. He still hadn't mentioned his family. Since the market and she characterized them as crazy and she felt bad about that.

"The finest bourbon is made in Kentucky." He poured her a glass and showed her how to warm it in her hands. He told her not to swirl. They sat side by side on the couch, between Good Boy and Hey Girl, and sipped.

When they stopped at Matthew's to pick up the Budweiser, he saw the bourbon on the counter and decided to bring it. Suzanne said bourbon wasn't for the weak or timid. She showed Matthew how to warm it in his hands. She'd left another message. He didn't listen to it in front of Astra, but he knew it was the message she left every day. "I won't stop calling until you talk to me."

She wouldn't talk to him before, why now? Did she want him to come home?

"Sweet and smooth as honey, like you said." Astra rested her bare feet on the table and leaned her head against his shoulder.

"I knew you'd have a taste for fine bourbon," he said. He stopped himself from saying fine bourbon wasn't for the weak or timid. He wouldn't go back to Suzanne if she asked.

"My taste in home decorating, however, is another story." She nudged the rock with her foot. "Mother gave this to me last night before she left town with Mr. Cooke."

Astra clinked her glass against Matthew's, finished off the bourbon, and set the glass next to the rock. She laid her hand on top of it. "I'd like you to meet my father, the asteroid."

Astra held the asteroid next to her face. "Do you see the resemblance?"

She'd picked up the asteroid more in the last twenty-four hours than she had in the thirty years her mother had it. She wondered if it was as close as she was going to get to a father.

After she introduced Matthew, she told him the whole ridiculous story, all the way back to her alien birth up to now and the lie her mother wouldn't stop telling. "Beats the stork, right?" Astra asked and he didn't laugh or even chuckle. He thanked her for telling him. He said he liked every alien part of her.

"If there's a resemblance, it's subtle," Matthew said. He was looking her up and down. He saw the smirk he'd come to know, the dimple it emphasized. The first three buttons of her blouse undone. "You're nothing like that rock."

"You're not just saying?"

"I'm not just saying." He took it out of her hands and set it aside. "You're much softer." He brushed his fingers across her cheeks. The length of her neck and he slipped them under her hair to a warm spot where he felt her spine. He started to kiss her.

Hey Girl nudged Astra in the hip and Good Boy woofed. Astra sighed and she and Matthew looked down at the dogs. They'd gone for their leashes. They held them in their mouths. Their big friendly eyes, drool.

Astra shrugged. "It's time for their walk. We walk every night before bed."

Matthew crouched next to Hey Girl and ruffled her fur. "After all that pecan pie, a walk would do me good. What do you say, may I come along?"

Hey Girl licked Matthew's face. Astra smiled. Hey Girl was an excellent judge of character. She didn't lick just any guy.

It wasn't long before they were ready. The dogs waited at the front door. Astra pulled on her rain boots. She checked her pockets for plastic bags.

"You'd better zip up." She grabbed one side of Matthew's coat and then the other. "It's chilly outside." She pulled him close and he kissed her, a kiss without thinking.

Fog was rolling in. The night air chilly, like Astra said it would be. Hey Girl and Good Boy stopped and sniffed things along the way.

"I thought Mother would take that stupid rock to her grave," Astra said. "All these years, it's been her, the rock and the house. The three inseparable and now I'm stuck with the rock and she's gone off with her boyfriend."

Good Boy stopped in front of John's Junk and started peeing on the reader board. Jesus Saves.

"Does this mean she's giving up on the house?" Matthew asked.

"Giving up the rock isn't giving up the house."

"She wanted me to help save her house. My first week in town, she invited me to lunch at Angelo's. She asked me then and said not to tell you."

The streetlight cast a fuzzy glow. Across the road, boats anchored in the slips, creaked and knocked against the docks. Astra stared ahead.

"Maggie was confident if I found the owner of Oak Enterprises, she could talk him out of the interpretive center deal. I told her I couldn't help and then I forgot about it. Until recently, I discovered the FishWrap is owned by Oak Enterprises."

Astra turned her head. "Mother's Oak Enterprises?"

"That's right. Oak Enterprises, the corporation that's financing the interpretive center also owns the FishWrap Bugle."

"What do you make of that?" Astra handed Matthew a plastic bag and nodded toward Hey Girl.

"I didn't know what to make of it."

"So naturally, you investigated."

"Yep and I came to the same dead-end that stopped your mom's private investigator. Delaware is a state where disclosure of stockholder names isn't required." He scooped and tied the bag and handed it to Astra.

"Maybe you aren't the super investigator hero we all thought you were."

"I've been saying. As far as the FishWrap interpretive center connection, Oak owns them, and if there's more of a connection, I couldn't find it. Case closed."

"Did you tell Mother?" Astra tossed the doggie bag into John's dumpster.

"I told her a few days ago. She didn't take the news badly. I was kind of surprised."

Matthew thought about the kiss. Astra said next time they would pick up where they left off. Next time, Matthew was thinking, next time could be tonight.

They'd been walking for a while. The dogs sauntering, Matthew with his arm wrapped around Astra. The cold didn't matter.

He was glad he told her the truth about what her mom asked him to do. He understood how Astra felt about secrets and liars. He wasn't a liar. He'd tell her about Suzanne. He just had to figure out how.

For now, it was time he explained his family. The part of them he meant to leave back in Kentucky. He supposed it was right to tell Astra though, considering she'd told him all about her alien-ness. But that didn't make dredging up the past easier.

"You know back at the market?" he asked and she looked at him. "It's not easy talking about my family. I know firsthand how it is to be an alien."

Astra stopped and Hey Girl bumped into Good Boy. "I'm so sorry I called your family crazy," she said. "I didn't mean them. I'm sure they aren't. If I'd known, I wouldn't. I mean, they must be very nice people."

She reached for Matthew's hands. They were so cold. "Wait, did you say you're an alien?"

"Let's keep walking." He blew warm air into his hands. "I'm not offended and yep, I did say I was an alien."

He pulled in a deep breath to get started and the cold burned inside his nose.

"It's not much of a story, really," he said and sniffed. She nodded for him to go on.

"All right. I'd never been outside of the holler until my aunt moved me to her apartment in the city. I was awkward, naïve and I had a real thick accent. Wasn't long before kids at school found out my family took up serpents and I found my coat pockets stuffed with worm snakes."

A shiver ran up and down Matthew's back and it wasn't from the cold.

"How awful. Kids can be so mean."

Matthew nodded. He remembered how fast his hands came out of the pockets, the coat on the ground and the little pink-bellied snakes wriggling on the floor. That day was the first he'd ever felt the skin of a snake or seen its eyes up close. He looked over at Astra. She had a disgusted look on her face.

"Yep, a whole new world and I was an alien in it," he said. "I learned how to fend for myself. My aunt looked the other way if I punched a kid for talking trash about my family. She believed in loyalty to your kin, no matter what they did to you."

He thought of Suzanne's family and how they treated him like one of their own after Aunt Vicky died his first year in college.

A cat darted across the street and Good Boy barked and tugged on his leash. Any other time, Astra would have scolded him, but she was thinking about loyalty. She remembered the night at the hospital when Matthew said he owed it to the men who beat him up. Loyalty, no matter what your family did to you?

"Are you related to the snake handling pastor?"

Matthew looked at her.

"The pastor who was arrested, was he family? Him or one of his partners, were they kin?"

"Uh. Well, uh."

She waited.

"No, not exactly related, not blood related," Matthew said and he breathed a bit easier. "In the faith, we're all family."

"Those men went to your church."

"Yep."

"The snake handling pastor was your pastor?"

He nodded.

"Huh –"

Matthew lengthened his stride and Astra hurried to catch up. She remembered him saying that turning in those men was a difficult choice to make, and that by doing it, he'd put a lot at stake. She wondered if he lost it, whatever it was he put at stake.

They walked without talking. Matthew focused on the sidewalk, the rhythm of the dogs. Questions whirled in Astra's head.

"Don't people who take up serpents get bit?" she asked.

Matthew sighed. "Yeah. Uh. Some. Some do. People get bit sometimes."

He wished Astra would stop asking questions. But then, he was the one who got her started. Of course she had questions, who wouldn't?

Matthew cleared his throat. "I was scared of snakes. At church meetings, when they came out of the boxes, I tried not to let on, but my insides shaking gave me away. I still don't like snakes much."

Astra thought of shoving her hands into her pockets and finding slithery nasty snakes in them. "Snakes aren't very likable creatures."

Matthew agreed. "My sisters teased me something awful. But Dad said not to worry, because when I grew up, God would give me the power to take up serpents and I'd have nothing more to fear."

"You wanted to?"

"It's not a matter of wanting to." Matthew stopped and turned up his coat collar. Hey Girl whined and licked his hand and he scratched behind her ears. "Believers do what God says and He gives them power. It's in the Bible."

He thought of his dad's strong hands, and he wasn't a large man, but when he pulled Matthew into a tight hug, Matthew felt like he could do just about anything.

They crossed the road diagonally. Half past nine and the businesses were closed, not a car in sight. A street over, waves were pounding the boardwalk.

Astra didn't know what to say. This new side of Matthew rivaled her alien-ness, she would have never guessed. He knew the Bible. She'd never owned one.

She offered him a Kleenex she found in her pocket and he blew his nose.

"Are the snakes a test?" she asked. "If you believe, you survive, and if you don't, then too bad for you?"

Matthew breathed in and then out. "Some folks think so."

"Did you ever take up serpents?"

He remembered his dad, two rattlers around his neck.

He shook his head. "Nope, not me. Kids aren't allowed."

He remembered tambourines, the floor vibrating. He remembered sweat and stumbling and falling down.

"Why did you go live with your aunt?"

Matthew blew his nose and made shivery sounds.

Astra realized she was asking too many questions, grilling him like he was a criminal. She looped her arm through his. "I think you're ready for a fire and a hot apple cider." She felt him relax. He said he was.

They waited for the dogs to finish sniffing the empty flower box in front of the bakery. Then they turned around, the wind on their backs.

A raindrop plopped onto Astra's cheek and she wiped it off.

"Rain," he said.

"A stray drop is all."

"I went to live with my aunt because she didn't want me growing up in the church that killed her brother."

Astra looked at Matthew. "The church killed her brother?"

He nodded. "Snakebite."

"Oh. I see. Was her brother your dad?"

"Yep, my dad. A big rattler came up out of its crate when he opened it. Bit him on the hand. That rattler was swift, I didn't see it bite him and I was right there, standing off to the side where the children were supposed to stay-put."

Matthew and Suzanne and a few other kids he didn't remember. Somebody, Suzanne's dad maybe, made her and Matthew go sit in the back of the church. Matthew's dad was on the floor by then and church folk were gathering around him. People were praying.

"Couldn't the medics do anything for him?"

"No one called them. Dad lived his life by the signs. The pastor said praying was all he needed."

"Everyone, including your mother, believed that?"

Matthew didn't remember his mom, not her eyes or her dress, only her sound, a low wail rising to a pitch he was surprised didn't break windows.

"I should have called for help when no one else did, or pushed through their prayer circle. I don't know. Maybe I could have convinced Dad to go to the hospital."

"You were just a little boy."

He shrugged. He'd never told anyone. Astra was the first. He looked over at her and she squeezed his arm.

"Dad died nine hours later. He suffered. The pastor said God means us to suffer. My sister said it was Dad's time. He's in a better place, most folks said. A handful believed it was a sign he wasn't living right."

Astra felt her cheeks heat up. How could they not call in the medics and then blame his dad for not living right?

A few raindrops came down on her head. She tugged on Matthew's arm. "From one alien to another, I know how painful it was to tell me."

"Thanks, I've never had another alien to talk to."

He'd never talked to anyone like that. He wondered if it was the way people in love talked.

"Aliens understand each other," Astra said. She held out her fist and he bumped his against hers.

Matthew stopped at the crosswalk light. Astra laughed and took his hand and pulled him across the street before the light changed. She'd been thinking about the kiss.

"I'm going to put Hey Girl and Good Boy to bed first thing," she said. "They wouldn't mind if you stayed over."

"I'm not surprised. Dogs usually take a liking to me."

She poked him in the arm. "Well, Mr. Charles, I've taken a liking to you too and I'm inviting you to stay."

"I'd like that."

He was glad he'd put all those family matters out in the open. Well, most of them. He'd call Suzanne. Make sure she filled out the papers right and had them in order. He should have done it months ago.

Now it started to rain. About three blocks from home and the clouds opened. A drencher and Matthew and Astra were soaked through before they thought to run.

Chapter 14

Matthew finished the beer Maggie gave him and set the empty on the floor next to Astra's.

He stood and offered his hand. "You're beautiful when you heft boxes. Let's get back to work."

Astra, slumped on the couch, didn't budge. She'd volunteered her and Matthew's services. This after she discovered her mother had signed the agreement with the county. A whole new perspective was the reason she gave. Whatever the reason, Astra was happy to help move her out.

She reached for Matthew's hand and pulled him on top of her.

"Break time isn't over." She held him there and kissed him.

They'd spent little time apart since Thanksgiving night. Now it was January and she wondered if time swiftly passing was a sign they were in love or just time passing.

They'd been carrying boxes all morning, sorting and labeling and it wasn't easy with the numbering system Maggie thought up. Matthew couldn't keep the ones and twos straight and had put a few items Maggie deemed important into the dumpster instead of the portable storage container the you-pack, we-store place, dropped off.

"The ones are throw and the twos are stow, how hard is that?" Maggie asked Matthew.

"And three is, I don't know, right?"

"No. Three is giveaway. See, if an item is too good to throw and I don't want it to stow, then it's three, a giveaway. Four is, I don't know, until I figure out what to do with it and then it will become a one, two or three, get it?"

That was when Matthew asked for the beer.

"Oh, excuse me, so sorry for intruding," Maggie said.

Astra pushed Matthew off.

Good Boy and Hey Girl had followed Maggie downstairs and they trotted past her, over to the couch, happy to see Astra and Matthew.

Maggie wasn't surprised they didn't hear her coming. She pulled a stray hair off her sweater and looked for others while they put themselves back together.

Then she held out a shoebox. "I wanted to show you this. I had no idea you were –"

"We weren't." Astra sat up straighter and glanced over at Matthew. He was straightening the back of his shirt. Astra felt like a fifteen year old.

"You asked about these a couple months ago. I knew I'd come across them eventually. I thought you and Matthew would have fun going through the box together."

"What's in it?" Astra reached for it and Maggie handed it to Matthew and turned to leave.

"Oh, should I knock on a box next time I come down?" Maggie asked before she headed upstairs, but Astra didn't hear. She was grabbing for the shoebox. Matthew wouldn't let her have it. He'd seen the words written on the lid in permanent marker, same as she had. He took the rubber band off. "Maggie wanted us both to look at these."

Astra folded her arms and pouted.

He picked out a photo and wouldn't let her see it.

She sighed loudly.

"Well, look here, three year old Astra." He held it next to her face. "You do resemble this beautiful little redhead here. No mistaking, that pouty face hasn't changed in twenty-seven years."

Astra took it out of his hand and studied it. "I think you are mistaken; this child is clearly ill-tempered and obstinate, and is lacking my charm and sweet disposition." She burst out laughing.

There wasn't anyone Matthew would rather be with. He'd been thinking about this since Thanksgiving.

"Astra, I'm in love with you."

She hadn't finished laughing and she didn't hear what he said. He'd timed it badly. But he'd already said it and he meant it. He held her by the shoulders. "I love you."

They picked through the pictures in the shoebox. Matthew's arm around Astra and they were both slumped on the couch and they couldn't stop laughing.

He surprised her, telling her the way he did. She didn't say I love you right back. She thought she ought to consider such a serious affirmation, though she'd considered it every day since Thanksgiving. Still.

She let him hold her shoulders. Let him say it again. Let the feeling wash over. There wasn't anyone she'd rather be with and she said so. She loved him. She knew for sure. This was the happiest Astra had ever been.

"Hey, look at this picture," Matthew said. "You never said you had a Newfie when you were a kid."

"I didn't."

She looked closer. Five years old, according to her mother's handwriting, and she was sitting in a red cart hitched to a Newfie, an all-black one that made Good Boy look rather small.

Astra scratched Good Boy with her foot. "I don't remember this, but the kid in the picture is me, all right. Isn't this Newf a beautiful dog?"

"Yep, sure is. Who's the guy?"

A man crouched next to the cart, his hand on Astra's shoulder.

"He lived next door. I was scared of his wife. I don't remember the Newfie. How could I not remember a dog as grand as this one?"

"You were only five. There's no house next door now. What happened to it?"

"Burned to the ground. Mother said he died in the fire. Oh, I hope his Newfie was all right."

"Dogs are smart enough to get out of a burning building."

"A Newfoundland would stay and try to save everyone inside. Newfies are brave like that."

Matthew hugged Astra closer. "Maybe your mom knows what happened. That's too bad about your neighbor. He's squinting here, but he looks mighty happy. Look at his hair. It's as red as yours."

Matthew went back to looking at pictures, but Astra couldn't stop looking at this one.

"Yes, Ray had a Newfoundland, a sweet and friendly dog, like Good Boy and Hey Girl." Maggie smiled at the picture.

"Why didn't you tell me there'd been a Newfie in my life?" Astra asked. Good Boy and Hey Girl were lying together at the foot of Maggie's bed. Astra and Matthew were sitting on it, the shoebox in Astra's lap.

"I didn't think to, I guess." Maggie tapped her fingernail on the picture. "Ray hitched his dog to the cart often, and he'd haul whatever Ray put in it, including you. Ray died in the fire not long after this was taken. We'd always been neighbors. I'd known him all my life."

"I'm sorry," Matthew said. "It's tough, coming to terms with an untimely death. Did they know what caused the fire?"

"Faulty wiring, the stove, they didn't know for sure, that house was older than mine."

"Mother, his Newf didn't die in the fire, did he?"

"Oh no, Ray's wife left with the dog that afternoon and was on her way to eastern Oregon to drop it off at a breeder's. For stud service, Ray planned on giving you one of the puppies. His wife must have taken it. She was a surly and disagreeable woman. Were there other pictures of

Ray?"

Astra and Matthew didn't remember seeing any. Astra turned the box upside-down and they spread out the pictures.

"Ray and his wife babysat you when I was working nights. Ray would take you outside and show you the stars."

"Oh." Astra thought back. "I remember that. We looked for Gemini. Yes, he said the twins were on the right side of the moon. Look for two bright stars."

"He had an interest in the stars. The night of the fire, you were supposed to be over at his place, but I wasn't feeling well, a stomach bug or something and I called in sick. I'm so glad I did."

A shiver went up Astra's spine. "You never told me."

Maggie kissed Astra on top of the head. "I didn't think to." She walked over to the dresser and laid the photo on top of it.

"What's this doing in with the pictures?" Matthew placed a small stone in Astra's palm.

"Is this grey rock special?" Astra held it out to show her mother.

Maggie was bent over the dresser looking at the photo.

"Mother?"

Maggie turned and saw Astra's hand extended. She sat next to her on the bed. Took the stone and turned it over and around. "Curious, if you look close, you'll see it isn't all grey." Maggie pointed out the green in it.

"It's real pretty," Matthew said.

Astra shrugged. "Why was it in the shoebox?"

"I don't know," Maggie said.

"You don't know?"

"It is a lovely stone." Maggie closed her hand over it.

Astra watched her mother walk over to her dresser. Open the panty drawer and open her hand. She tipped her palm and the rock dropped inside and she put the photo in after, Astra and the neighbor. She covered them with a handful of panties, pink and lacey and sheer.

Chapter 15

Miriam admired the perfect shape of the four poppy seed muffins. Topped with a bit of lemon zest mixed with sugar, they were the precise color of doneness. She baked them for Jim Conroy.

She checked the clock. He called yesterday and said he'd drop by the FishWrap at ten to see her. He wanted an astrological reading and she was excited. She'd wanted to do his reading for ages, a reading and zodiac love chart. She was a Pisces and Jim an Aquarius, an ideal love match. She couldn't wait to show him. She smoothed her dress, the green, green being her most excellent color, the perfect amount of cleavage. The zodiac could turn his heart. Finally open his eyes and see she is the woman for him, not Astra Billings.

Jim showed up at work early. Couldn't sleep, he'd been thinking about his appointment with Miriam. Miriam knew her signs and ruling planets, all that crap and she read your future and mapped out love charts for free. Jim's eye was twitching and he'd given up trying to stop it. He should have made the appointment for earlier. He was in a time crunch. The sooner he got Miriam working on his and Astra's love chart, the better.

He wasn't stupid. He had eyes. He'd seen Astra and Mr. FishWrap, why, they acted as if they were alone on the planet. Jim had to stop them before they announced an engagement.

Jim was a man of his word. When he told Astra he'd never give up on her, he meant it. He had his game plan. An official astrological report was the evidence he needed. The proof was in the stars. All he had to do was show her. She'd listen, she was her mother's daughter, after-all and came with the same inherent belief in the workings of the cosmos.

Jim gazed into Astra's office. She was rubbing her eyes. When she came in this morning, he recommended a good eight hours of sleep every night or else she'd come down with a winter cold and she told him to mind his own business.

Astra reset the alarm for Matthew this morning. She left at the normal time, but he'd worked long after midnight and planned on going in at ten. She thought she'd walk over to the FishWrap around then. He felt the onset of a cold last night and she wanted to see how he was feeling and while she was there, she'd take him into the back and kiss him good-morning. Astra smiled and checked the time.

Matthew heard the alarm and shut it off. He felt better than he did when he went to bed. The mega-dose of vitamin C Astra made him take must have done the job. He rolled over to wrap his arms around her and kiss her good-morning and found cold sheets and No-Name asleep on her pillow. Matthew looked at the time. She'd been gone for a few hours. Good Boy woofed and Matthew said to give him another minute. Later, Good Boy and Hey Girl jumped on the bed and licked Matthew and No-Name awake.

Miriam finished her coffee. Time was dragging, the muffins getting staler by the minute. The morning had been quiet and only a handful of employees had come in. Matthew left a note to let her know he'd be late. He was a nice guy, genuine and considerate, so true for a Cancer, a nurturing and understanding soul. Cancers can be vulnerable though; he sure was when he let Astra get her claws into him. Too bad for him, Astra was a Gemini, a perfect example of her sign, with that two-sided personality. She'd end up breaking Matthew's heart same as she broke Jim's.

Jim had a big smile on his face when he walked into the FishWrap. He saw Miriam behind the counter smiling back and he thought what a good bud she was. Always had been and Jim was excited to let her in on his game plan.

She said good morning and waved her hand over the muffins. "I made these for us and there's a fresh pot of coffee in the break room. We can talk in there."

He wanted to get down to business now, the whole reason he came in, but the muffins. He removed his hat and went around the counter. He thanked her for the muffins.

The front door swung open, the bell jangled. Miriam handed Jim the muffins and told him to go on back and get himself a cup of coffee and she'd join him as soon as she took care of the customer.

Jim wasn't listening. He stared at the woman standing in the entryway. She was unbuttoning her coat and revealing a generous amount of cleavage. He set the plate of muffins on the counter and grinned.

"What do you want?" Miriam asked the woman. Then she looked sideways at Jim and scowled.

The woman scanned the office. "If y'all don't mind getting Matthew, I'd appreciate it very much."

Miriam noticed the accent. She noticed lips, cheekbones, red gaudy jewelry.

"Excuse me?" the woman asked. "This is the FishWrap Bugle, isn't it?"

"Yes, it is indeed. I'm James Conroy, Sheriff's Department, nice to meet you." He was all teeth and gums. He extended his hand.

She did not smile. She called him officer and shook his hand in one quick motion.

"Excuse me. I'll handle this, Jim." Miriam glared at him. Then she turned to the woman. "Matthew should be in any minute now. If you want to wait, feel free." Miriam pointed to the beat up chair no customer ever sits in. "Or, leave your name, number and a message." Miriam pushed a message pad and a pencil across the counter.

"Fine." She scribbled on the pad and pushed it back to Miriam. "This is urgent business. Be sure and give this to him the second he walks in the door."

Miriam looked at the message. The Half Moon Inn was all the woman wrote.

"Who should I say was asking for him?" Miriam pushed the message pad back to the woman.

"Oh, sorry about that, I'm a little bit jet-lagged, I guess. Matthew has my cell number and my name is Suzanne." She wrote her name. "Suzanne Charles."

"Oh." Miriam was taken aback. "Matthew didn't mention a sister coming to visit."

"No, ma'am, I'm not his sister. I'm Mrs. Charles, his wife."

Miriam stared.

A smile played on Jim's lips. His game plan had been turned upside-down. He had a new one now and the odds were stacked in his favor.

A woman was leaving the FishWrap office the same time Astra opened the door to go inside. Astra held the door and the woman thanked her. Something struck Astra as familiar. She slid her sunglasses down her nose and watched the stranger walk away. Blonde curls, long legs, spiked heels. Astra wondered who this woman was visiting.

Astra entered the FishWrap thinking about the woman. Overdressed and breasts out of proportion.

Miriam was standing at the counter, same as always. Deputy Conroy beside her, a plate of muffins.

Astra glanced over at Matthew's desk. He hadn't come in yet. She was disappointed.

"If you don't mind telling Matthew I came by?"

Miriam didn't answer.

"Miriam?"

"You aren't the only one looking for Matthew today," Conroy said and sauntered out from behind the desk. "The woman you passed on your way in was too. Maybe you ought to sit down, Astra." He touched her elbow and nodded toward the beat up chair.

"I don't want to sit down." Astra drew her elbow close to her side. "What is this about?"

"His wife." Miriam's jaw set and she waved the pad the message was still attached to. "He has a wife. She came in looking for him. She was his wife; it's all here in the message." Miriam slammed the pad down on the counter.

"Who are you talking about?" Astra asked. "Who has a wife?"

Astra heard the door open, the bell jangle.

"He does. He has a wife." Conroy pointed.

Astra turned and the door shut behind Matthew.

Matthew smiled when he saw Astra inside. He missed waking up to her this morning. He was thinking about taking her into the back and kissing her when he pushed open the door, heard the jangle.

The door shut behind him and he stopped smiling.

Conroy was pointing, Miriam coming out from behind the counter. In an uproar that seemed to be directed at him.

Astra looked from Conroy to Miriam and back, her face all confused. Matthew reached for her shoulders and she stepped back into the counter.

"What's going on?" Matthew asked Astra.

"I don't know. They said that woman came in looking for you."

"What woman? Who's looking for me?"

The pink pad, Astra saw it, the message Miriam said was from Mrs. Charles. Astra ripped off the message and read it.

"Is this true?"

"Is what true? What is that?"

"This, Matthew, is this Suzanne Charles your wife?"

Matthew felt like he'd been punched in the face. He couldn't speak. He couldn't think.

"You missed your wife by a couple of minutes," Miriam said. "She's checked in at the Half Moon. It's in the message."

Matthew talked to Suzanne last week and she said she'd draw up the property settlement agreement and fax it for his approval. Why had she come all this way?

"Wait y'all, this is a bad misunderstanding," Matthew said.

"Tell me how this is a misunderstanding." Astra held out the message. Her hands were shaking.

Matthew wanted to take them into his own and tell her she was the one he loved.

"Take it," Astra shouted.

He took the message. There in pencil, in his wife's handwriting was her name all spelled out, Suzanne Charles.

"I can explain. I've been trying to get a divorce for the last year. I started the process long before I met you. And now the divorce is real close to being final. Come outside and talk to me. I'll tell you everything."

"She doesn't want to talk to you," Conroy said.

"Shut-up, Deputy," Astra said. "So, Matthew, this is true. She is your wife. You're married."

"Well, technically, I guess, but –"

"You lied to me, Mr. Charles."

"Let me explain. Please, I can explain."

"You had all these months to explain." Astra shoved him and he stumbled backwards into the chair no customer ever sits in.

Chapter 16

Good Boy and Hey Girl waited at the front door for Matthew. "He isn't coming home," I said. "Except to pick up No-Name, I suppose, and then they're both leaving and neither will be back."

The dogs whined and huddled closer to the door.

And I wished this day never happened.

Matthew followed me from the FishWrap over to my office. "Don't you hate when someone lies to you?" I shouted when he caught up and tried to explain.

He was still trying to explain as my office door was shutting behind me. Inside, I walked through a sea of people all doing their jobs, carrying on, and I busied myself wading through papers I should have filed months ago. When it was time to leave, I had trouble zipping my coat, locking my office door. On most days, Matthew and I went home together. On the way, we'd pick up Good Boy and Hey Girl at Mrs. Phillip's. We'd play ball with them before dinner.

I picked up their favorite ball. "Let's play." I tossed it and they watched it bounce off the door. "Come on you two, play with me. Please play with me." I went after it and threw it again and they trotted over to the window and looked out.

No-Name came out of nowhere and I scratched under his chin. "I'm going to miss you." He head-butted me and wandered off.

I kneeled between the dogs and hugged their necks. "I know you love Matthew. You love his cat. I know. It's okay to feel bad. I feel bad too. Real bad."

All the tears I'd been working to hold back escaped then, a wet explosion.

I don't know how much time passed, before the dogs nudged me and made a fuss. My cell phone was ringing.

"I know who it is and I don't want to talk to him," I said and wiped my face on my sleeve. "I can't talk to him. Okay? How about some dinner, you two? Come on; let's see what there is to eat."

I opened the fridge and we stared inside. I didn't remember it looking as empty as it did. There was half of a shriveled up grapefruit on the top shelf next to the soy milk. We heard knocking and the dogs raced to the door to see who it was. I guessed those guys from Spence's church. They liked to show up at dinnertime. They never rang the bell, they knocked.

Matthew had been sending them away. He was always polite to them.

They weren't going away. Good Boy was woofing. So I'd tell them to get lost. I shut the fridge and went to the door.

"Hi," Matthew said the same time he stuck his foot inside. "Please talk to me."

Hey Girl and Good Boy pushed me out of the way and Matthew loved them up the way he does.

"Same time my investigative piece came out in the paper, my father-in-law was arrested for animal trafficking and assault," Matthew said. "Suzanne walked out on me soon as she got the news. She was loyal to her daddy. Fact is, he convinced her to marry me in the first place. Thinking we'd have a family and get back to living by the signs. As it turned out, I wasn't the loyal husband Suzanne or her daddy thought I was."

We were sitting on the porch steps in the dark, me at the top, and Matthew down a few. When the dogs got insistent, he'd toss the ball out into the yard.

"So it was your marriage you put at stake by going to the police," I said. "You came out with the truth when you had everything to lose. Why couldn't you be honest with me? You had nothing to lose with me.

I would have understood. I thought you were a man of integrity." My eyes were filling up with tears. "I trusted you. I thought I knew you." I sniffed and gulped and checked my jacket pockets for tissue.

"I'm sorry." He was shaking his head. "I didn't know how to tell you. Suzanne and I were over long before I met you. She was supposed to be getting one of those do-it-yourself divorces. When I left Kentucky, she said she was on top of it and the divorce would be final in the next month or two. Come to find out, she'd missed filing dates and filled out the wrong papers. I'm sorry; you know how hard talking about the past is."

"I'm not worth the effort?"

"You are. I love you. That's why I've been on the phone with Suzanne since Thanksgiving trying to push the divorce through."

"Yeah, and you've been keeping it all a big secret."

He stared off into the yard and Good Boy picked up the ball and brought it over.

"We've been sorting through the legal papers." He threw the ball and Good Boy took off. "Last thing to do was come up with an equitable division of the property. We came to an agreement and she said she'd fax it."

"Then why is she here?"

"She wants closure. She brought the papers with her."

"She's stalling. Have you thought maybe she wants you back?"

I thought of the woman I held the door for. All dressed up at ten in the morning.

"I want you, I love you. I'm meeting Suzanne at Beacon Coffee at seven."

"Beacon Coffee, huh? Beacon Coffee and Wine is what the place is called. You say you want a divorce, but you're having drinks with your wife?"

"No, we're not meeting for drinks. She picked the restaurant. And she's not my wife, not really. I'll sign off on the agreement and she'll take it back home and file it with the court. Then it will be all over and I'll be legally divorced."

"She left you. Do you still have feelings for her?"

"No. I want you in my future. I hope you'll give me another chance."

He waited for my answer. I said nothing.

"Okay. I have to go now. I want to get this over with." He noticed No-Name in the window. "I'll come back for him tonight, after the meeting. Maybe you and I could talk then."

He didn't get up to leave. He set his eyes on me. The eyes I loved waking up to.

"Please, let me make it up to you," he said.

"Come pick up No-Name in the morning after I go to work. You go to your meeting now. Don't call me until you're through keeping secrets."

Chapter 17

Matthew saw Suzanne across the coffee shop. Sitting at the tall round table where he and Astra sit when they meet for morning coffee.

Suzanne was sipping wine. He saw a bottle, a second wineglass. He saw her hair down the way he liked. The way he used to like. Matthew's stomach was one big knot.

She raised her glass when she saw him. Left it on the table and met him half way. "Seems like an eternity since I laid my eyes on you." She embraced him.

"Let's get this over with."

She was dressed fancy in her high heels and jewelry, a little dress.

"Least you can do is say hello." She looped her arm through his.

"Hello, Suzanne."

He waited until she was seated and then he sat beside her.

She poured him a glass. “I remembered you prefer red.”

“I didn’t come here to socialize. I want to see the agreement.”

“Relax, you just got here.”

He smelled her perfume, the same sweet fragrance. The wine was deep red. A little wine would help him relax.

Suzanne leaned on her elbows and smiled. “You’re looking good.”

“Thanks.”

“Aside the fact you lost weight. You ate home cooking every day we were together. Remember? You always said I made the best chicken and dumplings.”

“You left me. Remember?”

Her brothers called him Judas. He remembered how it felt to have a shotgun pointed at his head.

He checked his watch; he hadn’t been at Beacon’s a half hour. “Let me have a look at the agreement now.”

“First, tell me, how’s Bartholomew? I miss the little guy. Sorry about leaving him the way I did. Greg doesn’t like cats and Mama sneezed anytime he got near. I knew you’d treat him kindly.”

“Yeah, thanks a lot. He was a monster traveling out here.”

Matthew didn’t mention that he and No-Name had become good friends.

“Well, thank you for taking care of him.”

They were interrupted by the waiter. “Matthew? What brings you in here after noon?” She looked Suzanne up and down.

“Uh – drinks. The merlot’s good.”

“It is, isn’t it? Missed you and Sheriff Billings this morning, I had your coffees started. Hope all’s well. So what can I get you folks to eat? The hummus platter is good.”

Suzanne made a face. “Hummus? Do you serve real food here?”

“We won’t be eating,” Matthew said. “If you don’t mind bringing the check, I’d appreciate it.”

"Will do."

Suzanne watched her walk away. "Did you see the shredded jeans that woman had on? I wouldn't leave the house wearing those, much less go to work in them."

"She's the owner. People don't dress up much around here."

Suzanne poured wine into his glass. "I met your sheriff this morning."

"You met the sheriff?"

Astra hadn't mentioned it.

"Tall and muscled but he struck me as not too bright."

"Oh." Matthew nodded. "You got that right."

The waiter left the check. "Take your time, you two."

"Don't need time, thanks." Matthew handed her his credit card and then he turned to Suzanne. "Let's get to the agreement now."

"Your newspaper office doesn't look like much; you must have taken a hefty pay cut. You got to miss the city."

"I don't miss it. This place suits me fine. The FishWrap is a good place to work."

"Well, aren't you the lucky one. Wish I could say the same. I got on half time at the drive-through market. Pay's lousy. I hate it. All my friends have moved away for jobs. Don't know how much longer I can stand it at Daddy's. You know, after living in the city with you for so long, and now the most exciting thing around town is watching those crab apples drop off Daddy's trees. He's getting out of jail real soon. Says for anyone living under his roof, church going will be required. Greg and John have been on me about it, making a big deal every Sunday when they and Mama go. No way in hell am I going back to that church. I'm so sick of them bossing me."

"What do you want me to say?"

She poured Matthew the last glass of wine. "All gone. If the factory hadn't closed and stole Daddy's pension and laid him off with no insurance, he wouldn't of got mixed up in selling those animals over the internet. It was only to get him by until he found a decent job. You can't blame a man for trying to earn a living. Daddy's a good man. He always treated you right and you went and paid him back with disloyalty."

"Was he treating me right when he stood by watching while his buddies beat the life out of me?"

"He tried to make them stop and he drove you to the hospital."

"And left me on the sidewalk with a death threat over my head. Look, Suzanne. Lots of folks are bad off these days and I'm real sorry about your daddy. It's true what you said; he and your mama were kind to me after Aunt Vicky died. But blind loyalty isn't something kin ought to expect in return. Speaking of loyalty, you weren't much of a loyal wife. It may have taken seven years of being married to you to open my eyes, but they're open now and I'm mighty grateful."

Suzanne stared into her glass. "I know you were hurt when I left. I did what I believed was right."

"Well, I sure do appreciate knowing that."

He had no feelings left for her. He was sure of it.

"We had some good times, you and me," she said. "You got to admit."

He raised his glass. "Here's to moving on. Here's to closure."

Matthew had never been inside the Half Moon Inn. Dingy motel room and it reeked of stale cigarettes. Suzanne claimed she accidently left the agreement behind in her suitcase. He didn't believe it. He knew he shouldn't be here.

"I wrote up the property division like we talked about." She was bent over the suitcase trying to find it.

"Good, then I won't be long looking at it."

She always liked wearing the little dresses. Liked how he looked at her when she did. He was looking at her now. He shouldn't be. He saw legs. He saw thighs. He saw a little bit of satiny red.

"I don't know why you couldn't have just faxed the agreement." He studied the check-out rules posted on the door.

"Closure." She was holding a manila envelope.

Matthew was relieved.

She took out the contents and laid the papers on the dresser, found a pen in her purse. "Here you go, take as long as you like." She stepped to the side.

He barely got a glimpse of the document before she took the pen out of his hand and slipped her hands around his waist.

"Don't sign it yet." She untucked his shirt.

"That's not what I came here for."

"I want to. It's okay, we're still married."

She was unbuttoning his shirt, kissing down his chest.

"No. This is wrong." He stepped back. "We're over. I told you."

She stayed with him. Unbuckled his belt, unzipped his jeans. The little dress slid off her body and dropped to the floor.

Someone knocked on the door.

"Who is that?" Matthew asked.

"Nobody, they got the wrong room."

She guided his hands to the red satin, pressed her body against his. "You want this as much as I do."

Another round of knocking and she told them to go away. They didn't.

"Are you expecting someone?" Matthew started buttoning his shirt.

"I don't know anybody around here, but you. No need to button, I'll get rid of them."

He told her to put on the dress, but she was already opening the door.

He continued to button his shirt. He didn't know how this had gone so far, so fast. He wasn't buttoning very well. He zipped his jeans.

"How'd y'all find me?" Suzanne asked. The door was open as far as the flimsy chain allowed and she was peering out.

"Who's out there?" Matthew asked.

"You got that Judas in there with you? Open up right now, Suzanne."

Now Matthew knew who was on the other side of the door.

"You and John had no business following me out here telling me what to do. I'm not letting you in."

"She doesn't want to talk to you," Matthew said. "Y'all better turn around and head home."

Matthew told Suzanne to get away from the door same time the door came off the hinges and the chain ripped out of the wall. Suzanne screamed and her brothers barged inside.

"Looks to me like we got here just in time," Greg said and John took a swing at Matthew and he ducked.

"Don't hurt him. He hasn't done anything wrong," Suzanne said.

"Stay out of this," John said. "And put some clothes on, for God sake."

"Come on, we can be civil here," Matthew said. "Let's sit down and talk about this."

"Nothing to talk about," Greg said. "We gave you fair warning. But you just couldn't keep your paws off our sister, could you?"

"All we're doing here is the paperwork that will make our split final," Matthew said. "If y'all would just leave us to it, I'll be out of here in five."

"You're a liar, Judas and you know God despises liars."

"He's not lying. I brought him here to sign the papers, like he said." Suzanne had picked up a damp towel she'd used earlier and wrapped it around herself. She adjusted a corner of it.

"What's the matter with you, woman?" Greg asked. "The devil's in him, can't you see? And now he's got you lying. God smites those who lie."

"Don't hurt him, please." Suzanne grabbed onto the back of his coat and pleaded with him to let Matthew go. He pushed her off and she banged against the wall.

"God despises cowards who shove women around," Matthew said and Greg lunged and Matthew hooked him in the jaw. Greg stumbled backwards into the dresser and the lamp fell and hit Suzanne's hard-sided suitcase. Suzanne screamed.

Matthew turned to see if she was all right.

John threw a powerful punch. Matthew saw it coming but he couldn't stop it.

Chapter 18

The snake stared. Didn't blink. It sensed his heat, Matthew knew. His jaw ached from the punch. He was lying flat on his back on the motel bed, no shirt. The snake curled up alongside him.

Be still. Matthew knew be still.

Eyes like a cat, diamonds down the back; it was a snake that could kill a man.

Matthew's insides were shaking like they used to. He remembered a heap of rattlers, his dad hugging them to his chest. Loud music, bass guitar, dancing and swaying.

"Gosh, after traveling in that hidey hole in the suitcase all day, a snake needs to get out and breathe, that's all he's doing," Greg said. "But look at the way you're shaking, Judas. You're getting our boy all riled up." He stroked the snake's head. "Who's the coward now? Look at your man, Suzanne, he's petrified. Sweating something awful; you know this snake has heat seekers, don't you, Matt?"

"Let him go," Suzanne said. "Don't let it bite him."

"Would you pipe down?" John took her by the arm and walked her over to the chair and pushed her into it.

"Think of this as a little test," Greg said. "If your man's on God's side, you've got nothing to fear. If he's living right, and not lying like you say, this rattler here won't do him any harm. Right, Judas?"

"Don't make a sound, Matthew." Suzanne whispered. "Don't move."

Greg hurried over to the window and pulled back the curtain. Matthew heard the siren too. Then he heard the snake's rattle. Saw a head rising out of the coil, saw the flicking tongue. The snake moved up the bed in graceful motions. Matthew felt the skin, smooth and dry against his own. He saw the eyes up-close.

"That snake's going to strike, Greg, get it off the bed." Suzanne was squealing and tugging on his arm.

"Somebody's gone and called the cops," Greg said.

"Get it off the bed," Suzanne said. "I'll go home with you. Just get it off the bed."

"Put the snake back in the suitcase," John said.

Matthew kept his eyes on the snake. He had to be quiet. Stop shaking. Shut off the damn sirens. He wanted to holler. Shut up. One bite and he'd be dead. Like Dad, it was a bad way to go.

"The snake's staying. We're getting out of here." Greg dashed into the bathroom and John bolted after him.

"Hey wait, y'all can't leave the snake here," Suzanne screeched.

Matthew didn't see it lunge. Didn't see its jaw unhinge. Or its fangs. But he knew it bit him. The pain. A pain like no other.

Suzanne rushed over to the bed on the side the snake wasn't on. "Oh dear God, you've been bit, the snake bit you. Your arm's swelling already. Rattlers are poisonous. You can't die like your daddy did. Please don't die."

The snake rattled. Its tongue flicked.

"Shut up Suzanne, you're upsetting it."

I pulled out my revolver. The room was a mess, a broken down door. I had a bad feeling. I'd seen Matthew's car parked out front.

"Sheriff Billings, Cedar County Sheriff's Department. Don't anybody move."

A woman dressed up in spiked heels, a nearly nothing bra and red satin panties held up her hands. She was bent over the bed talking crazy about being bit. I told her to shut up and move to the side where I could see her. And who was with her.

"Well, you must be Mrs. Charles," I said and lowered my weapon. "And Mr. Charles." Flat on his back in bed, no shirt and his buckle undone.

"Astra, it bit –"

"Cover up, Mrs. Charles," I said and nodded toward a towel on the floor. "Sorry to interrupt you folks. But we got a call, said you were breaking up the place. How about you enlighten me, Mrs. Charles?" I heard my voice rising. "What the hell are you and your husband doing here?"

"Please don't yell, you're scaring it," Matthew said and a snake reared up and its tail rattled. "It bit me, Astra, it bit me. It's going to bite me again."

"Shoot it before it does," Mrs. Charles said. "You have a gun. Shoot it, do something."

"Be quiet and don't move a muscle, either of you."

His arm was swollen and off-color. I called for backup, for animal control and medics.

"Matthew, hold your arm still," I said. "They'll be here soon and we'll get you to the hospital. You're going to be okay. Just don't move."

His wife was whimpering into her hands. The rattler was shaking its tail. I was shaking. I didn't know what to do, but wait.

It wasn't long before the snake backed down. Dropped off the bed and slithered under the dresser. I was so relieved, I almost burst into tears. Be calm, I told myself. Be professional.

Mrs. Charles was bent over Matthew telling him not to die.

"You get away from him. And put on your clothes."

"Excuse me, I'm his wife."

"I don't care who you are. You do what you're told. Now."

She marched over to her suitcase and I scanned the floor and around the dresser. "Were you two alone here?" I checked the bathroom. No sign of the snake.

"Just me and my husband," Mrs. Charles said.

Had Matthew broken the door down? I couldn't imagine him doing that. I returned my gun to the holster. Leaned over Matthew and laid my hand on his cheek. He was breathing uneven and noisy. "The medics will be here in a minute or two. Matthew, listen, you're going to be okay. You're going to be okay. I promise."

"A diamondback bit me. It hurts. People die from diamondback bites."

"You're not going to die. It's important that you hold still. Your arm's swelling. I have to take off your watch." He cried out when I did.

"What are you doing to my husband?" his wife asked. The towel was no longer around her and she was pulling clothes out of her suitcase.

"I'm sorry, Matthew. I won't touch your arm again. Leave it down at your side. Don't move it." I covered him up and walked around the bed.

"Aren't the medics coming?" he asked.

"Of course they're coming, I called them. Don't worry. They're right down the street." I kissed his forehead.

"Don't leave me, Astra."

"I won't." Tears welled up in my eyes. I pushed my fingers through his hair. I told him he'd be okay.

"Those medics are taking their sweet time," Mrs. Charles said and pulled a little tee-shirt over her head. "Don't they know people die from snakebites?"

His wife's moronic comments were helping me get a grip. "That kind of talk is uncalled for, Mrs. Charles."

She leaned over Matthew. "Is this the sheriff you have coffee with every day?"

"You're bumping the bed," Matthew said.

"I barely touched it. You and that woman are awful friendly. Is there something going on between you two?"

"You are upsetting him," I said. "Go sit in that chair." I thrust my finger toward the chair in the corner.

She didn't.

"Unless you'd like to go back home and tell the folks about the night you spent in the county jail?"

She muttered something about reporting me to my superiors and plopped into the chair.

"I don't hear the ambulance. They aren't coming," Matthew said and he groaned. His heart was racing and he wouldn't lay still. "It hurts like hell."

I called dispatch again and they said the ambulance was close.

"I know it hurts," I said. "Don't move. Please try not to move. They'll give you something for the pain as soon as they get here. It won't be long." I reached for his hand under the blanket.

"Don't they teach y'all what to do for snakebite at the Police Academy?" Mrs. Charles asked.

I wondered if the woman ever shut up. Besides the obvious, what did Matthew see in her?

"Does the snake belong to you, Mrs. Charles?" I asked.

"No." She crossed her legs and swung her foot.

"Then who does it belong to?"

She shrugged.

"You don't know?"

"It's my brother's snake. They left without it."

"They were here?"

She wouldn't look at me.

"Where are they now?"

"I don't know anything about them. Aren't you supposed to be getting the poison out? Or are you just going to let him die?"

"Will you just shut up?" I shouted. "I don't want to hear another word out of you."

Tears stung my eyes. Not now. Be professional.

"Snakebite's a bad way to go," Matthew said.

"The only place you're going is the hospital," I said. "They know what to do for snakebite. I want you to close your eyes. Try not to worry."

I stayed close to Matthew while the medics prepared him to transport. His wife was giving her statement to Deputy Conroy. I heard bits of it. Her brothers were God-fearing men.

Conroy nabbed them going out the bathroom window. Now those God-fearing men were handcuffed and locked in the cruiser waiting for Deputy McGuire to take them in.

They meant no malice. I heard Mrs. Charles say. This is all a misunderstanding.

A misunderstanding.

Twelve hours ago, Mrs. Charles didn't exist.

She looked over at me and glared. I saw dark circles under her eyes; she wasn't as beautiful as I first thought. Deputy Conroy was saying her name. Mrs. Charles. Mrs. Charles.

The medics said Matthew was ready to go.

Twelve hours ago, I was so in love with him.

I kissed his cheek. "Time to go."

"Bartholomew will need a good home," he said.

What kind of pain killers had they given him?

I brushed my hand across his forehead. "Shh. Don't you worry. You're in good hands now. You're going to be okay."

"Don't let Suzanne take him. Please, Astra. Say you won't."

"Okay, I won't. Tell me who Bartholomew is."

"He'd be happy living with you and the dogs. Remember, he likes tuna fish. And please tell him I'm sorry I didn't think up a new name for him that wasn't stupid."

"Oh, I get it. No-Name Cat does have a name. Don't worry. I'll take good care of Bartholomew until you come home."

"But what if I don't –"

"Sheriff?" One of the medics was tapping my shoulder.

"You will," I said. "You have to go now. Goodbye."

"But you're coming with me."

I stepped back. "I'm not. Your wife will ride with you."

"No wait. Wait. This isn't the way it looked. What you saw, you don't understand, let me explain."

"No need, I saw plenty."

"I don't want to be with her," Matthew said.

The medics were carrying him out the door. Mrs. Charles followed.

"You said you wouldn't leave me," Matthew said. "I want to be with you. I love you."

Mrs. Charles turned and offered one last glare.

Matthew was still pleading his case when they rounded the corner.

I sat on the bed. I would wait until the ambulance left. Then I would leave.

"Animal control hasn't found that snake yet, Sheriff Billings." Deputy Conroy sat on the bed next to me. "But they've only been here a minute or so. Hope it didn't go under here." He bent over and stared under the bed.

"I saw it go under the dresser." I sniffed and wiped my eyes with my hands.

"I heard the medics say there's an antidote for snakebite. Matthew has a good chance of a complete recovery."

I nodded. I folded my hands in my lap.

"I'm really sorry. I mean about him having a wife. I'm glad he's going to be all right."

"Me too."

He grabbed the box of tissue that was on the bedside table and handed it to me.

"I heard him calling for you, not her. Maybe you two can patch it up. Give it some time, you never know."

I shrugged. "Thanks."

I told him to finish up business and I left. I opened my vehicle and turned off the flashers. Shut the door and locked it.

Matthew seemed surprised I didn't go to the hospital. After he hurt me like that. He didn't even get it.

I walked over to the beach. The tide was going out. The stars gave off enough light. I tramped through beach grass and loose sand until I came to sand that was wet and hard as a road and I turned and walked north.

Chapter 19

Matthew crouched next to Samson, his arm around the dog's neck. Matthew and Mother were engaged in conversation. He looked happy enough. I'd let myself in the front door. From her living room,

I could see them out on the deck. Mother lounging in one of her new deck chairs. The ocean deep blue, waves pulling back.

It seemed only a week had passed since that awful day Matthew's wife showed up, not months. He looked good. He'd made a complete recovery. Samson had too. Mother told me. She told me the day Matthew flew out to Kentucky, the day he brought Samson home.

Matthew had been helping her fix up the beach cottage she purchased with the help of Great-great grandmother Hannah and the money the county gave Mother.

I had no idea Matthew would be here. I looked into the bag I brought. I should leave and come back another time. They hadn't seen me. I turned to go.

Samson gave me away. He yipped. Matthew turned his head and saw me and his smile went away. Mother waved me out.

I didn't go out. I walked as far as the slider. It was wide open. "I'll come back later."

"How are you doing?" Matthew asked.

"I'm fine thank you."

"Glad to hear." He leashed Samson and stood. "You don't have to leave. Me and Samson have to get home."

"There's no reason you and Samson have to run off," Mother said. "Or you either, Astra."

"Thanks for the chat, Maggie, but we have to go," Matthew said.

"Before he leaves, come out here and see what he's done with the deck," Mother said. "He finished it over the weekend."

I left the bag in the doorway and walked out onto the deck. "Hard to believe this is the same broken down deck that came with the house." I glanced over at Matthew. He made no comment. He'd built on a new section. I walked up steps to it. Samson followed me. Matthew had let the leash go slack.

"Isn't it wonderful?" Mother asked. "He built a space for my new hot tub." She was beaming.

"A hot tub?"

"As soon as it's delivered, I'm inviting the girls over."

"Sounds like fun." I turned to Matthew. "Thank you for spending so much of your time helping Mother out."

"I have time. Lots of time."

Samson licked my hand and I squatted next to him. Petted his spotted muzzle and his floppy ears and down his back; it was strong and his coat, a satiny blueblack. "I've heard so much about you, boy. My name is Astra." He nosed my cheek. "And you are Samson. Nice to meet you." I stood and he stayed by my side. "He's a fine dog, Matthew."

"He's usually standoffish at first. I said he'd take a liking to you, remember?"

I nodded and big stupid tears started rolling down my cheeks.

"I'm so sorry," Matthew said. "Come here, Samson. It's time to go." He and Samson hurried down the steps to the beach. They'd walked over. They passed a couple who were taking off their shoes and rolling up their pant legs. Samson barked at a gull. Matthew didn't look back.

Mother handed me a paper napkin. "I've had enough sun, haven't you?"

"I guess." I wiped my face.

She bent over a side table and picked up two glasses, crumpled napkins and a bottle of bourbon. "You know, this is excellent bourbon. A little housewarming gift from Matthew. Would you like some?"

I shook my head. I never thought to bring a housewarming gift.

"That was thoughtful of him," I said.

"Yes, it was. We toasted to my new start in life and to his."

"What do you mean his?"

"I mean his divorce is final, he got the papers in the mail this afternoon."

Mother served hummus and crackers and iced tea. She put out paper plates and napkins on the new coffee table made of glass and driftwood. She asked what was in the bag. I set it on the floor.

"I'll show you after tea." I picked up my glass. It was sweating.

Matthew was divorced. I didn't know how to feel. If only he hadn't lied, we'd be celebrating tonight.

The tea wasn't refreshing, the way iced tea should be; it was just cold and it was making my fingers numb. I set the glass down.

"Did you see I framed Hannah's picture?" Mother motioned toward the curio cabinet where she put Hannah's box and the silver frame next to it. "I thought she deserved a place of honor."

"She does, I agree. I think she'd approve of this little cottage. It suits you."

"It does, doesn't it? I feel grounded here. Life is good."

"I'm glad."

"I wish you and Matthew would talk. He's as sad as you are."

"I'm not sad."

"You aren't sad?"

I chose to ignore that.

She dipped a cracker in the hummus. "Have you thought maybe he had his reasons for not telling you about the wife?"

I walked over to the window. Her neighbor had mounted a whirligig to his fence. He was holding the hammer and watching the gull flap its wings.

"Matthew gave me his reasons," I said. "But not knowing how to tell me isn't a good one. Neither is it's hard to do. Why keep his wife a big secret? He should have just come out with it. Telling the truth would have been a simple thing to do." I plopped into the overstuffed chair next to the window.

"Maybe for you, it would have been simple. But Matthew's life journey has taken him down roads far different than yours."

"Let's not start the life journey –"

"Think about Matthew for a minute. He's been through many painful experiences. I'm not surprised he has a hard time talking about them."

"And I haven't had painful experiences? I told Matthew things I never told anyone else."

"Oh, are we talking about you?"

"I was just –"

"Perhaps if you tried to understand his perspective?"

"All right. Here's his perspective. He slept with me while he kept his wife a secret and then when it came out, he decided on one last fling with her."

"Isn't that your version of his perspective?"

"My version? I have eyes. I was at the motel, remember?"

"You may have eyes, but that doesn't mean you know."

"I know he lied to me. Why are we even talking about this?"

"Because people make mistakes and people learn from their mistakes and I would venture to guess that out of all the people in the world, you won't find one who hasn't lied. As a matter of fact, I don't think you're being honest."

"You don't think I'm being honest? The truth is; you're in my business again."

She shrugged. "Oh, there I've done it again, gotten in your business. Seems I do that a lot. I just don't believe for a minute that you've fallen out of love with Matthew. And I was thinking. Isn't denying those feelings a bit of a lie? That's all."

"That's all? So you're finished meddling?"

"Just think about what I said."

That was all I'd been thinking about. For months I'd thought about it. Falling out of love was supposed to be easy. It always was before.

I listened to the neighbor's gull clapping its wings and Mother finished off the hummus. She drank all of her tea.

"All right, teatime's over," She wadded up her napkin. "Why don't you tell me what's in the mysterious grocery bag now."

I walked over to the couch. "Speaking of honesty, I have something to ask you."

Mother cocked her head. "What is it that you'd like to know?"

"I want an honest answer." I sat beside her. Took the asteroid out of the bag, set it on the table and slapped my hand down on it. "Is this Ray? Ray McFarland? Is Ray McFarland my father?"

"Ray McFarland." She looked at me. She looked at the rock.

"Yes, Ray," I said.

Mother didn't put just any old thing in her panty drawer. Only items of significance went in. Like Hannah's box, the grey rock. I watched her put the picture of Ray and me and the Newfie inside. I watched her cover it with panties.

"Ray was my neighbor. I told you."

Ray with the brilliant red hair. Matthew said one out of ten have it. But still, there was the panty drawer.

"Ray was twelve when I came into the world. He said I had a very round head when I was a baby." Mother paused. "Funny the things you remember. We became good friends. He watched over me, you know, he was always there, the guy next door. He married when I was fifteen and they stayed married until he died. I was fortunate our paths crossed while he was here. He was a good man. When he moved on, everyone who knew him grieved."

"You didn't answer my question. So I'm going to ask again. Is Ray McFarland my father?"

Mother folded her hands in her lap and looked at me.

"A nod would be sufficient."

Chapter 20

Matthew shook his head. He was sitting on Maggie's deck finishing off his second micro-beer. "I don't understand."

She was sipping her first. Samson was chewing a bone Maggie had saved for him. Tuna steaks on the grill, and the smell made her stomach rumble. "What don't you understand?"

"I divorced Suzanne. I fixed what was wrong and Astra still won't talk to me."

Maggie wasn't surprised this was about him and Astra. Last time he was over, he said Astra made falling out of love look easy.

"I messed up bad," he said. "I wish she'd let me explain about the motel. Let me apologize and ask her forgiveness. I love her."

They ate dinner, neither said much. Samson finished his bone and sneaked under the table and rested his head on Matthew's knee. He licked Matthew's hand if it came anywhere near.

The waves were turning black and the chilly moist air gave Matthew goose-bumps. He was thinking about Astra. He saw her at Beacon Coffee sitting at their table this morning. He was at a table near the door and he could see her from it, hair pulled back, sunglasses propped on her head. People stopped and chatted with her, some longer than others and Matthew noticed more men than women. She looked happy enough. He left soon after, when he started feeling like a stalker.

Spence invited him to church. He said one good way to get over a woman was to find another and there were plenty of nice women at his church. Matthew thanked him and declined.

Maggie laid her fork and knife on her plate when she finished eating. Matthew did the same.

"I have a bit of advice for you, if you don't mind," Maggie said.

He looked over at her. He remembered, meet the sheriff.

"Forget about forgiveness," she said. "Instead, seek understanding.

I think you'll get a lot further."

"But asking to be forgiven is part of apologizing."

"Forgiveness isn't very useful except to soothe a man's conscious."

They started cleaning off the table. A breeze whipped up the flags Maggie had strung between the hot tub and the house and Samson was barking at them.

"I'm trying to understand. I planned on telling Astra about Suzanne. Soon as I fixed the mess Suzanne made of the divorce. See, the whole situation was out of my past and it was my problem, not Astra's." He followed Maggie inside and put the dishes in the sink.

"Why not tell Astra your problems?" She turned on the water and squirted in detergent. "How about I do the dishes and you get a fire going in the woodstove?"

He called Samson inside and Samson sprawled out on the rug in front of the stove while Matthew built the fire. Maggie didn't get it. Telling Astra before he had it figured out would have only complicated matters.

"Well, I see Samson is enjoying an after dinner nap," Maggie said. She came out of the kitchen drying her hands on a towel.

Matthew was kneeling by the stove. "Yep, we had a woodstove back home. He's real comfortable in front of yours." The fire crackled. The pine he used was pitchy. He added several more pieces and watched them ignite. "I was thinking. Even if Astra knew my problems right off, there was nothing she could have done."

"Nothing? Really?"

"Well, yeah, no one can sort out or resolve someone else's problems. Don't you understand?"

"I understand that you're awfully focused on yourself." Maggie sat in the chair nearest the stove. "Maybe if you thought more about Astra."

He sat back on his heels and looked at her. "I was thinking of Astra.

That's why I didn't pile my troubles on her."

"Oh, Matthew, you just don't get it." She leaned forward and put her hand on his shoulder. "Look, you excluded her, don't you see? She's in love with you. So naturally, she wants to be in your life, in every corner of it, whether or not your corner is nice and tidy or a big dirty mess, she wants to be there, in your corner. You know Astra doesn't like secrets. I suppose some are best kept secret. That's a choice, but it's a risky one. Believe me, secrets tend to alienate the ones you love the most."

Matthew opened the stove. He stirred the embers and added more wood.

Chapter 21

Mother told me to dress up. Wear heels. She was taking me out to lunch at a quaint little restaurant she and Will had discovered. She was parked out front tapping on her horn.

I hadn't dressed up for months and I had trouble deciding. I zipped the skirt and put on the jacket that matched.

"What took you so long? We have reservations and we can't be late," Mother said when I opened the car door. "Happy Birthday. You look lovely. You should dress up more."

"I would if I had anywhere to go besides work. I thought Will was coming."

"No." She grinned and headed north on the highway. Turned on the radio and opened the sun roof.

I hadn't seen Mother since the asteroid. The day she wouldn't say if Ray McFarland was, or, was not, my father. I left the stupid rock on her glass and driftwood table and went home. I was surprised to hear from her. But then, it was my birthday.

She slowed down at the top of the mountain and signaled to turn into Lahkanea Wayside.

"What are you doing?"

"It's such a beautiful day; I thought we'd stop here so I could take your picture, birthday girl."

"I'm thirty-one years old."

"Yes, you are. The light is perfect right now. I learned a few tips from Will about taking pictures." She turned off the car and reached for her camera.

"I thought you were in a hurry. What about the reservations?"

"We're on time. No worries."

I walked over to the ledge. A gentle rolling sea and the colors right out of a coffee table book. "Incredible."

I turned and Mother snapped a picture. "Perfect," she said. "Lahkanea is incredible, a great place to clear your head. You come away with a whole new perspective. Speaking of perspective, have you talked to Matthew?"

"Maybe we should get going."

She checked the time on her phone. "Not yet. Sit on the ledge. I want another picture."

I sat on the ledge and she started snapping pictures. "You're beautiful. Give me your best smile. Perfect. You've become the woman I hoped you'd become. Tough, resilient, a compassionate heart. You make me proud." She focused the camera. "Give me strong."

I flexed my biceps and stuck out my tongue.

She laughed and took the picture. "Now give me serious. Give me sultry."

I burst out laughing.

"I think I'll frame this one. Laughter is good for you. You've been so unhappy."

"Please, let's not ruin this."

"It's not healthy to deny your feelings. I hope you've been thinking about what I said. That's all. I have something I'd like to give you."

"I'm not a little kid anymore. I can wait for presents until the restaurant."

She was already over at her car opening the door. She came back carrying a plain paper grocery bag.

"Fancy wrapping," I said.

"This isn't a birthday present. This is something that belongs to you."

"Hmm, a bag of my baby pictures to toss out to sea?"

"No." She opened the bag and pulled out the asteroid.

"Oh. My. God. Not that thing again."

She set the rock on the ledge next to me. "I don't want it," I said. "You're the one who came up with the extraterrestrial encounter story and this rock is part of it. It belongs to you, not me."

"Telling you who your father is won't change anything. It won't change your past. It won't change your future. And it won't change who you are."

"But a father would take away every drop of alien that's in me."

"Do you really think that's true?"

A car pulled into the wayside and Mother whipped around. It didn't stop, it only drove through.

"So, a bit of advice Will gave me," she said. "There's a world out there and it's full of endless possibilities. You can keep going around the same block or you can get out and live. I'm living, honey. And I'm not taking the asteroid back. It's all yours." She started folding the grocery bag. "You decide what to do with it. Hell, you can throw it into the ocean if you want."

I looked at the asteroid. I looked out over the ocean. I heard Mother's car running and I looked up and saw her driving away.

Chapter 22

Matthew drove into the wayside expecting to see a crowd of gawkers and a cloud formation that wasn't a formation. Mr. Cooke told him to get on the story. There'd been a dozen calls already, reports of an encounter of an extraterrestrial nature up at Lahkanea. Leave right now and Matthew did.

He powered down his window. The crowd had dispersed, if there'd been a crowd. Not a cloud in the sky, no formation. Then he noticed someone sitting on the ledge on the other side of the parking lot. He pulled his sunglasses down his nose. A redhead, and she was alone, no car in sight. He took the sunglasses off. Yes, a woman, her hair brilliant red, and she was looking his way.

He'd been had.

She knew the minute she saw his car. Her mother set her up. An elaborate plan and well executed, Astra had to admit. Her mother had outdone herself. One corner of her mouth turned up and then the other. It was all so ridiculous.

Matthew parked a ways down from where she was sitting, but close enough to see her face. He got out of his car. Was she smiling? She was; she was smiling. She stood and he forgot about shutting the car door and walked toward her, walked, when he wanted to run.

"Seems we've been duped," Astra said and she apologized for her mother.

"No apology necessary. I can give you a lift home, if you'd like. Or if you'd rather someone else pick you up, you can use my cell phone. You look real pretty."

"Thank you." She felt her cheeks blushing.

"You're welcome. Happy birthday."

"You remembered."

"Course I did, I didn't take your birthday off my calendar."

She folded her arms and looked at him. "I'm pretty sure Mother isn't coming back. I'd appreciate a lift."

"Whenever you're ready. Mr. Cooke was in on this, you know. He sent me up here to cover an alien encounter."

Astra burst out laughing. "Alien encounter?"

"Mr. Cooke's story was a bit suspect." Matthew started laughing. "But he is my boss and he sent me out on the story."

"You'll be happy to know, his story wasn't so far off. In fact, if you'd like an exclusive interview with an alien, I know that guy." She pointed over to the ledge and Matthew saw the asteroid.

She sat on one side of it and invited him to sit on the other. "I believe you've been introduced. Ask him anything. Anything but his name, his name is a big secret."

"You are the only alien I want to talk to," Matthew said. He nodded toward the rock. "I don't want to be that guy with all the secrets."

She laid her hand on the asteroid and gazed one-thousand feet down into the water. A white capped wave crashed on the rocks.

Her hand slipped off the asteroid and she looked over at Matthew. And there it was, the smirk he'd come to know, the dimple it emphasized.

She held out her fist and he bumped his against hers.

Conversation Guide

New Halem Tales

13 Stories from 5 NW Authors

Conversation Guide

How it Began

New Halem Tales started as a challenge among writer friends, the 5 NW Authors. After a glass of wine, or maybe a few, Gwen made the challenge. "Let's all write stories that take place in the same town; maybe a small town on the Oregon Coast. We could kick it off with a weekend beach retreat… for inspiration."

We found our inspiration and returned with the foundation of our village. Together, we created New Halem on a bay with a sandy hook and an imposing mountain towering over the landscape; Lahkanea, a spiritual place filled with mystery, native traditions, and stories passed from generation to generation. The 5 NW Authors crafted their own tales of conflict, relationships, decisions, mistakes and unintended consequences.

The village newspaper, *The FishWrap Bugle,* chronicles the day to day lives of its good citizens. William Cooke is the publisher. There's Sheriff Astra Billings; By-the-Book owner, Adele Delacruz; the young actor, Kevin McLeod; the Parking Lot Prophet who lives in a truck and camper in a park by the sea and more. Sometimes one character appears in another's tale.

Everyone in New Halem is looking for friendship, solace, a fresh start, truth, forgiveness, and true love. We hope you find the 13 tales of this quirky village as much fun as we had writing them.

5 NW Authors

Conversation Starters

Charles Thompson

Will moves to New Halem to escape the attention of winning so much money and to keep it a secret. Were his "white lies" necessary? What would be a better solution?

Are you surprised that pirates and Spanish galleons visited the North Oregon Coast?

Where on the coast do you think New Halem would be?

Catherine Kigerl

What is the PLP's underlying mission in life? How does it evolve by the end of the third story?

How does he help Mayor Bumgartner, Linny Jones, Felicia Douglass and Sir Roberts?

Gwendolyn Van Hout Knechtel

Lonny has a classmate who made a cruel remark about the relationship between her Uncle Drew and his life partner, Daniel. What are your views on same sex marriage?

Lonny feels Ellen is a bully with her mean girl comments. If Lonny came to you for advice, how would you suggest she handle Ellen's behavior?

The Bauer family moved to a small coastal town to live their dream. Given the same opportunity, would you live in New Halem? Why or why not?

L. C. Mcgee

What is a meme: How does the author use the concept of meme? What are Kevin's thoughts when he talks to Brutus about memes?

How does ritual affect the aura or use of realism in the stories? What distinguishes one person's concept of reality from another's?

Give an example of a dream that seemed real to you. How did you react to that dream? What reflections did you have, if any, on the causation of the dream?

What paradoxes did the author avoid by using mind-travel rather than corporeal time-travel?

Kate E Thompson

Why would Maggie only say that an asteroid was Astra's father? Could it possibly be true?

Matthew moved to New Halem to escape a bad relationship and threats to his life by his wife's family. Was he justified to not tell Astra that he was married and in the process of getting divorced?

Why would Astra have such a hard time forgiving Matthew for his lies?

Who is Astra's father?

Meet the 5 NW Authors

Kate E Thompson

Kate E Thompson is a Seattle author. Her interests range from the 19th century woman's experience to genealogy to making handcrafted books. She's especially fond of reading old letters and diaries. She stops at all bookstores, art galleries and historical museums. Her dog, Ali, a Goldendoodle, is her loyal writing companion. Currently, she is working on her second novel, *A Family of Forgetters*, a historical fiction, coming of age, story about a Danish girl in 19th century Salt Lake City, Utah.

Learn more at kateethompson.com

Lonnie Mcgee

L. C. Mcgee, his wife and two fine cats live on the coast of Puget Sound. He enjoys reading, writing, writhing in coils (yoga), gardening and the occasional summer sail. Researching coastal indian lore is a hobby which is enhanced by his son's Tlingit ancestry. He is the author of the new Pacific NW Murder Mystery Series, *The Amber Crow*, where a mix of murder, mayhem, and an amber crow keep you guessing.

Visit his website for more about *The Amber Crow*, first in the Pacific NW Murder Mystery Series, along with *The Amber Crow and the Black Mariah* and *The Amber Crow and the Hooting Woman*.

www.TheAmberCrow.com.

Catherine Kigerl

Cathy has lived on the US west coast most of her life and holds dual Canadian-US citizenship. Her poetry book, *Stirring Up the Water* (under the name Cat Ruiz), was published in 2008 by Salt Publishing Ltd, Cambridge UK. She has completed a novella, *On the Far Bluff.* A college instructor in the Humanities, she resides with her husband in Washington State.

Gwendolyn Van Hout Knechtel

Born in Jakarta, Indonesia, Gwen lived with her parents and sister on Java until age four when political unrest moved the family to the Netherlands. After fourteen months they immigrated to the United States, first to Oregon then to Washington. A graduate of Fairhaven College and Western Washington University, Gwen is a teacher and resides in western Washington with her husband and family. Now in "late middle age" she celebrates daily, love of family, friends and creativity.

Whether dancing down hallways, spontaneously singing or keeping connected with loved ones, beach time strengthens her through life's journey. With one published story in *Lembas for the Soul* and a contributing author in *New Halem Tales, 13 Stories from 5 NW Authors*, she is currently working on *DORM 1973*.

Charles Thompson

Charlie loves the Oregon Coast, having lived and worked for several years at Scripps League Newspapers in Tillamook, Seaside, and Coos Bay. Most of his writing in those days consisted of columns, editorials and financial reports—so many financial reports.

Now with a Master's Degree in Education from the University of Washington, he has embarked on a very satisfying second career as the director of a healthcare initiative at Edmonds Community College. He still writes too many reports but he makes time to share a good story.

Charlie lives outside Mill Creek, Washington with his wife, daughter, two dogs and three cats. His interest in graphic design, photography and publishing technology combined with his creative art, writing and editing skills have fueled his most recent editorial adventure, TwoNewfs Publishing.

Learn more at TwoNewfs.com

www.ingramcontent.com/pod-product-compliance
Lightning Source LLC
Chambersburg PA
CBHW051134120726
47905CB00005B/1541

* 9 7 8 0 9 9 0 6 9 9 8 3 5 *